...to submit to the most
dangerous of desires.

W9-BQX-819

continued . . .

DARK GOLD

"Wish I had written it!"   —Amanda Ashley

DARK DESIRE

"Terrific."   —*Romantic Times*

DARK PRINCE

"For lovers of vampire novels, this one is a keeper."
                —*New-Age Bookshelf*

Praise for Christine Feehan's GhostWalker novels . . .

PREDATORY GAME

"[An] explosive, scintillating novel."   —*Romantic Times*

DEADLY GAME

"[An] action-packed, gut-wrenching, adrenaline-driven ride."   —*Romance Junkies*

CONSPIRACY GAME

"Love and danger are a winning combination in [*Conspiracy Game*]."   —*Booklist*

NIGHT GAME

"The sensual scenes rival the steaming Bayou. A perfect 10."   —*Romance Reviews Today*

SHADOW GAME

"Erotically charged."   —*Booklist*

MIND GAME

"Sultry and suspenseful."   —*Publishers Weekly*

WILD FIRE

CHRISTINE FEEHAN

JOVE BOOKS, NEW YORK

THE BERKLEY PUBLISHING GROUP
Published by the Penguin Group
Penguin Group (USA) Inc.
375 Hudson Street, New York, New York 10014, USA
Penguin Group (Canada), 90 Eglinton Avenue East, Suite 700, Toronto, Ontario M4P 2Y3, Canada
(a division of Pearson Penguin Canada Inc.)
Penguin Books Ltd., 80 Strand, London WC2R 0RL, England
Penguin Group Ireland, 25 St. Stephen's Green, Dublin 2, Ireland (a division of Penguin Books Ltd.)
Penguin Group (Australia), 250 Camberwell Road, Camberwell, Victoria 3124, Australia
(a division of Pearson Australia Group Pty. Ltd.)
Penguin Books India Pvt. Ltd., 11 Community Centre, Panchsheel Park, New Delhi—110 017, India
Penguin Group (NZ), 67 Apollo Drive, Rosedale, North Shore 0632, New Zealand
(a division of Pearson New Zealand Ltd.)
Penguin Books (South Africa) (Pty.) Ltd., 24 Sturdee Avenue, Rosebank, Johannesburg 2196,
South Africa

Penguin Books Ltd., Registered Offices: 80 Strand, London WC2R 0RL, England

This is a work of fiction. Names, characters, places, and incidents either are the product of the author's imagination or are used fictitiously, and any resemblance to actual persons, living or dead, business establishments, events, or locales is entirely coincidental. The publisher does not have any control over author or third-party websites or their content.

WILD FIRE

A Jove Book / published by arrangement with the author

PRINTING HISTORY
Jove mass-market edition / May 2010

Copyright © 2010 by Christine Feehan.
Excerpt from *Water Bound* copyright © by Christine Feehan.
Cover art by Dan O'Leary.
Cover design by George Long.
Civer handlettering by Ron Zinn.
Text design by Kristin del Rosario.

ISBN: 978-0-515-14790-2

JOVE®
Jove Books are published by The Berkley Publishing Group,
a division of Penguin Group (USA) Inc.,
375 Hudson Street, New York, New York 10014.
JOVE® is a registered trademark of Penguin Group (USA) Inc.
The "J" design is a trademark of Penguin Group (USA) Inc.

PRINTED IN THE UNITED STATES OF AMERICA

10 9 8 7 6 5 4 3 2 1

For Jennifer Wade,
with love . . .

For My Readers

Be sure to go to http://www.christinefeehan.com/
members/ to sign up for her PRIVATE book announce-
ment list and download the FREE ebook of *Dark Desserts*, a book of delicious desserts compiled by her
wonderful readers. While at the website, join the community and all the book discussions! Please feel free to
email her at Christine@christinefeehan.com. She would
love to hear from you.

Acknowledgments

As always, there are people to thank for all of their help. Domini, you're absolutely invaluable to me. Brian, you always say the right thing to get my mind working. Thank you both for your unfailing patience. And Denise, whatever would I do without you?

1

HE heard the birds first. Thousands of them. All varieties, all singing a different song. To an untrained ear the sound would have been deafening, but it was music to him. Deep inside, his leopard leapt and roared, grateful to inhale the scent of the rain forest. He stepped off the boat and onto the rickety pier, his eyes on the canopy rising like green towers in every direction. His heart shifted. It didn't matter what country he was in—the rain forest was home. Any rain forest; but it was here, in the wilds of Panama, where he had been born. As an adult he'd chosen to make his home in the Borneo rain forest, but his roots were here. He hadn't realized how much he'd missed Panama.

He turned his head, looking around, savoring the mingled scents and noises of the jungle. Each sound, from the cacophony of the birds to the shrieks of the howler monkeys to the hum of the insects, contained a wealth of information if one knew how to read it. He was a master. Conner Vega flexed his muscles, a small shrug only, but his body moved with life, every muscle, every cell, reacting to the forest. He wanted to tear his clothes from his body and run free and wild as his nature demanded. He looked civilized in his jeans and simple T-shirt, but there wasn't a civilized bone in his body.

"It's calling to you," Rio Santano said, glancing around at the few people along the riverbank. "Hang on. We have to get out of sight. We've got an audience."

Conner didn't look at him or the others maneuvering small boats up the river. His heart pounded so the blood thundered through his veins, ebbing and flowing like the sap in the trees, like the moving carpet of insects on the forest floor. The shades of green—every shade in the universe— were beginning to form bands of color as his leopard filled him, reaching for the freedom of his homeland.

"Hang on," Rio insisted between clenched teeth. "Damn it, Conner, we're in plain sight. Control your cat."

The Panama-Colombia leopards were the most danger- ous of all the tribes, the most unpredictable, and Conner had always been a product of his genetics. Of all the men on the team, he was the most lethal. Fast, ferocious, deadly in a fight. He could disappear into the forest and disrupt an enemy camp nightly until they were so distraught— haunted by a ghostly assassin no one saw—they abandoned their position. He was invaluable and yet volatile—very hard to control.

They needed his particular skills on this mission. Con- ner was born in the Panama rain forest to the tribe of leop- ard people indigenous to the area, and this gave them a distinct advantage should they come across the elusive— and very dangerous—shifters. Conner also gave the team the advantage of knowing the local Indian tribes. The rain forest, most of it unexplored, even for other shifters, could be difficult to navigate. But the fact that Conner had grown up here and used it as his personal playground meant they wouldn't be slowed down when they needed to move fast.

Conner's head turned in a slow freeze-frame movement indicative of a hunting leopard. He was close to shifting—too close. Heat poured off of him. The scent of the wild animal, a male in his prime, strong and cunning, ripping and clawing to break free, permeated the air.

"It's been a year since I've been in a rain forest." Conner dropped his pack at Rio's feet. His voice was husky, almost a chuffing sound. "Much longer since I've been home. Let me go. I'll catch up with you at the base camp."

It was a small miracle and a testimony to Conner's discipline that he waited for Rio's nod of consent before he began to walk fast toward the line of trees near the river. Six feet into the forest the sunlight became only a few dappled spots on the broad leafy plants. The forest floor—layers of wood and vegetation—felt familiar and spongy beneath his feet. He unbuttoned his shirt, already wet with sweat. The oppressive heat and heavy humidity took its toll on most people, but to Conner it was energizing. The natives wore a loincloth and little else for a reason. Shirts and pants grew wet fast, chafing the skin, causing rashes and sores that could quickly go septic out here. He peeled off his shirt and bent to take off his boots, rolling the shirt and pushing it inside a boot for Rio to retrieve.

He straightened, inhaling deeply, looking around at the vegetation surrounding him. Trees rose up to the sky, towering high like great cathedrals, a canopy so thick the rain fought to pierce the various-shaped leaves and hit the thick bushes and ferns below. Orchids and other flowers vied with moss and fungus, covering every conceivable inch of the trunks as they climbed toward the open air and sunlight, trying to pierce the thick canopy.

His animal moved beneath his skin, itching as he slipped out of his jeans and thrust them deep in the other boot. He needed to run free in his other form more than he needed just about anything. It had been so long. He took off sprinting through the trees, heedless of his bare feet, leaping over a rotten log as he reached for the change. He had always been a fast shifter, a necessity living in the rain forest surrounded by predators. He was neither fully leopard nor fully man, but a blend of both. Muscles wrenched, a satisfying pain as his leopard leapt to the forefront, taking over his form as his body bent and the ropes of muscles shifted beneath his thick fur.

Where his feet had been, clawed paws padded easily over the spongy forest floor. He went up and over a series of downed trees and through thick brush. Ten more feet into the forest the sunlight disappeared altogether. The jungle had swallowed him and he breathed a sigh of relief. He belonged. His blood surged hotly in his veins as he raised his face and let his whiskers act like the radar they were. For the first time in months he was comfortable in his own skin. He stretched and padded deeper into the familiar wilderness.

Conner preferred his leopard form to that of his man form. He bore too many sins on his soul to be entirely comfortable as a human. The claw marks etched deep into his face attested to that, branding him for all time.

He didn't like thinking too much—about those scars and how he'd gotten them or why he'd allowed Isabeau Chandler to inflict them upon him. He'd tried running to the United States, putting as much distance as he could between him and his woman—his mate—but he hadn't been able to shut out the look on Isabeau's face when she found out the truth about him. The memory haunted him day and night.

He was guilty of one of the worst crimes his kind could commit. He had betrayed his own mate. He hadn't known she was his mate when he'd taken the job to seduce her and get close to her father, but that didn't matter.

The leopard lifted his face to the wind and pulled back his lips in a silent snarl. His paws sank silently into the decaying vegetation on the forest floor. He moved through the underbrush, his fur sliding silently along the leaves of numerous bushes. Periodically he stood up and raked his claws down the trunk of a tree, marking his territory, reestablishing his claim, letting the other males know he was home and someone to contend with. He'd taken this job to stay out of the Borneo rain forest where Isabeau lived. He didn't dare go there, because he knew if he stayed there, eventually he'd forget all about being civilized and he'd let his leopard free to find her. And she wanted nothing— *nothing*—to do with him.

A low growl rumbled in his throat as he tried to choke off the memories. He burned for her. Night and day. It didn't matter that he'd put an ocean between them. Distance would never matter, now that he knew she was alive and he'd recognized her. He had all the traits of a leopard, the reflexes, the aggression and cunning, the ferocity and jealousy, but most of all the drive to find his mate and keep her. The man in him might understand jungle law was no longer a way his people could live, but here in the rain forest he couldn't keep the primitive needs from rising sharp and strong.

He thought coming back to his home would help, but instead the wildness was on him, gripping him by the teeth, slamming into his body with urgent need until he wanted to rake and claw, to tear open an enemy and roar to the heavens. He wanted to track Isabeau down and claim her whether she wanted him or not. Unfortunately, his mate was a shifter as well, which meant she shared all the same ferocious traits, including fierce, abiding hatred.

He looked up to the towering trees, the thick canopy shutting out the sunlight. Flowers wound up the tree trunks, a riot of color, vying with moss and fungus, all reaching toward the light above. Birds flitted from branch to branch, the canopy alive with constant motion, just as the spongy floor was with millions of insects. Beehives hung in great chunky masses, hidden by broad leaves, and snakes wound around the twisted limbs, nearly impossible to see amidst the multitude of interlocking branches.

He wanted to drink in the beauty of it all. He wanted to forget what he'd done to his own mate. She'd been so young and inexperienced, an easy target. Her father, a doctor, had been the way into the enemy camp. Get close to the daughter and you had the father. It was easy enough. Isabeau had fallen under his spell immediately, drawn to him not because of his animal magnetism, but because she had been his in a previous life cycle. Neither had known.

Unfortunately he'd fallen just as deeply under her spell. He was supposed to seduce her into caring for him, not sleep with her. He'd been obsessed with her, unable to keep his hands off of her. He should have known. She'd been so inexperienced. So innocent. And he'd used that to his advantage.

He hadn't considered anything beyond his own plea-sure. Like what would happen when the truth came out—that she didn't even know his real name. That she was a job and her father was the mark. He groaned and the sound came out a soft rumble.

He had never crossed the line with an innocent woman. Not once in his entire career until Isabeau—human or leopard. She had not yet experienced the Han Vol Dan, a female leopard's heat, nor had her leopard emerged. It was the reason he hadn't recognized her as a leopard or as his mate. He should have. The flashes of erotic images in his head every time she was close, the way he couldn't think when he was with her: These facts alone should have tipped him off. He was only in his second life cycle and he hadn't recognized what was in front of him. The need burning in him so strong, growing stronger each time he saw her. He'd always been in control, but with her a wildfire had swept through him, robbing him of common sense, and he'd made the ultimate mistake with a mark.

He'd needed. He had burned. He'd tasted her in his mouth. Breathed her into his lungs. He'd slept with her. Deliberately seduced her. Reveled in her until she was stamped into his very bones. He'd given in to his instincts and he'd done irreparable damage to their relationship.

Overhead a howler monkey screamed a warning and threw a twig at him. Conner didn't deign to look up, merely leapt into the low branches and made his way up the tree. The monkeys scattered, screaming in alarm. Conner leapt from branch to branch, climbing his way up to the forest highway. Branches overlapped from tree to tree, making it easy to navigate. Birds took to the air in alarm. Lizards and frogs scurried out of his way. A few snakes lifted their heads, but most ignored him as he made his way steadily into the interior.

Deeper into the forest, the sound of water was constant again. He had moved away from the river, but was coming up on another tributary and a series of three falls. The pools there were cool, he remembered. Often, when he was young, he would swim in the pools and doze on the flat boulders jutting out of the mountain.

The cabin where he was meeting Rio and the rest of the team was just ahead. Built on stilts, it was positioned in the crook of three trees. The cabin became part of the network of branches, easy for leopards to access. In the shadow of the tallest tree, he shifted back to his human form.

To the left of the cabin a neat pile of folded clothes had been left for him beside a small outdoor shower. The water was cold but refreshing, and he took advantage of it, scrubbing the sweat from his body and stretching out his muscles after his forest run. His leopard was nearly purring, happy to be home, as he dressed in the clothes Rio had left for him.

Conner paused on the small porch in front of the house built into the tree. He sniffed the air. He recognized the scents of the four men inside. Rio Santano, the man running the team. Elijah Lospostos, the newest member of the team. Conner didn't know him as well as the others, but he seemed extremely capable. They'd only worked together a couple of times, but the man didn't shirk and he was fast and quiet. The other two men were Felipe and Leonardo Gomez Santos from the Brazilian rain forests, brothers who were brilliant at rescue work. Neither ever flinched under the worst circumstances, and Conner preferred working with them to anyone else. Both were aggressive and yet had endless patience. They got the job done. Conner was pleased they were on board with this mission, whatever it was. He had a feeling the mission was going to be difficult, since Rio had specifically asked for him.

He pushed open the door and the four men looked up

with quick smiles but serious eyes. He caught that right away, as well as the elevated tension in the room. His stomach knotted. Yeah—this was going to be a bad one. So much for being happy about coming home.

He nodded to the others. "Good to be back."

"How's Drake?" Felipe asked.

Drake was probably the most popular of all the leopards they worked with and often ran the team on rescue missions. He was the most methodical and disciplined. Leopard males were notoriously bad-tempered, and when so many were in close proximity, outbreaks of anger quickly escalated. But not with Drake around. The man was a born diplomat and leader. He'd been injured so severely during a rescue that he'd had plates put in his legs, plates that prevented him from shifting. Everyone knew what that meant. Sooner or later he would be unable to live with the loss of his other half.

"Drake seems to be doing well." Drake had gone to the States, putting distance between himself and the rain forest in an effort to alleviate the pain of not being able to shift. He had taken a job with Jake Bannaconni, a leopard unknowing of their ways, since he lived in the United States. Conner had followed Drake to the States and had worked for Bannaconni. "We had some trouble and Drake was injured again, same leg, but Jake Bannaconni arranged for a bone graft to replace the plates. We're all hoping it works."

"You mean Drake might be able to shift again?" Leonardo's eyebrow shot up and some of the worry in his black eyes receded.

"That's what we're hoping for," Conner replied. He glanced at Rio. "I wouldn't have come back, with Drake in the hospital, but you said it was urgent."

Rio nodded. "I wouldn't have asked but we really need you on this one. None of us is familiar with this territory."

"Have you informed the locals?" Conner meant the elders of his own village. They were reclusive and difficult to find, but the leopards could send word when they were passing through one another's backyards.

Rio shook his head. "The client's representative warned us that a couple of the leopards have gone rogue and now work for this woman." Rio tossed a photograph on the rough tabletop. "They call her *mujer sin corazón*."

"Woman without a heart," Conner translated. "Imelda Cortez. I know of her. Anyone growing up in those parts knows her family. She's also known as *víbora*, the viper. You don't want anything to do with her. When they say she has no heart, they mean it. She's been murdering the local Indians for years, and stealing their land for her coca growing. Rumor has it she's been pressing deeper and deeper into the jungle, trying to open up more smuggling routes."

"Rumor is right," Rio said. "What else do you know about her?"

Conner shrugged. "Imelda is the daughter of the late Manuel Cortez. She learned her cruelty and arrogance in the cradle and took over his connections after his death. She pays top dollar to all the local militia and buys officials like they are candy."

His eyes met Rio's. "Whatever the operation is, everyone will be against you. Even some of my own people will have been bought off. You won't be able to trust anyone. You certain you want to do this?"

"I don't think we have a choice," Rio replied. "I understand she's a man-eater and prefers very masculine, dominant males."

The room went silent. The tension stretched thin. Conner's golden cat eyes deepened to pure whiskey, gleaming with some faint threat. A muscle ticked in his jaw. "You do it, Rio. I don't do that kind of work anymore."

"You know I can't. Rachel would kill me, and quite frankly, I don't have the same kind of dominant quality you have. Women always go for you."

"I have a mate. She may hate my guts, but I will not betray her any more than I already have. No." He half turned, ready to leave.

"Your father sent much of the information to us," Rio said, his voice quiet.

Conner had his back to the man. He stopped, closing his eyes briefly before turning back. His entire demeanor changed. The leopard blazed in his eyes. There was a threat in the movements of his body, in the fluid, dangerous glide toward Rio. The threat was sufficient enough to get the other three men on their feet. Conner ignored them, stopping just in front of Rio, his golden eyes focused completely on his prey. "My father observed the old ways. He would not ask outsiders for help. Ever. And he has not spoken to me since he disowned me many years ago."

Rio pulled a tanned leather skin from his backpack. "I was told you wouldn't believe me and was asked to give you this. They said you would know what it meant."

Conner's fingers closed over the thick fur, tunneling deep. His breath caught in his lungs. His throat burned raw. He turned away from the others and stood at the door, breathing in the night air. Twice he opened his mouth but nothing came out. He forced air through his lungs. "What's the job?"

"I'm sorry," Rio said.

All of them knew what a leopard pelt meant, and the

way Conner held it to him, there was no doubt he knew and loved the owner.

"Conner . . . man . . ." Felipe started and then broke off.

"What's the job?" Conner repeated without looking at any of them. He couldn't. His eyes burned like acid. He stood with his back to the others, holding his mother's pelt against his heart, trying not to let anything into his mind but the job.

"Imelda Cortez has decided to run her smuggling routes through the rain forest. She can't use her men because they aren't accustomed to the environment. The roads turn to mud, they get lost, the mosquitoes eat them alive, and even small cuts turn septic. She's lost a number of her men to injury and disease, and local predators. Once they're deep in the forest, they're easy to pick off with poison darts."

"She needs the cooperation of the Indian tribes she's been annihilating, but they aren't too fond of her," Conner guessed.

"That's right," Rio said. "She needed leverage to get them to work for her. She's started taking their children and holding them hostage. The parents don't want to get their children back in pieces, so they've been running her drugs through the new routes where it's unlikely government agents can track or intercept them. With the children hostage, she has the added bonus of not having to pay her couriers." Rio pulled a sealed envelope out of the backpack. "This came for you as well."

Conner turned then, avoiding Rio's all too knowing eyes. He held out his hand and Rio put the envelope in his palm.

"I'll need to know if your father believes our leopard species have been compromised," Rio said. "Have the two rogues working for her revealed what they are to her, or are they just taking her money?"

Conner looked at him then. The irises had nearly disappeared in his eyes. Flames smoldered in their depths. It would be the height of betrayal for a leopard ever to reveal to an outsider what he was. He ripped the envelope and pulled out a single sheet of paper. He stared at it for a long moment, reading his father's missive. The night insects sounded overly loud in the small room. A muscle ticked in his jaw. The silence stretched.

"Conner," Rio prompted.

"You may want to change your mind about the mission," Conner said and carefully, with reverent hands, folded and returned the pelt to the backpack. "It isn't just a hostage rescue. It's a hit. One of the two rogue leopards working for Imelda murdered my mother. She knows about the leopard people."

Rio swore and crossed to the stove to pour a cup of coffee. "We've been compromised."

"Two of our own betrayed us to Imelda." Conner looked up, rubbed at his eyes, and sighed. "I have no choice if we want to make certain our secrets remain just that, to the rest of the world. It seems Imelda would like an army of leopards. The two rogues have been trying to recruit, not only from our ranks here, but other places as well. The elders have moved the location of the village deeper into the rain forest in an effort to prevent her reaching out to others who might want her money. The only ones who can get to them are the two rogue leopards already working with her, and they would be killed instantly if they dared come near the village." He smiled and there was no humor in that flash of sharp white teeth. "They would never be that stupid."

"How did your mother die?" Felipe asked, his voice very quiet.

There was another long silence before Conner answered. Outside a howler monkey shrieked and several birds called back. "According to my father's letter, one of the rogues, Martin Suma, killed her when she tried to prevent the taking of the children. She was with Adan Carpio, one of the ten elders of the Embera tribe, and his wife, when Cortez's men attacked and took the children hostage. Suma led Cortez's men and he murdered my mother first, knowing she was the biggest threat to them." Conner kept his tone without expression. "Suma has never seen me, if you're worried about that. I've been in Borneo long enough to appear as one from that area. Felipe and Leonardo are from Brazil; Elijah could be anyone, few people have ever seen his face; and you're from Borneo. They will not suspect me. I'll get into the compound, locate the children, and once we move them to safety, I'll eliminate the three of them. It's my job, not yours."

"We go in together," Rio said. "As a team."

"You took this assignment in good faith that it was a rescue, and it is. The rest of it, leave to me." He turned his head and looked directly at the team leader. "It's not like I have a lot waiting for me, Rio, and you've got Rachel. You need to go back to her in one piece."

"This is no suicide mission, Conner. If you're thinking along those lines, then we end your participation right here," Rio said. "We all go in, we do the job, and we get out."

"Your elders do not allow retaliation when one of us is killed in our leopard form," Conner said, bringing up a painful subject. Rio had been banished from his tribe after tracking down his mother's killer.

"It isn't the same thing," Rio said. "Suma murdered your mother. A hunter killed mine. I knew the penalty and I still tracked him down. This is justice. He not only murdered a woman of our people, but he betrayed all of us. He could get us exterminated. We go in together. Before anything, the children have to be secured first."

"We'll need supplies dropped along a prearranged route to move fast. The team can take the children into the interior until they neutralize Imelda, but not without supplies to feed and care for them until they reach safety," Conner said. "I'll go in, mark the areas from above, and you'll make the drops. We'll also want to run a couple of escape lines. We'll need to map them out and cache clothes, weapons and food along the routes."

"We'll have to do it fast. We've got an opportunity for contact in six days. The chief of tourism is giving a party and Imelda will be there. We've arranged for a Brazilian businessman, Marcos Suza Santos, to be invited. We're his security detail. It's our only chance for an invitation to her place, otherwise we're going to have to break in. Not knowing exactly where the children are makes that very risky."

"I take it he's a relation to you two," Conner said, glancing at the two Brazilians.

"Uncle," they said together.

Conner squared his shoulders and returned to the table. "Do we have any idea of the layout of Imelda's compound?"

"Adan Carpio is the man who initiated the original contact with our team," Rio said. "He has provided sketches of the exterior, security, that sort of thing, but nothing inside the compound. He's trying to get information from some of the Indians who have been servants there, but apparently few ever leave her service alive."

"I know him well, a good man," Conner said. "There are few like him in the rain forest. He speaks Spanish and English as well as his own language and is easy to communicate with. If he says something, it's true. Take him at his word. Adan is considered a very serious man in the rain forest hierarchy, very respected by all the tribes, including my own."

From a leopard, that was high praise, and Rio knew it. "His grandsons are two of the children taken. Seven hostages were taken, three from the Embera tribe and two others from the Waounan tribe, sons, daughters or grandchildren of the elders. Imelda has threatened to chop the children into pieces and send them back that way if anyone tries to rescue them, or if the tribes refuse to work for her."

Conner's breath hitched in his lungs. "She means it. We'll have one shot to get in and get out clean. Adan knows the rain forest like the back of his hand. He's trained Special Forces from several countries in survival. He'll stand and be an asset, believe me. You can trust him." He scrubbed his hand over his face. "The two rogue leopards who betrayed our people—is Adan certain they're on her payroll or acting independently?"

Rio nodded. "Most of the information on them came from your father . . ."

"Raul or Fernandez. I haven't called him Father in years," Conner interrupted. "I use Vega, my mother's name. He may have written to me, but we aren't close, Rio."

Rio frowned. "Can he be trusted? Would he set us up? Set you up?"

"Because we despise each other?" Conner asked. "No. He's loyal to our people. I can guarantee his information. I can also tell you with certainty that he is not our client. He

would never even think to pay for the rescue of these children. He's taking advantage of whoever our client is and
adding the hit to our work. And he won't be working with
us or giving us aid."

There was another long silence. Rio sighed. "The names
on that list?"

"Imelda Cortez. No one can trust her with the information she has, and even if we take the children, she'll be back
for more. The other two names are the two rogue leopards
working for her who betrayed our people."

"Those two will recognize us as leopards," Rio pointed
out. "And they'll know you're from this region."

Conner shrugged. "They'll recognize your businessman
as leopard. Santos is bound to have leopard for security.
He'd be insane not to. As for me, there are three leopard
tribes residing in the Panama-Colombia rain forest, but we
don't mix that much. The traitors would probably recognize my father's name as he's an elder in the village, but
I use my mother's name. Plus, few people know of me—I
lived with my mother apart from our village."

There was a collective gasp. Mates stayed together—
always. Conner shot them a hard look. "I grew up despising
my old man. I guess I turned out just like him."

Conner felt the knots in his belly tighten. They were giving him no choice. He crossed to the window and stared out
into the darkness. The noose had slipped over his neck and
was slowly tightening, strangling him. If they wanted to get
to the compound to rescue the children, he had to charm the
socks off Imelda Cortez and get Marcos Suza Santos and
his security detail invited to her fortress of a home. Maybe
he'd entertained some romantic notion that he'd go back
to Borneo and find Isabeau Chandler, and she'd forgive
him and they would live happily ever after. There were no

happily-ever-afters for men like him. He knew that. He just couldn't accept that he had to let her go.

It was dead calm beneath the canopy, but in the utter darkness he could still make out the shapes of the leaves, feel the heat seeping into his pores, squeezing his heart like a vise. He was going to seduce another woman. Look at her. Touch her. Draw her to him. Betray Isabeau one more time. It was another sin among so many.

"Can you do it?" Rio asked, evidently following his train of thought.

Conner turned his head, a slow animal-like motion. His eyes held distance. Self-loathing. "I was born for the job." He couldn't quite cover the bitterness in his voice.

Rio inhaled sharply. He couldn't imagine betraying Rachel. "One of the others can try it. You can teach them."

Felipe and Leonardo looked at one another. How did one learn charisma? Conner had an animal quality about him that they all shared, but his was predominant, inherent, something he was born with and wore on the outside as well as the inside. He walked into a room and everyone was instantly aware of him. They didn't try to hide Conner, rather used his presence to their advantage. He could look bored, amused and indifferent all at the same time.

For the first time Elijah stirred, drawing attention to himself. He had a past in the drug industry and knew most of those involved by reputation. He was also a very dangerous, charismatic man. "I might be able to help with this matter. I have a past. This woman, Imelda Cortez, she will recognize my name if I use it. Just my presence alone will cast a taint on Santos." He cast a quick glance at Felipe and Leonardo. "I'm sorry, but you know it is the truth. She will have all of us checked out and my name is known to every law enforcement agency around the world. She might be interested enough to invite us because I'm there as well. I can try seduction."

Rio studied him. Elijah was his brother-in-law. He had inherited the drug throne his father and uncle had created. When his father had tried to go legitimate, his uncle had killed him and taken Elijah and Rachel in, raising them under his rule. Life and death was all Elijah had ever known. He wasn't ready yet for such a key position on a mission. There was no doubt his looks and magnetism would draw Imelda to him, but he didn't have the charm yet that Conner possessed. The four scars from a leopard's claw on the side of Conner's face only added to his mystique.

Rio let himself look at Conner. He'd been the one who'd selected Conner to seduce Isabeau Chandler. And in the end, Rio had been the one to kill her father. Conner had tried to save him, but Chandler had pulled a gun and tried to protect the leader of a terrorist camp. He'd given Rio no choice. Conner was in the line of fire, trying to talk the man down, but the doctor refused to take the out. Rio had pulled the trigger and saved Conner's life, but there'd been no way to save his soul.

Isabeau had been so shocked. Rio would never forget the look on her face when she realized Conner had used her to gain entrance to the camp. He cringed every time he thought of it and now he was asking Conner to do the same thing again to another woman. Imelda was no innocent like Isabeau, but it was still a lousy job anyway he looked at it.

Conner shrugged. "I appreciate the offer, Elijah, but there's no use in both of us losing out. You still have a chance. I lost mine a long time ago. You can't go to your mate with dirt all over you. It just doesn't work out."

"I'm pretty covered in it already," Elijah pointed out. "I've done things I'm not proud of."

"All of us have," Conner said, "but that's not what I'm trying to tell you. This is a different situation, and Imelda Cortez is the scum of the earth, but if you seduce her and sleep with her, when you do find your mate, you won't be able to look her in the eye."

Rio opened his mouth, but there was nothing to say. He could never have gone back to face Rachel with that kind of sin coating his soul black, yet he was asking Conner to once again bear that responsibility. What he was asking was wrong, but there was no way into the Cortez fortress without an invitation.

"You've been there once," Elijah pointed out. "It isn't fair to have you put in that position again."

"I know who my mate is," Conner said. "Isabeau Chandler belongs to me. I won't have a second chance with her, not after what I did. I would never take another woman and ruin her chances at her own happiness. I know all too well how that turns out." His voice had gone bitter and he made an effort to change his tone, shrugging casually. "I have nothing to lose, Elijah, and you have everything to lose. I'll do this one last time and then if you still want the job and it needs doing, you can make up your mind then."

"If you're sure."

"It's my mess. The man my father accuses of killing my mother is working for Imelda Cortez. His name, along with his partner's, is on that hit list. I'm going after both of them. Imelda wouldn't tell anyone about the leopard people. She'd use the information to her advantage, so right now we've got the opportunity to contain this."

Rio nodded. "She'll be looking for more leopard recruits."

"She won't find them in our village," Conner assured. "Raul moved the village deeper into the forest and the two rogues, Martin Suma and Ottila Zorba, are the other two names on the hit list. I recognize the name Suma from my village, but don't remember him. He didn't live with us. His parents took him out of the rain forest. He must have returned after I left. Even though Suma killed my mother, he wouldn't have a way of putting us together. Zorba isn't one of ours."

"Eventually," Rio said, "Imelda will send them to the leopard village to recruit for her if they don't find recruits elsewhere. She's got money. Most of those living within the forest don't give a damn, but some of the younger ones will want the adventure."

"If I don't get them first, the elders will have them quietly killed before they ever have the chance to speak to the young ones." Conner looked around at the team. "If you're all certain it's a go, then let's get it done. Do we know what the children look like? How many females? How many males? And be prepared. Imelda likes to use children to guard her compound. She often takes young ones, and puts guns in their hands as her first line of defense. She knows it's difficult for government officials to kill the children."

"You think she'll have children guarding the hostages?" Felipe asked.

"I'm just saying we could run into them and we have to be prepared, that's all."

Rio handed Conner a bottle of water and tapped the tabletop with his finger, a slight frown on his face. "Elijah, is it known that most of your operations are now legitimate?"

Elijah shook his head. "No. When my uncle was killed, it was assumed I had him killed to take over the entire operation for myself. I've been slowly selling off everything I can that was tainted. I did get out of the drug and gun business. We were never into human trafficking. There are rumors, but I'm considered ruthless."

"Then rather than change your name and pass you off as security, let's use your reputation. You'll have to be there as a friend of Santos," Rio said. "That will only make her more inclined to think Santos is a big fish."

"That leaves three of us for security detail," Conner said. "Will a man like Santos have more?"

"As a rule he has a four-man team and two dogs," Felipe said. "I didn't want to put any of his regular team in danger. We wouldn't be able to let them in on what was going on."

"And your uncle has agreed to this?" Conner asked. "Does he have any idea who he's dealing with?"

Felipe nodded. "He knows. And he knows she's a threat to our people."

"So who exactly is our client, Rio?" Conner asked. "You say Adan Carpio initiated contact. His tribe wouldn't know of us. My father wouldn't ask for our help. So who knew about us and how? I'd like to have all the cards on the table before we go any further."

2

THERE was a long silence. The men exchanged long glances. Tension stretched taut in the room. Conner broke the hush first. "You don't know who hired us? You didn't check them out before bringing us together in unfamiliar territory? At least unfamiliar to all of you."

Rio sighed. "Adan Carpio has given his word that he stands behind the client, Conner. You said his word was gold."

"Wait a minute, Rio," Elijah said. "You didn't investigate our client at all? You took this mission on faith?"

Rio shrugged and poured himself a cup of coffee. "Carpio contacted me, bringing me half the payment for the rescue along with the things from Conner's father and specific instructions. I checked out every detail and everything he told me was legitimate, so I went ahead and I contacted the team members."

"Tell me we weren't asked for specifically," Conner said.

"Only the two of us, Conner. They used an old code to find us, but still they knew it." Rio spun around, leaning one hip against the makeshift counter, and regarded Conner over the steaming cup. "Carpio said the client knew you and knew you did this kind of work."

The men looked at one another. Conner shook his head. "That's impossible. No one knows who we are. They asked for me by name?"

"Not exactly. The client described you in detail. Even had a sketch of your face. Of course, Carpio recognized you. Carpio went to your father to try to contact you, and as you gave your father my address for emergencies, he gave it to Carpio."

"But you don't know who the client is?" Conner insisted

Rio shook his head. "Carpio didn't want to identify him."

"I don't like this," Felipe said, clearly uneasy. "We should walk."

"I thought that at first," Rio said, "but Carpio appeared to be a man of his word, and he vouched for the client. I investigated everything he said before I called in the team, and Imelda Cortez's men did in fact kidnap seven children. Your father sent you your mother's pelt. I agree we have to be careful. Carpio is supposed to bring the client to us here. They should be here soon. Felipe and Leonardo, you can wait outside. Elijah, to the back. Let them through and then check the back trail to make certain they weren't followed or haven't left anyone waiting to ambush us."

Conner shook his head. "We've made it a policy to know who we're working with. No exceptions. Why all the secrecy?"

"Adan said the client wanted to talk to us in person. If

at that point we aren't satisfied, then we can give back the retainer minus our expenses and walk."

"And you believed him?" Felipe said. "It's a setup. It has to be. They have a description of Conner, but not his identity? Come on, Rio, someone's looking to kill him. They drew him out and you're hanging him out on the line for them to do their best."

"I don't think so," Rio disagreed. "Adan Carpio was not lying to me. I can smell lies."

"Then they're using him. Whoever it is, the client found the connection between Carpio and Conner and used it to draw him out." Felipe sounded disgusted. "We need to get him under cover. Now."

Rio glanced at his watch. "They'll be here soon, Conner. All of you can stay out of sight while I interview them."

Conner shook his head. "I'll stay with you. If it's just two of them, we can kill them if we have to. Anyone following in the forest the others can handle. I'm not leaving you exposed with no backup. Someone wants me, let them come for me."

Felipe shook his head. "I'll stay with Rio, Conner."

Conner pinned him with a steady, focused gaze. "My leopard is close to the surface, Felipe. I'm edgy anyway. My reflexes are going to be fast and instinctive. I appreciate that you'd take the risk for me, but it's my risk and my cat's ready for a fight."

Felipe shrugged. "We'll let you know if there's anyone on the back trail."

Conner waited until the three men left before turning to Rio. "What's going on?"

Rio pushed a cup of coffee across the table toward Conner. "I don't honestly know. I know what Carpio told me was true, but some of the things he said . . ." Rio toed a chair around and dropped into it. "The description of you was less than flattering and didn't mention the scars. Carpio didn't mention the scars either."

"He hasn't seen me in a few years. What description?" A faint grin tugged at Conner's mouth but didn't quite make it. "I thought I was considered a handsome sort."

Rio snorted. "Despicable was a word used. I kid you not. A ruthless bastard who can get the job done. The sketch of your face bothered me. It was good enough, apparently, that Carpio recognized you, so whoever our client is, they've seen you and can identify you."

"At least they know I'm a ruthless bastard and one wrong move is going to get them killed," Conner said, standing still at the open window, staring out with more than a little longing.

The wind shifted slightly, barely able to penetrate the stillness of the forest floor. A few leaves fluttered gently. Somewhere birds called. Monkeys shrieked. They weren't alone in their part of the forest. A faint rumbling started in his throat and he picked up his coffee cup with one hand, taking a small swallow. The coffee was hot and gave him a much-needed jolt. His leopard was roaring again, moody and edgy without his mate, and returning to the wild haven only added to his primitive feelings of need. He wanted rough. Hard. Deep. He wanted claws raking him, branding him. He rubbed a hand over his face, wiping off the sweat.

"You all right?"

What the hell did one answer to that? His leopard was clawing deep, raging for release when he needed to be at the top of his game. "I'm all right enough to back your play, Rio."

He kept his eyes on the forest, staring out the window. He heard the low chuff of a leopard. Another answered.

Felipe and Leonardo warning them they had two guests. Rio moved into place to one side of the door. Conner stayed where he was, his back to the door, depending on Rio while he quartered the area surrounding the house, looking for possible ghosts—men sliding in under cover while the front person distracted them.

The door opened behind him. He knew from the sudden draft. A scent filled his lungs. Rich. Potent. Wild. *Her.* He inhaled instinctively. His leopard leapt and raked. His mate. His woman. He would know that scent anywhere. His body reacted instantly, flooding his veins in a rush of heat, engorging his cock, sending his pulse rocketing so that it thundered in his ears.

Rio kicked the door closed with the toe of his boot, and jammed the barrel of his gun against Adan Carpio's temple. He knew better than to threaten the life of a leopard's mate. "If she moves, you die."

Conner half turned. He could barely move, his body trembling, the shock registering along with her absolute loathing.

Liar. The word lived and breathed between them.

Conner inhaled and took her loathing into his lungs. Her eyes never left his face. Burned over him, over the four scars there, branding him all over again.

Betrayer.

Time slowed down. Tunneled. He was aware of every detail of her. Her face. That beautiful, oval face with nearly luminescent skin, so soft a man wanted to touch her the moment he saw her. Her large eyes. Golden sometimes. Amber really. Or green. Emerald. Depending on how close her cat was to the surface. Her lashes, so long and curly, a sweep of fringe that accented her catlike eyes.

Isabeau Chandler.

She'd haunted him on the nights he managed to get a few hours' sleep. That long, sleek tawny hair, so thick. His fingers remembered tunneling through it. Her mouth, full lips, soft beyond anything he'd ever known. Talented. Inviting. A fantasy mouth. He could feel her lips on him, moving over his body, bringing him paradise. Completion. Peace. Her body. All feminine curves, every bit as alluring as her face. *His.*

Damn her to hell. She belonged to him. Not to the son of a bitch standing beside her with his cocky arrogance. Her body was his, her smile, all of her, every damn inch belonged to him alone. The man with her hadn't moved a muscle. Conner didn't really look at him, didn't care who he was. After all, he was already a dead man, and she should have known it. The law of the jungle. Higher law. *Their* law.

Conner felt every muscle lock into place. His head turned slowly, inch by slow inch in the stalking freeze-frame motion of a large jungle cat. He held himself still, his leopard barely held in check, dwelling on the strong fingers wrapped around hers. He shifted his gaze, a single sound escaping—rumbling up from inside his raging leopard, into his chest to come pouring out his throat. It was low. Chilling. There was nothing human in that sound. An animal's hatred. A leopard's challenge. One male to another. The low growl carried through the room, cut through the conversation and music so that all conversation ceased.

"Don't do it," Rio warned. "Step back while you have the chance," he cautioned the man.

Conner heard him as if from a great distance. His world had narrowed to one woman. No one, nothing could stop him, not even Rio. His cat was too fast. He knew it—they knew it. He'd have the throat ripped out in seconds. The growl persisted, a rumble never rising above a soft carrying note that raised the hair on the backs of necks. He knew killing the man was unacceptable in the civilized world, but it didn't matter. Nothing mattered but to remove the other male from the side of his mate.

Isabeau let go of her companion's hand and Rio jerked him back, away from her.

"I'm sorry, I didn't catch your name," she said softly.

Taunting him. Daring him to lie to her again. Her voice was low. Sexy. Sliding over his skin, teasing his body with memories of the way her mouth had moved over him. He clenched his teeth, grateful she'd at least stopped the body contact with another male in his presence. His leopard clawed for supremacy.

"Why did you bring me here?"

Her eyes slid over him, holding contempt and pure loathing. "Because you're the only person I know who is bastard enough, deceptive enough, who might be able to get those children back. You're very good at what you do. I'm only asking for a few minutes of your time to hear me out and I think you owe me that."

Conner stared her down for several long moments before gesturing toward the door. Rio hesitated. The only person who had a chance of killing Conner Vega was Isabeau Chandler. He wouldn't fight her. The last thing Rio wanted to do was leave and Conner could sense his reluctance.

"She deserves her five minutes," Conner said.

Rio gestured for Carpio to walk in front of him. Conner waited for the door to close before he turned fully toward Isabeau and allowed himself to breathe again. Her scent was potent, surrounding him, invading, swamping him. He could hear the insects in the forest, the hum of life buzzing in his veins. The rich sap running in the trees and the constant movement in the canopy overhead thrummed through his body, a thick, potent mixture of heat and desire. The drum of water, constant and steady, beat in rhythm with his heart. He was home—in the forest—and his mate was caged in the same room with him.

She moved away from the door—away from him, a delicate retreat from his predatory nature. His gaze tracked her, much like a wild animal following prey. He knew his stillness made her nervous, but he remained locked in place, forcing himself not to leap on her when every cell in his body demanded it. His gaze never left her, completely focused, automatically calculating the distance between them each time she changed it.

"Do you have any idea how dangerous it is to be here with me?" He kept his tone low, but the menace was there.

Her gaze flicked over him, filled with contempt, filled with revulsion. "Do you have any idea how dirty I feel standing here in this room with you?" she countered. "What am I supposed to call you this time? Do you have a name?"

He shouldn't tell her, but what the hell difference did it make now? She belonged to him and she was in the jungle. She'd brought him to her—*sent* for him. "Conner Vega," he answered, his gaze locked on hers, daring her to accuse him of lying. His voice wasn't quite normal, but at least he hadn't killed her companion. He'd held on long enough to get control and had allowed Rio to get the man out of harm's way. Death was in his eyes. He knew that, just as pure loathing was in hers.

Her eyebrow shot up. She made a little moue with her lips. She radiated heat mixed with fury. His heart jumped. His cock reacted, engorged and hot. Need punched, hard and mean. His crime was unforgivable. He understood that intellectually, but the animal in him refused to accept it. She was his—that's what the animal understood. She was alive, in the same world and she belonged to him. And right now, her body was throwing off enough pheromones to draw every male within a hundred miles. He drew a deep, shuddering breath of air into his lungs and held on grimly to his control.

"Is that your real name?"

"Yes. Why did you bring me here, Isabeau?"

Breath hissed out between her teeth. She had small white teeth. Her leopard was different—rare. A clouded leopard perhaps. There were so few of them. She was curvy, yet streamlined, muscles fluid beneath her skin, the mark of their species, her hair thick and long, nearly impossible to keep short. She didn't know her own power; he recognized that as well. She didn't know she was safe from him and her fear beat at him. Ugly. Like a sin. A man's woman should never be afraid of him or his strength.

"I left Borneo because I didn't want to take a chance of running into you. I can do my work here, the plants and species I'm looking for are in this rain forest. I needed a guide and the Embera tribe was kind enough to provide one for me."

And her guide would have been a man. A growl rumbled in his throat and he turned away from her, unable to keep his leopard from leaping at the scent of her, at the idea of her in close proximity with a man. He closed his eyes, trying not to allow the vision of her body wrapped around someone other than him.

She shot him a look as he began to pace, trying to rid himself of the ferocious need building in his body. He could barely breathe with the intensity of the demand. He'd never experienced anything like it. Sweat poured off of him.

Desire was wicked. Sharp—hammering at his skull, until even his teeth ached. His body painful. He was acutely
aware of the leopard prowling beneath his skin, so close
to the surface, waiting for one moment when he wasn't on
guard so the cat could take what was his.

"I'm so sorry I'm boring you, but I paid a good amount
of money for your time."

He knew she was misinterpreting his uneasy pacing as
disinterest, but he shrugged, not bothering to explain the
danger she was in. "Get on with it."

"I became friends with Adan Carpio . . ."

This time he couldn't stop the leopard's reaction, the
terrible fury, the jealous rage consuming him. He whirled
on her, flames feeding the heat in his eyes. She gasped and
stumbled back, flinging one hand out to catch at the back
of a chair for support.

"And his family. His wife. And children," she added
hastily. "Stop it. You're scaring me. I don't like feeling
threatened. *You* wronged me, in case you've forgotten."

His gaze moved over her face broodingly. Dwelled on
her soft, trembling mouth. On her throat—so vulnerable.
He could sink his teeth there in seconds. His gaze moved
down—touched her breasts. Her lush, full breasts—he remembered the soft feel of their fullness. She was a little
smaller than most of their women, probably the clouded
leopard in her, but he liked her that way. He liked every
single thing about her. Even her temper.

"I haven't forgotten anything." The growl rumbled in
his voice.

He was acutely aware of the incessant cicadas. Loud.
He could hear the sentries of the forest playing their mu-
sic. His people were in place, and yet uneasiness crept in.
He studied her expression. She was hiding something from

him. Color flagged her neck, crept into her face. She veiled
her eyes with her long lashes. He knew she didn't realize
the danger wasn't to her life, but to her virtue—and his
honor. But still, she was definitely hiding something from
him. Not her loathing. Not pure unadulterated hatred. Those
emotions were plain enough for him to see. No, something
else, something beneath the surface, and if he didn't find
out what it was, all of them could die here.

"I was there when Cortez's men swept into the village.
They killed several people, including a woman who was
visiting Adan and Marianna, his wife. Their grandson,
Artureo, hid me before he went to try to help the others.
He's seventeen, but very adultlike. He ran back to help
his grandfather and they beat him down with the butt of
their weapons and dragged him away. Everywhere I looked
there were people dead or dying or screaming for the loss
of their loved ones." She wiped her hand over her face as if
she could wipe away the memory.

Conner poured her a glass of water and thrust it into her
hands. His fingers brushed hers and the air fairly crackled
with electricity. She jerked her hand away as if he'd burned
her, spilling droplets of water across the floor. Sweat trickled down his chest. Desire clawed at him. Her close proximity in the confines of the small cabin shredded his nerves
of steel, leaving his body shuddering with a dark need so
intense he had to grit his teeth and turn away from her just
to draw a breath.

"I heard their demands and knew I had to try to help.
When we'd buried the dead, we tried to figure out how to
get them back. No one had ever seen the inside of the Cortez estate and lived to tell about it, at least not anyone we
knew. We couldn't rescue the children ourselves. I remembered what you did and when Adan's request for help from

Special Forces was turned down for political reasons,"
there was contempt in her voice, "I thought of you, and
how you'd infiltrated the enemy camp using seduction."
She shot him a look of disgust before she continued. "I
knew if anyone could get inside that camp, it would be you.
You're certainly more than capable of seducing Imelda
Cortez."

His heart squeezed down so hard, so tight, for a moment
he thought he was having a heart attack. He nearly staggered under the unexpected pain of it. His breath hissed out
between his teeth and he didn't even try to prevent the snarl
of rage from escaping. He took a step closer to her. "You
want me to seduce another woman? Touch her? Kiss her?
Be *inside* of her?" His voice was deadly quiet.

Her gaze flicked away from him. "Isn't that what you
do? Isn't that your specialty? Seducing women?"

He jerked the glass from her hand and threw it against
the wall with a leopard's force. It shattered, the sound loud
in the confines of the room; glass rained down like tears
onto the floor and mingled with the water. "You want me to
fuck another woman?"

Each word was enunciated. Distinct. Punctuated by a
threatening growl. Deliberately he was as crude as he could
be.

The arrow struck. Isabeau winced, but she lifted her
chin. "You obviously were very successful fucking me,
but then I was an easy target, wasn't I?" Bitterness fed her
fury.

"Hell yeah, you were," he retorted, his gut twisting into
knots beyond anything he'd ever known. His own mate
wanted to pimp him out. If that wasn't the best revenge a
woman could think of for a male of his species, driven to
be with their woman for nine life cycles, he didn't know

what else would be. He wanted to shake her until her teeth rattled.

She gasped, took a step toward him, her fingers curling into fists, but she stopped herself from attacking him, holding her hurt and pain in check, although she couldn't stop it from showing on her face. "I figured I wasn't the first. And I wasn't, was I?"

Mates didn't lie to one another and he'd done that enough. "Hell no, you weren't the first," he snapped. "But you're damn well going to be the last. Get yourself another man to do your dirty work for you."

He spun around, desperate to breathe air that was free of her scent. His cat had gone crazy, roaring with rage, raking at his insides until he was on fire.

"I don't need another man to do it," she taunted. "You were plan B. I told Adan I could get in by seducing one of the guards and I know I can. Did you really think I wanted to see you again for any reason? Adan refused, but I learned from the master. I guess I should thank you for that."

Fury rushed like fire through his veins. The animal rose to the surface in a heated rush of fur and teeth and claws, nearly exploding through his pores. He moved, a blur of speed, his hand palming the knife lying along his thigh, even as his body aggressively slammed into hers, driving her back against the wall, one hand pinning both her wrists above her head. He held her absolutely still, vulnerable, a leopard's strength running like steel through his body, his heart thundering in his ears as his gaze locked on to hers.

Her eyes were cat's eyes, although different in that the pupils were vertically oblong rather than linear like his, or round as some of the other cats showed. Right now, her eyes showed exactly what she was thinking, a fierce hatred, a hint of heat she couldn't stop that only made her loathe him more. Wholly amber, her eyes had gone just as focused as his, refusing to bend to him.

"I didn't make you a whore. You're doing that yourself."

"Fuck you, Vega. And get your hands off of me."

Instead he stepped even closer, shoving his knee between her legs, nearly lifting her off the floor. As it was, she had no choice but to go up on her toes. "You want me dead. I can see it in your eyes. You came here thinking you were going to kill me."

Air burned through her lungs so that she gasped for breath, the effort pushing her breasts against his chest. He felt the heat waves sliding over him like a tsunami, swamping him with need. Not just his need. Hers. She was so close to her heat and his close proximity was triggering her leopard. He could feel the burn of her body, and the unwanted desire in her eyes—desire she'd been hiding all along.

Her eyes stared directly into his, spitting flames. "Yes," she hissed. "As long as I know you're alive somewhere I think about you and I hate that you still have the ability to hurt me. Yes, I want you dead."

He slammed the knife into her hands, forced her fingers to close around the hilt. "Then fucking do the job right. Do it clean. Here's your chance, baby." He dragged her arms down until the razor-sharp point of the blade was against his chest, directly over his heart, his hands covering hers, preventing her from dropping the knife. "You kill me right here, right now, fast and clean, because I'll be damned if you do it inch by slow inch."

Her body shuddered. He felt her fingers flex. "You think I wouldn't?" She whispered the words even as her fingers moved under his.

"This is your only chance. Do it and walk away clean. If you don't, you won't be getting another chance, but you'll never seduce another man." His teeth snapped together and he deliberately jerked the point of the knife into his skin. Blood ran down his shirt.

Isabeau gasped and tried to pull back, but he was too strong, his hands clamped around hers, forcing her to push the knife into his body. She shook her head. Tears swam in her eyes. He went still, leaving the tip where it was.

"Look at me, Isabeau, not at the blood. Look me in the eye."

Isabeau swallowed hard and tilted her head to once again meet his compelling gaze. She had wanted him dead, prayed for him to be dead, dreamt of killing him, but she'd never imagined feeling like this. She was terrified by the look in his eyes. He would do it, force the knife into his heart. She'd never imagined him so strong, but she couldn't move away from him and she felt every muscle in his body coiled—ready.

"Shove the knife into my chest. You're no coward. You want me dead—just get the job done, don't play games. You seduce another man you'll get him killed too. This is between us. Don't drag anyone else into our mess."

Isabeau couldn't breathe and her vision had gone blurry. Tears burned in her eyes. In her throat. In her lungs. She'd thought she was all cried out, but just seeing him tore her apart again. The betrayal had been so devastating, the cut so deep, the wound as raw as ever. The idea of him with another woman made her physically ill, but rage was strong, strong enough, she'd thought, to carry this through.

His body was trembling, this man who had cut her heart into little pieces and left her without a father, with nothing, absolutely nothing, her life in ruins. She couldn't sleep at night with wanting him, with loathing him. He thought she'd sent for him for revenge, but the truth was worse than that—she'd sent for him because she couldn't bear not to see him again. She couldn't wash enough times to get him off her skin, the taste of him out of her mouth. Her heart was so shattered she didn't think she could ever feel its rhythmic beat again.

It had been hell, sheer torment without him, but now, seeing him, breathing him into her body, feeling him so close, the burning started all over again, like a wildfire out of control. He made her his puppet, his slave, a woman with such need no other could ever fill her or satisfy her. She hated him with every fiber of her being, yet the idea of him touching another woman sickened her.

And the way he looked at her. That focused stare, filled with possession, as if he knew she wanted him in spite of every sick thing he had ever done. So damned smug, knowing it would take one move on his part, crushing her mouth under his, knowing she longed to go up on her toes and fasten her mouth to his and she would melt into him, give herself away all over again. She hated herself with the same fiery passion she hated him. He'd destroyed her heart and he'd stolen her soul. She was left with nothing but ashes and pain.

For one horrible moment her fingers tightened on the hilt of the knife, but she could no more have shoved it into him than she could have done it to herself. He was a part of her. She hated herself, but he was a part of her and she knew she couldn't live with the knowledge that she'd killed him.

Her mouth trembled. Her hands. And then her body. She ducked her head and tears fell on the backs of his hands where he gripped hers so hard. "Tell me what you want,"

her voice barely a thread of sound as she capitulated, her
shoulders slumping in defeat. She was lost and she knew it.
"To get those children back. Tell me what you want, how
to do it."

His grip eased on her hands until she could slide them
away. She rubbed her palms up and down her jean-clad
thighs as if she could rid herself of the urge to rip and tear
at him—or touch him.

"Keep doing that, as if it's going to help you," he said.
"It isn't going to stop the itch, little cat, and we both know
it. You need scratching, you have one place to come. *One*,
do you understand me?"

"I'd rather die."

"I don't care. You want me to get those children out, I'll
do it, but you don't go near any other man."

"You can't dictate that to me."

"You persist in thinking in human terms, Isabeau," he
said. He stepped close again, inhaling her scent, forcing
her to inhale his. "I have news for you. I'm not human and
neither are you. You're in the rain forest, and here, we have
a whole different set of laws. Higher laws. You're close to
heat, close to the Han Vol Dan, the first emergence of your
cat. Her first need is your first need. No one touches you
but your mate. And whether you like it or not, that would
be me."

"You're crazy." She jerked back away from him. "I'm
human."

He touched his face, drawing her attention to the scars
there. Her brand. "You did this with your claws, little cat."

She closed her eyes tight for a brief moment but not
before he caught a glimpse of pain, of confusion and guilt.
She shook her head in denial, her breath coming in ragged
gasps. "How could I possibly do that to you?"

Conner knew she'd been so shocked by all the revelations that night. Her father dead on the floor—the evidence
of his guilt all around them. One dead prisoner and two others weeping. The discovery that the man she'd trusted, the
one she loved, used her to get to her father—that she didn't
even know his real name—the betrayal of that moment—
the shock. She'd stepped toward him in spite of the restrain-
ing hands holding her back—more evidence of the power
of her leopard—and she'd slapped him. Only in that split
second, before her palm connected with his face, the pain
had been so acute her cat had leapt to shield her, her hand
shifting to a claw. She'd gone white, her eyes too large for
her face, her knees nearly giving out so that he'd caught at
her to keep her from falling, even with his face torn and rav-
aged, blood dripping steadily.

Isabeau had shrunk away from him and he could see
clearly that over time, she'd convinced herself the entire
thing hadn't happened. It couldn't have happened. How
could it be possible for a woman to shift even partially into
a leopard?

She shook her head again. "My father was Dr. Arnold
Chandler. He may have lost his way and done some things
he shouldn't have, but he was human. People don't just
change and grow claws."

He heard the honest confusion and guilt in her voice and
reached out to curl his fingers around the nape of her neck.
"There are a lot of unexplained things in the world, Isabeau. You have dreams, don't you?" His voice thickened,
turned husky. "Of you. Me. The two of us in another time,
another place."

She looked more horrified than ever. Isabeau shook her
head frantically, as if the stronger her denial the more she
could make it real. "Never. No way. I would never dream

about you. You're a monster, someone who takes pleasure in preying on women."

The lash of contempt hit him like a whip and his cat raged and snarled. One eyebrow raised coolly and his eyes bore into hers, held her so she couldn't escape his focused stare. His head moved slightly and a purring growl rumbled in his chest as he moved his head close to hers. Her eyes went wide as his lips whispered over hers.

"You're lying, Isabeau. I can smell your need of me. I can feel your heat. You want me more than you ever wanted me. And you dream of me, just as I dream of you."

She shoved hard at his chest in an attempt to knock him away from her. He didn't so much as rock and she put the roped muscles of her cat behind it unknowingly. He felt the punch of her palms, the bite of her claws, and his cat leapt to meet hers, snarling for supremacy. He caught her wrists in a steel grip and held her against him. The moment he did, he knew it was a mistake. His control was already far too thin.

They stared at one another, lips inches apart, his golden gaze locked on hers. Desire was raw and unrelenting. He expected violence when the emotion was there, fierce and passionate, arcing between them, but when his lips touched hers, there was only a whisper, as if from the brush of a moth's wing, and God help them both, he didn't know if she moved or if he had. The jolt was electric, shocking in its intensity, igniting an instant fire that raced through his veins like a storm.

"I hate you," she hissed, tears in her eyes.

He felt the shudder go through her and there was no way for her to hide her body's reaction to him. "I know." He brushed back strands of her thick, tawny hair from her face. Tears caught on her lashes.

"You killed my father."

He shook his head. "I'm not letting you lay that at my door. I have enough sins without you blaming me for something I didn't do. You know better. You don't want to face it, but he killed himself the moment he threw in with that bunch for the money. They kidnapped and tortured people for money. How is that different from what's going on here?" His palm cupped her face, his thumb sliding over soft skin before she could pull away. "If you need a reason to hate me, you have legitimate ones. Stick to one of those."

Isabeau pulled away from him and crossed to the window, staring out into the forest. "Those children need to be rescued, Conner. It really doesn't matter what I feel right now. This isn't about what happened between us. It really isn't. I didn't bring you here for revenge. I wouldn't have sent for you, but Adan refused to allow me to try by myself to get inside her compound. Those children are in danger. She'll really do what she's threatened—send them home in pieces if the tribe doesn't cooperate." She turned to face him again, her eyes meeting his. "How do we get inside to find out where they're being held?"

He was silent a moment, watching her. She seemed more fragile than he remembered, more beautiful, her skin nearly glowing, her hair shiny and rippling with a silken invitation. She was telling the truth. "Then we'll have to get them out, won't we," he said softly.

Some of the tension eased from her body. "I thought you weren't going to help me."

"You really don't know about the leopard world, do you?" he asked.

She frowned and looked at her hand. "I didn't think that was real."

He held out his hand. "Look at me, but stay very calm. I mean it, Isabeau, don't make any moves or scream. My cat is hungry for you and I'm going to let him out just enough for you to know I'm speaking the truth. Don't incite him any more than your scent already has."

She looked more confused than ever, so he willed the change. His leopard leapt at his control, battering hard in an effort to emerge fully. Claws burst through his hands and fur raced up his arm. He felt the contortion of his muscles and, breathing deep, he fought the cat back. It took every ounce of strength. Sweat trickled down his body and muscles locked and froze as he urged the leopard under control.

Isabeau gasped, but she stood her ground. Most of the color leeched from her face, and her eyes seemed enormous. She rubbed at her arms as if they itched, as if her cat had leapt toward his beneath her skin. "How is this possible?" Her voice was a whisper of sound.

He glided toward her, afraid she might fall, but she stepped back and held up a defensive hand, shaking her head. He froze again, going completely still.

"The short version is, we're a separate species, not leopard, not human, but a combination of both. Our female leopards don't emerge until the Han Vol Dan, or the first heat for the leopard. Many females don't know they are leopard. My guess is, the doctor delivered you, and not realizing you were leopard, as we're a closely guarded secret, he decided to raise you when your birth mother died. We'd have to do some research, but he probably passed you off as his wife's child, or quietly adopted you."

"Why is it when I'm around you everything in my life goes to hell?" She pushed a shaky hand through her hair.

His leopard snarled a warning just as the cicadas ceased

their song. A chuffing sound followed by a grunt of acknowledgment came from outside the cabin.

"Who followed you, Isabeau?" Conner was on her fast, gripping her arm and pulling her into the protection of his body, and away from the window. "Do you have someone else with you?" He dragged her onto her toes. "Answer me, now, before someone gets killed."

3

ISABEAU swallowed hard, shaking her head, her eyes wide with fear, even as she fought him, more instinctive than wanting free. "I swear, it was just Adan and me who came to see you, no one else."

Conner responded by dragging her away from the windows and into the shelter of a small alcove where anyone looking in wouldn't be able to see her. He gave a series of chuffing sounds, warning the others that whoever was approaching the cabin had not come with Isabeau's knowledge.

Isabeau's heart was pounding loud enough for him to hear, her breathing coming in ragged gasps. He held her still, ignoring the heel drumming into his shin. Dropping his voice to a whisper, he pressed his lips against her ear. "You'd better be telling the truth, because whoever is out there will be hunted."

She forced herself to stop struggling, but her body remained tense, on the verge of flight. "I swear to you, Adan and I came alone."

"Who knew you were trying to hire a rescue team?" Her scent was driving him insane. Her body was soft and lush and he remembered every curve, every secret hollow. It was difficult to keep from nuzzling her throat. As it was, his head dipped low and found the soft joining of her neck and shoulder.

"Adan's wife. And he went to the grandfather of the other children, but no one else. Cortez pays spies. She has them everywhere. We had to be careful. We didn't even meet in the open. Adan went off for a while trying to track you down, but I don't know if he talked to anyone else."

Rio would be questioning Adan, and the tribal elder was too savvy to lie to a leopard. "You'll be fine, Isabeau. Nothing will happen to you with all of us around. They'll take care of it." But he felt caged. He didn't like the walls surrounding him. He needed to be out where he felt he could remove any threat to her. "Just relax."

Isabeau took a deep breath and instantly regretted it. There was no way to relax when he was so close. His heat poured off of him, his scent, wild and magnetic, and now she knew why. She wasn't as shocked as she'd been the first time she felt something running under her own skin, or when she'd slapped him and raked the skin from his face. Over time, she'd tried to convince herself she hadn't really done it, but the rare times she actually slept, she woke up screaming, seeing the blood running down his face.

She was confused by her own feelings. She was intelligent enough to recognize that her father had not been innocent and had placed himself in harm's way. She'd researched his business connections and had discovered for herself just how dirty he'd been. That didn't stop her from loving him or regretting his death. She didn't really blame

Conner for that. But he'd used her to get to her father, making her an unwitting accomplice in his downfall. He'd seduced her over and over. They hadn't been able to keep their hands off each other. They'd done things that had seemed so completely right at the time, but after—when she knew he didn't really love her—she'd been ashamed.

She was still ashamed. She could barely look at him without feeling his hands on her, his mouth, his body, hard and muscular moving over and in hers. She heard her own low moan of distress and ducked her head to avoid his eyes. Of course she'd researched the myths of leopard people and shape-shifters, but it seemed so outrageous it was easier to convince herself she'd been so traumatized, she'd remembered wrong.

He hadn't loved her. He *didn't* love her. Not then. Not now. It mattered little that lust burned hot in his eyes, that possession was stamped deep whenever he looked at her. He was bred for danger, it was in his bones, in his eyes and she'd been mesmerized by him. She hated that she'd made it so easy for him. She'd never looked at another man, never been interested in having a relationship with one. She couldn't believe it when he'd smiled at her from across a room and sauntered over to talk to her. She should have known.

"Don't," he commanded softly.

He'd always been able to read what she was thinking. He seemed so much older, so much more experienced. She'd felt safe with him. "By take care of it, you mean . . ." she prompted.

"You sent for us to get the children back, Isabeau. Don't pretend to be shocked when violence is involved. If someone is hunting you or Adan, they came to do some damage. We need to know if Cortez has been warned that the

Embera tribe is going to try to get the children back instead of cooperating with her."

His voice was very low and held little expression, but it felt like the lash of a whip to her, making her feel not quite bright. She was a woman unafraid of going into the deepest interior of the rain forest to catalogue and research the medicinal purposes of plants. She'd made a name for herself and was driven to succeed in finding new uses for the plants. She had been independent and happy—until she'd met Conner Vega. He'd turned her world upside down.

Was it fair to blame him for the things her father had done? Or for shedding light on his illegal activities? Maybe not. But she would never understand how he could have used her, clearly an innocent, to bring down her own father. It was wrong. There had to be lines one didn't cross. What kind of man did that? And what kind of woman still craved his touch when his character repelled her?

"I want you to slide down to the floor and sit against the wall. Stay low. We'll sit here and talk while they see who followed the two of you." He kept his hand on her arm to steady her as she obeyed him, bending her knees and sliding her back down the wall until her bottom touched the floor. "I know you're scared, Isabeau, but nothing will happen to you."

"Do you have a better plan for getting into Cortez's compound?" Isabeau needed something to distract her. She wasn't going to panic, she'd been in bad situations before and truthfully—how far did she trust him? If he could build the illusion of being in love strong enough to fool her, then he could do the same with the danger. With Conner, she didn't know what was truth or fiction.

He'd thrown her for a moment, that dangerous edge to him, more animal than man, deliberately showing her his ability to shift, to heighten her fears, put her in a vulnerable position, but she had resources. She was intelligent. She'd been in the rain forest hundreds of times, but she hadn't counted on being separated from Adan.

Conner was so close to her that she felt the instant he stiffened. He went to his feet, muscles flowing easily so he appeared silent, deadly, a cat stalking prey. The breath left her lungs in a rush as she saw him cock his head to one side and sniff the air. "Isabeau, we're getting out of here." He reached down his hand to her. "Something's not right."

"What is it?" She tried to listen, but as far as she could tell, the rain forest sounded the same, although the scream of the monkeys and the cry of the birds seemed overly loud.

"I smell smoke."

She let him pull her up. "Where's Adan?"

"With Rio. He'll be fine. Adan knows how to take care of himself in the forest. It's you I'm worried about. Let's get out of this trap."

"I didn't do this, Conner," she said.

"You wouldn't be stupid enough to kill yourself and Adan along with me," he said, not looking at her. He pulled open the cabin door a few inches and peered out, his hand tightening around hers. "Someone followed you, probably not knowing you were meeting us. And that means it's an assassination squad. Did they know you witnessed the attack on the tribe?"

Her face went pale, her eyes wide, just like when he'd shown her his claws. "The letter. Adan wrote a letter to the director of the interior of Indian affairs, detailing what had happened and asking for aid. When we didn't hear anything back, he sent word to some of his old friends, men he'd trained in survival. The official word came back that no one could risk the political fallout it would cause, bringing in a Special Forces team against Cortez without permission from this government. That's when I told him about you."

"Did he mention you? As a witness?" His fingers involuntarily tightened around hers until she let out a small gasp. He made an effort to relax. "I need to know if they've seen you. Did anyone know you were there when Cortez's men murdered some of the Indians?"

"Adan and his wife. No one else saw me."

"Did you see the letter? Did it mention you?" He hissed the words through clenched teeth, a low growl rumbling in his chest. His leopard was raging now, his mate in danger. Fire was something used by outsiders. And any outsiders coming this far into the rain forest had a purpose. The cabin was only a few miles into the interior, but nearly impossible to find unless one knew where it was, and Adan had assured them all this meeting place was secure.

He felt the shudder of fear that rippled through her body, and he made an effort to push his cat down enough to maintain complete control. "We're going to make a run into the trees. When we come onto the porch, leap over the edge."

Her gasp was audible. "This cabin sits on stilts. We're a story up."

"You're leopard. Trust her. She'll land on her feet. You must have noticed extraordinary skills by this time."

"But I'm not . . ."

He turned his head, his golden eyes glowing yellow-green—a cat's eyes—focused and unblinking. She trailed off and nodded her head.

"If you're too afraid, I can carry you, but I won't be able to shield you as well."

The thought of him carrying her in his arms, held close

against his body frightened her almost more than the guns did. She shook her head. "I'll try."

"You'll do it," he corrected, his voice gentling. "Jump over the rail on the left side. I'll be right behind you. Start running for the forest and don't look back. You've got about twenty feet to make it into the tree line. Keep running once you get there. Twenty feet is a long way, but if you let your cat lose . . ."

"I don't know how."

At least she wasn't arguing with him about being leopard. That was a start. "You'll feel her, muscles like steel, flowing like water, beneath your skin. She'll rise because she senses your fear. Your instinct will be to fight her, but she won't emerge, you're not ready yet. Let her come close. You'll run faster, take longer leaps and you'll be able to go up into the canopy."

His eyes held hers, willing her to believe him. She swallowed hard, but nodded her head.

"A leopard is tremendously strong. You have that, Isabeau. She won't swallow you, but for a few moments as she's rising, you'll feel that way. Don't panic. I'll be right behind you and I won't let anything happen to you."

Isabeau didn't know why she believed him after everything that had happened between them, but she couldn't help responding to his voice. The idea of a leopard living in her was absolutely preposterous, but she'd seen her own hand shift into a claw, felt the stiletto-like tips raking across his face. She woke up often, her heart hammering in panic, a scream of protest echoing through her room, looking to see if there was blood on her hands. His blood.

"You ready?"

She took a breath and nodded. Now she could smell smoke too. A series of shots rang out in the distance. She flinched, her stomach lurching. She'd seen what automatic weapons had done to the Indian village, but she didn't protest. She knew the thin walls of the cabin weren't going to protect her. They had a chance in the forest.

"No hesitation. We don't know how close they are until I'm out there. Once you go through the door, you have to commit, Isabeau. Straight to the rail and over it." There was a command in his voice, one that might normally have put her back up, but she found solace in it. He was the kind of man who survived this kind of attack. The safest place in the rain forest was right at his side.

"No hesitation," she agreed, and steeled herself.

He burst through the door, rushing in front of her, shielding her body right up to the rail. Isabeau refused to look down. She leapt and was astonished when she landed adeptly with both feet onto the rail and then she was sailing over it. She was aware of Conner right beside her, keeping his larger frame between her and the narrow path leading to the small clearing. There was a kind of singing in her veins, as if adrenaline had found a symphony and played the crashing notes as it rushed through her body. Strangely, there was a rush in her body, like the flow of the wind, the sound of the trees. She landed in a crouch, utterly astonished.

The buzz of a bee was loud in her ear. As if at a distance, she heard Conner shout, his hand caught hers and yanked her into motion. She didn't have time to analyze the shocking way her body reacted, muscles flowing like water. He pulled and she felt the coil of her body, the leap that covered more than half the distance to the tree line. A second leap and she was inside the cover of the broad leaves, running along a narrow rodent path.

Her sight grew strange, as if she was seeing in bands of

color, yet everything was totally clear. Her range of vision seemed enormous, as if she could see, without turning her head, a good two hundred and eighty degrees around her. Her vision was amazing to the front. Isabeau judged her ability to see at least one hundred and twenty degrees straight ahead. Her eyes didn't blink and detected movement in the underbrush as she ran—small rodents and insects as well as the fluttering of wings overhead. The deeper into the forest they went, the darker it became, but she could see quite clearly.

Sounds were enhanced, as if someone had turned on a loudspeaker. Her own breath rushing through her lungs sounded like a locomotive. Her heart thundered in her ears, but she could also hear the rustle of movement in the underbrush and knew, as she ran, exactly where other animals were. She caught the scent of a man's sweat and the arid smell of smoke. She could hear the crackle of flames and the screams of the monkeys and birds as they fled ahead of the blaze.

Her heart seemed to beat in rhythm with the forest itself, absorbing the frantic energy of the other creatures as she moved fast through the trees, deeper and deeper into the interior. She was acutely aware of Conner's hand pressing on her back, urging her to move even faster. She heard the whistle of a bullet and then a *thunk* as it slammed into a broad tree trunk a few feet to their right.

"They're firing blind," Conner said. "Keep going."

She wasn't about to slow down. She should have been terrified, but she felt absolutely exhilarated instead, almost euphoric, aware of each movement in her body, every separate muscle working smoothly and efficiently to carry her over the uneven terrain. A large fallen tree lay in her path and she didn't even slow down. Instead, she could feel the wonderful coiling of her body, the spring as she leapt over it, clearing the downed trunk by a good foot.

She smelled sweat off to her right just as Conner gripped her around the waist and tossed her to the ground, his body covering hers. He pressed his mouth to her ear. "Stay still. Absolutely still no matter what happens and look away."

She nodded her acceptance, although she didn't want him to leave her there alone, but she knew he was going to take care of the threat moving toward them. For one heart-stopping moment she thought he brushed a kiss along the back of her head.

"I won't be long." His lips moved against her ear and she felt her heart leap. Her fingers curled into claws and dug into the spongy, vegetation-covered ground.

"Don't get killed," she hissed back and then closed her eyes, feeling as if she'd just betrayed her father. She could pretend to him and everyone else that she didn't want him dead because she was afraid of being left alone in the rain forest, but she refused to lie to herself. She hadn't shoved the knife into his chest because the thought of him gone from the world was devastating to her. And it made her hate herself all the more.

"I'm a cat," he reminded softly and his voice had a roughened edge to it that slid over her skin like the lap of a cat's rough tongue. "I'm hard to kill."

He was gone, and even with her heightened hearing, she could barely follow his progress through the jungle of broad leaves. There was the soft slide of his body along the brush, no leaves crackling, only a whisper of movement as he crept closer to his prey. She turned her head slowly inch by inch, even though he'd told her not to look. Instinctively she knew it wasn't about drawing attention, as a fixed stare could do, but that he didn't want her to see death—and what it looked like.

Conner may have been in the form of a man but at that moment she knew he was all leopard, just without the form. She understood what he meant when he said to let her cat rise close to the surface. He looked like a large leopard, roped muscles sliding beneath his skin, his body moving in the freeze-frame stalk of a predator, head down, eyes focused on prey. He carefully positioned each foot, making certain he stepped in absolute silence as he crept toward his prey through the thick brush. When the man emerged just in front and to the left of him, halting to listen and look carefully around him, Conner was motionless, crouching low in a spring-loaded position, held frozen by the ropes of banded muscle power.

Isabeau's breath caught in her throat as she saw the man with the deadly automatic weapon slung around his neck emerge from the brush and turn his head to look directly at Conner. Her heart pounded in her chest and her fingers dug deeper into the thick vegetation, as if the cat in her was ready to spring, to attack. She held herself still, feeling that other presence now inside of her, smelling her—the itch under her skin, the ache in her mouth, the need to allow the animal to burst free.

Breathing deeply, she kept her gaze fixed on the life-and-death struggle playing out just feet from her. Overhead, wings fluttered and something heavy crashed in the canopy. A monkey screamed. The man looked up and Conner sprang. She saw the powerful movement, and yet she could barely comprehend the amazing physical leap that took him into the armed man. He hit with the power of a battering ram, slamming his prey to the ground, the sound terrible as the two bodies came together with tremendous force. Conner's body was so graceful and fluid flowing over the ground that she half expected him to use his teeth to tear out the man's throat and claws to rake his belly open. He rolled the man over and caught his neck in a powerful, unbreakable hold.

She would never forget that picture of him, all raw strength, his face a mask of relentless determination, the muscles in his arms bulging, the death grip, nearly identical to a cat sinking teeth into a throat and holding while prey suffocated. She should have been repelled. She should have despised him all the more. Broad leaves tried to camouflage the intense struggle as his prey kicked and hit at him, but she could see through the foliage. The man grew feebler until only the heels of his boots drummed into the soil. Then she heard the audible crack as the neck snapped and there was no more movement.

Conner released the man slowly, his head turning away from her, back behind them, as if he'd heard something else. His body remained coiled tightly, ready for another attack. He carefully removed the automatic weapon and belt of ammunition and slung it around his own neck. All the while he stayed very low, his eyes on something she couldn't see.

Isabeau strained to hear what had alerted Conner. Voices came. Faint. Two men some distance away. At first she couldn't make out the words, but then she realized she was listening with her own ears, straining, forgetting the cat inside of her, the amazing, acute hearing. She took a breath and tried to summon the feline closer to the surface.

"We can't go back empty-handed, Bradley," one voice said. "She'll bury us alive just to make a point. We need a body."

"How are we going to find that Indian?" Bradley snapped. "He's like a ghost in this forest."

"The fire will drive him to the river and the others will be waiting," the other voice said. "Come on. Just shoot and keep moving."

"I hate this place," Bradley complained.

Isabeau watched Conner. He wasn't surprised. He'd known all along what the attackers were doing. Everything living in the rain forest would be on the move away from the flames and heading toward the river. The forest was wet this time of year and the fire would burn itself out rapidly. They'd be safe from flames along the swollen banks of the river. Of course this was a trap. That was the point. Cortez had sent an assassination squad after Adan to make a point, because he'd written letters about the attack on his village and the kidnapping.

Imelda was going to kill Artureo. That happy seventeen-year-old boy who had been her guide for so many weeks. He'd been a good companion, explaining things to her every step of the way, patient and caring, interested in her work documenting the fauna. He'd been a font of information, explaining the tribe's uses for each plant. She couldn't bear the thought that he'd be killed because Adan refused to traffic in Imelda's drugs.

Her gaze went to Conner again—jumped to his face. That face etched with hard lines, with the four scars she'd put there. The tips of her fingers ached. He was a strong man. She could sense the danger in him, the wildness, as if his world really was reduced to kill or be killed. His code was different from hers, but maybe he was the only one who could stand up against someone like Imelda who had too much money and too much power.

Isabeau pushed herself to her feet and waited for him to tell her in which direction she should move. She wasn't afraid because she was with him—and that scared her more than her situation did. Deep inside, where no one else could see, she craved him. The man who had used her to set up her father and who'd then walked away, leaving her crushed. Devastated. Broken into little pieces. She wanted to rake and claw at her own face, at her heart, at whichever part of her was so weak as to still look at him with wanting—no, more—needing.

Conner straightened, his eyes settling on hers, wholly yellow-green now, pupils dilated, fixed and focused, penetrating. Even the green was disappearing, leaving a burning gold. She shivered. She would never get over that look, more animal than man. Why had she never noticed how different he was? He mesmerized for a reason.

He moved and her breath caught in her throat, watching the flow of muscles under the shirt clinging to his roped skin. As he drew close to her she felt his body heat, scented the wild cat hidden beneath his skin. Her cat leapt and for a moment there was a burst of joy spreading through her. Isabeau quickly clamped down on the emotion, shocked at her own treacherous cat.

He moved into her space, towering over her, one hand sliding along the side of her face, his thumb tipping up her chin. "I don't like the way you look at me. I'm not going to hurt you."

Her mouth went dry. "You've already done that."

"I won't again."

It hurt just to look at him. To remember. To still want him. She moistened her lips with the tip of her tongue. "I'm not afraid of you, Conner." But she was. Not physically. She didn't believe he would harm her, but he had an unbreakable hold on her.

He gestured toward the dead body. "I told you to turn

your face away. What did you think was going to happen when you asked for my help?"

"I knew exactly what to expect. There're two more quite close to us and more in front of us. Do you know where Adan is?"

His expression hardened, his mouth set in implacable lines. "What the hell is up with you and Adan Carpio? He's old enough to be your grandfather. He may not look it, but he is."

Isabeau looked away from his piercing eyes. Accusing eyes. What exactly was he accusing her of? Having an affair with Adan? That was totally absurd. And what difference did it make anyway? He'd used her. He hadn't fallen in love with her.

"Go to hell, Conner," she snapped, and jerked her face from his hand before she was tempted to touch those four scars. Her fingertips ached.

Without warning the sound of gunshots rang out and bullets bit into the trees all around them. Conner flung her down, his body completely blanketing hers, the gun in his hands as he swiveled around to face behind them. Several large animals crashed through the trees to the left of them and above them. Leaves fell from the canopy as a migration of monkeys passed overhead.

It was hot. Steam rose along with smoke. She could hear the crackle of flames and the sounds of animals panicking. Swarms of insects passed over their heads, and leaves shriveled and blackened as the heat swept through the trees, turning the forest into an oven. Her cat fought for survival, suddenly frightened. She instinctively struggled, wanting to run with the other animals.

Conner's palm curved around the nape of her neck and

he lowered his head to whisper into her ear. His voice was gentle. Soothing. Like a black velvet cloth stroking her inside and out. "*Sestrilla*, you can't panic. We can't move until I remove the threat behind us and the fire's coming. I'll get you out of here. Just stay with me."

She took a breath and forced herself back under control. She wasn't the panicking type, but the cat was definitely jittery. "It's not me."

Sestrilla. He'd called her that before. The word was foreign and exotic. She'd loved it before, when they'd lain together, their bodies wrapped around one another, but now she feared the power of that small word over her. She went soft and mushy inside. Opened to him. More vulnerable than ever.

"You and your cat are one. It doesn't feel like it to you, because she's just rising. But you're always in control. She's going to panic at the smell and feel of the fire, but you know you're safe. You have to trust me and she will too."

Trust him. Why had he used that particular word? Trust him? She might as well put a gun to her own head. Before she could reply, he pressed his fingers tighter around her neck, growling low in his throat. She froze. Her hands opened and she pressed her palms into the earth. Something heavy was running toward them.

A man burst out of the bushes just to their left, almost on top of them. His eyes widened and he fought to bring his gun around. At the same time, he tried to skid to a halt to keep from shooting past them. A wild yell of warning ripped from the man's throat, even as Conner squeezed the trigger, firing a single round. She heard the bullet hit, the terrifying sound of torn flesh, and it threw her back in time, to the moment when her father brought up his gun, aiming at Conner's head. The man's cry was cut off abruptly, but apparently his partner heard him and sprayed the entire forest with a hail of bullets.

She closed her eyes tight, trying not to smell the mixture of blood and gunpowder, but her stomach churned and bile rose in her mouth. Her father's body shimmered in front of her, blood splattering along the wall behind him. There was no face, only a mass of blood. So much blood. *Daddy?* A sob broke from her and Conner reacted immediately, pressing close to her, although his gaze was on the forest.

"Are you hurt?"

She fought for control, a little disoriented, caught between the past and the present. Now wasn't the time to lose it. What in the world was wrong with her? She could hear the blast so close to her ear, the scream of the bullet loud in the confined room. Her own scream, the shock hitting her body. She tried to reach him, before he crumpled to the floor. She didn't want him on the floor with all that blood.

Conner swore and rolled to one side, coming up on his knee, his body between hers and the gunfire. He nudged her. "When I fire, get up, stay low and run fast, staying to the right. We're going up, into the canopy."

She glanced up at the towering trees. Ashes fluttered through the air, looking like gray snowflakes. Her heart thundered in her ears. He wanted her to run, maybe right into more guns, with bullets spraying around them and a fire coming straight at them. And go up hundreds of feet into the canopy.

"Damn it, I'll get you out of this but you have to do what I say."

She didn't have much choice. If she stayed where she was, she was going to get shot. She nodded, setting her jaw.

He laid down a spray of cover fire and hissed *"Go!"* over his shoulder.

Isabeau scrambled to her feet and began to sprint to her right in a low crouch. It was easier than she thought, her cat nimble, moving over the uneven ground without hesitation. Once on her feet and in motion, the song of the forest was in her veins again. It was a little more chaotic and frantic, but her senses were acute enough that she could sort out her surroundings even while she ran.

She knew there were only animals ahead of her. She never heard Conner coming up behind her, but she caught the leap of her cat reacting to him. Stupid cat. Didn't it know he was more dangerous to them than any fire? She hated the surge of relief she felt at his presence, but told herself it was because without him, she didn't stand a chance of getting out of the situation alive. She resisted the urge to glance at him over her shoulder just to reassure herself that he was really there in his solid, masculine form. He gave her confidence, when he shouldn't have.

With the world around them turning a red-orange glow against the setting sun and the sound of the wind whipping through the trees generated by the fire itself, she felt more animal than human as she raced through the brush.

Conner caught the back of her shirt and halted her abruptly. "Here. We go up here. They won't be looking for us in the canopy. They're shooting blindly to drive us into another group. We can't be caught in a crossfire."

She was barely breathing hard, even after the hard run, her lungs and heart working more like the cat than the woman. She looked up the long tree trunk. The first branches were a good thirty feet above her head. "Are you crazy?" She took a step back. "I can't climb that."

"Yes, you can. You're powerful and strong, Isabeau.

You've lived one life cycle already as a cat—with me. It will come back to you. Trust your cat and let her loose. She won't fully emerge, but she'll get you up the tree."

"Have I ever mentioned, I have a problem with heights?"

"Do you have a problem with bullets?"

She blinked up at him, realized he was teasing her and sent him a scowl. "That's not funny." But at his raised eyebrow, a small smile managed to sneak through. He didn't look worried at all. He looked at her as if he believed she could do the impossible.

She took a breath and looked up the long tree trunk. It was covered in ropes of vines, a multitude of flowers and fungus. "How?"

He smiled at her, his teeth flashing white. "Good girl. I knew you'd do it."

She swore his canines might have been a little longer, a little sharper than they'd been before and ran her tongue over her own teeth just to check. They seemed normal enough and she was almost disappointed. His smile sent a flare of pride singing through her veins, and that was not tolerable so she kept her attention on the tree. "Then you know more than I do. Tell me how."

"Take off your shoes, tie them around your neck."

She hesitated, but he was already doing as he advised and she reluctantly followed suit, stuffing her socks inside the shoes and tying laces together so she could hang them around her neck. She felt silly, but she stood up and stood awkwardly waiting.

"Tell me how this works first."

"I'll be right behind you. You've seen cats climb. They use their claws to anchor themselves on the trunk. Leopards are enormously strong. You have her claws and her strength."

She held out her hands to him. "Does it look like I have claws?"

He took her hand in his, turning it, examining it. Her hand looked small and a little lost in his. His touch was gentle, but when she involuntarily tried to pull away, he tightened his grip, preventing her escape. His fixed gaze holding hers, he lifted her fingertips to his face, deliberately brushing the pads of her fingers into the four grooves there, following the scars from one end to the other. "You have claws."

She moistened her lips again, her heart thudding. "I didn't mean to do that. I didn't know." She hated that she apologized; he deserved the scars, but she was still ashamed of the violence, of the way she'd been so duped, of the things she'd done with him—and still wanted to do. All of it. She ducked her head, half convinced he could read her mind. "I meant to slap you, not scar you."

"I know. And I don't blame you," he said, reluctantly releasing her hand. "I think of it as your brand on me."

Her womb clenched and then spasmed. Her reaction was totally inappropriate and upsetting, but still she found herself damp and aching. He mesmerized people. It wasn't just her. She had to remind herself that if he turned that magnetic charm on Imelda Cortez, she would react exactly the same way. It wasn't real.

"Tell me how to do this." It was her only out and, although it was terrifying, climbing to the canopy was better than thoughts of Conner Vega wearing her brand.

"Step up next to the trunk. Pretend you're a tree-hugger." He slung the gun around to lie against his back, leaving his arms free.

Isabeau did what he said. Instantly he stepped behind her, his arms coming around on either side of her, his fingers curving, tips against the trunk. She felt him against her back. It was—intimate. Shocking. When he took a breath, so did she. Every nerve ending went on alert.

He tipped his head even closer until his lips were against her ear and his chin brushing her shoulder. "That's right. Mimic what I do. Don't be afraid. Don't look down. Just climb with me. I won't let you fall. Trust your cat. Talk to her. Now. Tell her to climb the tree. Tell her we need to escape the men and the fire. Feel her. Reach for her. She can't emerge fully, but she's already demonstrated to you that she'll come to your aid."

It sounded so preposterous but she heard him whispering in her ear, or maybe it was her mind. *Life or death. Survival of our mate. Take us up. It's harder in this form, but she can't fully emerge. Call to her. Let her smell you. Reassure her.*

Even as she watched, his hands curved into two claws. She smelled something feral—wild—untamed. The musk of a male cat in its prime. She felt the instant reaction inside her, her own cat leaping toward the scent, rising close, so close she felt hot breath in her lungs and strength pouring through her body. Adrenaline rushed through her bloodstream and she broke out in a sweat. Her skin itched and she felt fur sliding just beneath the surface of her skin. Her mouth ached, teeth hurting. Joints snapped and popped. Her fingers and toes tingled and burned.

Isabeau gasped and forced air through her lungs, pulling back. Her head hit Conner's shoulder and rested there while she breathed away the strange and frightening feelings.

"You're doing great, Isabeau. She was close. You felt her. She's rising to help you."

She shook her head. "I can't do it. I can't."

His lips brushed the side of her face. On purpose? An

accident. In any case his touch steadied her. He hadn't moved, pressing so close to her she could feel him like a protective blanket surrounding her. "Of course you can. Block out the fire. The guns. They don't matter. Only your cat. Get past fear. You won't lose who you are, you'll grow. Let go of you and reach for her."

It felt like giving herself to him all over again, but how could she explain that to him? His magic voice, so soft, and slow, like a thick molasses that moved over and into her, filling every empty space inside of her with him. Smoke drifted through the trees, animals scrambled above their heads and ash rained down on them. She heard the sound of gunfire, and a stray bullet hit around them, but he never flinched, never grew impatient. Just waited, his back exposed to danger, his body protecting hers.

She realized she felt completely alive for the first time since she'd learned the truth about him. And that scared her more than anything.

4

FOR a long moment, Isabeau allowed her body to lean back into the comfort of Conner's. It would be better to die trying to get away than to be shot down by Imelda Cortez's assassins or killed in their fire. It was a good argument for trying to climb the tree—much better than wanting to please him—to prove to him that she had as much courage as he did—okay, to prove to herself. A matter of pride. She closed her eyes and forced herself to think of a leopard, to picture the large cat in her mind. She needed the sound of his voice, his encouragement.

"Tell me what she's like."

She felt rather than heard Conner's swift indrawn breath. His lips whispered over the vulnerable spot between her shoulder and neck. "She's beautiful, like you. Very intelligent, and that shows in her eyes. Everything was always a challenge to her and she could be very moody, one moment loving, the next, raking me with her claws."

There was a soft, almost seductive note in his voice,

and he didn't seem to notice that he was talking as if he'd known her leopard intimately. "She loved the night, and often, we'd have to go out under the stars and just walk for hours. She's wary of outsiders, slow to trust, smolders with fire. She's so beautiful, Isabeau, and secretive, mysterious and elusive. She has such a quick, intelligent mind."

"What does she look like?" The words were strangled. He was describing her personality, yet not. She identified with everything he said, and his voice had grown husky, sexy, as he articulated his intimate knowledge of her innermost, guarded self.

"She's graceful. Petite for one of our kind. Her fire shows in her smoldering eyes right along with her intelligence. More gold than green, the pupils dilated and dark, shining, reflecting the light. Her eyes are piercing and gorgeous. Once seen, never forgotten. I can close my eyes and see them among all those dark rosettes scattering through her fur. She's tawny, like your hair." He nuzzled her thick hair with his face. "She's sleek and muscled, with tawny, golden fur and patterns of rosettes that resemble the night sky she loves so much. Her paws are dainty, like your hands."

His hands covered hers. "Do you feel her close to you?"

Isabeau did. The cat was nearly emerging, so much a part of her, it was nearly a memory. She could see the feline just the way he described, and her hands, trapped beneath his, ached and burned.

"It hurts, Conner," she whispered, frightened.

"I know, baby." His voice lowered an octave. Turned husky. "Remember the first time I made love to you? There was pain, Isabeau, but so much pleasure. Take a breath and let it out. Call her, just let it wash over you."

His voice was pure black velvet, an irresistible seduction. His warm breath. His heat. His body pressed so tightly against hers. Every vivid detail of that first time. His hands on her. His mouth. The way his body moved in hers, so confident, so experienced, hard and strong and right, as if they were made for one another.

"Just let go," he encouraged, just as he had so many months earlier.

His voice brought back a flood of memories, sending the crackling fire from the low-lying brush straight to the core of her body. She went damp. Her breasts ached, swelling with need, nipples hardening, desperate for his touch. His lips trailed kisses from her earlobe to her shoulder. His mouth nuzzled her, sending sparks of electricity leaping through her bloodstream.

Isabeau reached for the female cat lurking in her body. At once she felt the leap of response, as if her cat had simply been waiting. Her fingers and toes burned and sizzled, a red-hot fire. Involuntarily her hands curled. The skin felt as if it might split wide open. Her breath caught in her throat and she stiffened, feeling something moving *inside* her hands and feet. Just as she was about to pull back, Conner leaned down and sank his teeth into her shoulder, a bite very reminiscent of when he'd taken her virginity, distracting her, holding her in place, the pleasure and pain of it sweeping through her body, turning her liquid and acquiescent.

Stiletto-like switchblades burst through her skin, thick, hooked claws attached by a ligament to the bone at the very tip of each digit. The tiniest movement of her muscles and tendons allowed her to move her claws.

"Breathe, *Hafelina*, you've done it. We're going up."

Again there was no impatience in his voice, only pride.

Isabeau trembled as he took her wrists and extended her arms over her head, anchoring her claws in the tree itself.

"You climb with your dewclaws. Trust in your cat's strength. I'll be with you every step of the way and I won't let you fall."

She believed him. Part of the reason she'd fallen so hard and so fast for him had been the way he made her feel completely protected. She couldn't imagine anything happening to her as long as she was with him. No matter the circumstances, he was a man to inspire confidence.

She dug her claws into the tree. He stretched his own arms above hers, caging her in, making her feel safe as she pulled. She was shocked at the strength running in her body. It was exhilarating to climb with such ease, claws curling into the trunk, roped muscles sliding beneath her skin as she heaved herself upward toward the canopy. She didn't look down, but up, at the broad branches interwoven like a highway. The thick veil of leaves hid the life of so many creatures hundreds of feet above the ground. It was an entire new world up there.

She nearly forgot about the fire and the guns. There was more of a wind and she smelled the smoke, shocking her out of her surreal experience and back to real life. That had always been the way it was when she'd been with Conner. Each thing they'd done together, every place they went, had taken on a life of its own. She'd almost been afraid to go to sleep, afraid she'd miss something. Life with Conner was vivid—electric—passionate—everything she'd always wanted.

She climbed methodically, finding a rhythm in the movement as she pulled herself up the tree trunk. Conner always covered her, in perfect sync, as if they were dancing—or making love. She felt the muscles in his body, hard and defined, sliding against hers. His thick thighs stayed beneath her at all times, his arms surrounding her, his chest tight against her back so they moved together, almost as if they were one person, not two.

Raindrops splashed down as the roiling clouds above the canopy burst and dumped sheets of water onto the smoldering trees, effectively dousing the crackling flames. Black smoke rose to mix with the thick grayish vapor surrounding the canopy, creating a thick veil. Conner stepped easily onto a branch and pulled her next to him, keeping his arm around her waist. She felt like she'd stepped into the heavens.

Conner was right: The gunmen couldn't possibly see them up in the thick branches, not with the thick mist blanketing them.

"I want to keep moving. I doubt they'll notice the marks we made on the trunk, but I don't want to take any chances. The others will have made for the river and if they run into trouble, we'll be there to help them."

She stared down at her hands. The claws had retracted as if they'd never been. She turned her hands over and over, inspecting them. "I saw it, but I can't believe it."

"Come on." He took her hand. "It will be slippery with the rain, so watch your footing and don't let go of me. If you slip, Isabeau, trust your cat. Don't panic."

"You say that a lot to me."

"Our ability to land on our feet is legendary for a reason," he reminded. "It's true. Even if you somersault upside down, your cat will right you in under two seconds. You'll be fine and I'll be right behind you."

She took a breath, a nervous laugh escaping. "I think I'll just take your word for it and skip the actual experience, if you don't mind."

He grinned back at her. There, with the smoke and clouds surrounding him, his scarred face strong, his eyes a deep whiskey holding a trace of amusement, she found him far too attractive. She had to look away. Animals were everywhere, the canopy in constant motion, saving her from embarrassment.

"This is amazing."

"Yes it is."

The coloring on the birds, up close, was vivid—brilliant blues and greens and even reds. She'd never really noticed individual feathers and how large and sharp beaks could look. He tugged on her hand. "Let's go. We've got to get out of this tree."

"They'll never believe we could get up here."

"Cortez has two rogue leopards on her payroll. They could follow us."

Her heart jumped. "Men like you?"

"Men a lot worse than I am." His gaze slid over her face. "You may not believe me, Isabeau, but I do have a code. I screwed up with you, but I've got one. These men don't."

She ducked her head. She didn't want to talk about the past. It was too painful. He'd shattered her, left her half alive, an empty shell who would never be able to love another man. She knew that with absolute certainty. It would always be Conner she craved, as much as she despised him.

She followed him, surprised by the ease with which she was able to balance as she stepped over the network of limbs and onto a branch from the neighboring tree. The rain increased in strength, as it often did in the wet season. It wasn't cold, and with the onslaught of moisture and heat, steam rose around them, turning the canopy into an eerie world.

His fingers tightened around hers, signaling silence. She heard the sound of voices drifting through the veil of mist and a thousand butterflies took wing in her stomach. Her mouth went dry. Conner never even hesitated, walking along the branches as if they were a sidewalk, going from tree to tree. Twice he made a chuffing noise as if warning some larger creature of his presence, but most of the time, the sounds he made were somewhere between strange purrs and low, rumbling growls. Instead of menacing, the notes were soothing.

She became aware of the creatures in the canopy. Where before the animals had been frantic, racing away from the fire and shrieking warnings to one another, now they were much calmer—like she was becoming. It was his voice— that beautiful, reassuring, comforting voice. It made no sense. She should have been terrified. She was a hundred feet above the forest floor, surrounded by smoke and mist so thick it was nearly impossible to see the hand in front of her face, carefully placing her feet on slippery branches. Somewhere below, men with guns hunted them and she was with the man who had shattered her world and left it in ruins.

Birds settled in the trees around them rather than flying in fear. Monkeys merely looked at them curiously, but the frantic chatter had faded to normal. The rain poured down steadily and life seemed to return to usual just that fast. She looked at the man leading her with such confidence along the twisted highway of branches. It was Conner. The sheer force of his personality extended calm not only to her, but to the animals.

She followed him, trying to figure out how to stop her reaction to him. How did one block his voice, his charisma, his sheer magnetism? He was the type of man who stood out in a crowd. How was she supposed to keep her blood cool and her pulse normal after sharing a wildfire with him? Every time he looked at her it was there again—that wild, passionate response she couldn't prevent.

She should have known. She wasn't the kind of woman a man like him would want. His gaze was too focused, too absolute, making her feel as if she were the only woman in his world. As if he could never see anyone but her. It was the animal in him. The leopard. Stalking prey. She'd been his prey. A single sound escaped, a low and wounded cry she hastily choked back.

At once he whirled around, his body graceful and fluid, almost balletic on the narrow branch. He bent to her, pulling her into the shelter of his body. "What is it?"

You. The accusation was there in her mind. In her heart. God help her, in her soul. He was what was wrong. The way he moved. The sound of his voice. The memory of his hands and mouth and his body belonging to her. Isabeau shook her head. She hadn't known it would be so difficult to see him—to smell him. The wild, dangerous scent of him.

"It's just a little scary up here," she lied. And she heard the lie in her voice. She could tell by his eyes that he heard it too.

"Lies have a scent all their own," he said.

"Do they? You taught me a lot of things, but you neglected to teach me that."

"It wasn't all lies, Isabeau."

She shook her head, her heart so painful she brought her hand up to press against her chest. "I don't believe you. And it doesn't matter anymore, does it? We have to find a way to get those children back. That's all that matters." She forced herself to say it. She wasn't a coward. "You weren't wrong about him—my father. I did a lot of digging and found out the truth. He was involved with the terrorist cell you uncovered. He was taking their money." Her eyes met his. "That doesn't mean I didn't love him, or that what you did was right, but he wasn't innocent."

"I'm sorry, Isabeau. Finding those things out must have hurt."

"Not as much as watching him die." Or finding out that the man she loved above all else had only used her to get close to her father. She had believed in him with every fiber of her being—she'd given him everything she was or would ever be. And it had all been a lie.

Conner's heart clenched. Isabeau would never be adept at hiding her feelings from him. Hurt wasn't the word for what he'd done to her. He'd shattered and disillusioned her. There was guilt and humiliation mixed with her pain. "You have nothing to be ashamed of, Isabeau. I'm the one who acted without honor. You did nothing wrong."

"I fell in love with the wrong man."

"You didn't, *Sestrilla*, I'm the right man. It was just the wrong time for us."

She lifted her chin, eyes flashing fire. "Go to hell, Conner. I'm not your job this time. Don't bother practicing on me; you really don't need it."

Her voice cut like a knife, enough to make him wince. He deserved it, though. His gaze moved over her face with brooding intensity. She looked rebellious, defiant, so beautiful he ached inside. He'd told himself he'd walk away from her, but how? How could he give her up? He was already so in love with her there was no way out. He brought her hand up to his chest, pressed her palm over his heart. "You were never my job, Isabeau." He was going to find a way to win her trust back. There had to be a way.

She swallowed hard and looked away from him, but not before he caught the sheen of tears. "Let's just go."

"Damn it, Isabeau. How are we going to get past this?"

"Get *past* it?"

Furious, Isabeau wrenched her hand free and pulled away from him, stepping backward—into empty space. She threw out her hands, but she was already tumbling. Terror gripped her as she looked up and saw the mask slipping from Conner's face to be replaced by fear. She saw his jaw harden as he leapt from the branch after her. Then she was somersaulting through open air. Panic flooded her body with ice-cold adrenaline.

Breathe. Reach for your cat. She swore she heard Conner's voice, as calm as ever, flooding her mind, driving out fright to be replaced by a strange calm.

She felt her body twisting until her upper body was pointed down, and her legs followed suit. She seemed to be tumbling out of control and she gave herself up to the cat struggling to come to her aid. Her skin itched and fur burst along her body, slowing her descent. Instinctively she spread out her arms and folded in the middle. Her spine flexed. Her ears burned, almost as if her body tuned itself to know which way was up and which way was down. Her eyes focused on the ground rushing up to meet her.

She found herself tucking her arms in and extending her legs so that her body rotated, the front coming around much faster than the bottom half. Immediately she tucked her legs and extended her arms to bring herself all the way around. She'd rotated completely in midair, just as Conner had said she would. She tried to relax as she felt the burning sensation in her feet and hands, indicating claws breaking through her sensitive skin just before she hit the ground. The pads helped, but she hit hard, her legs and hands absorbing the tremendous fall through the paws.

Pain crashed through her body, her wrists, elbows, knees and ankles crumbling beneath her as she sprawled out on the forest floor.

"Don't move," Conner hissed as he landed beside her in a perfect crouch.

She hated him in that moment. He had to be good at everything. She'd fallen from the canopy in the rain forest, managed to right herself and still got hurt. His hands moved over her, examining her quickly and efficiently for damage.

"We just landed in the middle of enemy territory," he reminded. "Don't make a sound."

She realized she was moaning softly and forced herself to go quiet, although she couldn't stop the tears tracking down her face. She winced when his fingers moved over her left wrist.

"How bad," he mouthed.

She looked up at his grim face and tried to look brave when she really wanted to curl into a ball and sob. The pads of his fingers brushed gently at her tears, making her heart ache.

"A sprain, I think. The rest of me, just the shock, jamming everything as I landed. I was lucky." She remembered to whisper the words, using a thread of sound that his acute hearing could easily pick up.

Her body was tuning itself once again to the rhythm of the rain forest. She heard the rustling in the underbrush and knew it was a man, not an animal, brushing against leaves quite close to them. Too close. She smelled sweat and fear and rot. Her eyes met Conner's. There it was again, that implacable, ruthless, *dangerous* look that meant she was safe.

He put his finger to his lips and indicated for her to move back into the cover of the brush. She used her toes and elbows to slide on her belly, easing her way over the thick carpet of decayed leaves until the broader, thick leaves of the bushes provided a screen for her.

All the while she scooted back, Conner held his ground, shielding her with his body. He made it difficult to despise him totally when he continually put himself in danger to protect her. And she wanted—*needed*—to despise him. She had to stay alert to keep from falling under his spell. Out in the forest where a higher law prevailed, life seemed very black and white.

Only when she was safely under cover did Conner begin to move. The gun was always ready, his gaze restlessly examining every inch of their surroundings, missing nothing. He slowly drew back into the brush to lie beside her. With infinite patience he pushed the gun into her hands, settling her finger on the trigger and cautioning her again to silence. His hand, almost in slow motion, went to the small daggerlike pieces of metal in the loops of his belt. He palmed two of them without a sound.

She'd never really noticed them, so small and harmless-looking, but she saw, before his fingers concealed them, that they were lethal stiletto-like daggers. An assassin's weapon. She closed her eyes for a moment, wondering how she'd ever gotten to this place with this man. He touched the back of her hand and waited until she dared to look at him again. He winked and just like that the tension eased.

Night descended fast in the rain forest and, although she was used to camping for long periods of time while she worked, she was used to being safely off the ground and out of the way of the millions of insects that turned the forest floor into a living carpet. She could feel bugs mov-

ing over her skin and might have tried to move in order to
dislodge them, had Conner not touched her hand and given
her that slow, sexy wink.

Isabeau's breath caught in her throat and she froze as
two huge boots stepped inches from her head. Conner
never moved. He lay beside her, his breath even and silent, but she could feel the tension coiling in his body, the
bunching of his muscles as he gathered himself, preparing
for the spring. The man crouched down and began to inch
his way through the brush. Steam rose from the ground,
surrounding his boots and calves with every step he took.

The sight should have struck fear into her heart, but
Conner was too solid next to her, too much of a hunter,
his eyes fixed on his prey, unblinking, like the eyes of a
leopard. His eyes blazed, the amber darkening to yellow-
green, smoldering with tension, with fire, but mostly with
a cunning intelligence. His gaze was penetrating and she
couldn't take her eyes from his face, not even to see where
the man creeping through the forest was headed.

Isabeau heard her heart pound, but Conner never moved,
using all the natural patience of a leopard, completely motionless as the man turned his back and took several steps
away from them, alerting to a soft noise just ahead. Her
breath stilled in her lungs as she caught Adan's scent. He
was close and the man hiding in the brush heard him.

Conner slid forward, a slow, belly-to-ground stalk, pro-
pelling himself forward inch by inch. He crawled and froze,
using the meager cover to inch within a foot of his prey.
The closer he approached, the slower he moved, continuing
the freeze-frame stalk until he was nearly on the man. Once
locked on, his dilated gaze never moved from his intended
target. He exploded off the ground, leaping on his prey,
the two daggers grabbing, holding and puncturing. He held

his prey easily with his great strength, while the large man resisted, trying to fight back, dropping his weapon in the process, unable to cry out.

Isabeau tried to look away, but the sight of the life-and-death struggle mesmerized her. Mostly she looked at Conner's face. His expression never changed. His eyes looked savage, that strange burning gold now, but his face was a mask of implacable resolve. She couldn't imagine him defeated by anything. He seemed invincible. He looked ruthless. Deadly. And God help her, she was drawn like a moth to a flame instead of being repelled as she should have been.

Conner lowered the body silently to the ground and let out a series of chuffing noises. The sound pierced the veil of mist rising like clouds around them, reverberating in the darkness, mixing with the natural sounds of the forest. Far off, she heard an answer, the common prusten greeting of a leopard, much like the snorting of a horse. Another answered with a combination that resembled the coo of a pigeon and water running over rocks. A third leopard chimed in with short muffled sneezing, forming a triangle with Conner and Isabeau in the center. The vocalization lasted less than half a second, but the sounds were chilling.

There in the night, already facing unseen enemies, to be surrounded by dangerous, wild animals was terrifying. She knew leopards were more widespread than any other cat, because they were more adaptable—more cunning and bold. They were known to stalk people in villages, going right into houses and taking their prey. They were secretive and supposed to be solitary, so why were there at least three of them? Unless the fire had driven them to the river just as it had Conner and Isabeau. She knew leopards were extremely dangerous—much like Conner. Or maybe he was more so, being man too. Did that give him more intelligence? More control? And maybe he wasn't the only leopard on his team.

Her mouth was so dry she feared she couldn't find it in her to swallow, and somewhere the trembling had started. Conner made his way back to her in that silent way of his and lifted her off the ground, setting her on her feet. Pain jarred through her body and her wrist throbbed where she'd sprained it. She stood quietly while he brushed the insects from her shuddering body. She didn't live like this, with great adventures. She lived a life of solitude, hidden from the world in her precious rain forest, working with her plants. Most of the time she was alone or with a guide, and she certainly didn't get involved with drug cartels or dangerous men—until Conner.

"I'll get you out of this," he said.

His voice was gentle, a slow drawl—like a drug to her, something once experienced, always craved, like his touch. Like the focused, piercing stare from his eyes. So intent. So completely locked on to her. It was exhilarating and unnerving all at the same time. The brush of his fingers against her skin sent tremors through her body, ripples of awareness through her until her very core turned a heated liquid. Surrounded by death and danger, she was more susceptible to him than ever.

"I know you will." She kept her voice low, afraid of giving herself away. "Those were leopards, weren't they?"

"Friends. I warned them they had two more coming at them. Rio's got Adan safe."

"The leopards aren't real leopards," she guessed. She should have known it was Conner's friends answering his call. Isabeau let her breath out. Friends. They had friends in the midst of this madness. "Are they like you?"

"Like us," he corrected and reached to pull leaves from her hair. "They're like us, Isabeau."

She didn't move, absorbing the feel of his fingers in her hair. He had a way of making her feel special and cared for—protected and loved—yet she knew it was an illusion. She'd hired him for those traits—to seduce another woman with that magnetism. Now she wasn't so certain she could watch him do it.

"I shouldn't have brought you here." The confession slipped out in spite of her resolve not to engage with him over the past.

His roughened palm cupped the side of her face, the pad of his thumb sliding seductively back and forth, nearly mesmerizing her as completely as his voice did. "No, you shouldn't have, not if you wanted to be safe. But it's too late for regrets. We're already here and we're in this mess all the way. We can't leave those children to Imelda Cortez and we can't pretend we're indifferent. I expect a little hate, Isabeau, but that's not all you feel for me and I expect honesty between us."

Fire flashed through her, a storm of such heat she shook with it. "You *expect* honesty between us? *You*?" She poured contempt into her voice. "You wouldn't know honesty if it bit you in the butt. Don't you dare lecture me. You *lied* to me. Used me. Made me believe you loved me and we were going to have a life together. And then you killed my father. Everything about you is a lie, an illusion. You aren't even real."

Rage burst like a firestorm in her stomach, churning wildly, exploding in fiery conflagration she couldn't—or didn't—want to douse. There was a part of her that knew her sexual hunger was a good percentage of what was fueling the flames of anger—that the intensity of her righteous,

feral anger was her cat's heat and her absolute physical
need of the dominant male standing in front of her, but it
felt so good to throw the gun to the ground and swing her
clenched fist at the smug male smirk, wanting to wipe it
off his face.

Amusement crept into the amber of his eyes as he
evaded her swipe, his teeth flashing at her. "Are you trying
to hit me?"

"I'm going to kick your ass," she spat back, circling
around him, a slow hiss escaping her throat. His laughter
only drove the flames of her fire higher.

"Hafelina." His voice smoldered with sex and her
treacherous body reacted with a spasm of need.

"What does that mean?" she demanded and threw a kick
at his thigh.

He slapped her foot away from him. "Little cat. And
you're behaving like one right now. I don't want to hurt
you, Isabeau, so stop this nonsense."

"You think you're the only one with training?" Now it
was a matter of pride that she score a hit on him. Just one.

She attacked hard, a series of lightning fast kicks. He
blocked every one with an almost casual slap of his hand.
The taps stung, but didn't really hurt. She didn't take her
eyes from him, a sexual fury manifesting itself in violent
rage.

"Do you know what a cat does when she's in heat and
her male is circling her?"

His voice lowered an octave. Purred at her. Stroked her
sensitive skin and found raw, burning nerves. Liquid heat
scorched her. Her breasts ached. Her skin felt too tight,
need and an angry hunger she couldn't control mixing
together.

"I'm not in heat," she hissed, and drove in again, this

time with her hands, throwing a left, a right and then an uppercut.

He blocked every move with an open palm, that same casual slap that was as maddening as the raw, edgy hunger that drove her need to attack him.

"Sure you are." His voice dropped even lower and his eyes drifted possessively over her body. "You're hot as hell. Your scent is driving me insane."

She flushed, turning nearly crimson, and rushed him again. He sidestepped and caught her, spinning her around until her back was against him, her arms pinned to her sides, trapping her tight against his body. His scent was potent, wild, sexy. Every ragged breath burned through her lungs. Adrenaline was hot and liquid rushing through her veins.

She hissed again. He lowered his head, holding her in an unbreakable grip, his strength enormous. He lapped at the side of her neck, in a slow, languorous display of ownership, sending shivers through her entire body. Tongues of flames licked over her skin. His teeth scraped along her neck, down her throat and then his lips pressed against her ear.

"The female leopard always rebuffs her mate, giving him a show of claws, hissing and spitting like the little cat you are. All the while she's seductive, driving her mate into a frenzy of hunger even as she pushes him away. Her body calls to his. Like yours does to mine. Do you know why, *Hafelina?*"

She went very still, sensing danger. Absolute danger. His teeth slid down her neck, nuzzled at her shoulder. "Because you belong to me."

His teeth sank deep into the back of her neck, the pain and pleasure of it seared her heart, sizzled through her

veins and scorched her most feminine core. Her womb
spasmed, and clenched. Damp heat gathered between her
legs. She couldn't stop herself from rubbing against him,
almost desperate for relief. His knee came up between her
legs, driving into her clenching heat. Sparks burst behind
her eyes. Her breath caught in her throat and every muscle
in her body tightened. She nearly sobbed with the pleasure
crashing through her body.

It was humiliating, but she couldn't stop the way she
moved against him, frantic now, every nerve ending raw.
He growled a soft warning when she struggled. His mouth
moved over her neck, his tongue swirling over the stinging bite, sending waves of scorching heat through her over-
loaded system.

"I'm your mate, Isabeau. Now. Always. There is nothing else. You belong to me and I belong to you. You don't
have to like it, but you can't deny it. Your body knows it.
Your cat knows. Fight me all you want, but you know it as
well."

She hated the knowledge in his eyes when she looked
over her shoulder, into his heavy-lidded stare. He looked
so sensual. So male. So intense. He looked at her as if he
knew no one else would ever satisfy her. No one else
could hold her so still, so hypnotized, his thigh rubbing
over and into her, sending waves of pulsing need crashing
through her. His hold was possessive. He rubbed his face
over her neck, her shoulder, her hair, almost as if he was
leaving his scent all over her. Claiming her. Warning off
all other males.

Muscles bunched in her stomach, arousal teased her
thighs and breasts, her breath turned ragged. A sob escaped.
His body was full and heavy, pressing tightly with urgent
demand against the small of her back. His scent filled her

lungs. He was everywhere and her skin felt too tight, her clothes hurt.

Keeping her arms pinned with one arm wrapped tightly around her, his fist bunched in her hair and he dragged her head back. She looked into his golden eyes, dark now with heat. Intense hunger. So much possession. She watched his mouth come down toward hers and she should have moved—should have fought him—but her breath left her lungs in a rush and she was lost in her own need. His mouth was hard and demanding, a crush of command, a taking, a branding and she tasted lust, tasted sin and sex. She tasted *him.*

She'd forgotten that addicting taste. Her mouth opened to him and she indulged her need, feeding there, feeling taken when all he was doing was kissing her, over and over, his lips rough, his mouth hot, his tongue stroking caresses into a fire that threatened to consume her. She heard her own strangled whimper, a sound of intense need escaping before she could think to prevent it.

She could no longer think clearly, her brain fogging over, her skull too tight, the throbbing beat of hunger like a jackhammer in her head. Her breasts ached, nipples hard and straining against the thin material of her bra. She couldn't stop rubbing against him, needing the hard pressure of his thigh to relieve the terrible ache that wouldn't stop, yet knowing it wouldn't be enough until he filled her completely. His mouth moved on her shoulder—a burning brand and he whispered low and sexy in her ear.

"Stop fighting it, *Sestrilla,* let it happen."

His voice, that sexy, velvet whisper of sin triggered the drenching orgasm that flashed through her body like a firestorm. She writhed in utter shame, as her heart slammed too hard in her chest and the waves of heat rippled and pulsed through her.

He knew. He knew what he did to her, she could hear it in the humming satisfaction rumbling in his chest, the purr emanating from his throat. Tears burned behind her eyes. She hated her lack of control, the raw need that tormented her in his presence. He should have been the last person whose touch she needed, yet here she was, a few hours in his company, allowing his touch—*craving* his touch.

How did she wrench her soul free from him? Take her heart back? Stop her body's response? He'd left her empty. Broken. He was a terrible obsession she couldn't get over, no matter how hard she fought. She had no idea how to stop the deadly hunger every time she looked at him. His voice alone triggered it. She was caught in his trap, in the illusion he wove and she couldn't break free.

He'd leave her again. He'd come to the rain forest to seduce a woman. *She'd* brought him to the rain forest to seduce another woman. *And he'd taken the job until he knew she was the client.* What was wrong with her? Where the hell was her cat now? The treacherous animal coming close to the surface, revealing her heat, her hunger and then deserting when Isabeau needed her claws and strength the most. She felt limp. Shattered. Humiliated. She was no match for a man like Conner Vega. She wasn't even in his league.

"Let go." Her voice shook, but she got the words out. Her body shuddered with illicit pleasure even as it began cooling rapidly after the terrible burning need that had raged. She was left drained and sated and confused.

"Isabeau, look at me."

The sound of his voice made her close her eyes like a child trying to block out the ghost that always haunted her.

"Just let go." Because if he didn't, she was going to burst into tears and sob loud enough for any enemy in the vicinity to come running.

"Relax. We're not out of the woods yet, honey. I can't have you fighting with me when we're in the middle of enemy territory. Just calm down for me."

"I'm perfectly calm." Shattered. Broken. But calm.

5

"EVERYTHING will be all right, Isabeau."

The devil's whisper. That sinful, sexy, *lying* voice. She'd succumbed to his power the first time she was tested. At that moment, she despised the cat inside of her nearly as much as she hated her human self. Isabeau forced her body to relax, showing him the fight was gone.

Conner loosened his hold on her reluctantly, as if he didn't quite trust her surrender. She glanced at his face and saw herself as a shadow in the reflection of his eyes. She felt like a shadow, insubstantial beside his power. She ducked her head, unable to face even just the shadow of herself. She never wanted to look in the mirror again.

"I'm your mate, Isabeau. There's no shame between mates."

She lifted her chin and stepped away from him, her knees rubbery, her heart still thundering. "You're nothing to me. And whatever is happening to my body, has nothing to do with you. Any man would have been satisfactory."

She made the mistake of looking at him. The amber in his eyes crystallized, turned gold and then yellow. Flecks of green merged, his pupils fully dilated and his stare focused and deadly. He stepped close to her, invading her space. If there was rage, it smoldered beneath the surface. His face was hard, mouth firm. A muscle bunched in his jaw, but his gaze held steady, a clear warning.

"Say whatever you have to say to keep your pride, Isabeau. Words don't matter much. But you think long and hard before you endanger someone's life. That's on you. Mating is a higher law and there's no getting around it. You can't pretend it away. This is between us, no one else. We'll work it out."

She blinked rapidly to stop the burning tears. Damn him. He'd destroyed her. He couldn't have known how deep a blow he'd struck. She wasn't the kind of girl boys had flocked to when she'd been growing up. There were no dates or dances in school. Boys had rushed to her friends but never to her. Same with college. She had never discovered why others avoided her. She tried to learn the art of flirting, of conversation. She'd made it a point to be friendly, but she was always pushed aside and had finally accepted she wasn't attractive to the opposite sex and women found her too intimidating to be her friend.

Conner had come along and made her feel beautiful. He'd made her feel wanted. Of course, his name hadn't been Conner and he'd been lying to her about his feelings for her. And she should have known. Men like Conner, dangerous, magnetic, charming and sexy, simply didn't look at women like Isabeau. He'd made love to her over and over, and all the time he'd been doing his job. Someone had paid him to seduce her in order to get close to her father.

The shame was overpowering. She felt like such a fool.

To believe, after all the years of knowing that men didn't find her attractive, that a man like him would fall head over heels for her was ridiculous. She felt almost like she deserved what happened to her for her own stupidity.

"You killed my father." She flung the accusation at him, so mixed up she couldn't breathe properly. Her breath came in ragged, harsh gasps, her lungs burning, as if she was starved for air. He sounded so calm. So in control. She wanted to slap his face all over again.

"I had nothing to do with your father's death. That was his choice and you damn well know it. I told you before, I have enough sins on my soul, Isabeau, without you adding things I'm not responsible for." He towered over her for a long moment, his expression grim, his eyes deadly, and then he drew in a breath and touched her hair with gentle fingers. "I know it's difficult to be with me, but you're doing fine."

"You call this fine? I'm a wreck. I'm so mixed up," she admitted. Because her pride was already long gone. He could smell her arousal, her body's call to him. There were no secrets between leopards. "I can't even think straight." She pushed a shaky hand through her hair—the strands he'd just brushed a caress over. She couldn't deny the mating thing, not really, not when her body was insane for his, but she was still human and she had a brain. She had to find control. "Maybe everything you're saying about the leopard and the mate is the truth, but I refuse to allow it to rule me."

"You have so much more power than you realize, Isabeau, but it will come to you," he assured.

She hated the gentleness in his voice—the caress—that sexy note that stroked her already raw nerves. Now that she knew it was practice, a tool of his trade, one would think she wouldn't be susceptible, but it seemed her body believed him in spite of her brain.

"I'll teach you the things you need to know to live with your cat. You'll find you already have the strength and power to deal with her. She won't accept any other male and she'll drive you toward me, but you already know that."

"She isn't going to get her way."

"Look at me."

The quiet command in his voice was impossible to resist. She found herself looking into the eyes of his cat and it was both exhilarating and terrifying at the same time. His eyes had gone so yellow they were golden and lethal, a cat's deadly stare, wholly focused and possessive.

"It isn't any different for me. No other woman would be accepted by my cat. When you slapped me you left your mark in my skin, on my bones. Your cat claimed me whether you knew what you were doing or not. I can't sleep. I can barely function. I'm edgy and moody and two breaths away from fighting every moment of the day. That's the reality, Isabeau. I have to accept it just as you do."

He was telling the truth. She saw it in his eyes. Heard it in his voice. She shouldn't have felt satisfaction, but it was there, as petty as that was. One more thing to hate about herself, but if she spent her life craving a man she could never be with, he could damn well pine away for her. She let her breath out and some of the tension eased from her taut muscles.

"I didn't know. About the mark. I didn't know."

"I know. Your cat knew. She was angry and she had every right to be. Let's call a truce until we get the children home safe. We'll sort this out later."

"You'll still help us then?"

"Yes." Conner spoke tersely, aware he could never walk away from her. She still didn't know just how strong the pull between their cats would be. He knew how strong the pull between the man and woman was, but she had every right to reject him. He had to find a way to redeem himself and if that meant he had to seduce another woman, as abhorrent as it would be for him—and for his cat—he would do whatever it took to convince her he was serious about atoning. Words weren't going to convince her, only action. And action was something he was good at.

"Can you teach me more things like climbing the tree?"

He nodded. "You've learned martial arts, and you're not bad, but you aren't utilizing your reflexes. You need to be more confident. We can work on that as well." He flashed her a faint grin. "Of course I'm not certain I want you to learn to be a better fighter. You have a penchant for using your skills on me."

She managed a slight smile, her stomach settling. "I liked being in the canopy," she admitted, striving for civility. She'd summoned him to her and now it was a case of "being careful what she wished for." She had to live with her decision and apparently so did he. Finding she wasn't alone in her desperate, clawing need, made dealing with it much easier.

"I do too." He stepped away from her and gathered the fallen man's weapons along with the gun she'd left on the ground. "Let's rendezvous with the others and make our plans. We've got a lot to do before the party if we're going to pull this off. And we have to find a way to safeguard Adan's grandson."

Relief flooded her body. "Do you think there's a way? Or do you think she's already had him killed?"

"It wouldn't make sense for her to kill him until she's

disposed of Adan. She'd want to make a point, but if Adan capitulates, by some miracle, it would be a huge victory for her. He's the most respected elder the tribes have. If he caves, so will the others."

"So she sent these men out after him knowing they might fail?"

"This is his turf. He's at home in the rain forest; these men aren't. She has two rogue leopards on her payroll. She would have sent them if she wanted to make certain Adan died. He trains Special Forces from all over the world in survival. She knew he might survive and she's hoping if he does, he will have gotten the message she's willing to play hardball with him."

"He won't open her routes for her. He feels very strongly on the subject."

"I imagine he does," Conner agreed. "She's murdering his people, forcing them into servitude. He's a proud man who managed to bring his people into this century, yet still keep his culture intact. He'll fight her with every breath in his body."

"Then how?"

"We just need him to buy us some time. She doesn't know, or care anything about the tribe, so Adan can make up ceremonies that have to be done before he leaves and buy us a couple of days there. She'll be gloating, figuring now that she's bent the will of the most influential tribe elder, everyone will fall in with her plans. Once he's in the forest, she'll have to send her rogues to watch him. She'll have no choice. None of her other men would have a chance of staying up with him and she'll need to know he's complying with her orders."

Isabeau was horrified. "Conner, he won't deliver the drugs and they'll kill him."

"Adan doesn't die so easy. And we want the rogues to trail him. We need them out of the compound."

"Dead. You mean you want the rogues dead." Her eyes met his steadily.

"What did you think we were going to do? Smile and ask pretty please? You sent for me because I'm a bastard. The biggest bastard you know. That's what you need to get those kids back and to make certain it doesn't happen again. She'll tear those villages apart once we leave if she's alive. You wanted me here because I'm the one you know who can get them back. You knew exactly what you were getting, so don't act shocked. Anyone who hires us knows what has to be done, they just don't have the guts to do it themselves."

She ignored the bitterness and glimpse of hurt in his normally expressionless voice. "I have the guts. Adan said no. And for your information, I wasn't putting judgment on you."

His eyebrow shot up. "You accused me of killing your father. I stood there like a damned idiot and almost got shot for you."

"What are you talking about?"

He studied her pale face for a long moment. His eyes slowing changed back to dark gold. "It doesn't matter, Isabeau. We have a truce. Let's just keep to that."

She frowned at him, her expression genuinely puzzled. "I don't understand what you meant. I saw you."

"You saw your father put a gun to my head. He nearly blew my brains out."

"You had him trapped. What was he supposed to do?"

"I went in unarmed. I tried to talk him into surrendering, into walking out with me and letting the team take down his boss, but he wouldn't listen." He made certain to look her in the eye. She wouldn't want to believe him, but her cat would know he was telling the truth. The cat was becoming strong enough to emerge, and the closer she got to the surface, the more she would enhance Isabeau's abilities. She would know if he lied and if he told the truth.

Isabeau refused to be a coward, looking him straight in the eye and forcing herself to remember the terrifying moment when she'd stepped into the room and saw her father falling, blood splattering the wall behind him. There'd been so much blood. At first she hadn't known what happened. There was no sound, a silencer on the weapon used. She had opened her mouth to scream, and her lover had been on her so fast she couldn't even see him move, his hand clapping hard over her mouth, taking her to the floor, his eyes cold and hard and so demonic she'd been terrified.

She'd lain under his body, watching the blood turn black and thick around her father, and the man she'd loved with her soul, now a stranger who was clearly working with the man who had shot her father. Funny, she could barely recall the other man, only the gun and her father falling and Conner's face, carved of stone, grim, without a trace of love or caring. Without a trace of remorse. He'd held her there while others moved in with guns, his hand clamped tight so she could barely take a breath. She'd watched them, grim and silent, weapons crisscrossing their bodies, move through the room, stepping over her father as if he were a piece of garbage and not a man who had laughed and played with her, teaching her to drive, sitting up all night with her when she was ill.

Isabeau swallowed hard and looked away from him. It was totally dark now, but she could see when she should have been blind. She didn't want to see. Maybe staying blind in the darkness was the best way for self-preservation, because God help her if she came to terms with what Conner had done.

"We've got to go," Conner said.

She nodded, letting her breath out in relief. She couldn't think about that night. She'd spent too much time delving into her father's affairs, feeling as if she was betraying him. She'd spent too many sleepless nights, had too many nightmares.

"Put your shoes back on, you can't walk barefoot."

She sank down without arguing and pulled her shoes on, watching as he did the same. She knew by the way he tilted his head that he was listening to something. She caught vibrations of sound, like an echo almost, but couldn't sort it out.

"Are they close?" Instinctively she lowered her voice.

"Someone is coming this way. It isn't one of ours."

"How can you tell?"

"They're too loud. And I can smell their sweat. It isn't a leopard scent or Adan's. We'll be fine. He's alone and he's being stalked."

"Why can't I smell him?"

"Your cat retreated. Women move closer and closer to their leopard emerging, but she comes and goes quite often at first. No one knows why. Maybe she's just as nervous as you are. My cat has settled, which means yours has moved away from us."

She shook her head. "It's hard to believe. If I hadn't seen or felt it, I'd think we were both crazy."

His eyes went soft. Liquid. Sexy. Her breath hissed out. She couldn't blame her reaction on her cat when her cat was far away. This was woman, pure and simple, so attracted to a man she went damp just looking at him.

"I know this is a lot for you to take in all at once, Isabeau, but it will get easier. And you haven't run screaming even with all the death you've seen today and the revelations about who and what you are."

There was pride in his voice—respect even. That was his talent. He could make her feel special. More than special, extraordinary. The admiration in his voice stroked like fingers over skin. How did he do that? His voice was so compelling. So real. There was no way to desensitize her skin after he'd touched her with his fingers, or after hearing his voice. It was impossible, at least for her. Her nerves were raw—little electric sparks arced over her breasts and down her stomach.

She wasn't experienced enough, or sophisticated enough to be casual with him. Everything he did and the way he talked affected her physically and emotionally. He was so far out of her league she didn't have a prayer of hiding anything from him, so she shrugged her shoulders and made certain her shoes were tied.

"I'm not fragile, Conner. I knew what I was getting into, or at least what it would take to get the children back."

A blood-curdling scream filled the night. Chills went down her spine and she swiveled toward the sound. The harrowing cry was cut off in mid-note. Isabeau stood shivering, realizing that once again, Conner had inserted his body between her and whatever had made that god-awful, horrible sound. He always protected her, even in the cabin when he thought she might want him dead. Even when her father had been killed. It hadn't felt like protection then— he'd prevented her from crying out—but his body had shielded hers throughout a terrible shootout.

She didn't want to notice that about Conner, how he protected her, because that small little voice in her head would begin dreaming, whispering that she mattered to him. He was a master manipulator, and she'd paid him to come. He hadn't sought her out on his own. He hadn't fallen to his knees and begged forgiveness. Even when he told her his cat wouldn't accept anyone else, he had been matter-of-fact and unenthusiastic.

He skirted the dead body of the man he'd killed earlier, leading her into the darkness, padding ahead in silence. She couldn't even hear him breathe, but she felt his presence— very solid—close to her. She felt like his shadow, attached, yet not, and the thought made her smile. Everything in her life was so mixed up, so upside down, yet she was more alive than she'd been in a year.

She'd spent a good portion of her time in the rain forest, and she'd learned to really respect it. One had to be careful all the time, much like divers in an ocean. Her beautiful surroundings could turn on her in a moment, yet being with Conner took that edge of fear away. She believed nothing could happen to her as long as she was close to him. He exuded absolute confidence, and it carried over to her.

Was it possible to learn to be like him? Could she learn his abilities? Have his power and strength? She wanted it to be true. She loved climbing the tree and making her way through the canopy. It felt like living in the clouds in spite of the fire and the fleeing wildlife. She'd felt the heartbeat of the rain forest through her cat, the joy and freedom of being so close to nature.

"Why weren't they afraid of us? The animals. Didn't we smell like predators to them? I can smell your cat when you're close to me and you can smell mine."

"Our people have always been guardians of the rain forest. Over the years, of course, our people have intermarried with humans and have gone to the cities, but the instinct to protect is in all of us and the animals respond to it."

He reached back and took her hand, tucking her fingers into his back pocket. "Stay close to me. We're coming up on the river. They'll have an ambush set."

Her heart jumped the moment his fingers brushed hers. It was worse holding on to his jean pocket. The heat of his skin seemed to surround her, envelope her, just put her in a cocoon of warmth. She could actually feel him moving, the ripple of his muscles, the fluid steps, more animal than man. She tried to feel her cat, to emulate the flow of his body, but she seemed that little bit out of sync, occasionally stumbling over the uneven ground now.

She'd always had good night vision, but her sight wasn't like it had been earlier when her cat had been close. She knew the difference now, just as she knew she was fairly experienced in the rain forest, not like Adan, but she'd been superb with her cat close.

"Feels good, doesn't it?"

His voice was a bare thread of sound, projected—almost—into her mind rather than heard. She felt the vibration go through her brain like a heat wave. She curled her fingers around the edge of his pocket, an involuntary reaction, and instantly he halted and half turned to her, bending his head close, his palm cupping the side of her face, thumb brushing a reassuring stroke along her cheek.

"You aren't afraid, are you? I won't let anything happen to you, Isabeau. I know you have no reason to trust me, but I give you my word I'll guard you with my life. There's no need for fear. We've got friends close by. If it's too difficult here on the ground, I can take you back up into the canopy and you can wait while I help them clear the way to safety."

She shook her head. "I want to stay with you. I'm not afraid."

"You're shivering."

Was she? She hadn't noticed. It wasn't because she was afraid of the men sent to kill them—or rather to kill Adan. Excitement. Anticipation. Even being close to Conner again. "Just nerves," she said, simplifying without lying. "I don't want to have to kill someone. I think I could if I was defending someone else, but I'm afraid I'd hesitate and get everyone killed."

There was a part of her that wanted to jerk away from him and tell him to quit touching her, but another, more masochistic part craved each brush of his fingers, every intense, compelling look from his shattering gaze.

"I don't want you having to do the things I do, Isabeau. There's no need. I'll teach you all the things you need to know to defend yourself and anyone you love, but when it comes down to it, you lose a little part of yourself every time you kill. It isn't as bad in leopard form. Our cats are pure predators and that helps, which is why many of us choose that form when hunting." He indicated the night.

She listened. At first she only heard her own heart pounding. The sound of air moving in and out of her lungs. She was acutely aware of Conner so close to her, his body heat warming her, his large frame protecting her. To her right she heard the soft brush of fur against something rough— a tree trunk she guessed. She inhaled and scented something wild. Her skin tingled as she recognized the scent of a leopard.

Conner stepped closer to her, his arm sliding around her to bring her tight against him. His lips pressed against her ear. "He's hunting something close to us. Reach for the information. Even without your cat close, you can use its senses. You have a kind of radar. You must have known who was at your door sometimes before you opened it."

She nodded.

"A cat's whiskers are embedded deep in tissue and the nerve endings transmit information to the brain. You can use that information as a guidance system, sort of like feeling your way in the dark. You can read objects, where everything and everyone is in the forest, how close you are to it and what it is." His fingertips slid over her face. "Like Braille. Right now, Elijah knows exactly where his prey is, his position and where he needs to strike to deliver a killing bite."

Conner couldn't resist touching her. Cats were tactile and he needed not only to keep his hands on her, but to rub his scent over her. She rubbed her face along his chest and throat, without even realizing she was doing it. He remembered how often she'd done just that when they'd lain together, naked, skin to skin. He should have realized then. Scent and touch was tremendously important to their species—a necessary thing.

Isabeau had taught him to play. With her, he'd felt different—*more*. Often, when he'd be curled up on the bed, cat-napping after a long and satisfying sexual encounter, she would stalk and pounce on him, so they would end up in a rough-and-tumble play that led right back to much more sensual play.

He'd missed everything about her, especially the way she rubbed her scent all over him, like now. Just the feel of her soft body pressing close to his, the feminine fragrance rising around him, wrapping him up in her, so that when he inhaled he took her into his lungs. He wanted to hold her forever, to bury his face in that sweet spot between her neck and shoulder and just breathe her in until he knew she was real again.

He tensed when Elijah made his move, just a scant thirty

feet from them, leaping on the gunman, dragging him to the ground and holding his prey with a suffocating bite to the throat until all struggle ceased. He heard the soft thud of the body, scented blood and then death. All the while, he kept his arms around Isabeau, grateful he had a reason to be close to her.

He knew the exact moment she scented death. Her body trembled slightly, and she snuggled a little deeper into him, but he was proud of her. She stood. There in the darkness, with enemies in the night, and violence and death, she stood. That was the kind of mother he wanted for his children. A mate who would stand with him no matter the circumstances.

How the hell had he been so blind? How could he have blown his chance with her? He'd more than disappointed her. Her first experience, her first love, had betrayed her, left her with nothing but a dead father and too many questions. She hadn't even known his real name. How did one get forgiveness for that kind of betrayal?

Something moved off to their left and just in front of them. Leaves crackled. He felt Elijah's sudden stillness. His hand slipped over Isabeau's mouth, a gentle reminder to stay quiet. She looked up at him and his breath caught in his throat. There was no fear there. Her eyes were beautiful, like two jewels pressed into the pale moonlight. He held a finger to his lips and indicated she stay where she was. She nodded in understanding, but when he slowly loosened his grip to step away from her, she caught his arm.

He leaned into her, pressing his lips to her ear. "I'll be right back. Don't move. Not a muscle."

He didn't like leaving her, but the enemy was too close and Elijah couldn't get to him before the man would discover them. Their adversary was moving closer, the tread

of his boots loud in the night. Conner let his lips drift over
her ear and into her hair, savoring her for just one moment
before he moved away to intercept. He didn't look back,
but he listened. There was no rustle of clothing, no sound to
indicate she'd moved, yet she must have been a little afraid
left by herself deep in the rain forest with a leopard close
by and men with guns hunting anyone human.

Pride stirred in him as he slipped close to the enemy. He
crept close enough to reach out and touch the man. Dressed
in combat gear, crouched low, his automatic rifle cradled in
his hands, the man's face was grim and businesslike. Conner caught the scent of fear as the head swiveled back and
forth.

"Jeff," he hissed. "It's Bart. Answer me."

Conner could have told him that a leopard had killed
Jeff just a few feet away, but there was no point. Instead, he
slipped out of the heavier brush into the open, directly behind Bart. As he reached for him, he heard a soft movement
near Isabeau. She gasped, the sound audible in the night.
Bart whirled toward that slight noise. His eyes widened
as he saw the dark shadow inches from him. His mouth
opened, no sound emerging as he brought the gun around,
finger on the trigger, already firing as he tried to line up the
gun with Conner's chest. The muzzle blazed blue-white.
Behind and around Conner, bark and leaves flew into the
air.

Isabeau cried out, a choking cry of pain, and he scented
blood. His cat went insane, snarling and raging even as he
caught Imelda's soldier by the throat, claws bursting through
his fingertips. The man's screams were cut off abruptly to
a small gurgle. Conner threw him aside and spun around,
rushing back through the thick brush to Isabeau.

He skidded to a halt just before he came through the

brush out into the open. The scent of a male leopard mixed with man was heavy and mingled with blood—Isabeau's blood. She was breathing. He could hear her, the air rushing in and out of her lungs, ragged and harsh. He felt her pain, knew she was hurt and his cat grew frantic. The scent of the other male inflamed the leopard even more, so that he clawed close to the surface, demanding to be let loose.

Conner forced himself to think, not react. He could see the stranger, eyes glowing red like a cat's in the darkness. The hand on her throat was not human, the claws digging into skin. He held Isabeau in front of him like a shield, his attention on the brush to his right. Snarling, showing a mouthful of teeth, he snarled a warning toward something Conner couldn't see in the brush.

Elijah. The leopard crouched, waiting for his opportunity. Cats had patience, especially leopards. They could wait for hours if they had to, and right now it was a bit of a standoff. Isabeau didn't look toward Elijah, or even back at her assailant. She kept her gaze glued on the brush where Conner breathed away his fear. She knew he was there. And she knew he'd come for her. There was no panic in her eyes.

Blood dripped steadily down her left arm where a bullet must have grazed her. Conner's gaze locked on to his enemy. Leopard for sure. Most likely one of the rogues. He would never get out of the rain forest alive. Not with Elijah waiting in the brush. Or Rio creeping up behind him. Not with Adan closing in from one side, poison darts ready, or the Santos brothers crawling, belly down, approaching from the other side.

Conner was aware of all of them, but dimly, as if far away. Every fiber of his being was focused on the leopard holding his mate hostage. He stepped out of the brush, facing the man. Isabeau gasped and shook her head. His cat leapt, hissing and growling, wanting to rip and slice his opponent to shreds. There was no way to calm his cat, so he didn't try to suppress the animal's natural instincts. He just took a firmer grip. Of course he wanted to destroy the man touching his mate, but keeping her alive was more important than anything else, especially pride.

"Let her go," he said quietly. "She can't help you."

The rogue snarled with a great show of teeth and dug his claws deeper into Isabeau's throat in warning. Droplets of blood ran down her skin. Conner marked each one, assessing the damage the leopard was doing to her throat.

"Are you all right?"

Isabeau pushed down the burning pain in her throat, nodding, terrified, not for herself, but for Conner. He stood without a weapon, facing the man holding her, and she had no way of warning him that her captor was enormously strong. She'd never felt such strength running through someone—like steel. He could snap her in half easily should he be so inclined. She tried a cautious movement. Instantly the claws went deeper.

Isabeau coughed, and tried to drag air into her burning lungs. She kept her eyes on Conner. He looked utterly calm—completely confident—and it gave her the ability to stay cool.

"Which one are you? Suma or Zorba?" Conner asked.

The leopard snarled again and Conner's cat clawed for supremacy. His eyes must have changed because the man's expression changed. Fear entered for the first time, cracking the air of superiority. "What difference does it make?"

Conner shrugged. "The difference between dying slow in agonizing pain or quick and merciful."

"I don't much like my choices."

"Then you shouldn't have put your claws into my mate."

A nervous tic broke the concentrated stare the leopard was trying to maintain. Conner noted that and immediately changed his opinion. This one couldn't be either Suma or Zorba. They were older, more experienced, and neither would flinch at trying to take another leopard's mate. It was strictly taboo in their society and carried a death sentence, but either of the two rogues wouldn't have cared, believing themselves above the law.

"I just want to get out of here in one piece. I don't want her hurt."

Conner lifted his eyebrow. "You have a strange way of showing that with your claws in her throat. Your own elder would sentence you to death for harming a woman."

"You have no idea what's going on."

"Tell me." Conner kept firm control of his cat, who was angry with him now for not leaping forward to kill.

The smell of Isabeau's blood drove the animal insane. Conner might not have been able to stay in control had she looked terrified, or cried, but she kept her eyes locked with his, silently telling him she knew he would get her out of the situation. He had no idea if she knew the others were closing in, but he knew. He was counting on Adan's poison dart.

One slash of those lethal claws and the rogue would kill Isabeau. If the cat knew he had no chance, he just might be spiteful enough to take her with him. Leopards were notorious for their black tempers. All of the members of his team were fast—as men or leopards—but those claws were already too close to her jugular, and all leopards knew exactly where to strike a deathblow.

"You shouldn't be out here. There's an Indian stirring

up trouble. If I kill him, I have a job. It's no big deal. He's a pain in the ass to everyone, holding up progress and killing innocent men who get in his way. We have a chance at making a lot of money with him gone."

"So Cortez promised you money to kill Adan Carpio and you decided all those children were expendable."

The leopard blinked. "What children? What are you talking about? This isn't about children."

"Suma left that part out when he approached you, didn't he?" Conner held up his hand to stay the execution. They were all in place. The leopard was young and impressionable. And stupid. He'd looked up to the wrong leopard. "Suma led an attack on Carpio's village. They killed several people in the attack and kidnapped children to force Adan into opening up drug routes. Suma betrayed our kind to an outsider and he also murdered a female leopard. Is that the kind of man you want to work for?"

Isabeau's swift indrawn breath was audible. The leopard nearly let go of her, retracting his claws in his shock. "That's not true."

"Isabeau is going to walk toward me and you're going to let her. You're surrounded with no way out. Keep looking at me," Conner commanded when the young leopard started to turn. "I'm the one who is going to decide whether you live or die, not anyone else. What you do right now is going to be a life or death decision."

"How can I trust you?"

"No matter what, I'm going to teach you a lesson," Conner said. "You don't get to walk away free when you made my mate bleed. As for trusting me, you'll have to decide what you want to take a chance on. You touch her again, I give you my word, you're a dead man."

Conner never took his gaze from that of the young leopard's. He knew the man could see the truth in his eyes. He knew he could see his raging leopard, the demand to kill. The young man sniffed and caught the scent of the others surrounding him. He swallowed and stepped back away from Isabeau, raising his hands slightly.

"They really killed a female leopard? You're certain?"

"She was my mother," Conner said. "I'm certain."

Isabeau gasped, and made a small sound of distress.

The young man paled. "I didn't know. There's no mistake?"

"Suma works for and recruits for Imelda Cortez. She's head of the largest drug cartel in the region and she's directly responsible for the murder of the tribes and destruction of our forest," Conner continued. "That's who he revealed our people to and that's the man you were working for."

The leopard swallowed and held his hands out away from his body, raised his head to expose his throat. "Carry out the sentence then. Ignorance is not a defense."

6

CONNER let his gaze unlock from that of the inexperienced leopard's and allowed himself to look at Isabeau. His breath caught in his throat. Her face was pale, her eyes glazed with pain. Blood dripped from her throat and arm. She swayed slightly as if unsteady. Something inside him crumbled and another part of him wanted to leap on the leopard cub and rip him to shreds. It would be so easy to tear out his throat in retribution. Every instinct urged him to do just that.

For a long moment the forest seemed to hold its breath. The cat inside him prowled back and forth, occasionally throwing himself at the bonds holding him, testing Conner's strength and resolve. Felipe and Leonardo moved out into the open, circling the young leopard. Elijah shoved his head through the leaves. Close. Too close to Isabeau.

His cat snarled, his gaze swinging toward the new threat to his mate. Red haze burned through his mind. A warning went off in his brain. The cat was too close, raking to get free. His muscles contorted. His mouth ached. Fingers curled. Sweat broke out on his body as he tried to fight the cat back.

Isabeau walked right up to him, unafraid, although her body trembled. "Conner?" Her voice was soft but demanding.

He reached for her, brought her against him, holding her close for a moment, listening to the reassuring beat of her heart, the steadiness of her breath. It took a few minutes to take control of his cat. The scent of the other leopards and the strong smell of blood nearly drove him mad, but her ready acceptance of his touch managed to calm him enough to stay in control. He bent his head to her throat, examining the puncture wounds. The young leopard had been careful to miss her jugular. Blood welled from the cuts, but they were definitely not lethal. The cub hadn't meant to kill her. It wouldn't stop Conner from teaching him a lesson, but it would save the boy's life.

He brushed the pads of his fingers over the claw marks and then used the rough velvet of his tongue to heal them, the way of his cat. The coppery taste mixed with the fresh rain and the fragrance of her skin. She rested her forehead against his chest, obviously exhausted. He needed to get her to shelter soon.

"I have to look at your arm, *Sestrilla*." He ripped her sleeve away to expose the wound. A chunk of her arm was missing, up near the bicep, but it was a flesh wound. They'd been lucky. "Infection happens fast in the forest," he told her, his voice as gentle as he could make it when his cat refused to settle.

"I've got a few things in my bag that will help," she confided. "I study medicinal plants, so I always carry a few."

"Do you have painkillers?"

"They don't work so well on me," she said, attempting a small smile.

He was grateful for that little smile. She was comforting him, and that turned him inside out . He could tell it bothered her that his usual calm was gone on her behalf. She was having a hard enough time keeping him at arm's length, and having his cat *and* the man be so agitated over her injuries and the threat to her was disturbing.

"We've got to go," Rio said. He was in the forest, out of Isabeau's sight.

Conner knew it wasn't modesty. Leopards weren't modest about nudity. When they shifted, they generally carried or cached clothes in the areas they lived, but they often shifted in front of one another. Rio was more concerned for Isabeau, who wasn't raised leopard, and for Conner's reaction. Isabeau was near the Han Vol Dan, the emerging of her leopard and her leopard's heat. She was putting out enough hormones to rock all the males, mated or not. He wasn't taking a chance of Conner getting more aggressive.

"We've taken care of most of them, and the others have turned tail and run, but they might suddenly get their courage back. Let's get to shelter."

"What about me?" the young leopard asked.

There was silence. Conner looked over the top of Isabeau's head at the young man. He'd been like that once, looking for adventure and something besides the village.

"You'll be coming with us. I have a few things to say to you."

The kid put his arms down as he let out his breath in obvious relief.

"Don't look happy about it, kid," Conner snapped. "I'm going to beat the hell out of you."

"Jeremiah. My name's Jeremiah Wheating." He flexed

his claws and grinned at Conner. Now that he was safe, he was back to looking cocky. "I'll look forward to it."

Conner had the urge to cuff the kid. Seriously smack him. His mate was still bleeding and the kid was looking like he was full of himself all over again. He turned away from the young leopard to keep from springing on him and ripping the smirk from his face. With gentle hands, he wrapped up Isabeau's arm and, because he couldn't help himself, he pressed a kiss over the bandage, uncaring what she—or any of the others—thought.

"Let's move out. Adan? You all right?"

"Still deciding whether or not to shoot our young friend," Adan answered from where he was hiding in the brush. "It's more tempting than you could possibly know."

"Oh, I think I have some idea," Conner said. He slid his hand down Isabeau's arm until his fingers tangled with hers. "Let's get moving."

"Where are we going?" the kid asked eagerly. He nearly bounced as he hurried after them.

Elijah launched himself into the air, leaping on the kid's back, hitting him with enough force to knock him over. The boy rolled in the leaves and insects, and Elijah kept going without breaking stride, his large paws making no sound as he paced alongside Conner.

Conner sent him a small nod of appreciation. Isabeau turned her face against his side and muffled a small laugh.

"You did good, Isabeau," he praised. "You didn't panic."

"I knew you'd come," she said, shocking him.

There was a quiet acceptance in her voice. She might not realize it, but she trusted him a lot more than she let on. "He didn't threaten me at first. He was shocked when he came out of the brush and I was there."

Conner sniffed his disdain, his cat chuffing in annoyance. The kid hadn't used his leopard senses even when he was hunting. His disdain for Adan had left him handicapped. He hadn't done his homework. He didn't even realize who he was hunting. Adan's skill in the rain forest was known far and wide, yet the young man hadn't been aware of him.

"What village do you come from?" Conner asked, suddenly suspicious.

"My village is in Costa Rica," Jeremiah said cheerfully. He shot Conner a quick grin. "I've been around. It's not like I've never been out of the forest."

This time Rio charged him, knocking him flat. He hit the kid hard enough to produce a grunt of pain. As Rio moved off the boy, he cuffed him hard with his large paw, his claws retracted, but definitely a reprimand.

Jeremiah rolled, came up in a crouch, scowling at the large leopard as he dusted himself off. "Hey! I have been around."

"Obviously you didn't learn respect," Conner pointed out. "You have five elders here and an elder from one of the local Indian tribes as well as a female. So far I haven't been impressed."

The boy had the grace to look ashamed. "I just want to see some action," he said.

"How did Suma contact you?" Conner asked.

"Internet. He put an ad up asking for help. I figured I was just the thing he needed." Jeremiah stuck out his chest.

"Young. Impressionable. Stupid." Conner spat on the ground.

"Hey!" Jeremiah's cocky grin faded to another scowl. "I just want some action. I don't want to spend my entire life locked up in some boring village with the elders telling me what I can and can't do. I'm fast."

"You have to be more than fast in this business, kid," Conner said. "You have to know when to depend on your cat and when to depend on your brain and when you need to blend them both. You're all over the place. Right now, you're walking so hard, any leopard in the forest would be able to hear you." He shot the boy a hard look. "Adan would have heard you coming a mile out."

Even in the darkness, the kid's flush was apparent. He made an effort to walk quietly. "You could teach me."

"Do I look like someone who wants to teach some damned cub wet behind the ears? You sank your claws into my mate, you ass." His cat rode him hard all over again, furious that he didn't attack the kid right then. His breath came out in a long hiss and his muscles contorted.

Isabeau stumbled, whether deliberate or not, he didn't know, but his arm slid around her waist and he simply lifted her, cradling her in his arms. She stiffened, opened her mouth to protest. Her gaze met his and she stayed silent.

He *needed* to hold her. Her weight was nothing to him, but the feel of her in his arms was everything. He nuzzled the top of her head and glared at the youngster. The kid didn't have any idea yet how difficult it was to find a mate. He had no idea about life or danger. The idea of living on the edge was a terrifying lure to the young. He knew because he'd been the same way. He'd been young and cocky and full of his own strength without a clue of what mattered or would ever matter.

Conner closed his eyes briefly and wondered why the universe was slamming him so damned hard. He couldn't just turn the kid loose to get killed—and Suma would kill him. Jeremiah Wheating wouldn't stand by and watch children be killed. The moment Suma took him to Imelda Cortez and the kid realized what was really going on, he'd see himself as the hero and get himself killed. Conner had no choice but to look after the little punk.

He sighed and looked down into Isabeau's upturned face. She smiled at him.

"What?" He asked it almost belligerently. She had too much knowledge in her eyes.

"You know what. I don't think you're as much of a bastard as you want everyone to think you are. Not by a long shot."

"I came close to killing him. And he damn well deserved it."

"But you didn't."

"The night isn't over yet."

She just smiled and his belly tightened. He didn't want her getting the wrong idea about him. The kid was going to learn a lesson tonight. Isabeau would think he was a brute, and the kid would sulk for a while, but his cat would be happy again and maybe give him a little respite from the clawing need and the sharp, angry reprimand.

The cabin was just ahead, built high in the trees, hidden by the heavy vines and broad leaves surrounding it. He had mapped it out for the others just in case they were separated. He had lived there for several years with his mother, separated from others while she mourned the loss of her husband. His father had never been her true mate, but she had loved him.

The cabin didn't hold happy memories for him, but the moment he'd stepped foot in the rain forest it was the first place he'd gone. He'd spent two days making repairs and stocking it so they'd have a base camp if needed. It wasn't for sentimental reasons. He wasn't a sentimental man. He should have checked in immediately with Rio, but he needed the time to readjust. And he'd gone looking for his mother. Now he knew why she hadn't been there.

Strangely, the cabin looked as though it had been occupied recently, lulling him into a false sense of security. He'd even found a couple of his old toys, a truck and an airplane carved from wood out on the table. He'd imagined his mother looking at them and remembering their times together in the cabin. Now he didn't know what to think.

He set Isabeau on her feet and leapt up to catch a vine. Pulling himself, hand over hand, he gained the small porch and dropped the ladder made of tight vines down to the others. He shoved bundles down to them, knowing the men would need the clothes after they shifted, and then he dropped back to the ground.

"I'm not certain I can climb," Isabeau admitted. "My arm has really stiffened up." Even as she voiced her doubt, she reached up to grasp the ladder.

"I can take you up," Conner said, "but you'll have to go over my shoulder."

She gave an experimental pull, winced and let out her breath. "It's a long way up. I think I'm going to forgo my pride and just let you take me up." She stepped back from the ladder.

Conner signaled Adan to go up and pointed to Jeremiah. "You can wait down here for me. We're going to have a little talk before I invite you in."

The kid's eyes showed his nerves, but he nodded gamely. Conner took Isabeau up without further delay. She was swaying on her feet and needed her wounds attended to. He wanted her on antibiotics and whatever medicine she was carrying. They had a first-aid kit stashed with the antibiotics, but no painkillers. She'd warned him she didn't do well on them, but he wasn't certain what she'd meant. He'd never conceived of her getting shot. If the juvenile leopard hadn't taken her hostage, it never would have happened, another sin against him.

He put Isabeau in the most comfortable chair—his mother's chair—and poured her fresh water from the small tap at the sink. "It's good water from a spring we found," he offered.

Her hand shook as she took the water. She looked exhausted, her clothes soaked, her body shivering in shock, but she managed a small smile.

"Don't worry about me. It's a scratch, nothing more. I've had worse working."

He thought she was the most beautiful woman in the world. It didn't matter that her hair hung in wet trails, or that her face was drawn and pale. She had courage and she didn't complain when she'd just been through a terrible ordeal.

"You might remember I have some skills as a medicine man," Adan said, keeping his distance across the room. "She has plants and herbs I can use in her bag." He held it up almost as an appeasement, leery of Conner's leopard.

Conner glanced in the small mirror his mother had insisted they have over the sink. His eyes were still wholly cat. His teeth ached and the tips of his fingers and toes burned with the need to allow his leopard freedom.

"Are you comfortable with Adan cleaning your wounds? He's an adept medicine man." His mother had often taken Conner to the village whenever he was injured, and it was always Adan who had taken care of the minor damages. There had been a doctor a greater distance away who took care of any injuries from fighting young leopards.

"Of course," Isabeau agreed readily—too readily for his cat.

"Stay inside," Conner managed to growl, his smooth voice turning to gravel.

The animal snarled, forcing Conner to turn away from her. She was learning about leopards. Intelligent. Cunning. Fast. Foul tempers. And jealous as hell. He walked out onto the porch and breathed in the night, flexing his aching fingers. He needed a good fight. It was common for the males to give one another a good workout when females were close to the heat and they were all stirred up and unable to do much about it. Or when they were just plain angry.

Conner didn't use the vines, but leapt to the forest floor, landing almost in front of Jeremiah. The boy drew in his breath sharply and peeled off his shirt, flinging it aside. Conner was already stripping. Fast. Efficient. Eager now, his leopard raking and roaring to be free.

Jeremiah was built with strong lines. Ropes of muscle moved beneath his skin, and when he shifted, he was a big leopard, stocky and ferocious. Conner could see why the kid was eager for a challenge. His leopard, eager for the fight, waited for the younger man to make the first move. To prod him a bit, he snarled, exposing his teeth, and flattened his ears, his eyes focused on his prey.

Jeremiah reacted as expected, wanting to prove himself—still smarting over the reprimands Rio and Elijah had delivered and the lectures Conner had given. He snarled, exposing his canines, and took two experimental swipes at Conner, hoping to slap his face hard enough to knock him sideways and establish dominance fast.

Conner slipped both paws and growled, the sound swelling to a roar that shook the surrounding forest. Ears flat, lips drawn back, his tail switched viciously at the taunt.

Without warning, Jeremiah launched himself, claws extended, intending to rake Conner's side and gain respect.

Conner was too experienced to ever allow such an attack
to work. Using his extremely flexible spine, he twisted in
midair, allowing the lethal claws to miss by an inch, and
turned in pursuit of his prey, swiping laterally, taking fur
and skin from Jeremiah's exposed side and belly.

Conner was heavier, more experienced and far more
muscular. He changed direction in midair using hip rota-
tion so that when he landed, he was nearly on top of the
younger man. He didn't want to end the fight so soon,
needing the physical workout. He slammed into Jeremiah
with the force of a battering ram, driving him off his feet.
The smaller leopard turned as he went down to protect his
soft belly, rolling and scrambling to get back on his feet.

Conner sprang, using the leopard's natural agility and
grace, knocking Jeremiah over and over so that he rolled
across the clearing and up against a broad tree trunk. The
two went at it, snarling, growling, bodies rolling on the
ground. Blows landed. Claws occasionally ripped furrows in fur and skin. The hard jolt of large paws landing
gave Conner satisfaction. It felt good to use up his energy
and his cat's anger in the rough-and-tumble way of his
people.

Jeremiah surprised him. The kid held his temper and
took a punishment without shirking. He got in a few solid
blows Conner would feel for days, but he didn't resort to
illegal moves or try to rip his opponent into shreds. Conner
had a lot more respect for the kid when they lay panting,
side by side, nursing their wounds and eyeing each other
warily.

"Are you two going at it all night?" Isabeau called from
above them. "Or are you hungry?"

The two leopards looked at one another. Jeremiah rubbed
a paw over his twitching nose and shifted. His naked body

sprawled out on the grass, covered in sweat and blood and bruises.

Isabeau squeaked and turned away. "Take a shower before you come up. And put some clothes on."

Conner studied the kid as he sprinted for the shower, clearly motivated by the idea of being fed. He looked to be somewhere between twenty and twenty-four. He had the muscle mass and the coolness under fire. He was young and eager and had no idea of what he was getting into, but he was game. He didn't whine and he hadn't run, even when Conner had given him a good beating, testing the kid's resolve to take his punishment.

He moved like water over rock. They'd have to work on his stealth. He sounded like a damned rhino crashing through the brush, but he also was a bit of an eager puppy. He looked up and met Rio's eyes. They'd all watched—partly to test the kid—partly to make certain Conner didn't allow his cat to kill him. Rio nodded, confirming the boy had earned enough respect that they'd give him a try.

Conner waited until Jeremiah had gone up the ladder and the others had gone back into the cabin before he walked over to the shower. Feeling a little lazy, but good, he shifted and allowed the water to pour over him. It was cold, but invigorating. He could feel the bruises already starting to form up and down his body. There were one or two places where the boy's claws had ripped skin, but his cat was calm, the first respite he'd had since he'd laid eyes on Isabeau.

He let the cold water pour over his hot skin and allowed himself to breathe, really take a breath. Before, Isabeau's scent had been drawn into his lungs, surrounding him, inside him, overwhelming his senses until he felt a little crazy. He had to come to some kind of a balance in order to function properly. They had to get the children back and that would mean proceeding with the plan to get into the compound.

He dried off slowly and turned alternate ideas over and over in his mind. The thought of touching someone other than Isabeau was abhorrent to him. The idea of a woman as cruel and immoral as Imelda kissing him or touching him would inflame his cat to madness. He wasn't certain he could actually do it. Not now. Not with her close and certainly not with her on the verge of the Han Vol Dan.

Isabeau had no idea what would happen when her cat emerged. She would never, under any circumstances, tolerate another woman near her mate. Conner shoved his fingers through his damp hair and stared up at the cabin, hesitant to go back in where his cat would react to the close proximity of the men around Isabeau. He was in for a long night. His body was not going to get a reprieve from the relentless urgent demands.

She had more power over him than she knew. On the nights he'd managed to sleep, he woke with the sound of her laughter in his mind. The image of her diving into water, looking over her shoulder, enticing him. His memories were mixed now, old and new. Past life and present one. All Isabeau. Everything good in his life was now simply Isabeau.

He'd been walking through the motions for a year. Hiding in the States. He'd heard her voice everywhere he went. His skin ached for the touch of hers. He couldn't find a way to keep the blood in his veins from thickening and heating every time he thought about her—which was all the time. He hadn't realized—until he saw her again—just how numb he'd been. Everything in him came alive when she was near.

Now he was faced with seeing her every day. Teaching her the ways of their people. How to protect herself in the rain forest. He had no idea how to stop wanting her. How to stop needing to kiss her and just try to be casual and indifferent around her. Not only did he have her and her emerging cat to worry about, but the kid was going to need training and looking after. He sighed. His life had turned very complicated, yet he felt more alive than he ever had.

Isabeau was close. Her warmth. Her scent. Her cat. He lifted his face to the rain and let it drop on his face, trying to cleanse his mind of her. She was swamping his senses. Driving out all sane thoughts until he was going to be useless to Rio and the others if he didn't get a handle on his cat. And damn it all—he couldn't blame the out-of-control emotions all on his cat. The man was feeling the same driving hungers—the same desperate need.

He'd fallen so hard for her. So fast. He'd been in too deep before he'd even realized she was burrowing into his heart and soul, winding around his bones and pressing her stamp deep into them, invading every blood cell until he couldn't escape her lure. There was no way to free his soul once he'd fallen in love with her. He'd destroyed everything between them, shattered her in one horrible blow, but he hadn't managed to disentangle himself from her in the process.

He knew being leopard mates played a huge part in the physical draw between them, but he loved her. The man and leopard both loved her. There was no one else for either of them and there never would be. He closed his eyes and listened to the sound of her laughter. That little note in her voice had always managed to arouse him and soothe the beast in him at the same time. There were so many facets to her, so many intriguing parts to her character. He loved everything about her, everything from her generous heart to her nasty temper.

"Conner?" Isabeau called down to him. "Come and eat."

He looked up because he couldn't stop himself. One hand was wrapped around the post as she peered down at him. Her waist-length hair was unbound, flowing a little with the meager breeze moving through the canopy. Her jeans and tee emphasized the lush curves of her body, and he felt his cat purr low in his throat at the sight of her.

"I'll be right up. I'm going to poke around a little, see what turns up."

She put her hand on her hip, drawing his attention to the fact that she wasn't using her injured arm. "Nothing's out there, Conner. No one would ever find this cabin unless they knew where to look. There are enough cats here to smell anything within miles. Just come up and eat."

It wasn't so much her words as her tone that had him moving fast over the rotting vegetation to grasp the vine. In the midst of all the men, she was nervous without him there. And any way he looked at it, that was a good sign. He went up fast, hand over hand, using his leopard's enormous strength to pull himself up to the porch. He dragged up the ladder after him so that there were no signs to give them away. Even if someone found the small makeshift shower, it was ice cold and no more than a crude but effective rain carved out of a sparse waterfall rushing down the slope.

He straightened slowly and drank her in. She stood, a little hesitant, but she didn't retreat. She was waiting for him. He watched her inhale deeply, and involuntarily draw his scent into her lungs. His body tightened in reaction. He supposed he'd have to get used to the relentless ache. His gaze dwelt on the puncture marks on her neck; satisfaction welled up that he'd given the kid enough of a beating that he'd feel it for days. She looked a little bruised and battered, but beautiful, with her exotic looks and cat's eyes.

Isabeau blushed. "You're looking at me that way again."

"What way?"

"Like you're about to pounce on me any moment. I'm looking for a little comfort, not an ambush of some sort."

He moved in close to her, reaching to tuck strands of hair behind her ear, the brush of his fingers gentle. "You were courageous tonight, when the kid grabbed you. You didn't panic."

She flashed a tentative smile. "I knew you'd come. He was so shocked to see me there, at first I think his intention was to get me out of the line of fire, but just then Adan stepped out of the brush with his darts. I think it was clear that I knew Adan, and Jeremiah used me as a shield. He could smell the other leopards and knew he'd walked into a bad situation."

"Are you making excuses for the kid?" Unable to stop touching her, he stroked his fingers down the long fall of silken hair.

"He's pretty bruised."

"He's damned lucky he's alive," Conner pointed out. He took her elbow and tugged her back away from the edge. "Don't defend him. He should have known better than to put his claws in you."

"That wasn't as bad as being shot," she said, attempting a small laugh.

He didn't smile—couldn't smile. A few more inches . . . "That man is dead. Jeremiah is very lucky. I wasn't in a good mood."

Isabeau burst out laughing. "Really? I would never have guessed."

He loved the sound of her laughter. He loved that she could laugh. Standing there battered and bruised with punctures in her neck, defending the kid who did it, he felt respect rising like the sun. The image struck him as pertinent. He hadn't felt as though he was anywhere near the sun for a long time, and suddenly the world around him was bright again and that had everything to do with Isabeau.

He deliberately lifted an eyebrow. "Are you saying you think I have foul moods?"

"I think it's entirely possible, yes," she teased.

Something squeezed his heart hard so that he felt an actual pain in his chest. She wasn't looking at him as if he was loathsome. It wasn't complete and utter love like he'd seen in her eyes before, but it was a start.

Isabeau looked away from Conner's focused eyes. He was looking at her with that possessive, hungry look that always made her so crazy for him. She wanted a truce, but she didn't want to make a fool of herself. And she didn't want to betray her father's memory. She didn't like being inside the cabin, so close to so many people she didn't know. She hadn't realized how comfortable she felt with Conner.

She'd thought she didn't trust him, but the moment he was no longer at her side, she'd panicked. "The rain sounds different up here."

He nodded without taking his gaze from her face. She could feel his eyes burning a brilliant gold right through her.

"When I was young, I used to sleep out here on the porch so I could hear it. I love the sound of the rain," Conner admitted.

She sank down onto the wooden planks and looked around at the leaves sheltering the cabin from view. "I've always found the rain soothing, but there's a pattern to the way it hits the leaves that makes it sound different. I can almost hear it set to music."

Surprise crept into his expression. "I used to think that. I'd lie awake listening and add in instruments to create my own symphony."

"Do you play an instrument?"

Conner sat beside her, drawing his knees up, back to the wall of the house. He shrugged his shoulders, looking a bit uneasy. He lowered his voice, keeping an eye on the door. "I play a couple of instruments. It was mostly me with my mom. Being alone a lot we read books, did a lot of school-work and we both liked to learn to play whatever we could manage to get our hands on."

"So your mom played too," she prompted, surprised that during all their conversations he'd never told her about his mother, his life or his music. Important things. Things a lover should have known. She wanted to look away from him, upset that he hadn't shared who he really was with her. Their time together had been the most wonderful of her life, yet it hadn't been real. *He* hadn't been real. The man sitting there, slightly uncomfortable, exposing his vulnerable side was the real man. She couldn't look away though; she was fascinated, once again mesmerized.

Conner was a hard, dangerous man and he carried that aura like a shield around him. He'd always seemed invincible—impenetrable. She'd never seen a chink in that armor until now—this moment. His face was the same. The strong jaw, the scars and weathered lines, the fierce burnt gold of his eyes, the sensual mouth that would drive any woman crazy—all showed a man with absolute resolve. But his eyes had gone different. Softer. Almost hesitant. She couldn't help but be intrigued.

"Yes, she played," Conner admitted, his tone dropping even lower. There was a soft note that was all leopard mixed in with his human voice.

Isabeau watched him swallow, his gaze moving over the broad leaves surrounding them, hiding them from the rest of the rain forest.

"She loved the violin."

"Did you play the violin?" She couldn't stop herself from learning whatever she could about the real man, not the role he played.

"Not the way she could play." He had a faraway look in his eyes when he turned his head back toward her. There was a small smile on his face as if he was remembering. "She used to sit out here with me while the rain came down and she'd play for hours. Sometimes the animals would gather so she had a huge audience. I'd look out and the trees would be covered with monkeys and birds and even a sloth or two. She was gentle and beautiful and it showed in her music."

"She taught you herself? Or did she send you for lessons? And where would you even find schools and music teachers? You couldn't have lived here for long."

"We stayed to ourselves. When we left our village . . ."

Isabeau caught a note of pain in his voice. The boy was remembering some childhood trauma, not the man.

"We kept to ourselves for several years. My mother didn't want to see anyone. She was very strict about schooling and she was smart. If you look in the wooden boxes beneath the benches, you'll find they're filled completely with books. She was a good teacher." A slight grin touched his mouth. A little mischievous. "She didn't have the best student to work with."

"You're extremely intelligent," she said.

He shrugged. "Intelligence had nothing to do with being a wild boy out in the middle of the rain forest thinking I was king of the jungle. She had her hands full."

Isabeau could imagine him, a curly-haired towheaded boy with golden eyes, leaping from tree branch to tree branch with his mother chasing after him. "I can imagine."

"I snuck out a lot at night. Of course, I didn't realize then that, being an adult leopard, she could hear and smell better than me and knew the moment I moved. I learned a few years later that she trailed after me, making certain nothing happened to me, but at the time, I felt very brave and manly." He laughed at the memory. "I was also feeling pretty cool that I'd managed to put it over on her that I was out every night playing in the forest."

"It must have built your confidence though. As much time as I've spent in the rain forest, I stay in camp at night."

"I was a kid, Isabeau. I hadn't learned all the dangers in the forest. Mom would tell me and I'd just shrug my shoulders and think it could never happen to me. I was invincible."

"Most kids think they are. I know I did. I liked to climb on the roof of our house at night. Any place high. My father would get so upset once he found out. I forget how old I was when I first started. I think he said around three."

He flashed a companionable grin at her. "That was the leopard in you. They like to go up all the time. The higher the better."

"And I took tons of naps. I was always sleepy in the day."

He nodded. "And up all night. Mom actually made me do lessons at night when I was a teen. She said I'd do my best work then."

"And you played music at night?"

"I couldn't sleep sometimes—most of the time. And she was . . . sad. We'd sit listening to the rain and then we'd come out here with our instruments. She'd have the violin and I'd have a guitar and we'd play together. Most of the time the animals would come. A few times I glimpsed leopards, but they never came close and she pretended not to notice them, so I followed her lead."

"I wish I could have met her."

He blinked and his expression settled into the familiar mask. "She would have loved you. She always wanted a daughter."

"You said she was killed by Suma? Why? Why would he kill a female leopard?"

His jaw hardened. "Suma killed her in the village. She tried to defend Adan's family."

Her breath caught in her lungs. "That was your mother? I heard you tell Jeremiah that Suma killed your mother, but I had no idea that was the Marisa I knew from Adan's village. I did meet her—more than once, but of course I saw her only as a human, not a leopard. She was so sweet to me. She treated me as a daughter." She felt burning in her eyes and looked away. "For a while she made me feel less lonely. I was pretty broken up." Her throat burned. Maybe he'd believe it was over the death of her father. She'd been shocked—traumatized, but Conner's deceit had shattered her.

He stared at her almost in horror. "You spent time with my mother?"

As if that was all he heard and he didn't seem happy about it. Isabeau tried not to be hurt all over again, but it was a blow nevertheless.

"She often would come to my camp with Adan's grandson, or even by herself, and she sometimes stayed several days with me. She would bring a little boy with her. They'd even go out looking for plants with me. She was very knowledgeable. Sometimes all I had to do was sketch a plant and she'd identify what it was and where it was as well as the various uses for it. She could take me right to it. She never mentioned playing the violin though." She made an effort not to sound defiant.

"My God." He scrubbed his hands over his face and then he stood abruptly.

She caught the sheen of tears in his eyes before he leapt from the platform to the ground below, leaving her alone.

7

SHE knew. His mother knew he had betrayed his own mate. Shame was a living, breathing entity. Bile rose as he landed in a crouch on the forest floor. Thunder pounded through his skull. He had scent-marked Isabeau a thousand times, so deep he knew his scent was in her bones, and his mother would have known the moment she was close to Isabeau. Had she died believing he had betrayed and abandoned his mate the way his father had done her?

He raised his head and roared his anguish. She'd suffered enough without believing her only child—the son she loved—had repeated history. His father, Raul Fernandez, had thrown them—him—out, and his mother had chosen to go with him. In his anger at her decision to keep her child, his father had forced them from the village, their only protection, so that his mother had to make a home in the forest for her son. Conner knew his father had believed they would die alone there, and he'd cruelly left them to their fate. He despised the man with every breath in his body.

The thought that his mother might think of him like that . . . He stripped off his shirt and jeans and willed his cat to the surface. He needed to run. To think. To not think. *She had known.* Of course she would befriend Isabeau and try to help her. Marisa Vega had a kind heart. There wasn't a mean bone in her body. She had mated with his father in good faith, believing he loved her as she loved him, but his true mate had died years earlier.

At first Raul had insisted Marisa, twenty years younger than he, was in her next life and born early, and was truly his mate. He'd been lonely and wanted a woman and Marisa had been young and beautiful. He had courted her, made her love him, but after Conner was born, he became angry and resentful—filled with guilt—because all along, he'd known it wasn't true.

Raul had hated the sight of Conner from the moment he was born, refusing to interact with him—the living reminder that he had betrayed his true mate. Conner would never forget the night his father had given his ultimatum to Marisa, stating coldly she must get rid of her child or go. When she refused to abandon Conner, Raul had told Marisa he didn't love her. Conner had been very young, still small, crouched outside the door, listening to the man say cruel, demeaning things to the mother he adored, and he had felt the first stirrings of his cat's terrible temper. The man had driven them both away using every means he could. Conner had known, with a child's intuition, that his father couldn't stand the sight or smell of him. Now, that same hatred had spilled over to his mother.

Conner stood on his hind legs, his golden, spotted coat stretched to his impressive height as he raked at the trees, shredding bark, leaving deep gouges, wishing he could do the same to the man who had hurt his mother so deeply.

She had never been angry at Raul, never said a bad thing
about him, but she'd kept Conner away from the village
until he'd come of age. She'd asked him, as a favor to her,
to go back and talk with his father, to try to make peace.

Sap ran like a river and blood from his skin mingled
with it as he dug through the thick wood, ripping and tearing, his anguish filling the night over and over again as he
poured out his grief and rage. He never told her the things
his father had said to him; he was a grown man and to hurt
her more wouldn't have accomplished anything. He also
didn't tell her that he'd beaten his own father to a pulp in
the house where he'd been born, leaving Raul bruised and
battered and bleeding there on the floor instead of throwing
him out of the house as his father had done to his mother.
He'd wanted to humiliate Raul in front of the villagers, but
he knew Marisa wouldn't be happy with him, so he hadn't
thrown him out the door for everyone to see he'd been defeated in combat—both as a cat and as a man.

The rain poured down, a steady drizzle that showed no
sign of letting up. He turned his face toward the sky and
let the drops run down his cheeks, hiding any tears burning there. He'd known hatred, but his mother hadn't. She'd
done her best to raise him to be like her, a gentle, loving
creature who didn't hold grudges. She hadn't succeeded,
and right at this moment he detested that he had many of
his father's dominating, cruel traits.

He couldn't bear the idea of his mother thinking he
hadn't loved Isabeau. What if Isabeau had told her the story
of his deceit? He swiped at a rotting log, rolling it over and
sending insects in all directions. He kept tearing at the log,
ashamed and disgusted with himself. He should have come
home. Told her about Isabeau. Asked her advice. Instead,
he'd slunk off to Drake, the only man who had ever treated

him decently. Wanting what? Some kind of absolution? Knowing already what his mother would have said to him.

Long, night-piercing roars and growls emerged from his throat, filling space from floor to canopy with the threat of violence. He'd hid like a coward far away where no one could see the way Isabeau had shattered him, broken him inside to little pieces. He'd been in too deep by the time he'd known who she was and he'd allowed their relationship to go too far. The two women he loved he had hurt. And his mother was dead . . .

He raged to the heavens, pouring his grief out to mix with the rain. In his animal form it was more acceptable to allow wild emotions free, something that was far more difficult as a man. Splintered wood flew in all directions. Dirt and debris followed. Nothing escaped the terrible retribution of claws as he tore up trunks and smashed through the root cages of several large trees.

Small rodents shivered in tunnels and dens. Birds took to the air in agitation, adding to the chaos. The large leopard smashed a tall termite cone, flung the debris in all directions and dug his claws into a muddy slope, dragging himself up the steep incline to the next line of trees where he marked every one of them with deep gouges.

His nose wrinkled and he opened his mouth, testing the air. At once his lungs were filled with the scent of his mate. The leopard whirled around, his teeth showing, his golden eyes piercing, ferocious, the snarls still rumbling low in his throat. She stood a few yards from him, her chin up, eyes steady, but she was trembling and he could smell fear.

"They told me it was dangerous to follow you," she greeted.

Her voice wobbled a little bit, but the leopard found it comforting. She had come to him of her own accord through the rain forest at night. It wouldn't have been hard to follow the trail of his destruction, but she looked alone and fragile, and far too scared. Conner took hold of his cat, forcing the rage back, raising the flat ears and doing his best to look tame and gentle within the powerful body of the big leopard. It wasn't easy. When he took a step toward her, her breath caught in her throat and her hand tightened on the torn tree branch she was using for support, but she didn't back up.

Her body tensed. He froze in position, not wanting her to run. He was in control of the leopard, but if Isabeau fled, her action would trigger the leopard's hunting instincts. He knew the cat would never harm her, but it would be unacceptable to frighten her.

"I know I said something to upset you, Conner," Isabeau continued. "I wanted you to know, I didn't mean to bring up unpleasant memories. Your mother was wonderful—a kind, loving person who really helped me when I needed it."

Another roar of anguish welled up. Conner fought it back. She looked so young to him, so inexperienced but brave, and love welled up for her so that his chest felt tight and his heart ached. How could he have blown it so badly? Handled everything so wrong? The moment he knew he was in over his head, he should have told her. He'd taken a chance talking to her father. It should have been her. He should have trusted her enough to give her the chance he gave her father. He hadn't even considered the idea. He knew Marisa would have asked him why. She believed in talking. She was an intellectual and believed problems were solved by talking them over.

Isabeau took a cautious step forward. "I swear, Conner, I wouldn't use your mother to hurt you in any way. Yes, I was angry with you over what you did, but I have come to some understanding about why you did it. Your mother was an exceptional person and I know she loved her son. I didn't know your real name and she never mentioned yours. She just referred to you as 'my son.' She said it lovingly, Conner. Proudly. You were everything to her."

He watched her, afraid to move, afraid of doing the wrong thing and making her run. She kept moving toward him, in a slow, freeze-frame stalk, one hand out tentatively. Her hand was small, and trembling. He kept his mouth closed over his teeth, and a close watch on the leopard. The cat trembled and slowly sank its hindquarters down, first into a sitting position, and then finally to a prone one, although the golden eyes never moved from her face.

Isabeau took a cautious look around at the torn trees and shredded bark and then looked down at the leopard's heavy paws. Traces of blood streaked the golden fur where he'd deliberately smashed his paws, using them like clubs against the tree trunks. The sea of rosettes created an optical illusion so that the large cat appeared to be moving when he was actually stationary. His penetrating stare was nearly lost in the sea of black spots. His sides heaved with every heavy breath. She knew she would never forget that smoldering hunger in the leopard's eyes, or the sharp intelligence.

It might not have been such a good idea to follow him. All the others had shouted to her to come back, but she'd hastened down the ladder and sprinted after the leopard once she'd heard the terrible anguish in his voice. She couldn't bear to hear him. She knew grief when she heard it. The idea that he couldn't express that same grief as a man tore at her heart. She'd known his mother, what kind of woman she was. Conner had to have loved and admired her. What son wouldn't have?

She took the last three steps to the leopard and let her fingertips brush over the powerful head. Her hand trembled and she sunk her fingers into his fur in an effort to stop shaking. "Are you all right?"

The leopard arched his neck under her scratching nails, turning his head from side to side, allowing better access. She sank down onto the one flat rock she could find near him, circling his neck with her arm, shocked that fear was receding so rapidly. The leopard stretched out beside her while she stroked the fur.

What did she know of leopards other than they were considered dangerous and cunning? Just looking into his eyes she could see that same keen intelligence that had attracted her to Conner. He was there—the man. And he was suffering. She wasn't certain what she'd said, but she knew she'd been the one to upset him.

"I talked to her about what happened," she admitted, searching for the right thing to say. "She knew I was upset. How could she not? I'd lost my father and then discovered terrible things about his business. And finding out the man I thought loved me had deceived me in order to get to my father—that was difficult, Conner—but I was coming to terms with it with her help. She didn't know it was you. How could she?"

His eyes went sad. Stricken. Those fierce, burning eyes, so open to her when the man wasn't, and she saw the truth. Marisa had known. Somehow his mother had known, and Conner knew how. She let out her breath and buried her face in his roped, muscled neck, unable to look at him. Conner had to think his mother thought the worst of him when she died. As much as Isabeau thought she wanted him to suffer—it wasn't like this—not about his mother.

She rubbed her cheek against his fur, needing as much comfort and soothing as he did. Did he think she'd done it on purpose? Tried to make him look bad in front of his mother? It hadn't been like that at all. "I was hungry for companionship—for a mother or big sister. A female I could talk to. My own mother died when I was a young child. I can barely remember her. Well, I guess she was really my adopted mother. I didn't know my birth mother."

She hadn't known she was adopted until after her leopard had clawed Conner's face. Instinctively her fingers went to the cat's face. Sure enough, there were four deep furrows there. She stroked small caresses along the four scars. She was somewhat sheltered from the rain by the thick leaves overhead, but every now and then a few drops ran off the broad leaves in a steady trickle down her back. She squirmed uncomfortably.

Instantly the leopard was on his feet. Sitting, he was taller than her. His face broad and strong. He looked up at the surrounding trees as if studying them before turning back to her. He waited while she slowly got to her feet. She knew he wanted to get her off the ground and up into the trees, a leopard's instinctive reaction.

"We can go back to the cabin and sit on the porch," she suggested hastily.

She was a little nervous surrounded by absolute darkness, those golden eyes glowing at her. And she didn't want to see any insects coming at her in swarms. For the most part, mosquitoes and other stinging or biting bugs kept a distance from her, but there were always the swarms of ants to contend with. She would never admit it aloud, after all her chosen profession kept her in the rain forest, but ants in particular gave her nightmares. It was rather comical to be standing with her fingers buried in the fur of a leopard and be scouring the churning vegetation for ants.

Isabeau took a tentative step in the direction of the cabin. She'd always had an amazing sense of direction, even in the interior of the rain forest, although she never entered without a guide, but now she felt even more confident. She took another slow step, her heart hammering hard, wanting him to follow her. The leopard moved to her side, keeping his neck under her palm and his body against her leg as they moved together through the heavy brush.

Wanting to keep his mind fixed on her and away from the loss of his mother, Isabeau continued talking. "When I was a child, I remember my father used to try to take me to those parks where they have roller-coaster rides, and I hated them. I was very adventurous, so he could never understand why I didn't like the movement. Every time I rode one of them, something inside me would go crazy. It must have been my cat, but of course I didn't know it at the time." She sighed. "I guess I didn't know a lot of things then."

They walked in and out among the trees. She could hear her heart pounding. She was going to tell him—and betray her father even more. But she owed him that much.

"I told your mother about the roller coaster—and the men my father always met at the parks." She could hear the tremble in her voice, but she couldn't quite control it and knew Conner could hear it too, especially with the sensitive ears of the leopard.

Beneath her hand, the roped muscles tensed, but he didn't break stride. He kept walking with her and that gave her the courage to make the confession. "I never paid attention to the men he often met there, because I didn't like them. There was something off about their smell." Her fingers curled deeper in his fur. "I could smell things miles away. It drove me crazy. These men would come up to him when we would get a snow cone. Dad always took me to this one stand, and the same two men would meet him and hand him a package. He would give them an envelope. I was a child, Conner, and didn't realize, or even question, that he was getting paid for something, or that the reason those men smelled 'off' was because they were doing something wrong."

She hadn't realized how easy it would be—or what a relief it was to be able to tell him. In his leopard form, she didn't have to face his burning eyes and know he was judging her. As a child, she hadn't had an inkling of what her father was into, but as a grown woman, she should have been able to fit the pieces of the puzzle together. She should have known: All the signs were there, she just hadn't opened her eyes.

"He did it for me," she said softly, hating the truth. "He wanted the money for me." Her throat burned. Her father was a doctor, dedicated to saving lives. He'd taken an oath to save others, yet he'd sold information to a group of terrorists—information that led to the kidnapping and deaths of many people over the years.

The leopard pushed his head close to her, nuzzling her thigh as if to comfort her. She was grateful Conner didn't shift to his human form. She needed to get this said, and it was so much easier talking to the leopard there in the darkness. She took another breath and lifted her face to the cleansing rain. The drops were slowing, so it was more thick mist than driving rain, but it felt good on her burning face.

"I know this will be difficult for you to believe, but my father was a good man. I don't know what happened, why he thought we'd need that kind of blood money. He made good money as a doctor. After he died, I inherited everything. I went over his books carefully."

She tripped on a small branch hidden deep in the layers of leaves and decaying vegetation, stumbling a little. The cat moved fluidly in front of her, preventing her from falling onto the ground. She had to grab handfuls of fur to keep herself upright, her fingers curling into the pelt. For a moment she buried her face in the neck, rubbing her wet face into the thick fur. It was amazing to feel so comfortable with the animal when the man made her crazy inside. She gave a small self-deprecating laugh. "Maybe you should just stay a leopard."

She felt the large cat stiffen, his muscles coiling tight as his head came up alertly. He opened his mouth in a silent snarl, showing teeth, his eyes blazing. She looked in the direction he was looking, back toward the cabin. She couldn't see or hear anything at all, but she trusted his animal senses and stepped back behind him. They waited in silence and then Elijah stepped out of the trees.

"Rio sent me," he said hastily. "He was worried your woman might run into trouble." He stopped abruptly the moment he saw the crouching leopard, but he appeared relaxed.

Isabeau tried to place him from her past. He was good looking. Intriguing even. The same dangerous aura that surrounded Conner enveloped him as well, and he looked vaguely familiar. A man like Elijah was memorable, yet she didn't recall anyone else who had stormed the compound where her father had gone to warn his friends. For all she knew, this man could be the one who shot her father.

"I'm fine. I found him without any trouble," she replied.

"I see that." Elijah studied her face. "I didn't shoot him—your father, I mean. I didn't shoot him."

She swallowed hard, but didn't respond to the bait.

"That's what you were wondering. I would have done it without hesitation," he admitted honestly, "to save Conner's life, but I wasn't first inside. I'm wondering what you were doing there."

She went rigid. No one had thought to ask her that question. Not one person. Not even Conner before she'd raked his face. She'd been so shocked, so traumatized, but even then, she'd waited for the question, wondering how she would answer it. Now, here in the jungle with the mist cloaking her and a leopard pressing close to her legs, she knew.

"I was worried about the way my father had been behaving. It wasn't rational. I knew he was upset, but he'd become secretive and . . ." She trailed off, realizing what it had been that had sent her following him. She *smelled* his lies. The memory swept over her fast, her stomach reacting, churning with bile, just as it had when she'd followed her father down the streets of the city and then the trails by the river, deeper and deeper into the Borneo rain forest. Her heart had sunk in her chest, and she'd known he wasn't going on a medical call.

He'd gone through guarded gates and she had parked her car in the forest itself and continued on foot. She'd stood for a long time in the trees when he drove behind those large gates, debating what to do. All the little clues from her childhood had begun to fit like pieces of a giant puzzle.

The waterways weren't safe. Everyone knew that. People were kidnapped so often and held for ransom, no one even blinked anymore on hearing the news. Most of the ransoms were paid and the prisoners released. It was business. Just business. But there were a few groups she'd read about, terrorist camps that tortured and murdered prisoners, always milking the families of those they kidnapped for more until there was no more and the bodies were sent back in pieces. The money was used for guns and bombs and more terrorist camps.

She'd been horrified, and then she'd been in denial. Of course her father wasn't involved in such a thing—and she'd decided to bluff her way inside. The leopard rubbed along her leg, probably sensing her distress. She realized she had fisted her hands in the leopard's fur, burying her fingers deep, trying to push back her thoughts.

"I know what you're doing," Isabeau whispered. "You don't want me angry at Conner so you think by making my father look bad, I'll forgive what he did."

"I don't need to make your father look bad, he did that all on his own," Elijah said. "But the thing is, you don't have to defend him." He ignored the threatening roar of the leopard, although he adjusted his position slightly, preparing for defense. "My father left me a drug empire when his own brother killed him. I don't have any reason to defend his lifestyle choice. It makes a great cover for me to move between the underworld and the business world, but no matter what, that's my legacy and I have to deal with it. I choose my life. You choose yours."

She felt her cat leap in anger. In a few sentences he'd reduced her real grief to self-pity. And maybe it was time someone did. She was tired of carrying her anger and wrapping it around her as armor. She'd run like a child and hid in the rain forest instead of tracking Conner down and confronting him as she should have. She'd loved him with every breath in her body, but she hadn't even tried to find out why he'd used her feelings for him.

She hated that this man, looking so cool and calm, with the mist swirling around him and the night shining in his eyes, was the one to make her look at herself. She should have looked in the mirror and found the courage herself. She'd never been much afraid of anything, certainly not expressing her opinion or confronting someone if she had to. Yet she'd run like a rabbit, and hid herself away with her plants and work instead of picking up the pieces. Instead of admitting her father had been a criminal, she should've at least demanded some kind of closure with Conner.

When had she become such a coward that she needed a snarling leopard to threaten his friend because her little feelings might be hurt when someone told the truth? She was ashamed of herself. She straightened, letting go of her death grip on the cat's fur. "Self-pity is insidious, isn't it?"

Elijah shrugged. "So is righteous anger, of which I've felt plenty in my lifetime. Come on back to the cabin, you two. We have a lot of work to do in the morning. And, Conner, someone has to take that cub in hand. You didn't let us kill him, so he's on you."

Isabeau scowled at him. "He fell in with the wrong crowd. He didn't deserve to die. Are all of you this bloodthirsty? He can't be more than twenty."

"He sank his claws into a female, and you wouldn't be saying that if Adan was lying dead at your feet," Elijah pointed out, his tone mild.

She noted that he'd put the sin of clawing a female before killing Adan. She had a lot to learn about the world of leopards. It was strange how she was more comfortable with these men than she should have been. She looked up at the high canopy where the wind swirled the mist into strange shapes that wrapped around the trees, forming gray veils she couldn't see through, not even with her superior night vision. This, then, was the world where she belonged.

Conner had said there was a higher law. Before she closed all doors and made judgments, she needed to learn the rules. In any case, while she was in the presence of so many leopards, she needed to learn as much as she could from them.

"I don't think he would have killed Adan without provocation," Isabeau defended. "He was actually quite gentle and a few times he whispered to me that he wouldn't really hurt me."

"That's bullshit with his claws in your throat and blood dripping down." Now there was suppressed rage in Elijah's voice.

Isabeau felt the echo of it in the shudder that went through the leopard pressed so close to her. Jeremiah had come very close to death. *For touching her.* That was where the anger was coming from. Not because he'd threatened any of them or Adan. She was somehow sacred to all of them. Because of Conner? Because she was a female leopard? She didn't know, but there was solace in the knowledge. A kind of security she'd never felt before.

There was also a newfound confidence that came with her knowledge. She realized Conner hadn't shifted at the sight of Elijah, not because he was in a better position to protect her as a leopard, but because he didn't want to embarrass her with his nudity in front of another man. He'd deliberately stayed in animal form, although he couldn't join in the conversation. She stroked a thank-you down his back, trying to convey silently her appreciation.

Modesty was a foreign concept to these men, she was certain of that. Isabeau walked in silence for a few minutes, enjoying the way the mist enveloped them so closely. She couldn't see very far in front of her, and the steam rose from the ground so that their bodies appeared to be floating through the clouds without feet.

"It doesn't hurt," she assured, when she caught Elijah examining her throat as she came up beside him.

Elijah fell into step with them, taking up a position on the other side of Conner so that the long, powerful body of the cat was between them. He moved easily, with that same fluid motion Conner had, as if he flowed over the ground in silence.

"The kid needs another beating," Elijah hissed.

The cat made a rumbling sound of agreement deep in his throat, and Isabeau smiled. "I don't think either one of you is very far from your cat."

"Law of the jungle," Elijah said as if that explained everything.

And to them it did, she realized. Another bit of information. Their lives were not more complicated because of their leopards, they were less so. They saw the world in black and white rather than in shades of gray. They did what it took to get a nasty job done, and if that meant seducing a woman to save children, so be it.

Why her heart squeezed painfully in her chest she didn't know. The thought of Conner touching—kissing—holding another woman made her feel sick. And she'd brought him here to do just that.

"I guess I don't understand these clear lines you all have drawn out for yourselves. Who determines what's right and what's wrong?" she asked.

The leopard nudged her thigh again, brushing close to her, and she felt her own reaction, the leaping of her senses toward him, a reaching she couldn't prevent, as it happened too fast, too automatically. The least little touch of man or beast and she reacted with hope, with need, with an almost obsessive response.

Elijah shot her a look. "Are we talking about Jeremiah? Or Conner?"

"Both. All of you."

"Talk to Conner," Elijah advised. "He's more knowledgeable of our ways than I am. I came to the clan late. And everyone makes mistakes, Isabeau. You. Me. Conner. Your father. My father. We all do."

She kept pace with the leopard, looking straight ahead. Water splashed from the sloped hills into a narrow streambed. They walked over the rocks and continued wading through the water toward the other side where the bank was less steep. Isabeau felt a pang of uneasiness and then deep inside, her cat stirred, shuddering awake.

Something tugged at her ankle from behind and then she was down and the water closed over her head. Almost immediately she was tumbled over and over, as if in a washing machine, rolling while something wrapped tightly around her, holding her in strong, steel-like coils. She heard herself screaming in her head, but she had the presence of mind not to open her mouth beneath the water.

Her arm, where her wound was, burned and throbbed. Her left wrist, trapped in the thick coils, felt as if it might burst from the pressure. She tried not to struggle, telling herself Elijah and Conner would both come to her aid and not to panic. The snake rolled her over and she felt the cool night on her face. She gulped air, drawing a deep breath before it rolled her over again. Her face scraped along the rocks as it took her down along the bottom.

Elijah leapt over the leopard, a knife in his fist. Conner exploded beside him, roaring a challenge, whirling around and sinking his teeth deep into the writhing coils, holding the snake, preventing it from taking its prey into deeper water. The green anaconda was large, close to four hundred pounds of solid muscle, and it was hungry, determined not to lose its prey. The head was close to Isabeau's head, the fangs dangerously near her neck. It didn't have a fatal bite, or venom, but it would anchor itself there and hold her until it could constrict and suffocate her.

Elijah tried to move around the churning water to get to the head, but the snake continued to thrash and roll, keeping the water roiling, preventing the man from doing more than angering it by slashing at the coils of thick muscle as he moved around the constantly writhing snake. The cat gripped the tail of the anaconda in its mouth and began a steady backward pull toward the bank in an effort to drag the snake to shallow water to keep Isabeau from drowning.

The snake was quite large and obviously female by its size. She was dark green with dark oval spots decorating her scales up and down her back. Along her sides were the telltale ochre spots of the anaconda. Her head was large and narrow, running straight into the thick, muscular neck, so it was difficult to tell where the two separated, especially in the churning water. The eyes and nostrils set on top of its head allowed it to breathe while mostly submerged. At home in the water, it was using its adeptness to its advantage, fighting the pull of the relentless leopard.

As Conner took two more steps back, gripping more of the snake to get more leverage, Elijah circled to the front, reaching below the surface of the water and dragging Isabeau and the snake out so she could draw in another breath. Unfortunately, as she gasped, her lungs burning for air, the snake constricted tighter.

"Conner, hold the damn thing," Elijah snarled, his teeth snapping together in frustration.

Time seemed to slow down for Isabeau. She could hear the leopard snarling, but her pulse was hammering loud in her ears. Her lungs felt starved for air and fear was a vile taste in her mouth. Every instinct she had told her to fight, to struggle, but she forced herself to stay calm, refusing to give in to the panic that threatened to reduce her to a screaming, mindless victim.

In her mind she chanted Conner's name. She knew the instant he shifted—or maybe her cat knew. She couldn't see him, and she could still hear the growls rumbling, reverberating through the water, but she knew he was using the combined strength of man and leopard to drag the snake onto the embankment.

Elijah kept going in and out of her line of vision, his face grim, his eyes locked on the head of the snake, the knife trying to slice through scale and muscle to sever the head. The snake knew it was in trouble now, and the only avenue left to it was abandoning its meal and escaping. The moment the snake loosened its coils, Conner reached past the thrashing body, wrapped his arm around her leg and yanked her to him. He all but threw her behind him. She caught a glimpse of that rock-hard, masculine body, ripped with ropes of muscles, as he plunged into the shallow water to help Elijah.

The snake coiled around the man in an effort to escape the blade of the knife, trying to use sheer weight and muscle to drive him back into deeper water. Conner gripped the thrashing body and held while Elijah killed the snake. The animal went limp and both men stood, bent, chests heaving from the tremendous fight against such a strong creature.

Conner turned to her, crouching low in the water to run his hands over her. "Are you all right, Isabeau?"

She considered screaming. Or bursting into tears. She'd

nearly died, crushed by a snake, or drowned. But he looked perfectly calm as if it was an ordinary occurrence and no big deal. She swore he even looked regretful as he watched Elijah drag the carcass onto land. Was she all right? She looked down at her body. She felt bruised and maybe a little battered, but nothing was broken. She was soaked, but the rain had already done that.

She slowly took stock of her situation. She was still in the stream, up to her ankles, and she'd just survived an honest to God anaconda attack. Her heart pounded like thunder in her ears, her breath came in ragged, harsh gasps, but every single nerve ending was alive. The world was crisper, fresh, more beautiful than she'd ever seen it.

The mist hung in soft veils surrounding the black, whispering leaves peaking through as the wind swayed the canopy slightly. The water ran over the rocks, a dark, gleaming ribbon of silver as it moved. She could see the long, thick body of the snake lying on the bank. Beside it, Elijah sat, a small smile spreading across his face. She couldn't stop her gaze from straying back to Conner, where his naked body rippled with defined muscles.

Conner grinned at her, a slow, very much alive grin that took what little breath she had and replaced it with a rush of heat and adrenaline. He raised a dripping hand to his hair and slicked it back away from his face. "What a rush, right?"

She nodded, fascinated by the sheer magnetism of his face. There was joy—*life*—shining in his eyes. Flames leapt and burned brightly in the golden eyes. He winked at her and butterflies began a serious migration in the pit of her stomach.

"Sorry about the lack of clothes. I thought your life was more important than your modesty."

"At the time I did too," she admitted. Although now she was more concerned with her virtue—what little she had left. She wanted him to stand up. His strong thighs hid the front of his body from her, but her mouth was watering. She knew what was there. And she knew he'd be rock hard. He usually was around her, and she hadn't seen much difference since they'd been in each other's company.

"I hated that we had to kill her," Conner said, and this time there was no mistaking the regret in his voice. "She was a female looking for a meal is all. I hate losing any of them."

"I'm grateful I wasn't her meal," Isabeau admitted.

"I should have been more careful," Conner said. "They lie under the banks in the natural caves there where the water is shallow and a little sluggish. We aren't at a very high elevation and I should have been more alert."

Elijah snickered and Conner sent him a glowering warning. Elijah just laughed. "Clearly, your mind was where it shouldn't have been."

Conner's glower turned to a smoldering glare. "Why weren't you alert?"

The glare didn't have any more effect than the glower. Elijah laughed out loud. "Trying to converse, you mangy cat. It isn't easy trying to get your sorry ass out of trouble. It takes some thinking."

Isabeau burst out laughing. "Both of you are insane."

"*We're* insane? You're the one standing there laughing after a snake tried to swallow you whole," Elijah pointed out.

"I'm sure it would have dislocated all her bones first," Conner said.

She shoved him, hoping for a big splash. Her push barely rocked him, but he flashed her another wide grin that shook her up, and his smile was worth missing out on seeing him going facedown in the water. It was the respect on his face. In his eyes. He was proud of her and there was respect in Elijah's eyes as well. She couldn't help the small, blossoming glow spreading inside of her.

"We'd better get you back and out of those wet clothes," Conner said. "I'm going to shift."

It was all the warning she got before his muscles contorted and fur slid along his back and belly. Claws burst through the tips of his fingers. She was shocked at how fast he could assume his other form. She fell into step beside him, unafraid, even though her heart pounded and she was aware of every movement in the forest. She was alive. Totally, absolutely alive.

8

IT was happening all over again. Isabeau took a quick, surreptitious look around, hoping no one would notice her squirming. Her skin burned, felt too tight, every nerve ending raw and jumping. She rubbed her arms, and with even that light touch, her skin hurt. Deep inside the itch had grown to a demanding ache she couldn't ignore.

She'd slept the night way, curled against the large leopard, the rain a steady, soothing rhythm, the fur thick and warm. His heartbeat had been in her ear as she'd pillowed her head on soft fur. There'd been no sign of this madness then. She'd even managed to get the picture of Conner crouching naked in the stream out of her mind. Now, she couldn't take a breath without scenting his fresh, wild musk—an enticing lure she couldn't seem to ignore.

Without even looking for him, she was acutely aware of him. She knew his exact position at any given moment. Conner Vega was fast becoming the bane of her life. She tried desperately just to breathe normally, but her lungs burned right along with her skin, air coming in ragged, harsh gasps.

The men shot her small, quick glances throughout breakfast, but no one really looked at her—and that told her that in spite of her best efforts—they knew her ripening condition. It was a humiliating and extremely uncomfortable position to be in. Her hunger deepened when Conner came back from his morning shower, dressed casually in jeans that hugged his strong legs and cupped his butt. The last thing she needed to do was to be looking, but, honestly, how could she stop herself? She pressed her fingertips to her temples hard in an effort to get control. Her teeth ached from the strain of continually clenching them.

The men had a low conversation after breakfast while she drank coffee that tasted so bitter she could barely get it down. Adan had left. She'd put down the sudden uneasiness she'd felt at her only real ally leaving, but no matter how much she wanted to deny it, since awakening this morning, a slow heat had begun building in her body. Thick, like magma in a volcano, the heat moved through her veins and spread like an insidious addiction throughout her body.

It didn't help that after breakfast the team decided to work with Jeremiah and her on fighting skills. Of course it was Conner touching her, totally impersonal, his hands placing her body in the correct position until just the brush of his fingertips made her want to scream with need. She was *not* going to miss this opportunity to learn from them, but their bodies were soon glistening with sweat and almost immediately the men shed their shirts.

She put everything she had into the workout, appreciating the difficult physical techniques of punching and kicking. She worked her body hard in an effort to sublimate. If she couldn't have hot, sweaty sex and lots of it, she hoped to work herself to the point of exhaustion. Each time Conner corrected her stance, or her leg when she pivoted and kicked, it was all she could do not to jerk away from his scalding touch.

She deliberately put distance between them, trying to work on the spinning, jumping kicks and accurate punches. She heard Conner and Rio talking about sparring and stood with Jeremiah, trying not to notice the amorous glances he shot her way. Her cat wanted to rub along the tree branches, basically rub anything at all. All she wanted to do was rub herself all over Conner, but if they wanted sparring then that's what they'd get.

Felipe was first to stand opposite her, his fists doubled, his hands up and his eyes focused on her. She could see he was trying not to breathe—not to inhale her scent. She'd never noticed that his lashes were so long, curling a bit at the tips. He had a nice nose and a firm jaw. He was extremely handsome, not quite as muscular as Conner or Rio, but lithe and supple . . .

"What the hell are you doing, Isabeau?" Conner demanded. "He just nailed you six times in a row and you didn't even try to block."

"He did?" She blinked rapidly and looked around at the circle of faces, a little confused. Had Felipe actually moved? "He didn't hit me."

"He pulled his punch because if he touched you, I'd knock his teeth down his throat," Conner bit back, clearly exasperated. "You still have to block."

He looked very sexy when he was angry. She'd never noticed that before. She reached out to rub the frown from his face. He jerked back, his breath exploding out of his lungs. She dropped her hand, pouting a little. "I'm trying, Conner."

"Well, try harder," he said gruffly.

His voice was thick and sexy, and another rush of heat slipped like fire through her veins. She liked that. Felipe was replaced by Elijah. Elijah seemed as if he was paying more attention to Conner than to her. Experimentally, she threw a series of light punches and kicks, determined to drive Elijah back. He didn't retreat as he should have, but flicked his hand toward her with incredible speed. She could actually see the flow of his muscle, the firmness of his jaw, the sensual shape of his lips.

Flesh smacked flesh and she blinked. Conner's open palm had captured Elijah's fist just a scant inch from her face. "Isabeau," he snapped between his teeth. "You aren't trying."

"I was. Really," she protested. How was she supposed to concentrate when Elijah's entire body seemed made of flowing muscle? It was poetic. And sexy. Hot. Downright hot.

Conner made a sound that bordered on a snarl. Elijah backed away from Isabeau, dropping his hands and shaking his head. Tiny beads of sweat dotted his forehead. "I'm done here, Conner."

Isabeau looked hopefully at Leonardo. Surely she could land a kick or two on him. The man looked as if he was terrified—going to his doom. That should tell Conner she was scaring the men.

Her body felt wonderful, very alive, every nerve ending sensitive and responsive. Every movement stretched her top taut over her peaking nipples, brushing them with the most delicious strokes, sending streaks of arousal dancing through her belly. When she moved with the sensuous flow of muscle, she was acutely aware of the mechanics of her body as she'd never been—of her own femininity and how perfectly wonderful jeans were, rubbing in all the right places when she picked up her leg to throw a kick.

Leonardo broke out in a sweat and abruptly dropped his hands, backing away from her as she glided closer. Conner stepped between them and caught her by the shoulders. "What *exactly* is that?"

"What?" She smiled at him dreamily. If she moved just a little closer to him, she could probably rub along his chest. She stepped into him.

"That noise. You're purring," he accused.

"Really? Am I?" She slid her body right up against his and rubbed her breasts along his chest, needing to leave her scent on him, enjoying the streaks of fire sizzling through her veins as her sensitive nipples tightened even more. "Did you know that you have the most amazing mouth?"

Rio made a noise somewhere between frustration and amusement. "This isn't working, Conner. I think we're going to work with Jeremiah's shape-shifting for a while." He pointed to a clearing a small distance away. "Over there."

Conner turned his head to see the young leopard staring at Isabeau with a rapt look on his face, mouth open, nearly salivating. A soft hand inserted itself between Conner's body and hers and rubbed the front of his jeans, right over his thick, aching groin, jerking his attention back to Isabeau. The purring had increased and her eyes had gone a little glazed. Swearing, he captured her wrists and yanked her hands to his chest, pinning them there. "Good idea," he all but growled back. The kid needed distraction.

Isabeau's cat needed to emerge soon or this wave had to be over before all the men went into some kind of snarling sexual frenzy. He could smell the testosterone rising. Things were going to hell fast. He needed to take control.

"You're going to get someone killed," he hissed at the cat.

He made the mistake of pulling Isabeau into his arms. All those soft curves melted into him. She leaned her face into his neck and licked. A delicate taste, her tongue like velvet stroking over his leaping pulse. His throbbing cock felt that tantalizing caress and jerked hard against the straining material of his jeans. Fire raced over his skin, burned into his bones, danced in his veins until he couldn't think for the lust coursing through him.

"Come with me now." He had the presence of mind to drag her into the trees, away from the sight of the others. She had no sense of self-preservation, going with him without a struggle, looking up at him with eyes drenched with desire.

His breath hissed out of his lungs and his mouth came down on hers before he had a chance to save them both. Temptation beat at him like a drum, pounding through his veins, through his cock—his entire nervous system inflamed—intoxicated—with her. He took her mouth with his own, long, drugging kisses until he couldn't tell where he was anymore. Everything distanced, the trees, the brush, even the scent of the other men. There was only Isabeau, soft and warm, a siren dragging him deeper into her web of pleasure.

He'd been there before. Every bit of honor he possessed had gone up in flames once the taste of her had become an addiction—and it was starting all over again. He dragged his mouth from hers and stared down into her liquid eyes, fighting for breath, fighting his own needs.

"You have to get control, Isabeau." His voice was hoarse. "Every man here is leopard. Do you have any idea of the havoc you're wreaking?"

"I love your voice." Her hands slipped under his shirt to find bare skin. "And your mouth. When you kiss it's like fire spreading through me."

Her voice was more seductive than anything he'd ever known, pouring over him, filling him, eating away his discipline. He closed his eyes briefly, attempting to remember how much trouble he'd gotten into before because he hadn't been able to resist her lure—and she hadn't had the added temptation of her cat emerging.

"Isabeau." He gave her a little shake. It didn't stop her wandering hands. "Look at me. You don't want to do this. A few hours from now you'll hate me even more than you already do. I let you down once and I'll be damned if I do it again."

Who the hell was he kidding? He didn't have that kind of control. Not in a million years. He wanted her with every breath he drew. Not because of her cat, but because she was Isabeau Chandler, the woman he loved above all else. He dragged air into his lungs. He loved her and he knew the difference having been without her. He wasn't going to let history repeat itself.

"Stop it, Isabeau." His voice was harsher than he intended.

She went rigid, dropping her hands as if he'd burned her. She stepped back away from him. "I'm so sorry I made you uncomfortable," she said, her voice trembling. "We certainly wouldn't want that, would we? The great Conner Vega. Funny how when seduction is your idea, there's no problem."

"Is that what you have in mind, Isabeau? Seduction? You're playing with fire."

She looked him up and down. "I doubt it. I don't think there's much left there." Deliberately she turned and allowed her gaze to sweep the other males, open speculation on her face. "Sorry I bothered you."

He caught her arm and swung her back to him when she would have walked away. "Don't even think about it."

Her eyebrow shot up. "I have no idea what you're talking about." She looked at his hand and he let her go. She turned her back on him and walked away, her hips swaying, her hair a little wild, disheveled and tumbling around her face and down her back as if unknowingly he had loosened her ponytail. He didn't remember doing it, but the feel of silk was still on the pads of his fingers.

Isabeau blinked back the tears burning in her eyes. She'd thrown herself at him and he'd turned her down. Her pride was on the ground, trampled. He didn't want her. She ducked her head, bending at the waist to drag in air. It was a mistake. She could scent all the men now, a heady mix of lust and male potency.

If you don't knock it off, you female hussy, I'm going to strangle you, she hissed at her cat. She wanted to claw her way down Conner's muscular back. Who would have thought muscles could be so defined? She knew it wasn't the cat—or at least just the cat. She wanted Conner, and her cat emerging was a great cover. *But he didn't want her.*

How could that be when she wanted him with every fiber of her being? She couldn't close her eyes without images of him haunting her. She couldn't take a breath without needing him. Damn him for rejecting her. He had been the one spouting the law of the rain forest was a higher law, and yet when she'd taken the chance, he'd shut her down. It had taken every ounce of courage she possessed to get him to kiss her, hoping he'd take it from there. If he didn't want her anymore, well . . . She lifted her head and looked at the men talking to Jeremiah in the clearing just a short distance away.

She'd told Adan she would try to seduce one of Imelda Cortez's guards because she knew she would never feel for another man the way she felt for Conner. Seduction still had possibilities. Maybe being a leopard meant she could be promiscuous and not care. Maybe her moral scruples would be overcome much easier than she'd ever believed. She moved closer, wanting to hear what they were saying.

She was acutely aware of Conner joining the other men. He stood out. For her, she feared he would always stand out. The light fell across his hair and body, illuminating him in the darkened, dappled clearing. He ran his fingers through his hair, slicking it back haphazardly in the way she found sexy. She almost hated him in that moment. She looked away from him and her gaze met Jeremiah's.

He kept casting Isabeau small amorous glances, unable to keep his eyes off of her. Clearly he found her attractive. He flexed his muscles for her and she tried not to be amused. It wasn't fair that she thought of him as a young boy when he was nearly her age. Conner just seemed so much more of a man, with a man's ripped physique.

Jeremiah flexed again and shot Conner a quick glance before sending her a smile. Rio called out to him and he took off running, stripping as he went, tossing his shirt aside and ripping his jeans down, glancing back at Isabeau as he did so. The material trapped his ankles and he went down, head over heels, rolling across the clearing, half-naked, tangled in his jeans.

"What the hell was that?" Rio demanded.

"I know exactly what that was," Conner said ominously, stalking across the clearing to Jeremiah.

"Conner!" Elijah moved quickly to intercept. "He's just a kid."

"He knows the rules."

Jeremiah scrambled to his feet, looking defiant. "Maybe you're just worried because I've got larger than average equipment and you think she'll prefer me?"

"Because of the size of your dick?" Conner looked him up and down and there was contempt on his face. "Sorry, kid, that's not going to cut it. You can't even get your pants off when you need to. I doubt you'll be too impressive trying to perform."

Outraged, Jeremiah tore his jeans from around his ankles and threw them in disgust, rushing at Conner. Elijah caught him and threw him away from the other man.

"Idiot. You're going to get yourself killed. Can't you tell when a man's mate is in the Han Vol Dan? Have some fucking respect."

Jeremiah stopped in his tracks and looked at Isabeau. They all did—with the exception of Conner. She tried not to turn bright red. She looked at the ground, wishing it would open up and swallow her. She turned and walked into the comparative shelter of the trees to watch as Jeremiah dressed and prepared to start over again.

Watching him run, strip and shift made her itch to try shifting. She'd been over her father's office carefully, getting into his private papers, and there had been no mention of the leopard people. She didn't believe that he knew. Her mother must have died in childbirth just as Conner had speculated and no one had come to claim the infant. He had relocated from the Amazon to Borneo around the time of her birth. There was a good chance her people were there. Maybe she should go try to find them.

She couldn't go back to Borneo. She couldn't stay in

Panama. Conner was everywhere. She would have gone anywhere with him, even knowing he had brought about the downfall of her father. She pressed a trembling hand to her mouth, ashamed of herself. It was a convenient excuse, a way to keep her hurt alive. Her father had brought about his own downfall. Conner's sin had been in seducing her when he didn't mean it.

He hurt her pride. He was still hurting it, but he wasn't responsible for the things her father had done. He'd used her just as she was asking him to use Imelda Cortez in order to get back the missing children. Did the end justify the means? Didn't that make her a hypocrite?

She pressed her fingers to her temples and willed her body to calm down. She didn't want to leave without seeing this through. She owed it to Adan and even to Conner's mother, who had befriended her, as well as all the children who had been taken. She took a deep breath and let it out, pacing back and forth to get rid of as much excess energy as she could before going back to join the others.

Isabeau walked with her head up, refusing to be intimidated or humiliated by the group of men. Whatever she was, whatever was happening to her apparently was normal in their world and she refused to be afraid. She might desperately want sex, but she didn't lack courage.

She watched the mechanics of the change over and over. Eventually she got over seeing a naked body and became fascinated by the actual shifting. It looked as if it could be painful, although it seemed to happen so fast as Jeremiah ran that maybe it wasn't that bad.

Rio, Felipe and Elijah shook their heads and looked at one another as they timed Jeremiah's run for the umpteenth time.

"Too slow, Jeremiah," Conner snapped. "Do it again.

And this time think about someone shooting at you while you're running. You're younger than any of us and you should be faster. You need to shave fifteen or twenty seconds off of your time."

Jeremiah shot Conner a look of utter disgust. "Jealous bastard," he muttered under his breath. "It can't be done."

Jeremiah should have known better. Conner had excellent hearing. Conner stalked across the forest floor to loom over the younger leopard. "You don't think it can be done? Not only can it be done, you young lazy cub, but it can be done racing through the trees, not in some nice clearing like this one."

Jeremiah compounded his sins by sneering openly. "I don't believe you."

Rio came up behind him silently and cuffed him on the back of the head, the blow hard enough to rock the kid. "Stop whining and try to learn something. If you're going to be working with us, you have to know how to stay alive. You didn't even hear me coming."

Isabeau turned away to hide her smile. Jeremiah really was a large child, wanting the respect of the other leopards, but not wanting to work that hard for it. They were all exasperated with him. They'd been working all morning and it was becoming clear he was a bit self-indulgent and lazy.

"You said your family was from Costa Rica?" she ventured, forcing herself to keep a straight face.

Jeremiah nodded. "But I'm doing this on my own. My parents don't need to know," he added hastily.

Rio whirled around. He'd been stalking across the clearing, his shoulders stiff with annoyance. "Your parents don't know where you are?"

"I thought maybe your mama raised you," Elijah muttered. "And you were an only child."

Jeremiah glared at him, drawing himself up to his full height and pushing out his chest. "I'm from a huge family, the youngest of eight. I have seven sisters. My father wanted a son."

The men exchanged knowing looks.

"And he got you," Elijah muttered under his breath.

"That explains a lot," Conner said. "Well, boy, this isn't home and your sisters aren't here to coddle you. Improve your time or get your sorry ass back to Mama where it's safe. If you stay with us, someone's going to be shooting at you."

Jeremiah flushed. "I'm no mama's boy, if that's what you're implying. I'm just saying, my time is fast, probably faster than any of yours."

Conner sighed. "Who has the slowest time of any of us shifting on the run through the trees?" He looked around at the men.

Felipe raised his hand. "I think it's me, Conner."

Conner stepped back and waved Felipe forward. Felipe glanced at Isabeau and raised an eyebrow at Conner.

"She has to learn. And she's sure seen enough of Jeremiah's naked ass."

Isabeau blushed, cursing under her breath as once again attention centered on her. She was trying to fit in, whether they all believed it or not, and she didn't need the added burden of them constantly throwing out reminders that she was female and basically going into heat like a freaking cat.

She let her gaze drift over Conner. She'd spent the night curled up next to a leopard, as warm and safe as she'd never even dreamt of being. Listening to the steady rhythm of the rain and the leopard's heartbeat had allowed her to drift off to sleep fast, even in the midst of so many strangers. She'd felt comforted and completely at ease. Now, watching him in action, the fluid grace, the play of muscle beneath his skin, the burning eyes and focused stare, her body had gone into meltdown. She could barely keep her eyes from him. And she was acutely aware every single second why she had brought him to Panama—to seduce another woman—and that he had rejected her.

Conner cleared his throat. "Isabeau?" he prompted.

She flushed, realizing Felipe was waiting for her permission. "I need to learn how to shift as well," she said, trying to sound nonchalant, as if she was used to seeing naked men all day long.

Felipe took her at her word, peeling off his clothes without further modesty while he sprinted. She had to admire the efficient way he stripped, a smooth, practiced motion that took only a couple of seconds. The moment he kicked off his shoes and shed his socks, he was running, stripping as he went, already shifting as he shucked his jeans and shirt, the muscles contorting as he picked up speed, so that he was leaping, covering large areas of space before his shirt floated to the ground.

Conner hit the stopwatch and walked over to Jeremiah. The kid's mouth hung open as he stared at the large leopard in utter astonishment.

"I could barely see him do it," Jeremiah said, admiration in his voice. "I swear, I almost think I can't believe my eyes."

"No wasted motion," Isabeau pointed out, unable to stay in the background. She hurried up beside Jeremiah to look at the watch. "That's not even seven seconds. How can that be?"

"I'm not certain I really saw it," Jeremiah said, still staring at the watch.

Isabeau crowded closer, brushing the naked leopard with her arm. Conner growled deep in his throat and the kid jumped back. All the men stiffened and turned to see Conner's head moving slowly, following Jeremiah's shriveling body, gaze burning brightly and focused on his prey.

"Conner," Rio said sharply.

Shocked by Conner's reaction, Isabeau instinctively moved away from Jeremiah. "You can't possibly think . . ." She trailed off, one hand going defensively to her throat, although there was a mean-spirited part of her that found the situation amusing. "He's a kid."

"He's closer to your age than I am," Conner snapped.

She couldn't suppress her laughter. "Come on, Conner, don't be ridiculous."

"Hey!" Jeremiah said. "Women can't get enough of me."

Conner snarled, his teeth elongating, curving, his claws bursting from the tips of his fingers. Isabeau made it worse by doubling over in laughter at the outraged look on Jeremiah's face and the other men rolling their eyes, shocked that the boy didn't have enough self-preservation to step back farther from Isabeau and close his mouth.

"Are you saying my woman wants you?" Conner demanded, stepping in close to the boy—too close. "That she prefers you to me?"

That sobered Isabeau immediately. She straightened, her eyes going green and glowing like two jewels. "I'm not your woman, you miserable excuse for a mate."

Everyone ignored her. Jeremiah sucked in his breath. Those lethal claws were far too close to the most precious part of his body, and Conner looked mean enough to rip body parts off.

"No, that's not what I meant," Jeremiah protested,

realizing his mistake too late. Cats were notoriously bad-tempered with men around their mates, especially if the mate was close to a heat. He realized none of the other men had gone near Isabeau.

"What exactly did you mean?" Conner bit out.

Isabeau was very aware of the other men moving in now, presumably to save Jeremiah should it be necessary. Suddenly the situation was no longer about her. Jeremiah was in real danger from a man who had earlier rejected her advances. Whatever was driving him was real and dangerous.

She stepped close to Conner and put her hand on his arm. She could feel the steel and adrenaline running through him like a river of fire. She was beginning to understand the terrible toll of the leopard on the men. The cat's laws were impossible for the man to ignore. They always walked a fine line when it came to their animal traits.

"I-I meant that was a great time Felipe had, and I need to work much harder if I'm going to even come close to that," Jeremiah stammered.

"I bumped him," Isabeau pointed out. "Please, Conner, I'm asking you."

Conner stood for a moment, his body fighting to rid itself of adrenaline and then abruptly he turned, his arm sweeping around her, forcing her away from the other leopard, his head close to hers so his lips could brush against her ear. "That was him getting aroused by your scent. His first damn mistake."

He took her deep into the rain forest, away from the others and the scent of aroused male that drove his cat—and him—insane.

She blushed a bright crimson. How could she not? She wasn't used to discussing anything having to do with sex in a casual setting, and the way these men treated nudity and the heat of a female cat bordered on the mundane. It wasn't offensive, exactly, it was just a little disturbing to know that all of them could tell she was entering into some sort of a cycle. Not just that they could tell—more than that—they were all hyper-aware of it.

"I hope it was more than my scent," Isabeau said, trying to lighten the moment, but meaning it all the same. "I don't want to be wanted because of the way I *smell.*"

He inhaled deeply, deliberately taking her fragrance into his lungs. She could send flames leaping in his blood without even trying, but right now, with her innocent frown and the long sweep of her lashes, he could barely keep his hunger in check. "Scent is important to cats." He rubbed his face against the bare skin of her neck. "So is scent marking. Any man stupid enough to cross into my territory is going to have a fight on his hands."

She jerked away from him. "I used to be your territory. Back when you were someone else, remember?"

"I remember every moment." His golden eyes burned deep into hers. "Do you?"

She bit back a retort. She was not going to fight with him. He could reduce her to tears in seconds. She was no match for him—she never had been. "You can't do this, Conner. You don't want me, but you're going to kill anyone else who does? That doesn't even make sense."

"I don't *want* you?" He bit the words out, a growl rumbling in his chest. His fingers tightened on her upper arms and he drew her tight against his body, deliberately letting her feel his thick arousal. "Want is an insipid word, Isabeau, for what I feel for you. I'm not going to blow it with you because I can't keep my hands off of you. That happened once and I'll be damned if it will happen again."

"You couldn't keep your hands off of me?"

"Don't act like you don't know that. I knew better. Seducing a woman doesn't always involve taking them to bed. I couldn't stop myself, and look what my lack of control did to us." For a moment there was naked pain on his face. "It was bad enough knowing I'd betrayed you, but to find out that before her death my mother knew what I'd done . . ." He trailed off, shaking his head. The mask—and resolve—slipped back into place. "When I take you to bed it will be because you want us there, not because your cat is screaming for relief."

She flushed all over again, but her pride didn't matter as much as his words. She held them close to her heart, for the first time feeling as if her mixed up world could come right again. Was it only her cat that wanted him? She didn't think so, but she wasn't sure, and Conner was right, she had to be certain. It made things easier knowing he hadn't totally rejected her.

His hands framed her face, his thumb sliding over her lips as his gaze burned into hers. "You're mine, Isabeau. You'll always be mine. Make no mistake about it. Whether you choose to forgive me and give us a second chance, or you don't, you'll be my only."

Her heart stopped. Just stopped. She could feel it there in her chest, twisting tight and then beginning a frantic pounding. For once her cat stayed quiet and she was allowed that perfect moment. She looked up into his face, a face that was etched forever into her mind—into her soul—and knew she was lost all over again. "Why didn't you come after me?" That had hurt more than she could say.

"I made up my mind to come," he admitted. "Six months ago. I knew I had to try to explain when I really had no excuse. I had a job to do, Isabeau, and the moment I realized I was slipping, taking us both in too deep, I should have shut it down. I'd like to say I didn't because the kidnap victims mattered so much to me, but I've thought a lot about that and it isn't the truth. Once I was with you, once I had gone over the line, there was no going back for me. I couldn't find the strength to do the right thing and give you up."

His words were stark. Raw. And they were truth. She saw it in his burning eyes, heard it in his velvet voice and smelled it with a leopard's acute sensory system. She could only stare at him, trying not to let the happiness blossoming in the pit of her stomach and spreading throughout her body with absolute joy show on her face. Her tongue touched her lower lip and instantly his gaze was there, following the small movement.

She held still. Absolutely still. She even held her breath. He'd rejected her advances earlier—she wasn't making a fool of herself a second time, even when he'd assured her their time together hadn't all been a lie. The truth washed over her and into her, bringing such relief her legs trembled. Or maybe it was arousal teasing along her thighs and sending her temperature soaring.

He lowered his head. Slowly. Waiting for her reaction. She stood still beneath his hands, watching his gaze drift possessively over her face. Watching the way his eyes changed, going leopard, blazing with hunger. His mouth was everything. Seductive. Heart-stopping. Perfect. And then his lips touched hers. A mere brush. Her stomach flipped. Her womb clenched. Liquid heat gathered. His mouth moved again over hers, a small back and forth movement designed to tempt her—to drive her wild. And it did.

Her breasts ached, nipples peaking into two tight buds, straining against the material of her shirt in an effort to get closer to his heat. His tongue licked her lower lip. Savoring her taste. His teeth nipped, and the bite of pain sent another spasm crashing through her core. He made a sound, a low growl in his throat that drenched her immediately in need.

"I missed you every single second," he whispered. "I dreamt of you when I could close my eyes and most of the time I couldn't sleep with needing you."

He kissed her, a long, drugging kiss that intoxicated every one of her senses. When he pulled away, it was to press his forehead against hers as he drew in a harsh breath. "I love the sound of your laughter. You taught me so many things, Isabeau, about what matters. When you find everything and then lose it . . ."

His mouth found hers again, over and over, each kiss more demanding than the last, more filled with hunger, so that he was nearly devouring her, sweeping her away on a tidal wave of desire. He'd always been able to do that, remove every vestige of sanity so that she was no thinking person, but a creature of pure feeling. She'd never known she could be passionate or sexy until Conner had come into her life, and everything had changed—*she* had changed.

His fingers bunched in her hair, pulling her head back, anchoring her in place, while his gaze burned a brand over her. Lines of passion etched deep in his face, dark lust glittered in his eyes. Her heart jumped. Another rush of heat spread like liquid fire. Her knees went weak. She'd always been susceptible to his sensual appetites, but now his hunger was a drumbeat in her veins.

Her breath hissed out as his mouth descended again. The gentleness was gone, replaced by raw passion. He took her response in his confident, dominant way. His hands were strong, his body hard, the heat rising between them like the steam in the forest. Her body went boneless, soft, melting into his. He growled, a low, vibrating note that sent fire licking like tongues over her skin. His hands slid down her spine to the curve of her bottom and he lifted her. Instinctively she wrapped her legs around his waist, locking her ankles.

The vee between her legs fit tightly over the thick bulge, welding them together. All the while his mouth ate hungrily at hers. Her world tunneled—narrowed to just Conner. His hands. His heat. The taste and texture of him. She was aware of every ragged breath, of the bite of his teeth, of the roughness of his caresses, even the feel of his skin beneath the material that kept her from touching him.

Everything receded until her mind was consumed with only Conner. He tasted like sin. Like a mixture of heaven, for the pleasure—and hell, for the craving that would always be for him. His mouth moved from hers and began traveling slowly, seductively down her face, the side of her neck, her throat and then shoulder. She felt the edge of his teeth and shivered in need. She didn't want soft and gentle. She needed his rough possession, claiming her, branding her, taking her in a firestorm of heat and flame that would end the world around them, leaving them nothing but ashes, clean and fierce and forever welded together.

His head came up alertly and his golden gaze swept the forest around them. The men, off in the distant clearing, melted away, simply disappeared as though they'd never been. Conner allowed her shaky legs to drop to the ground even as he inhaled deeply, drawing in the air—and information.

9

SHAKEN, her entire body trembling, Isabeau clutched at Conner's shoulders for support. "What is it?" She couldn't think, couldn't breathe right.

"We have company coming this way," he said. "The forest is getting mighty crowded these days." He wrapped his arm around her and drew her beneath his shoulder, sliding back farther into the brush. "We'll be fine. The boys are closing in on them."

"Them?" she echoed faintly. If survival meant being alert at all times—she wasn't going to make it. He had caught the scent of the intruders, or felt them in some way, while she'd been overcome with her own passion. How did he do that? She was almost upset with him, even though she knew it was a skill he needed—*they* needed—to survive.

"Two men. They move like they know the forest."

"I don't understand." She didn't understand what he meant, but more than that, she didn't understand how her body could be screaming for relief, every nerve ending crying out for him to stay—to keep his attention solely on her. It was stupid in the face of danger, but she'd been so consumed by him, aware only of him, thinking he had the same awareness and need and obsession with her.

"Most people come into the rain forest and try to dominate, hacking their way, but these men are familiar and comfortable with it, telling us perhaps they inhabit the interior on a regular basis." His palm curled around her nape and he dipped his head, skimming the side of her neck with a trail of kisses. "I could kill them just for interrupting us."

It was his voice, shaking a little, rough—even harsh, revealing he meant those damning words that ironically allowed her to forgive him for his survival skills. She leaned into him and let him hold her close, trying hard to cool the rush of heat that had sent her body into meltdown.

"Take a breath. It helps."

"Does it?"

He laughed softly, a mere thread of sound. "Not really. But we'll pretend. When I'm with you, Isabeau, it's a little like lighting a match to a stick of dynamite. I can't seem to control it." His teeth nipped her shoulder and he buried his face briefly against her neck, obviously struggling to cool the heat of his body as well. He was still thick and hard and, in spite of the potential gravity of the situation, she felt happy.

"At least it's both of us."

"How could you think otherwise?" He lifted his head and his gaze jumped from the forest to her and stared with that focused piercing intent that always managed to set fire to her blood. "Is it your cat who wants me?" His voice was velvet soft. Almost a caress. But there was just the slightest hint of uncertainty in his query.

"Why would you think that?"

A leopard grunted. Birds took flight. Several howler monkeys called out a warning. She couldn't help the little gasp of alarm that just seemed to slip out.

Conner pushed her behind him. "Never panic, Isabeau. In any situation your brain is always your best weapon whether you're in leopard or human form. There's always a moment when you'll have the advantage. All these defense techniques we're teaching you are great, but conditioning and thinking are always going to be your best weapons."

He spoke matter-of-factly, imparting the information even as he crouched lower in the brush, shifting position so he could find the slight breeze moving through the forest. Low, on the floor, there was rarely a wind unless a big enough storm generated it. Mostly the wind stayed in the canopy, but with his acute senses he could gather the information needed. Isabeau tried to follow his example. She was determined to learn, to be an asset to him.

She caught a faint scent drifting in the air and recognized it immediately from Adan's village. His people used roots for soap. She waited a few moments, aware Conner must have known, yet he didn't show himself and neither did any of the others. They weren't trusting, and maybe that was a lesson in itself.

Two men emerged into the clearing. Both wore only loincloths, one in sandals, the other barefoot. The rain forest was so humid, clothes hampered anyone routinely moving through the interior, and most wore the minimum. She knew that from experience. Even she dressed in as little as possible when she worked. She recognized the older man as one of the elders, Adan's brother, Gerald. The other was Adan's son, Will. She started to move around Conner to greet them, but he pulled her into his arms, one hand sliding over her mouth.

Her gaze met his and her heart jumped. In that moment he looked less a man and more a leopard. They stared at one another. He looked every inch predator, his eyes cold, burning with a lethal glow that sent her heart hammering hard. He slowly loosened the hand on her mouth and held up a finger between them, all the while staring down into her eyes.

She couldn't have moved if she'd wanted to. She found herself mesmerized—hypnotized—by his stare. She knew it could happen with a large cat. They had power in their focused stare, the enthralling moment when prey froze, waiting for that killing blow. She couldn't breathe, locked there, trapped in the glow. She remained absolutely still. Silent. Unable to disobey him.

He turned his head slowly, breaking the contact, focusing on the two men striding across the clearing in the direction of the cabin. She didn't turn her head, but rather shifted her gaze, afraid of making a movement, holding her breath. She could feel Conner beside her, utterly still, the tension coiling in him, his muscles locked and ready.

The men had blowguns in their hands and were advancing with care, watching the surrounding forest, stepping cautiously as was their way. Isabeau had seen them many times, moving with ease through the heavy brush. A leopard grunted. The two men froze, went back-to-back, hands steady on their weapons. Another leopard answered from a point in front of them. A third replied to their left. Conner made a sound, deep in his throat. Rio's call came from behind them, cutting off their escape route, so that the men knew they were completely surrounded.

Gerald slowly put his weapon on the ground and raised his hands, one holding a book. When his nephew hesitated, he snapped a command and the younger man sullenly placed his blowgun beside his uncle's. They stood with their hands raised.

"Stay put," Conner warned. "If they make a wrong move toward you, I won't be able to save their lives."

"They're my friends," Isabeau protested.

"No one is our friend on a job. They could have changed their minds and want this handled a different way. Just do what I say and keep out of sight. Let me talk to them. If anything goes wrong, drop to the ground and cover your eyes. And, Isabeau . . ." He waited until her gaze met his. "This time do what I tell you."

She nodded her head in agreement. She certainly didn't want to see leopards killing two men she knew.

Conner moved out of the brush onto the edge of the clearing. "Gerald. Your brother said nothing of your coming."

The two men swung around, the older one keeping his hands high and out from his body, the younger one going low, almost into a crouch, hands reaching for his weapon.

"You'd never make it, Will," Conner said. "And you know it. You pick it up, I guarantee, you're a dead man."

Gerald snapped at his nephew in their own language. Conner had spent enough time in their village as a youngster to understand, but he politely pretended he didn't know Will was being harshly reprimanded. They'd been friends once—good friends, but that had been a long time ago.

"We felt you needed to know the truth before you set out on this mission," Gerald called to him. "Adan sent me with your mother's book."

"Why didn't Adan bring it to me himself?"

"My mother had it," Will said. "Marisa thrust it into her hands when the men came, and my mother dropped it. She didn't remember until later, and my father was already gone when she went looking for it."

Conner remained still, almost rigid, forcing his lungs to continue breathing in and out. He knew his mother kept a diary. He'd seen it enough times as a boy growing up. She journaled nearly every day. She loved words and they often flowed in the form of poetry or short stories. Will conjured up vivid memories better suppressed there in the rain forest with danger surrounding them, but it was a plausible explanation.

"There's much to tell you," Gerald said. "And your mother's book will bear out my words of truth."

Conner gestured for him to put his hands down. "We have to be careful, Gerald. Someone tried to kill your brother last night."

Gerald nodded. "I'm aware. And there was a division in the tribe on how to handle the situation with getting the children back."

"Does that division include you, Will?" Conner asked.

"My son, Artureo, was taken," Will said, "but I stand with my father. Nothing we do will ever be enough for Cortez if we don't stop her now."

Conner beckoned them forward. Gerald stepped away from the weapons, and walked toward Conner. Will followed him, looking far less hostile. They drew thin mats from the small packs they carried slung over their shoulders and laid them on the ground, lowering themselves into a vulnerable sitting position. Conner gave a small hand signal to the others, advising them to back off and simply watch.

"Thank you." He took the book Gerald offered as he sat tailor fashion opposite them. "Will, it's good to see you again, old friend." He nodded his head toward the younger man. They'd spent a few years of their childhood playing together. The tribesmen took wives at a much earlier age, and by seventeen, Will had had the responsibilities of a son.

Will nodded his head. "I wish the situation was different."

"I knew one of Adan's grandsons was taken. This is about your son?"

Will glanced at his uncle and then shook his head, his eyes meeting Conner's.

Conner braced himself for a blow. There was no expression on Will's face, but there was a great deal of compassion in his eyes.

"No, Conner. This is about your brother."

Conner's first inclination was to leap across the small space separating them and rip out Will's heart, but he forced himself to sit quite still, his gaze locked on his prey, and every muscle ready to spring. He knew these men. They were honest to a fault, and if Will said he had a brother—then Will believed it was truth. He forced air through his burning lungs, studying the two men, his fingers tightening around his mother's book.

Isabeau had mentioned a child. "Marisa came with the child" or something to that effect. His mother was always around children; he hadn't thought much about that. He hadn't inquired as to whose child it was.

"She would have told me if she had another child," he said. He couldn't imagine his mother hiding her child, not for any reason. But she had stayed near Adan's village, even after he'd left. Could she have found love with a member of the tribe? He raised his eyebrow, silently demanding an explanation.

"Not your mother's child, Conner. A babe was brought to our village by a woman, one of your people. She didn't want the child."

Conner's stomach lurched. He knew what was coming, and the child in him remembered that feeling of absolute rejection. Without thinking, he turned his head to look at Isabeau. He rarely felt the need of anyone, but in that moment, he knew he needed her support. She came out of the brush without hesitation, striding across the clearing, looking regal, her face soft, her eyes on him. She flashed a small smile and greeted the two tribesmen as she sank down close to Conner. She laid her palm on his thigh and he felt it burning there. He pressed his hand down over the top of hers, holding her to him while she looked at him.

He didn't want that moment to end and the next to begin. She smiled at him, showing him without words she would support him whatever was coming. She knew he was upset, yet she didn't ask a question, simply waited. His mother had been like that. Calm. Accepting. Someone to stand beside a man and face the worst. He wanted that trait in the mother of his children.

"My father had another child." He made himself say the words aloud. Saying them served a dual purpose. Isabeau would understand, and he could better grasp the reality.

Will nodded. "You were already in Borneo. Your father had another woman and when she became pregnant, he told her she should abort or get the hell out. She wanted to stay with him, so she had the baby and gave him away. She went back to your father."

"Damn him to hell. How many lives does he have to destroy before he's satisfied?" Conner spat on the ground in disgust.

Isabeau shifted slightly, just enough to lean into him, as if shouldering whatever burden he had. He loved her for that small movement. His fingers tightened around hers, his thumb brushing back and forth in small caresses over the back of her hand.

"You know your mother, Conner," Gerald continued. "She took one look at that child, without parents to love him, and she immediately bonded. She was living in the cabin with the baby part of the time and the village during the rainy season."

"That's why she was in the village," Conner said.

Will nodded. "The boy was in Adan's house playing with my cousin when Cortez's men attacked. Your mother tried to stop them from taking the boys. They thought your brother was one of us. He's only five, Conner."

"Why wouldn't she tell you about having a half brother?" Isabeau asked.

Conner hung his head. "She knew I would have gone to the village and killed that son of a bitch. I despise him. He uses the women and if they become pregnant, he throws away the child—and the woman—if she won't get rid of it."

The bitterness in his voice sickened him, but he couldn't help it. He always had a handle on his emotions—except when it came to his father. The man hadn't been physically abusive to Conner, but emotional abuse was far worse, in Conner's opinion. It was like Marisa to put her child first and build a life for him. And she would have done the same for his brother, even though she hadn't given birth to the boy. He knew he couldn't do less.

He brought Isabeau's hand to his jaw and rubbed absently over the faint shadow while he turned the problem over and over in his mind. If Imelda's rogues took too close a look at the child they might recognize the leopard in him. With a female it was nearly impossible at a young age, but boys . . . one never knew when the leopard would emerge and there often were signs.

"What's he like?" Conner asked.

Beside him Isabeau stirred, drawing instant attention. "What's his name?"

Conner nodded and used the pads of her fingers to press tight against his throbbing temples. "Yes. I should have asked that."

"Your mother called him Mateo," Will said.

Conner swallowed hard, picturing his mother with the small baby. He should have known. Should have gone home to help her. "What's he like?"

"Like you," Gerald answered. "Very much like you. He will be grieving for your mother. He saw her killed."

That wasn't good. His leopard would try to emerge, to help the boy. Conner remembered the anger beating at him continually as a child, rage throbbing like a heartbeat in his veins. The boy would believe he had no one now. If he was like Conner, he would die before he could ever ask his father for help. He would want vengeance.

"Will Artureo be able to keep Mateo under control? Keep him from revealing his leopard even under duress?"

There was a small silence. "He's a headstrong boy," Gerald said. "And devoted to your mother." He glanced uneasily at Isabeau.

"She knows everything," Conner said. "You can talk freely."

"One of the men shot her when she tried to get Mateo back. They thought she was dead."

"I saw her go down," Isabeau admitted. "Artureo hid me in the trees and ran to help. They took him too. I never saw her animal form. I didn't know about her being leopard."

"Marisa crawled into the brush and shifted to her other

form," Gerald said. "The big man, Suma is his name, I saw him shift and he finished her off. No one would go into the forest after them once he took his animal form. The boy saw his mother die, the only mother he'd ever known. I heard him scream, Conner, and it was awful to hear."

Conner pushed down his own rising grief. His mother would expect him to get the boy back—not only get him back, but take full responsibility for him. He turned his head slowly to look at Isabeau. He had no choice now. He would have to do whatever it took, pay whatever price demanded of him.

Isabeau could see the despair in Conner's eyes, the sorrow and shock. And the distance. Her stomach did a small warning somersault and settled slowly. "Whatever you need, we'll help," she offered.

He let go of her hand and inclined his head toward Gerald and Will. "I thank you for making the journey here to give me this news in person. Assure Adan we'll get the children back. Tell him to keep to the plan. Will, I'll find your son. You know me. I'll bring him home."

Will nodded his head, his eyes steady on Conner's. "You're the reason I'm siding with my grandfather on how to handle this. We'll help should you need us."

Conner stood up, reaching down to draw Isabeau to her feet beside him. He waited until the other two men stood as well. "We're counting on your cooperation. It's essential that your tribe believe Adan is going to do as Cortez wants."

Gerald nodded and held out his hand. Conner watched them leave with a sinking heart. He almost forgot to give the signal for safe passage, allowing the two tribesmen to get through the gauntlet of leopards on their way back toward their village. Rio trotted up a few moments later, still pulling on his shirt.

"Forest is getting crowded. What's the news?"

"This just got very personal. It seems I have a little brother and Cortez took him along with the other children. If she finds out he's leopard . . ." Conner's voice trailed off. They'd never find the child. She'd hide him away and raise him herself.

Rio frowned. "That should get us some help from your village . . ."

Conner spun around, the growl rumbling in his chest a clear warning. The sound burst from his throat, a full-throated roar. "We will not go near that village. Let's get this bitch done." He spun on his heel and stalked across the clearing back toward the cabin.

Isabeau looked up at Rio. His frown had deepened and now there were worry lines etched into his face. "His father abandoned the child," she explained. "You can't let him go near that man." In a way, she felt as if she were betraying Conner, but instinctively she knew Rio had the best chance of keeping Conner from doing anything rash.

"Thank you," Rio said, as if reading her innermost thoughts. "I needed to know."

Scent. Isabeau looked around her and realized the leopards relied on scent to judge emotions in situations. They could read a lot more than their human counterparts. All of them used their leopard senses even while in human form, which afforded them advantages in any situation. She needed to learn how to do that.

She followed at a much slower rate, turning over and over in her mind the expression she'd seen on Conner's face. All the while she tried to recall his scent. What had gone through his mind in that moment? Resolution for certain. He was determined to get his brother and that meant . . .

She swallowed hard and stumbled a little. He'd told her he wouldn't seduce Imelda Cortez. They were going to try another way in, perhaps using one of the others, but that look on his face . . . He'd made up his mind to use whatever means possible and he wouldn't give the assignment to another—not when it was his own brother. Not when he believed his mother would expect it of him. *Conner was going to do exactly what she'd asked of him—seduce Imelda Cortez.*

Her heart squeezed down so hard it felt like something had gripped it in a vise. The pain was excruciating, so much so that she brought both hands to her chest and pressed hard, going down on one knee there on the edge of the trees. Bile rose in her stomach and churned, threatening to explode along with her protest. Her throat felt raw, her eyes burned.

What else could he do? What would she do? She wanted to scream a denial, to race to his side and rake at him with the claws of a cat for shredding her heart all over again. She'd let herself fall in love with him again. No, that wasn't true. She'd always loved him. She'd wanted him to come to her for forgiveness. She wanted him on his knees pleading with her and in the end she'd forgive him and they would live happily ever after.

He was supposed to love her so much he would never think of touching another woman. When he'd told her he wouldn't try to seduce Imelda Cortez, she'd been secretly thrilled. She'd wanted that reaction. She'd needed him to chase her, to court her, to prove to her that she was his love—his only love. The cat had complicated things. Now she didn't know if it was the cat he wanted, or her.

"Isabeau?" Conner was beside her, his arm sliding around her waist, shadows in his eyes. His gaze moved over her inch by inch, trying to find the reason for the pain. "What is it? Let me see." His hands went to her shirt as if he might lift it up to examine her chest for signs of injury.

She pushed his hands down and circled his neck with her arms, locking her fingers behind his neck. She loved this man with everything in her. Childish behavior had to be over, now, before it was too late and she lost him forever. She'd been living in a dream world, not reality. Yes, he'd seduced her for all the wrong reasons, but *they* had been right. They were right. If he felt for her half of what she felt for him, he couldn't have stopped himself any more than she could now.

"What is it, *Sestrilla*?" he whispered against her ear, holding her close to him just like she knew he would.

She could feel the care in his touch. The strength, yet gentleness. That soft word he called her, foreign, yet so loving the way it rolled off his tongue. "Tell me what that means." She laid her head against his heart, listening to that steady, reassuring beat. "I need to know what that means."

"Isabeau." She heard the sound of sorrow. The sound of a heart breaking.

"Tell me, Conner." She refused to let him go, even when his hands so very gently were trying to pry her from him. She strengthened her hold and pressed her body tight against his. "I need to know."

"It's an ancient word in our world and means 'beloved one.'"

Her heart turned over, settled, everything in her simply became clear. He'd always called her *Sestrilla*, long before the first time he'd slept with her.

"You're my beloved too."

She felt the breath he took. Ragged. Harsh. Deep. He rested his forehead against hers, his long lashes veiling his expression, but she could see the deep lines etched into his face. There was so much regret, so much sorrow, as if a great weight was on his shoulders, as if he'd already lost everything that mattered to him.

"You don't understand, Isabeau," he said gently.

She felt his voice inside of her, wrapping around her heart, sliding deep into her veins where heat rushed and her own heart pulsed to the tune of that smoky, hypnotic drawl.

"What don't I understand, Conner?" she asked, her voice soft—loving.

He groaned and pushed into her forehead with his. "Don't. Don't, honey. I can't live with losing you all over again. Let me just believe it was too late for us all along. It was over and there was no chance for us."

"I brought you here under false pretenses, Conner. I'm not so innocent in all this. I needed to see you. I didn't know Adan would know you from a drawing, but once I realized he could find a way to reach you, every single fiber of my being wanted to see you again. I made it happen. And deep down where I couldn't look, I knew how you would feel about seducing another woman. I wanted to . . ."

"Don't." He put his finger over her lips. "Don't say it. You don't have to say it."

She pressed her lips to his fingers. Stroked a caress with her tongue. "Yes I do. I wanted to punish you. I wanted to hurt you. I'm ashamed of that."

"Damn it, Isabeau, do you think this makes it any easier?"

"It would if you'd let me have my say," she nearly

growled. Her cat actually jumped beneath her skin and she heard her vibrating in her throat.

She caught Conner's faint grin. It didn't quite reach his eyes, but he'd always liked her little flare of temper. She narrowed her eyes. "I mean it. I have something important to say and you could listen before you argue."

"Yes, ma'am." He kissed her.

She should have been prepared for it. His hand had shifted to anchor in her hair as he bunched silky strands in his fist. His mouth captured hers in one heart-stopping moment. He tasted wild. Masculine. *Hers*. She moved closer to him, refusing to let his kiss end, taking over, her tongue sliding along the seam of his lips, teasing and enticing. Tempting. She rubbed her body over his. Seducing.

For a brief moment she felt his resistance running like a steel wire vibrating through his muscles and then, abruptly, he capitulated completely, his arms tightening around her, his mouth becoming commanding, feeding on her, his tongue sweeping inside, melting her with his heat. Fire flared instantly, tongues of flames rushing over her until she burned for him—until he burned for her.

Satisfaction gave her more confidence. She bit at his lower lip, her hands sliding beneath his shirt to find bare skin. One leg curled around his thigh as she pressed closer, offering him everything. Determined to have everything. She wasn't letting him go—certainly not to guilt. Her hands moved over his bare skin, feeling the texture of him while her mouth absorbed his unique taste.

"Come on, you two, you're killing us," Rio said. "We've got an escape route to map out and we need you for that."

Conner lifted his head reluctantly. "Be right there," he called over his shoulder, his eyes blazing heat into hers.

"You know what I have to do," he said in a low voice. "How do you ever expect me to look you in the eye again?"

"Because I'm the one asking you to do it," she whispered. She put her fingers over his mouth before he could shape a protest. "Because your mother was my friend and her son is your brother. Because your family is my family and I will do whatever it takes to keep them safe and get them back. I know little Mateo. Marisa brought him to my camp all the time. I didn't even realize she wasn't his natural mother any more than I knew she was your mother, but I saw their bond, Conner. We're in this together, Conner. Don't make me less than you, or make your sacrifice less than mine. You're worth everything to me. However—we do whatever we have to do."

He shook his head. "You're an amazing and courageous woman, Isabeau, and I don't deserve you, but you can't possibly know just how repulsive you'll find the situation when you see me with her. And you'll have doubts. Justifiable doubts. Worse, your cat will lose her mind over this. She'll be dangerous and you'll spend every moment trying to control her."

"How bad will it be for you, Conner?" she asked. "While you're worried about me, I'll be worried about you. You're the one who has to push your cat down and force yourself to look into another woman's eyes. Maybe for some men, it would be easy, but I think I've learned enough about you to know it will be abhorrent to you."

"Are you sure, Isabeau, because if you stay tonight with me, I won't be able to keep my hands off of you."

A slow smile welled up from her heart. "Well, that's a good thing." She forced herself to look away from the heat in his eyes toward the forest. "So how do we plan out our escape routes?"

He dipped his head to trail kisses down her face to the corner of her mouth. "We get to work, map them out, drop the supplies and make certain they're cached where animals won't dig them up. And then we think of every conceivable thing that can go wrong and put plans in place to cover those contingencies."

"Oh. Easy stuff. I was expecting it to be difficult." She flashed another grin at him.

Conner let her go reluctantly and stepped back, an answering smile beginning to form on his face. There was wariness in his eyes as if he was afraid to hope, but he linked his fingers with hers when she held out her hand and began to walk with her toward the others. "I'll send Jeremiah up in the trees. We'll see how fast he can climb. He'll need to pick up his speed. The more practice he gets, the better. He has to get faster or it's too dangerous for him."

"You're really worried about him."

"He took his beating like a man. He owns up to his mistakes. He's got courage. He's cocky, but then weren't we all at that age?"

She found herself smiling again. She loved the way he could be so intimidating, so dangerous looking and yet beneath that untamed exterior he had a heart. He'd probably hate that she thought that, but she knew just by his voice that he was going to make certain Jeremiah had the best chance possible to survive joining their team.

"Stop looking at me with stars in your eyes, Isabeau."

His voice had gone husky. Gruff. His eyes had gone all cat. Her womb clenched. Spasmed. Spilled liquid heat. She cleared her throat. "How long before my cat emerges all the way?" Isabeau asked. "Will we have enough time? I don't want to go through it without you."

"Not long. You're close," he said, his gaze drifting over

her in a possessive, hungry way that took her breath and
sent her temperature rising fast. "Too close."

There was still that hint of shadow in his eyes, as if he
knew something she didn't—and she conceded he probably did. She didn't expect it to be easy to watch him with
Imelda Cortez, the thought frankly sickened her, but she
wasn't going to lose him. Not again. There had to be a way
for them to get through this intact and still get the children
out. She glanced up to see they were getting close to the
others. A few more feet. She caught his arm.

"Whatever it takes, Conner. I would hope you wouldn't
even have to kiss her, but I'm not going to put limitations
on what I'll accept. You can't go into a life-threatening
situation with that on your mind. If we do this, we both
commit. Together. Agreed?"

He groaned softly and pulled her close again. She could
hear his heart. "I know you believe you're that strong, Isabeau, and I love you for it, but your cat is going to have her
say and it isn't going to be easy. Cats are jealous and tem-
peramental and we can't always control them. You saw me
with Jeremiah—and I like the kid. If you despise a woman,
how do you think your cat is going to react knowing I'm
flirting with her—or worse?"

"If your cat can handle it, then mine will have to, won't
she?" She lifted her chin. "I want the children back—all of
them—but especially Mateo because he's ours. And he was
Marisa's. I want this woman stopped. If anyone comes up
with another way into her stronghold, we'll take it, but if all
we're left with is securing an invite through you, then we'll
have to take it." She suddenly caught her breath. "Elijah!
Conner, Elijah could do it."

He shook his head, dashing her hopes. "Three reasons.
One, Mateo is my brother, and pretending to want to sleep

with this woman will be a crap job I won't push off on someone else. Two, Elijah, as good as he is, and he is good, very cool under fire, is relatively inexperienced. And three, Imelda won't go for someone she would conceive of as being equal to her. She wants a dominant male, but not one her equal. I've studied her, and Elijah would pose a threat. He might want to take over her position of power. A bodyguard wouldn't do that."

She let her breath out and forced a smile. "Then we go with our plan."

They returned, hand in hand, to the cabin where the others waited. Conner mapped out several escape routes through the rain forest, showing them the safest areas where they might shelter the children and keep them moving as well as the best campsites for them. They'd have to go in and mark the drop sites.

"I'll go and take Jeremiah with me," Conner concluded. "We'll go as leopards. It will be faster and safer. It will give Jeremiah the experience he needs in climbing fast and leaving no trace. Rio always flies the helicopter. Elijah is our supply man."

Felipe grinned at Jeremiah and showed off his muscles. "Leonardo and I are the big guns—the brawn."

"You mean not the brains." Jeremiah smirked.

That earned him a light cuff from Rio, but Jeremiah only laughed, not in the least deterred. Isabeau could see they were already developing a camaraderie of sorts with the newest member of their team. He might be on probation and in training, but they already treated him with growing affection.

"So we go in, Conner and Felipe will be personal protectors for Marcos," Rio got back to business, "and Leonardo and I will be the same for Elijah."

"Don't worry about our uncle," Felipe hastened to assure. "He might be in his sixties, but he's fast and cunning when needed. I wouldn't want to go up against him. And with Elijah, we've got six of us, all leopards."

"What about me?" Jeremiah demanded.

Rio shrugged. "You know Suma is going to be there and he's tried to recruit you. He can't see you. How are your shooting skills?"

Jeremiah looked happy all over again. "I'm a crack shot."

"Don't say it if it isn't true," Conner cautioned.

"High wind. Over a mile."

The men looked at one another. "We'll give you a chance to prove what you can do," Rio said. "If you aren't exaggerating, you'll be watching our backs for us."

"And me?" Isabeau ventured. "I could go in as Elijah's girlfriend. None of them has ever seen me. Elijah could be here to see me and knew his old friend Marcos was coming."

"No way." Conner stated it as a fact.

"She has to be protected," Elijah pointed out. "We can't just leave her out and you know it, Conner. She could prove to be a valuable asset. They have two rogue leopards. Those leopards won't be thinking of anything but Isabeau."

"That's really going to make me agree, now isn't it?" Conner said, sarcasm dripping in his voice.

"Not his girlfriend," Rio said. "Something closer. A sister or cousin. A relative. That makes it war if they touch her. A girlfriend might be considered disposable and the rogues are going to know she's leopard. They'll buy it. He came out to see her and bring her some news from home. In the meantime, they'll suspect that Marcos and Elijah are having a secret meeting. Cortez won't be able to risk the bait. The pot's too sweet. Elijah and Marcos, allies who could open doors for her, and you, Conner. Not to mention all the leopards."

Conner rubbed his temples and looked down at Isabeau's upturned face. She looked so innocent. She had no idea of the monsters they were dealing with. She'd seen their work, but she didn't have the capacity to understand the depths of their depravity and greed.

"If we tell you to get out, Isabeau . . ."

"I actually am extremely intelligent, Conner. I'll take orders from those with the experience."

There was no point in protesting. There wasn't another answer. And she did have a sharp mind. She might be an asset. "Let's get the escape runs done and then we'll think of every single thing that could go wrong and make plans to cover that as well."

10

THE escape routes were difficult to set up. Isabeau, riding in the helicopter with both Rio and Elijah, found herself using binoculars and straining her eyes to spot the small balloon tied to a tree. It was Jeremiah's job to climb the tree and mark the spot with a balloon, signaling to the helicopter where they were to drop the supplies along the escape route. Conner would then cache the supplies and mark the spot so any member of the team would know where to recover the food, water and arms. Even with the bright balloon, the canopy was nearly impenetrable, a world high in the air that cut off everything beneath it from the sky, making it very difficult to spot the target.

The rain forest looked different from the air. The mist seemed to hang like lacy veils throughout the canopy. The trees derived a great deal of moisture from the clouds they were shrouded in. Isabeau felt almost as if she could reach out and touch the drapes of film clinging to the branches and leaves. She even forgot to be scared, although the helicopter continually bucked as the wind came in gusts. Rio kept it just above the tops of the trees once they'd spotted Jeremiah's balloon.

She admired the efficiency with which they worked and realized they had definitely perfected the smooth way the team ran. She wanted to be a part of it, or at the very least, feel as though she contributed in some way. She tried to learn by watching them and even envied Jeremiah a little that he was able to actively participate.

Once back at the cabin, where they ate and hashed out every conceivable thing that could go wrong, and how to prepare for it, Isabeau found herself melting back into the shadows to watch Conner while they talked. She loved seeing the light play over his face, deepening the effect of a hard, dangerous man. He was intelligent and confident, and the sound of his voice became a drumbeat in her veins. Every breath he took expanded his chest and rippled the muscles beneath the thin material of his shirt.

Conner looked magnetic all sprawled out in his chair, lazy, as only a leopard could be. His jeans were snug, encasing his long legs as he tipped back his chair, his eyes half closed, his attention on the conversation—at least it appeared to be wholly focused there. His gaze flicked up and found her in the shadows, and her heart began to pound to that same drumming in her veins. She felt her womb clench and heated liquid dampened her panties.

One smoldering look. She remembered that so well. He rarely had to say anything—just looking at her could put her into a state of arousal. He was dangerous, sexy as hell. She couldn't take her eyes from him. When he spoke, his voice poured into the room with the same intensity as his molten gold eyes. He mesmerized her in the way a leopard might its prey. Once his gaze found her, focused on her, she couldn't find breath. She couldn't think clearly.

Isabeau tried to analyze how he had such a hypnotic, disturbing effect on her. Her entire body reacted to him. Her breasts ached, felt swollen and sensitive and *needy*. Her body pulsed with that need, that terrible craving she couldn't seem to sate. He looked intensely masculine, a sensual temptation she couldn't resist.

His hand casually snagged the neck of a water bottle and he tipped the contents down his throat, the action tightening her body. A frisson of awareness went down her spine. She loved the way he moved, the easy strength, the sureness he exuded. Everything about him appealed to her—even his arrogant dominance. She couldn't blame her reaction to him on her cat. This was the woman—or maybe both—who craved him.

He looked sinful with his legs stretched out in front of him and that thick, tempting bulge she was so familiar with straining his faded, worn jeans. She wanted to crawl over him and rip away the offending material to get at the hidden prize. Her mouth watered remembering the taste and texture of him, the way his hand gripped her hair and the sound of his growling moans. He had been so patient with her as she worked at learning how to pleasure him, and he'd always made her feel as if everything she did was sexy and exciting. He'd whispered instructions and she had obeyed, shivering with need, with wanting to please him. Whatever she did for him was rewarded a hundredfold. He could do things, knew things about her, she could never share with another man.

Her gaze dropped to his hands, carelessly circling the bottle, remembering the feel of his rough palms on her breasts, between her thighs, fingers sliding deep to stroke

and caress and drive her insane with need. She swallowed
hard as he tipped the bottle to his lips again, drawing her
attention to his mouth. Hot. Sexy. So seductive she could
never have resisted. His mouth had been ruthless, driving her up so fast she remembered she couldn't catch her
breath. His hands on her hips, pinning her down, holding
her open for his feast, had been strong and exciting, thrill-
ing even. When his tongue penetrated, stabbing deep, flicking, his strong teeth teasing, she'd been shocked. She'd used
her heels to try to push out from under him, but he'd held her
fast, throwing her into a ferocious orgasm—one she'd never
forget. It had been the first time she'd screamed under the
ministrations of his mouth—and she'd never stopped.

She wanted to scream again. Loud and long and feel the
pleasure rising like a tidal wave. She watched with fascina-
tion as he tipped the bottle again. Under cover of the act,
those golden eyes found her in the shadow. There was dark
lust blatant in his eyes. He did nothing at all to hide what
he wanted from her as his gaze traveled possessively over
her body.

She froze, much like the prey of a leopard might, her
breath caught in her lungs, her stomach muscles bunched
and tightened. Under his direct stare, she could feel the
damp moisture gathering between her thighs. Arousal
made her shiver with need.

Around him, the men shifted uncomfortably, and Rio
shot Conner one emotion-laden look. Conner stood without a word, setting the water on the table and holding
out his hand to her. "We're leaving. Be back tomorrow
sometime."

His voice was rough with the same dark lust that had
taken hold of her. She wasn't alone in her torment. She
could see the impressive bulge had grown even thicker

than it had been. She put her trembling hand in his. He was warm—hot even—she could feel the heat pouring off his body to envelope her. She didn't look at the others, didn't even care that they probably scented her arousal. Her heart was pounding and her body pulsed with liquid desire. Her breasts felt heavy, aching, her nipples tight, hard buds. Her thighs quivered and lust danced in her veins, little electrical shocks running rampant through her muscles and over her skin.

Conner snagged a large backpack and then drew her out onto the verandah. She followed him down the ladder without a word. The rain had started again, a soft drizzle that barely penetrated the canopy. The few drops that managed to land on her seemed to sizzle and turn to steam with the heat emanating from their bodies. He didn't say anything at all, didn't look down at her even after they were well away from the cabin and in the safety and shelter of the trees.

He didn't have to say anything. The air thickened around them so every step became difficult. Each breath she drew into her lungs was harsh and ragged. His palm burned into the small of her back, just above her buttocks, as they moved along a narrow, overgrown path. His steps were sure in the dark, his eyes giving off the peculiar nightglow of his leopard.

She'd never been more aware of her own femininity. Her body had gone soft and pliant, pulsing with aching need, with every step, her core clenching and wet. The sound of cicadas rose and fell, the ever-present shrill adding to her raw nerve endings. In the distance, through the inky darkness, she could hear a chorus of frogs and then the call of a bird. A twig snapped. Conner never hesitated. He walked with absolute assurance, all flowing, fluid grace and rippling ropes of muscle, so that each time he brushed against her sensitive skin, her breath caught and a multitude of butterflies took wing in the vicinity of her stomach.

Without warning he turned abruptly, dropped the pack and yanked her to him. His hands gripped hard and she felt the tension running like a river, sending a thrill of anticipation down her spine. Deliberately, she licked the length of his jawline and then trailed kisses along his shadowed jaw before sucking his earlobe into her mouth and then tugging with her teeth.

His breath exploded in a harsh gasp and he drove her backward until she clung to him to keep from falling. His teeth raked down her throat and nipped her shoulder before his mouth returned to claim hers, his tongue sweeping inside. He didn't just kiss her, he claimed her, devouring her as if she was his last meal.

"You know how fucking long it's been without you?" His voice was a cross between a growl and an accusation. He dragged her body tight against his, pressing his heavy erection against her throbbing mound.

A low moan escaped as she wrapped her arms around his neck. "I can't wait."

"I should make you wait." He trailed kisses over her face, then caught her mouth with his again, a ruthless brand that sent the fire already burning between them out of control.

Isabeau nearly sobbed as she tried to pull his shirt off. "I can't wait, not another minute. I need you inside me." She was past all pride with him. It had always been like this when they came together. She had no control and didn't pretend any, not when he was grinding his heavy erection against her and her entire body cried out for his.

"You don't leave me again, Isabeau. You understand?" His voice rough, harsh even, a sensual, hungry sound that made her knees go weak.

His hands were everywhere, tugging at her clothes, sliding against bare skin, urging her to step out of her jeans when she was barely aware of what was happening. A few raindrops managed to slip through the broad, leafy canopy and sizzle against her hot skin. The cool drops nearly burned, she was so sensitive.

His mouth was on hers again, hot and hungry, their tongues stroking caresses, dueling, while moans escaped to blend with the incessant shrill of the cicadas. Breath came in ragged gasps, and she couldn't get close enough, sliding her hands over his bare skin, yanking at the waistband of his jeans so she could slide her hand inside the material and stroke his thick arousal.

His breath exploded from his lungs. He cupped the soft weight of her breasts and bent his head. His golden eyes burned with liquid fire as he watched her watching his mouth descend. She'd forgotten how intense the sensation of his mouth on her breast could be. She shuddered, throwing her head back, arching her back to give him better access, a soft cry escaping.

His teeth tugged at her nipple and moisture pooled hot between her thighs. She shivered with pleasure, writhing under his mouth's assault. The way his teeth and tongue stroked over her breasts was addicting—intoxicating, so she felt almost drunk with pleasure. Streaks of fire whipped through her blood and licked at her hot core, driving her need beyond anything she'd known. She nearly sobbed, her nails digging into his hips, trying to connect their bodies.

"Say it for me, Isabeau. I want to hear you say you'll never leave me."

She would have promised him anything, and what he was asking was no more than she wanted with every breath she took. "Never, Conner."

"I'm holding you to your word."

Even the way he said it made her hotter, that was how far gone she was. He lifted her up, so that she was straddling his groin, and then he looped one thigh over his arm, forcing her completely open to him. He was enormously strong, his powerful thighs like twin columns supporting the both of them, his hands gripping her bottom. She felt the broad, flared head of his erection pressing into her entrance and she tried to push down, to claim him, but he held her just above her prize, the head lodged in her so she felt every inch of his slow, steady entrance.

Conner's cock was thick and long and his invasion would, even with her slick welcome, stretch her tight channel impossibly. She hadn't been with anyone else in all that time, and he knew it would be uncomfortable for her. He wanted to go carefully, make certain she experienced pleasure, not pain. His breath hissed out in a long rush, his teeth coming together as the scorching heat gripped him, consumed him, took him nearly beyond his control.

Her small, sobbing pleas only added fuel to the fire. He could feel tongues of flames licking up his legs to burn his balls and settle like a conflagration in his groin. She was searing him, velvet soft, hotter than hell, so tight she gripped him like a vise. He growled a command, incapable of speaking lucidly, but it didn't matter. She knew what to do, he'd made certain of that. He'd never understood men who didn't talk with their woman about the intensity of pleasure between a man and a woman. He believed in finding out everything he could about his mate, what pleased her, what turned her into a sobbing, pleading lover willing to give him the same careful consideration.

She began to move, a slow, delicious ride he felt all the way from the top of his skull to his toes. Every movement

sent electrical impulses rocketing through him. He was
desperate for her. In her innocence, she had no idea what
she did to him. Her body fit his perfectly. Her breasts were
beautiful, brushing his chest with each bucking motion of
her hips. Her silken hair seared his skin. He fought to calm
his racing heart and stay in control, but her body just grew
hotter and tighter with each stroke.

He felt her wince as he fully seated her, piercing her
cervix. He murmured softly to her, waiting for her body to
grow used to accommodating his. All the while, he kept his
teeth pressed tightly together, breathing through the brutal
pleasure. "You good?" The words came out harsher than he
intended, but she didn't seem to mind, tossing her head and
nodding emphatically.

He bent his knees and drove upward, his soft growl a
dark, dangerous sound that silenced the cicadas closest to
them. She sobbed out her pleasure. The angle he had, with
her thigh draped over his arm, allowed him to create friction along her most sensitive spot. He bent his head to the
temptation of her throat and gave a series of erotic licks, his
teeth scraping back and forth, taking several hungry bites.

He pounded into her melting heat, needing her shudders, her little breathless cries. He had to find a way to hold
her to him through the coming storm. He was desperate to
tie her irrevocably to him. He wanted her orgasm to be the
best she'd ever had, wanted her to associate all that mind-
numbing ecstasy with him alone. He couldn't ever lose her
again. He wouldn't survive it, and the coming days would
test the strength of what they had together.

He was relentless, driving deeper and deeper, even when
he felt her body clasp his in a viselike grip. He kept surging into her, over and over, burying himself in paradise,
while lightning forked over his skin and rockets exploded

in his skull. Her sheath pulsed around him and her muscles clamped down again. "Don't, honey. Don't move." His voice was more of a hiss than an actual command. He was certain he was half insane with sheer pleasure.

Her body melted around his, the inferno growing impossibly hotter as he plunged again and again, until he felt every nerve ending he had center in his cock. She stiffened. Her eyes went wide. There was a hint of fear mixed with anticipation. Her eyes went opaque and she dug her nails into his shoulder.

"Conner?" Her voice was soft. Shaky.

He loved her like that, looking at him with that sultry mixture of innocent and siren. Her body rode his, hot liquid bathing him with each thrust of his body. He felt her body gathering, spiraling, the erotic tightening causing the exquisite friction to heighten.

"Close baby, hang on."

She shook her head frantically as her body coiled tighter, the tension building until she feared she couldn't stand it. There seemed no release from the terrible coiling heat always building. His shaft slammed into her, driving deep, pushing her up, higher and higher until she was nearly sobbing, half in fear, half in erotic frenzy.

"That's it, honey, let go. Fly for me. Right now. With me," he commanded and deliberately bent his head and bit down gently, that soft junction just between her throat and shoulder. It wasn't where his cat preferred, but it was what her cat liked and he knew she would subconsciously obey, setting her body free to experience the shattering series of orgasms.

He felt her body clamp down, the velvet sheath spasming, rippling, then gripping and milking. He threw back his head and roared his own release. Around them the in-

sects and frogs ceased their nightly chorus and gave them
the floor, the sound of their voices rising in lust and love,
mingling together to form a deep harmony.

He buried his face in her neck and held her in his arms,
absorbing the form and shape of her, the miracle of her. It
had been so long since he'd held her, loved her, taken all
that she was and given her everything he was. "I missed
you." It was a ridiculous declaration. "Missed her" didn't
begin to cover at all how he felt. He'd been alone no matter
where he was, how many others surrounded him. He could
barely breathe without her. But that would be even sillier
for him to say.

He trailed kisses along her vulnerable throat, all the
while listening to her heartbeat, that racing rhythm so satisfactory to him. She was soft and pliant in his arms, her
body melting into his. Joined as they were, he could feel
every aftershock and the continual grip and release of her
muscles around his shaft. He waited until the shudders had
calmed and her breath was nearly under control before he
gently pulled away from her encompassing heat and allowed her legs to drop to the ground.

Isabeau swayed in his arms and buried her face against
his chest. "It's not supposed to be like that. I lose myself
in you."

"That makes two of us," he whispered, his teeth tugging
at her earlobe. He loved the way she looked after sex, the
slight sheen to her skin, her limp sated body, the glazed
look in her eyes. Her mouth was swollen from his kisses
and her body was flushed and marked by his. He bent
his head to the mark between her shoulder and neck and
pressed kisses there until he felt her shiver. "We need to
go. We're close to our destination, Isabeau. A safe place to
spend the night."

She lifted her head and blinked at him. "I can hear the sound of water."

"We're going to a waterfall I know of. We need to finish up here, honey," he prompted.

Isabeau smiled up at him even as she slid down to her knees, her arms using his stronger body for support. The pads of her fingers traced over his flat, hard stomach, along the rigid, defined muscles there and then slid around to his buttocks, massaging as she drew him into her. She looked intensely beautiful, her hair disheveled, spilling around her angelic face, her lashes veiling her eyes, and her hands sweeping up his thighs. Just looking at her with the mist rising around her, caressing her breasts and narrow waist, made him semi-hard all over again.

Her mouth was warm and moist, a heated bath of intense love, her tongue like a cat's velvet rasp as she licked and sucked gently, removing their combined scents, paying special attention to the underside of the broad mushroom head and lapping at the base of his shaft and finally his sac. She always took her time, no matter the situation, no matter where they were. She always shattered him with the way she made him feel so loved as if this small task was the most important thing she could do and she loved and enjoyed doing it for him.

And that always made him as hard as a rock, all over again. Very gently he drew her to her feet, his gaze holding hers captive. As she held him. Not with her body or fantasy mouth. Not even with mind-blowing sex. With this—moments like this one. He took her mouth with his, reveling in the taste of the two of them, that explosive mixture of sin and sex and love and lust. She made him soft inside, and he knew he wanted her in his life for always.

"We're just getting started, Isabeau," he warned, his

eyes going antique gold and dark, his lust not nearly sated.
"I'm going to keep you up all night."

Isabeau shivered at the look in his eyes. She'd seen it before and when he said he'd keep her up all night, she knew
he meant it. He could be brutally attentive, driving her beyond all thought until she was helpless in his arms, unable
to do anything but exactly what he wanted. She'd never
known anyone could feel the way he made her feel. And
she was just discovering her own power. Who would ever
have thought she could make a man like Conner Vega shudder and moan, his golden eyes going dark with hunger?

"I'll go anywhere with you, Conner. Lead on." She
reached for her clothes.

Conner took them from her hands and stuffed them in
his backpack. "I want to look at you." He ran the pad of
his finger down the slope of her breast, watching her reaction. When she shivered and her nipples beaded, he smiled,
leaned forward and flicked each one with his tongue. "I've
been dreaming about the taste of you. I want to eat you like
you are candy, Isabeau. For hours. Just lay you out like a
feast and consume you."

He was quite capable of carrying out his threat too. She
knew him and his appetites. Already his shaft was hard
and thick, lying against his muscled stomach like a hungry
beast just waiting. She reached out with caressing fingers
and danced them over him before cupping his balls. He
never moved. Never pulled away. Just watched her touch
him possessively. Her treasure. Hers alone.

"How is it that the leopard people can survive in the rain
forest when other large predators are so rare?" she asked
as she reluctantly allowed her fingers to slip away and she
took a step in the direction he'd indicated. "Tell me about
them."

He shrugged into his backpack and then took her hand, carrying it to his chest as they walked. Like all leopards, he was comfortable with his nudity, especially in the rain forest. It was natural to him, but not to Isabeau. He could sense her discomfort, but for him, she did it without protest. She'd questioned him when he wanted her to do something she was afraid of, or something that embarrassed her, but she'd never said no without trying it first. He'd been so careful of her trust—because all along with her he'd been lying. It astonished and humbled him that she could give him that kind of trust again.

"We don't hunt the animals the way other predators need to do. We might hunt to learn the skills, but we don't kill our prey. We watch over the other animals. To sustain a large predator, you need an abundance of animals for them to eat." He indicated the forest floor. "We're in a section of thick vegetation where other animals can live, but as a rule, the floor is bare because the sunlight can't penetrate enough for other things to grow. Carnivores just have far fewer food resources here than herbivores."

"That makes sense."

The sound of water grew louder as the trail narrowed and began to slope upward. The vines and flowers were thicker along the tree trunks, the leaves broader and wilder with so much water available. Many plants had taken root on the trunks themselves, never actually touching the ground and living in the wide branches entirely. The roots of the strangler fig trees looked like great forests themselves, twisted cages for creatures to hide within. In the darkness she could hear continual rustling in the canopy overhead and in the leaves on the forest floor.

Her nudity made her feel vulnerable, although she had to admit, there was something very sensuous and erotic about walking completely naked in a rain forest at night with a man like Conner. He had a way of protecting her as they moved through the brush, so that even leaves never actually touched her skin. His hand did often. He brushed his fingers down her spine, sending awareness shivering down her back. As they walked he casually slid his hand over her bottom possessively, keeping her very aware of him.

The waterfall came into sight as they rounded a bend, and she stopped abruptly just to stare at it. She'd always loved the majesty and elegance of waterfalls. This one was much larger than she'd pictured in her mind. It spilled in a narrow ribbon from a rocky ledge above, collecting in a wide pool made of more rock. From there it cascaded in a long veil to a deeper pool below and raced into the river itself.

"It's beautiful."

"Yes, it is," Conner said.

But he was looking at her. Isabeau could see the glittering hunger intensify. They were completely alone in a wild setting. A natural setting for him. And he wasn't tame. She felt the little thrill of fear. She didn't want him tame. She loved the way he made her feel—a little off balance and wholly his. He stepped close to her and his hands caught hers. He brought her palms up under her breasts until the soft weight rested there and she was virtually offering him her body.

His smile was slow. Wicked. Seductive. She craved that look on his face, the hooded eyes, dark gold burning with lust for her. His mouth, so seductive and skilled. His hands, experienced, knowing just what her body needed. And the way he looked at her, as if she belonged to him, as if her body was his and he could do whatever he wanted with her. What he always wanted seemed to be to bring her to screaming, mindless pleasure.

He bent his head and drew one breast into the warmth of his mouth. Instantly her body wept with need. He tugged at the nipple with his teeth and another rush of liquid made her womb spasm and clench in emptiness. He suckled, his mouth growing hot and rough, nearly throwing her into another orgasm right there. He dropped his hand, forcing her to hold her own breast for his assaulting mouth. He slid his palm down her belly to the throbbing mound between her thighs.

Unable to stop herself she moved her hips, seeking more. He removed his hand and continued to suckle at her breast. Tiny bites accompanied the tug of his teeth on her nipple and the soothing laving of his tongue. Heat rushed through her body and then his fingers were back, tracing small circles on her inner thighs, moving upwards toward the heat of her center. His slow pace was torturous given the need building so fast and ferocious in her.

"Please," she whispered before she could stop herself. Her blood pounded in her veins, thundered in her ears and throbbed deep in her sheath.

The fingers traveled through her trimmed wet curls and stroked lightning through the velvet folds. She moaned softly, the sound harmonizing with the symphony of night sounds. She looked at his beloved face, the lines set deep with desire, his pupils nearly gone now as his eyes went all cat. A frisson of delicious fear went down her spine at the look of hunger and determination etched into his face. Two fingers sank into her tight depths and she gasped and bucked against his invading hand.

He switched his attention to her other breast and when she held it for him, his second hand slid to her buttocks and pressed her onto his fingers. "Ride me, honey," he whispered.

What else could she do? Her body temperature was rising out of control and her tight, hot muscles grasped greedily at his fingers. She began to thrust her hips around his hand as he drove his fingers deep inside of her.

Conner's body hardened past the point of sanity. Her soft body was so willing with him. He used his fingers like his cock, thrusting into her, absorbing the feel of her damp heat growing hotter and hotter. Her breath came in ragged gasps and her heart beat out of control. The sensations he was creating were causing her body to coil tighter and tighter, edging her toward release. He wanted her needy. Hungry for him. On the edge. But he didn't want to tip her over.

His teeth tugged at her nipple and he felt the answering spasm in her wet channel. Abruptly he pulled his fingers free. "We're almost there."

She whimpered and dropped her hand between her thighs almost compulsively, but he caught her wrists and pulled her to him.

"Soon. Be patient." He gave her a small smack on her buttocks and nudged her along the trail that led behind the waterfall to the chamber where he had first stashed supplies on his original arrival to the rain forest a week ago, before he'd reported to Rio.

"You started this," she pointed out, trying not to squirm.

"And I'll finish it." His gaze darkened more. "I want you wanting me."

"I think that's rather obvious," she said, pouting a little.

He helped her the last few feet across the rocks. They ducked quickly through the outer edges of the spray and made it to the safety of the chamber. It was large and rounded, with smooth stone making up the walls on three sides. Years earlier, when he'd first discovered the secret place, he'd carved a hold in the rock wall for his torch and later a kerosene lantern. The lantern was long gone, but the torch he'd replaced a few days earlier. He lit it so she could really see the interior of the chamber.

Isabeau didn't care where they were, only that they were finally together. She missed his company. She missed his body. And she missed the things he could do to her body. He was watching her through half-closed eyes, his face in the shadows while the light cast a glow around her like a spotlight. She moved, a slow enticement meant to center his attention on her.

"How the hell did I ever make it without you?" he asked. He drew a mat from his backpack and spread it out over the top of what could have been a large sandbar resting on top of the smooth rock.

It was the first time that she'd noticed there was sand. She climbed up on it, standing just at the edge of the mat and curled her toes in the sand. It was incredibly fine. "How did this get here?"

Conner took her hand, drew her to him and wrapped his arms around her. Although she was standing on several inches of sand, she was still shorter than he was. He rubbed his chin on the top of her head. "My mother gave it to me as a gift when I was young. It was my birthday and I thought she'd forgotten. I used to use this as my hiding place." He looked around. "I felt very grown up here and when puberty hit, my fantasy girl was always here to help me out."

Her eyebrow shot up. "Really? What was she like?"

"Quite beautiful, but she never quite measured up in my mind to the real thing." The smile faded from his voice. "I've had a year of bad nights, loneliness and an aching cock, Isabeau. I was lost without you." He pulled back to look at her face. To judge her reaction. He didn't like talking about his feelings, love and lust and anger mixed altogether.

"I know." She rained kisses along his jaw. "I'm here. We're together."

He drew her down slowly, his grip like steel, forcing her to sprawl across the mat. She could feel the tension running through his body, and just like that her body responded with heat. Maybe the fire had never really cooled. His hands stroked every inch of her, as if he was painting her with smooth brushstrokes—or memorizing every inch of her. His inspection was thorough and he took his time. Just when she thought she might start moaning and pleading, with no warning at all he brushed those strong fingers over her wet mound and she cried out with the exquisite pleasure.

Shadows moved across the curved walls of the small chamber. The sound of water was constant and loud, the spray, a thick veil cutting her off from the rest of the world. Isabeau lay across the thick mat in the rock chamber behind the waterfall, and turned her head to watch the water cascading down in glittery white sheets, enjoying gentle touches to her body, but always aware of the gathering heat, a firestorm that would come crashing down on her.

Conner. Her ruthless lover. When he touched her, she was lost. And right now he wanted to claim every inch of her. She couldn't resist his particular brand of possession. The animal in him raged close to the surface, and the intensity of his touch reflected his hunger for her. He had made certain she was comfortable—he would always see to that—before he took his time doing everything he wanted to her. She heard her own breathing, ragged gasps she couldn't quite control. Anticipation was turning her on as much as looking at him did.

Conner knelt between her legs, surveying Isabeau for a long time before reaching out and dragging the second sleeping mat from his pack. He folded it and pushed it beneath her buttocks, raising the lower half of her body and opening her more fully to him. He studied her again. He loved the way she looked with her hair spilling around her and her body bare and open to him. There was moisture seeping between her thighs and he could scent her arousal.

He casually dropped his hand down to cover her tempting mound. She jerked, sensitive already with anticipation. He loved her welcoming moisture. There was something so satisfying about seeing his woman like this—so ready for his attention. Conner was ravenous for her and he didn't pretend anything else and he loved that neither did she. She wasn't ashamed of wanting him, of showing him how much she wanted him. And that was an aphrodisiac, pure and simple. Everything about Isabeau was to him.

Very slowly he lowered his body over hers, blanketing her completely like a cover, just holding her, absorbing her. She was so soft, that long expanse of skin and feminine curves. He sank into her heat, listening to the rapid beat of her heart. Her arms went around him, fingers lacing at the back of his neck. She didn't stir, didn't complain about his weight. She just absorbed him the way he was absorbing her as if she understood that great need to just hold her.

After a few moments, he rubbed his body along hers, scent-marking, claiming her, his shadowed jaw sliding down her neck where he nipped and kissed her before bringing up his head to fix his focused gaze on hers. He lowered his head slowly, watching her eyes close just before his mouth found hers. Every time he kissed her, it was as if he was lighting a match. Heat flared. Flames blazed, the fire leapt and there was no turning back. Her kisses had been his downfall from grace and honor back when she was completely an innocent. Now, her mouth moved under his, her tongue stroking and inciting so that he burned clean and hot and out of control.

His hand slipped to her breast and he felt her jump. Her hips bucked and her legs widened to give him better access. Conner kissed his way down her throat to her breasts, feasting there until she was making the little whimpering noises he loved. His body had been hot and hard and aching relentlessly since she'd wrapped her lips around him in the forest. He could feel her stomach muscles bunching when he tugged at her nipples and it was too tempting to stop there. He made his way down the slope of her belly and took control of her legs, spreading her wide, placing them over his arms as he bent his head to taste her.

"It's been so fucking long," he whispered and dipped his head.

Isabeau sucked in her breath, her fingers fisting in the mat to hold on as the rough rasp of his jaw along her thighs sent a thousand flames burning over her. Her entire body quivered. Her breasts heaved and she couldn't stop the helpless jerk of her hips. His hands tightened, just as she knew they would. He sent her one glittering look that meant hold still, and she tried to obey, tried to draw air into her lungs.

Need was a living, breathing thing, gripping her in its fiery thrall. He pinned her thighs and spread her legs farther so that her breath came in harsh gasps. She heard herself scream when he lowered his mouth and lapped at her, licking like a large cat with a bowl of warm cream. Fireworks exploded in her head as his tongue stabbed deep, plunging into her over and over again until she thought she might come apart in a million pieces. He took his time, savoring every drop, using his teeth and tongue to draw out more whimpers and soft pleading sobs, begging for release.

Then he was rising above her, gripping her ankles, yanking her legs over his shoulders, holding her open to him. He looked fierce, his erection thick and hard and long, pressing, burning, demanding at her entrance. She felt him there and held her breath. He plunged deep, driving through tight hot folds, and she screamed again, the friction sending fiery tongues of heat streaking through her body. She felt her muscles grip him like a vise, stretching for his invasion. Her body shuddered with pleasure as he buried himself completely and then withdrew to plunge again. His rhythm was fast and hard, almost brutal, driving her up fast so that her breath came in ragged gasps and her body rose helplessly to meet the driving needs of his. He arched over her, bracing himself with his arms, her legs forced back, giving him the ability to go deeper.

Pinned beneath him, with her body going up in flames, he kept up the powerful strokes, hammering home over and over, drawing her deeper and deeper into a vortex of fire. Her body felt as though it was melting around his, scorching hot, her orgasm just out of reach, but building, always building. She writhed under him, desperate for release.

He held her with his strength, his rhythm steady, fast and hard, driving so deep she was afraid he was piercing her cervix with every stroke. Every nerve ending on fire, she felt her muscles clamp down hard on him. She stiffened, but he just gripped her harder and plunged again, sending her body flying into a million fragments. A haze covered her eyes and she felt flames streak through her veins as an explosion tore through her body, ripped through her stomach and breasts and down her thighs, settling in her deepest core as she felt her muscles grip Conner's. She felt his hot release spill deep inside her, triggering another wildfire rushing over and through her.

Conner's breathing was rough as he collapsed over her, holding her to him. She could feel his heavy erection, so desperate, almost brutal, slowly ease while her body bathed his in their combined liquid heat. His hands framed her face and his tongue speared deep into her mouth. "I love you, Isabeau," he whispered, looking down into her eyes. "When this is over, marry me and have my children."

Her heart stuttered for a moment. She was in an awkward position with her legs up around her ears and his body buried deep, but his eyes gave no quarter. She had nowhere to hide. He wanted truth. She couldn't find the breath to speak so she nodded. She felt the tension ease in him and he rolled off of her.

"I'm going to be really nice, honey. I'll let you sleep for half an hour and then you're going to be begging for mercy." He crawled up beside her and collapsed again, flinging one arm possessively around her waist and closed his eyes.

AND he wasn't lying.

ISABEAU spent the next four days with Conner as her ruthless taskmaster, a ruthless commander who demanded perfection of both Jeremiah and her. She had to shoot guns for hours, take them apart and put them back together as well as keep working on combat techniques. Jeremiah had it worse. He had to shift on the run, and the entire team was merciless with him. Fortunately, he was so proficient with a rifle, she could tell they were all impressed with him.

The next four nights were spent behind the waterfall, with Conner as her demanding lover, a man never quite sated and always pushing for more. There were times she wasn't certain she would survive the intensity of their love-making, but she really didn't care. All that mattered was the feel of his body inside hers and the love in his eyes when he claimed her.

11

"REMEMBER to stay close to Elijah no matter what happens." Conner kept his hand on the car door, refusing to open it, although everyone was waiting. "Once we go in, don't look at me. Anyone in there can be working for her. You have to put on the best acting job of your life. And Isabeau—" He caught her chin in his hand, his glittering eyes staring straight into hers. "So will I—I'll be acting too."

Isabeau swallowed hard and nodded. "I know, Conner. I can do this."

"If you get into trouble, signal Rio or Elijah. They'll get you out of it."

"We've gone over this a hundred times." Her mouth was dry and fear had gripped her in spite of all her good intentions. She wanted to cling to Conner, but instead forced a small smile. "I'm ready."

"We're going over it again, just to be sure. Jeremiah will be outside up high in the trees with a rifle. He can shoot the wings off a butterfly; he'll protect you outside. If there's a problem . . ."

"I take the barrette out of my hair."

"That's the signal to shoot. If you're in trouble, use it."

"Conner, I'm going to be fine."

"She won't come in until late. Don't get antsy or alarmed. Her security detail will come in first and sweep the room, looking for people like us. You're going to stand out, honey. You're a female leopard and the two rogues are going to sense you're close to the Han Vol Dan. That will agitate them, make them more aggressive. You cannot be alone with one of them. Do you understand?"

"You aren't speaking a foreign language," she hissed. He was making her more nervous. It wasn't like every single man on the team hadn't already pointed that out to her. Even Jeremiah.

His eyes narrowed. Burned. "What? If you aren't going to take this threat seriously, Isabeau, you can damn well stay here. In the car."

She threw her hands into the air. "Conner, you're making me crazy. I'm scared enough. You don't have to keep going over this. I know what we're doing. I know what you have to do and I'm going to be all right with it. I'll stay very close to Elijah, unless you've scared him into thinking you're going to kill him if he looks at me wrong."

She sounded so exasperated, Conner found some of the tension easing from his body. He sank his fingers into her silky hair. "I'm sorry, beloved, I want you safe. I can't think about much else right now. Letting you go in there is unbelievably difficult."

She framed his face with her hands. "Letting you go in there is worse for me. I'm not afraid of Imelda Cortez."

"You should be."

She gave him a slight smile. "I should have said my cat isn't afraid. She's so close, Conner, and I want her. I want to be able to use her strength to help you."

"Just stay clear of the rogues. They won't be able to resist trying to get you alone. Stay with . . ."

"Elijah. Yeah. I think we started this conversation here. Go inside. I'm going to be fine." She leaned into him, kissing him, grateful for the tinted windows.

"Damn it, Isabeau," Elijah snapped. "When you get out, all of us will have to hug you, rub our scent over you, otherwise the rogues will be able to pick up Conner's scent exclusively."

Rio glared at Conner. "That's a rookie mistake."

"Great," she muttered rebelliously, "they're going to think I'm the loose, easy chick."

"I'm beginning to think Conner's right and you should stay in the car," Rio said.

Isabeau rolled her eyes and reached across Conner to shove open the door. She wasn't staying in the car.

Conner simply shrugged before flashing his teeth at Isabeau in a conspiratorial smirk. He exited the SUV and took his first good look at the estate where Philip Sobre, the chief of tourism resided. The man had done well for himself. The six-story sprawling mansion was on a slope overlooking the forest. The panoramic views swept around the verandah and from every deck and window in the large house. Trees, centuries old, rose up in grandeur, to surround the house and lead the way to the small lake shimmering just a distance away.

The temperature had begun to fall and Conner could hear the familiar sounds of the rain forest as evening settled in. The frog chorus had already begun in the many small ponds and puddles of water as the amphibians defended their territories and did their melodious best to attract mates. Higher up, hidden on the massive trunks and branches, the tree frogs chimed in with their strange knocking sound, a song that was more obnoxious, but strangely comforting.

He stepped out of the way and allowed Elijah to help Isabeau from the vehicle. All the while he kept his gaze moving around them, surveying the estate, he was acutely aware of her. The way she moved. The sound of her voice. The way the shadows caressed her face lovingly.

A myriad of insects had joined the frogs, with the cicadas taking a prominent roll in the chorus. Farther out, in the inky darkness, his cat could sense and identify other smaller rodents foraging on the forest floor. He had the sudden urge to throw Isabeau over his shoulder and disappear into that darkness where no one could ever find them. He turned his head to look at her, in spite of his commands to her that they should appear indifferent. He couldn't help it.

And that, he supposed, was the main problem he had with Isabeau. From the beginning, he lacked control and discipline when he was around her. He'd taught her to please him. He was the dominant in the relationship, yet she held him in the palm of her hand. She was wrapped so tightly around his heart there was no escape. There was no way to blame it on his cat—or hers—this was all about the woman, the whole of her.

Their eyes met. God, she was beautiful, a bright spirit, shining from the inside out. He was going into a party filled with corrupt individuals who wanted every last dollar they could rob from the poorer people around them. She went into a rain forest and studied how plants could be used to heal people. The woman he was going to seduce was the worst of all, with no regard for human life. His woman was willing for her man to do whatever it took in order to save children not her own.

"I love you," he said. Stark. Raw. In front of them all.

She flashed a small smile and there was pride in her eyes. "I love you too."

He turned and fell into step with Marcos Santos, Felipe and Leonardo's uncle. His heart ached and it was difficult to fall into his role as the personal protector. Rio touched his shoulder lightly and he flicked his glance to the team leader.

"We'll take care of her," Rio assured him.

Isabeau was smart and she'd learned fast. She had been in the rain forest on and off most of her life. And she read people very well. He had to believe in her abilities. He nodded his head at Rio, and continued to scan the area around them as they began to make their way up the winding path to the main house.

The rain forest was kept at bay by a host of workers continually at war with it. At every opportunity, the forest tried to reclaim lost land. The roots from the fig trees formed great cages all up and down the property and flowers curled up the trunks in a riot of color. Philodendron leaves as big as umbrellas shot up the trunks and every conceivable post, turning the grounds into a massive forest of greenery.

The plants sheltered the house from the surrounding forest more effectively than the high fence that had been added. Already the plants wound their way up the chain and in a few years, he could see the house would be hidden completely from outsiders. But for now, the view inside the banks of windows and along the balconies and verandahs was fairly clear for Jeremiah.

The security force Philip Sobre used was everywhere, walking patrols along the grounds, making a show of weapons, but he noticed no one was looking in the high canopy just outside the grounds. Jeremiah would have it easy at least until the rogue leopards came. The men here now, hired to protect those coming to the party, were not real professional soldiers or bodyguards. Conner suspected they were men from a local police force making some extra money.

As Marcos approached the front door, Felipe laid a hand on his shoulder and they stepped back to allow Conner to go in first without them. Conner set his face in hard, unreadable lines and approached the door, opening his jacket so there was no mistake he was armed. The doorman checked the list, nodded and allowed him in. He went through each room carefully and it was a damn big house. He took note of the security cameras, windows, exits and staircases. They had studied a layout of the house already, but the blueprints weren't exact. He spoke low into his radio, giving the other members of his team the remodels that weren't in the floor plans.

Several doors on the second floor opened into a courtyard where more exotic plants grew amidst a series of fountains leaping from a pool of koi. He sent the entire layout to his crew and Jeremiah, letting Elijah and Rio know the easiest rooms in which to protect their "clients," before allowing Marcos to enter.

Philip Sobre, the chief of tourism, rushed forward to greet Marcos Santos. Of course he ignored both Conner and Felipe. As an important guest, Marcos was shown personally into the house.

"I've brought a personal friend along with me, Elijah Lospostos. I trust my secretary sent you a note, as I was already en route when I realized he was in your country. He is in the country to visit his cousin who resides here.

She's with us as well—Isabeau Chandler," Marcos said. "If they're not welcome, we can meet another time." His tone was casual as only an extremely wealthy businessman used to getting his way could have been. "Elijah has his own security with him. One of his personal protectors is my own nephew. Elijah is like a son to me, as is my nephew." He half turned as if he might leave.

Philip bowed several times. "Of course your friends are welcome." And he was under strict orders to see to it that Elijah Lospostos felt very welcome. He waved Elijah's personal protector through, glaring at his doormen when the man would have stopped and checked for other weapons than the one in plain sight.

Elijah barely nodded at the man, flashing his white teeth briefly, looking more dangerous than the wild animals surrounding the estate. He wrapped his arm around Isabeau and drew her inside. Isabeau was dressed for the occasion in a long, swinging skirt that brushed her ankles and a short top that accented the curves of her body. She had the radiance and allure of a female close to the Han Vol Dan. Her scent was feminine and enticing. She was a vision in blue, and Philip stumbled when he saw her. He took her hand, gazed into her eyes with far too much greed, bending over her hand as though he might kiss it.

While she smiled gently, Elijah firmly removed her hand before those cold lips could touch her skin. "This is my favorite cousin." Again his white teeth flashed and this time they looked a bit sharper. "She is very dear to me." It was a clear warning and any man within hearing distance couldn't mistake the menace.

"Isabeau," Philip whispered. He couldn't seem to tear his eyes from her.

Elijah studied their host closely, inhaling his scent. They

had done research on the man. He was greedy and excessive in his decadent lifestyle. There were reports of women carried from his home while he looked on, wrapped in a silken robe and sipping a glass of whiskey with a small smile. Everywhere they looked the signs of his opulent lifestyle were apparent.

Marcos took a drink from a tray, his faded, burnished eyes taking in the server. He shifted his gaze to Conner, who barely nodded. The woman was dressed in dark trousers and a white blouse. There was a faint bruise on the side of her face covered by thick makeup. Her hand trembled slightly as she offered the silver tray.

Rio indicated they move deeper into the house, into one of the rooms Conner had deemed the safest. There were several exits and a more open floor plan. Philip followed them, chattering about the new hotel being built and how much it was needed. The jobs, economy and all the new tourist opportunities it presented. Marcos murmured politely, listening attentively, and Conner retreated back into the shadows, knowing he would appear more mysterious and more dangerous when Imelda Cortez's security people examined the tapes before allowing her inside.

He had studied Imelda's profile carefully, as he did any mark. She wanted a dominant man, one very dangerous, one that would thrill her, scare her a little, but one she could dispose of when she tired of him. No, Elijah had the charisma and danger she sought, but he was too powerful, she would never succumb to the temptation, Conner was certain he was right about her.

Isabeau wandered around the room and stopped in front of a display. Whips, floggers, canes and other various instruments of torture were displayed in a large glass case.

Philip came up behind her. Close. Too close. "Do these instruments interest you?"

Isabeau turned her head to look at him over her shoulder, her expression one of disdain. "Hardly. I prefer much more pleasurable forms of entertainment."

"Perhaps I could change your mind. Pleasure and pain are often mixed with surprising results."

Isabeau raised an eyebrow. She had only minutes to gather impressions of Philip Sobre, but she doubted she would need much more than that. Elijah's job was to act the overprotective cousin while she was bored and amused and as alluring as possible. Sobre was reputed to have visited Imelda Cortez's compound quite often for several months. The visits continued, but were much less frequent now. She had the feeling Philip and Imelda shared a similar fetish for using whips on others, not on each other.

"The giving or the receiving?" she asked with a small and what she hoped was a mysterious and mildly interested smile. "I think I'd much rather be the giver." Her cat stirred, rebelling at the way the man stood so close, breathing on her with mint-scented breath and his hot eyes. Her skin itched and she felt the movement inside her, a slow extension of claws unfolding.

"I agree with you there. It is exquisite to watch the whip cutting across flesh." He inhaled and the musky scent of arousal reached her nose. "Wielding the whip, gaining control and acquiring that perfect touch is an art form."

"One you've studied?" Isabeau turned to face him, leaning one hip against the wall and looking at him over the glass of wine she was pretending to sip. Philip Sobre was a sadist. He was sexually aroused at the thought of ripping into someone helpless with his whip. The rumors about

Imelda Cortez were rampant. Her cruelty was legend, as was her father's before her. They would naturally gravitate toward one another. And Philip was in a position where he would have an endless supply of victims to share with Imelda.

"Of course," Philip said. "Extensively." There was something hot and speculative in his eyes that made her stomach lurch in protest.

She'd lived a great deal of her life in the rain forest. The economic disparity between the rich and the poor was enormous. The smoldering heat of the jungle often brought out the worst in people, and the distance from civilization sometimes attracted the most depraved, who thought themselves above the law and entitled to do whatever they wanted. They believed the natives were beneath them and no one would miss a few if they disappeared. She'd seen the attitude many times in her life, but Philip was blatant about it.

She hung on to her smile and was grateful when Elijah crossed the room to her side and took her elbow. She knew Philip perceived Elijah as a shark, just as he thought of himself. Elijah bent to whisper in her ear, his eyes on Philip.

"Keep it up, you look very cool and calm and just that little bit disdainful. My guess is the feed from the videos is being reviewed right now. She'll be intrigued by Sobre's interest in you. There's no way they'll miss Conner prowling in the shadows."

She smiled up at him and touched his cheek affectionately, looking as loving as possible. It was strange. She knew Elijah's background, what he'd come from, what he'd done in his life, most of it not good, and yet he had a clean scent. Depravity clung to Philip. It was difficult to avoid looking toward Conner as Elijah led her back to

Marcos, who greeted her by raising his wineglass and telling her a joke. She was very aware of Philip joining them, standing next to her, which told all of them that despite the clear warning Elijah had given him, he felt very safe under Imelda Cortez's protection.

Cortez definitely ruled here. Signs of her were in the security system and the guns Philip's guards possessed. The weapons were too sophisticated for the men who held them. This was Sobre's personal army, not Imelda's, and Philip was too lazy, or too cheap to employ mercenaries or ex-soldiers. Maybe he didn't believe he needed security in the same way Imelda did. But Imelda and Philip definitely were affiliated, or he wouldn't have the guns and security system. As chief of tourism, he was in a position to help her get her drugs out of the country. And he got a fat paycheck for his services.

Isabeau was aware of Philip working his supposed charm on Marcos. Marcos was an older man and Cortez probably thought she could seduce him or blackmail him into going into business with her if her business offer wasn't as sweet as he'd like. Elijah was a different matter. Young. Virile. His reputation was that of a ruthless dictator in his cartel. His men were loyal to a fault and his enemies tended to die fast. None of them had expected him to be with Marcos.

In another hour Imelda would be there and the tension would skyrocket. In the meantime, the team would try to get as much information out of Sobre as they could without ever asking about Cortez. He had to bring her up and Isabeau was certain he would. He was already dropping the names of celebrities who he'd had to dinner or one of his parties. He was a vain, pompous man, but she wasn't going to underestimate him. He hadn't gotten where he was by being stupid.

"You have a lovely home, Mr. Sobre," she said. "It was . . . unexpected."

He preened and strutted a little. "We're quite fashionable even here in this place." His eyes held hers. "We make our own rules here and live the way we choose."

She gave him her sweet, empty smile over the rim of her crystal glass. "Well you seem to be doing a fine job. Where in the world did you find all these servants?"

Deliberately she used the word servant, making her tone a little dismissive when she indicated the uniformed women. Almost all of them were women, but she noticed a few men moving throughout the room. She was certain they weren't part of his security. Their eyes were downcast as they replenished the trays of food and moved through the guests. A few of the expensively dressed women ran hands over the men, touching them inappropriately. She would bet that the men and women going upstairs were taking advantage of other services his servants were required to give—and most likely the guests were being filmed secretly while they enjoyed themselves.

She knew the team believed they only had an hour or two before Imelda arrived. Everything Isabeau knew about the woman pointed to someone who would deliberately make those around her feel small. Imelda would be cold and cutting and even cruel to those she believed less than she was. If Imelda really was the one giving orders to Philip, he had only until the woman showed up to convince Isabeau he was someone important. After that, Imelda would undercut him.

Because he thought she was Elijah's cousin, Sobre banked on her knowing what Elijah did for a living. As head of a dangerous family-owned cartel, Elijah would be regarded in the same vein as Imelda. They all had to wonder if Marcos was related to him and part of that cartel or whether they were coming together to work out an alliance.

Marcos patted one server's butt and the woman averted her eyes and allowed him a closer inspection. Isabeau kept her expression the same when she wanted to throw her glass at the older man. What did she know about him? What were the others doing allowing him to behave like that? She forced herself to inhale, to take in the scents around her for her cat to process.

Fear was uppermost. Hatred. Rage. All boiled beneath the surface. She certainly smelled lust, but not coming from Marcos. He was playing a part. Just as she was. Just as Conner would be doing. She had to believe that.

She looked at Elijah. He had known. They'd all known. This was more than drugs and kidnapping. They hadn't told her the things they'd expected to run into. She would never have been able to smile at Sobre had she known coming in. She was made deliberately to look like the innocent in the middle of a jungle full of predators. She'd bet her life that they'd discovered some of the precious tourists Sobre lured to his part of the rain forest disappeared without a trace. It would be so easy.

What was she thinking? That the suave man handing her another glass of wine was really a serial killer of young men and woman? That he used his position for his own sadistic pleasure? To cover her frightening thoughts, she lifted the glass to her lips. She actually took a sip before the scent hit her. It was drugged. She moistened her lips and looked again at Elijah. This time he reacted, smiling back at her and taking the drink from her hand, bringing the contents to his mouth. Her breath caught in her throat and she nearly shouted at him to stop.

The server knocked hard into Elijah, sending the drink flying. The glass shattered all over the floor and the contents ended up on his immaculate shirt. The tray clattered to the floor, food scattering everywhere.

"Teresa!" Philip roared, his fist missing Isabeau by a mere inch as it shot toward the woman's horrified face.

The crack of flesh hitting flesh was loud. All conversation ceased and the room went eerily quiet. Conner stood in front of the woman, Philip's hand in his fist. No one had seen him move. He looked hard. Dangerous. His golden eyes burned into the smaller man.

"Perhaps you didn't notice, but you bumped the woman and knocked her into Mr. Lospostos." His voice was so quiet, Isabeau doubted anyone other than their small group could hear his words. "And you nearly struck Miss Chandler."

Philip Sobre looked murderous and then the dark promise was gone from his eyes and he was smiling. "I guess I didn't."

Conner let go of Philip's fist, his arm dropping back to his side. Isabeau knew the cameras had recorded every moment and Imelda would be intrigued with that interesting move on the bodyguard's part. He'd stood up for a servant. And he'd moved so fast he'd be a blur on the camera. She'd be more than intrigued. She'd want to get up close to such a daring, dangerous man. Not once had he looked at Philip's bodyguards, as if they were beneath his notice and no threat to him.

Isabeau's heart began to pound, and she could taste fear in her mouth. Conner was setting himself up, and these people were all killers. She even suspected the weasel Philip—who was smooth and charming all over again and ordering his servers to help Teresa clean up the mess—of being a killer. He appeared to ignore Conner, but she saw him glance several times toward the shadowed wall where Conner had once more disappeared.

If Adan had known about Sobre, he would never have allowed her to talk him into bringing in a team to kidnap back the children. So how had Conner gotten his information, because they definitely knew something was wrong with the chief of tourism and had come prepared. What other sources did they have?

"Come with me, Isabeau, while I get a clean shirt," Elijah commanded. With another smoldering look at Philip, he took her arm and walked her toward the entrance. "You're biting your lip."

"Am I?" She felt like she could breathe again, out of the presence of the chief of tourism and his penchant for hurting others.

"You do that when you're upset."

"How did you know about Sobre? He's a sadist, isn't he?"

"He's a killer. He likes to hurt people. He gets off on it. Men and women both from what I understand and he's got a perfect partner in Imelda. She shares his dirty little secret, in fact, she encourages it. As long as he kills his victims, she can control him."

"They sound like a perfect couple."

"They were a couple for a while. I suspect Imelda wants a dominant personality, and Philip would never be that to her. He's too afraid of her." Elijah stepped back to allow Rio to open the SUV door for him. Elijah waved her into the car.

"When we go back inside, I want you to look as if you've received a lecture from your badass cousin. Sobre will expect that I don't want you near him—which I don't. I know exactly the way his mind works. He thinks I have a weakness for my cousin and as he would never stop himself from taking what he wants, he believes neither would I."

"He makes me sick. His smell. His eyes. The way he looks at me. *Everything* about him. Something was in that drink."

Elijah nodded. "I got a whiff of it." He unbuttoned his shirt. "If the server hadn't bumped me, I would have found a way to drop it. Don't you find it interesting that he didn't want me drugged? Cortez is more anxious to talk to me than I expected."

"How did Rio know about Sobre?"

"Adan gave Rio Marisa's diary as proof of who he was. He needed to establish that he meant us no harm. She was investigating Sobre. She'd been suspicious of him for some time. Apparently . . ." He pulled a black shirt from a small suitcase, flashing her a small grin. " . . . always be prepared."

She rolled her hand in a circle over and over indicating for him to continue. "Apparently what?"

"Several women had disappeared in the area over the past few years, enough that Marisa became suspicious. She was the 'medicine woman' around these parts and many people, both from the tribes and other villages, sought her out, so she heard things more than others."

"And she heard about Sobre?"

Elijah nodded as he buttoned his shirt. "She zeroed in on him after a young woman from England disappeared. The woman had come here with three friends to hike in the rain forest. She somehow got separated from the others and they never found her."

"Why Sobre?"

"Sobre had told them about a particular trail, one little known and he didn't recommend a guide. At least that's what the other two women said. He claims he mentioned the trail in a conversation to them and even handed them cards with the names of tour guides on them."

"What else?" She knew there was more and she didn't know whether to be angry or just sick about walking into Sobre's lair without her team fully disclosing what they knew.

"Sobre came here when he was seventeen years old. He's now fifty-one. Marisa discovered that girls have been disappearing for thirty-four years."

She pressed her fingers to her mouth. "My God, he's a serial killer for real."

"That was the conclusion Marisa came to."

"Do you think Sobre knew she was on to him? Could he have deliberately used Suma and the raid on the village to target her?"

"Maybe, but we'll probably never know. Imelda Cortez has most likely known about this and probably not only encouraged him, but helped him. They have a bond, those two, and it's sick and perverted and definitely unhealthy."

"You already knew it going in," Isabeau said, "and you didn't tell me."

"Imelda Cortez would never go out into the open unless she completely controlled the situation, which meant, if she was attending this party at Philip Sobre's residence, she had him in her pocket. It wasn't that difficult after reading Marisa's suspicions to know where to start our research. She wasn't far off the mark. Every one of our leopards instinctively despised the man," Elijah pointed out.

"And Conner just set himself up," Isabeau said. "Sobre

despises him and will look for any excuse to kill him after that public humiliation, and Imelda will want him because he made Sobre look small. Am I right?"

Elijah nodded. "That's why we came, to get our foot in the door."

"And Conner wanted Sobre's attention off me and onto him," she guessed.

"That too. It was important that you handle Sobre without tipping him off, Isabeau. This is your first time going into a situation like this and none of us knew how you'd handle it."

She raised her chin. "What if I'd gone off with him?"

"No one ever took their eyes off you. That wouldn't have been allowed. I'm the big bad cousin and Rio and Felipe are our personal protectors. If I ordered one of them to cart your ass to the car, they would do so without hesitation and no one would be suspicious." His hand was on the door handle, but he wasn't opening it.

"I can handle it," she assured him.

"You're certain? There can't be any mistakes, Isabeau. Too many lives are at stake and we have no proof of anything. In any case, you can bet any law enforcement around here is either in Imelda's pocket or terrified of her. Hell, most of it is getting paid extra money to guard Sobre's party."

"I said I can handle it. Conner's hung out there on the line," she said. "I've got his back. And don't think I won't do whatever it takes to make certain he gets out of this alive."

Elijah studied her determined face and then nodded. "Good girl." He ruffled her hair and rubbed at her face, putting spots of color on her skin and making her lips a little swollen as if he'd been kissing her. "Let's hope Conner doesn't rip out my heart and shove it down my throat."

She forced a smile. "I'm going to make certain I blink back a couple of tears and really make you look bad."

"Badass cousin doesn't want his kissing cousin flirting with anyone else and you've been thoroughly reprimanded and then we made up."

"Sobre won't cross you, not without Imelda's permission," Isabeau pointed out.

"And that's what is going to keep you safe. Stay close to me now. Touch me occasionally, but be subtle about it. I want them to see the relationship without us shoving it down their throats."

"Like we're hiding it."

"Or at least that we don't want it common knowledge. Now, Isabeau, there is a risk. On one hand, as long as they think they have a chance of doing business with me, this is the perfect way to keep you safe, but if they decide they need to keep me in line, or try to influence me with a threat, you'll be the first in harm's way. They think like that."

She nodded. "I'm aware of that. Really, Elijah, I can do this. My relationship with Conner aside, it was my idea to bring you all here and I'm willing to take the risk right alongside of you."

He pushed open the door and Rio stood facing the house, his expression remote, as if she were just another body to guard. It was amazing to Isabeau just how they all managed to look grim and dangerous and so businesslike at the same time.

She flashed Elijah a small smile when he put his hand casually on the small of her back. "I'll bet Sobre would give anything to have our bodyguards."

"Personal protectors," he corrected and winked at her.

She walked closer to Elijah then she had before, but still maintained a distance that could be considered discreet. The doorman waved them inside. The music seemed louder and the rooms much more crowded. Elijah took her elbow with a proprietary air and guided her through the throng of people. Rio led the way with Felipe bringing up the rear. She noticed the crowd parted for them and no one bumped into them.

Marcos, with Leonardo beside him, was in a corner talking to Philip. Teresa, the server, stood beside Marcos looking miserable. Every now and then Marcos would rub her arm or the small of her back and she would jump, but she didn't move. As they approached the small group, Philip looked up, his quick perusal taking in her slightly disheveled appearance. Isabeau made certain he caught the sheen of tears before she blinked them away. Philip's gaze dropped to Elijah's fingers digging into her elbow before he looked back at Marcos.

"Teresa will be more than happy to make you feel very welcome, isn't that right?"

The server nodded, more miserable than ever. Philip scowled at her and she forced a smile. "Of course."

Marcos patted her butt with familiar intent. "Later. Don't get lost."

Teresa quickly made good her escape. The floor where the spill had occurred was immaculate, and Philip was all smiles now that he thought Marcos would use his upstairs rooms. Isabeau reached up and rubbed at imaginary lipstick at the corner of Elijah's mouth and then quickly dropped her hand.

"You haven't tried the mushroom cakes," Philip said to Elijah.

"They're wonderful," Marcos agreed, looking as if he and Philip had become good friends. "And the crab cakes are even better. You really must try them, Elijah."

Elijah nodded with a faint smile. "You've always been a great judge of food, Marcos. I know you'd never steer me wrong."

"He's a good judge of women as well," Philip said, his grin malicious as he looked Isabeau over. "Teresa is beautiful."

Elijah slipped his arm around Isabeau and moved her out of Philip's way as he led them to the long buffet table. He did it casually, as though he was simply helping his cousin, but he knew Philip would take the gesture as ownership. Isabeau belonged to Elijah and everyone else needed to stay clear of her. Philip had a secret smile on his face as he pointed out the various delicacies to them.

"Would you like to dance, Isabeau?" he asked, with another smirk.

In character, she glanced hesitantly at Elijah, who stared back at her grim-faced. Hastily she shook her head. "No, thank you. I think I want to try the crab cake."

"You'll find my chef is amazing," Philip said.

Elijah looked him over, his expression bored. "It's amazing how you can lure anyone to this place."

Philip's face flushed just a little, but he managed to keep his smile at the implied insult. "Secrets, everyone has secrets. It's a matter of capitalizing on them."

A slow smile, with just a faint touch of admiration lit Elijah's face for a moment. Isabeau was impressed with that look. It was as if he'd waved a magic wand in front of Philip. "I suppose it is. Isn't it interesting how the right leverage changes minds?"

Philip puffed up again, looking extremely pleased, as

if in that one moment he'd won over Elijah Lospostos, the infamous drug lord. Isabeau realized Philip's downfall was his vanity. He didn't have enough people to admire his abilities and he needed an audience. His criminal activities isolated him from most. There were only his victims and Imelda Cortez to see him as he really was, and Imelda was dangerous to him. Here was a group of sharks. He recognized them and wanted to be part of them.

"Elijah," Marcos said, "perhaps we can stay a few extra days and enjoy the offerings in Philip's little city here."

Isabeau couldn't believe the transformation from a good-humored, loving, avuncular man to one of greedy excess, looking to run wild and partake in whatever depravity he could. His face was a little flushed, his eyes clouded, as though he'd drunk just a little too much, his gaze on the women a little too hot. She found herself uncomfortable, almost believing his act. Elijah brushed his hand along her back, just skimming, barely touching her, but she knew Philip caught the movement out of the corner of his eye. She played her part, glancing up at Elijah with a slight smile, the color elevating just a little in her face.

Her cat leapt, slamming close to her skin, protesting the touch of another man. She heard the snarl in her mind, and the urge to break away from them and get out of there was strong. Her skin itched.

Rio turned his head to look at her. In the shadows, Conner stirred. Felipe and Leonardo shifted just enough to block her from sight of most of the other people in the room. Elijah bent his head close but didn't touch her.

"Breathe her away. Keep her calm," he advised, looking unbelievably intimate, his face a mask of tenderness.

Isabeau took a deep breath, trying not to panic. She knew the cat wanted out. She didn't like the overpowering smell of decadence and corruption. Her joints ached. Her jaw. Even her teeth hurt. Her fingers curled and the tips burned. To her horror she could see skin splitting along her palm. Gasping, she closed her hand and willed her cat to obey.

12

ISABEAU would *not* let her cat emerge here, in the middle of this insane party, and blow their chances of ever taking these disgusting people down. It wasn't going to happen. She hissed at her cat, suddenly furious that the creature would take this moment to decide to emerge. She'd had her chance in the rain forest when Conner was with her and it could have been a wonderful experience.

"You. Will. *Not*." She hissed each word between her teeth, keeping her face close to Elijah's chest. She dared not touch him, even though she desperately needed reassurance. She was grateful Conner didn't rush to her side. She doubted she could stay in control if he had. She would have flung herself into his arms, in the midst of her rising fear. She tried to think like him. He was always calm. He refused to show fear, or let fear paralyze him. What had he said? Her cat was part of her. And she certainly could control herself.

She took another breath and forced her will on the

raging cat, breathing for it, calming it, whispering to it in her head. Conner was her mate. There was no other. This was all for Conner. To protect him. To protect his cat. She lost track of what she was saying and even time passing, trusting Elijah and Marcos to keep the conversation flowing around them. Philip would continue to believe she was under Elijah's control and he wanted her to stand beside him, his decoration, and nothing more.

It took several minutes for the cat to submit to her control, subsiding, but making her needs known, leaving Isabeau in a heightened state of sensitivity and awareness. All senses were acute. Her body ached, every muscle, every joint. Her breasts were so sensitive, each time she moved, her nipples brushed against her lacy bra and sent an electrical current sizzling straight to the junction between her legs. She ached for Conner, for relief.

It was a fitting revenge, she thought. She'd denied her cat's emergence, but she couldn't stop the needs of her species. The Han Vol Dan. That mysterious moment when her cat was set free and wholly united with her human form. The shocking heat of the female leopard, emerging with a desperate, insatiable hunger that could never be sated by any other than her mate.

"Good girl," Elijah whispered in her ear, looking intimate, but careful not to touch her and incur the wrath of her leopard.

Before she could reply, the room went silent as four men dressed in black pants and black shirts swept through the double doors. The entrance was meant to be dramatic and it was. They carried automatic weapons, wore dark, mirrored sunglasses and looked like television gangsters to Isabeau. Her stomach tightened as she sensed the instant reaction of Elijah's leopard.

The tension in the room was shocking, stretched nearly to a breaking point as the men shoved couples against the wall and began systematically searching them. It was a show of power, pure and simple—a lesson to show just who was really in charge. The indignity on the faces of the various couples was apparent, but not a single person protested.

The driving, pounding music accompanied the sound of harsh breathing and grunts and little outraged gasps as the women were searched. Elijah and Marcos watched impassively as the four men came closer and closer to them, but neither moved. Isabeau remained close to Elijah, her stomach knotting as the security team got closer. She knew this type of search was unusual and was simply Imelda's way of making a dramatically grand entrance, but with her heightened sensitivity she could feel the men around her, their energy growing more dangerous as the guards approached.

Just as two of the men dressed in black reached Marcos and Elijah, Conner emerged from the shadows, placing his body solidly in their path. Rio, Felipe and Leonardo were there as well. They'd moved so fast she had thought she must have blinked. Elijah very gently drew her behind him.

Conner stared directly into those mirrored glasses. "I don't think so." His voice was quiet, but it was a whip, a challenge.

"We'll be searching everyone."

Conner's smile was slow, and there was no humor in it. "You'll be dead before you lay a finger on the three of them. But you're always welcome to try."

Isabeau's mouth went dry. He was provoking the guards deliberately. They were sending their own message to

Imelda. The woman was known for her insanity. She could order her men to open fire with the automatic weapons, killing everyone in the room. The other couples in the room were clearly shocked, gasping. One woman began to cry but her partner quickly shushed her.

Conner never broke off his stare, his eyes pure cat. He looked relaxed. He looked . . . lethal. He made the men he was facing look small.

The man closest to him spoke into his radio. "Martin, we have a problem in here."

Almost immediately two men entered the room. Both had the build of the leopard and moved with fluid power. Isabeau's cat reacted with a snarl and leap. She saw, because she was watching him, Conner's fingers flex just once when the man who was reputed to have killed his mother entered the room. Isabeau recognized Suma from the village and her stomach rebelled at the sight of him, almost as much as her cat did.

Used to instant obedience and the cowering of any opposition, Martin Suma and Ottila Zorba shoved their security force aside and were almost toe to toe with Conner before it hit them what exactly they were facing. Martin found himself staring into the focused eyes of a killer. Conner smiled. It wasn't a pleasant smile. The tension in the room stretched nearly to a breaking point as the two stared each other down.

Ottila, not the one locked in combat with Conner, surveyed the security for the two visitors, recognizing them instantly as leopard. He inhaled sharply and drew the scent of a female close to the Han Vol Dan into his body. At once his cat reacted, all male, hunger invading, a dark need that was all encompassing. He looked past the others and focused on the object of his desire.

Martin caught the scent next and his gaze flicked to the woman standing behind the man he knew as Elijah Lospostos, head of a major drug cartel and by all accounts a very powerful and dangerous man. Only then did he realize not only was the security team leopard, and the woman, but the two visitors as well. He was facing seven leopards, all of them armed. Self-preservation was strong and dictated that he back off immediately.

Isabeau saw the knowledge hit the two guards almost at the same time. Their eyes glittered with malice. She never wanted to meet either of them alone on a dark night. These were the men who had kidnapped the children and killed several villagers and Conner's mother. She couldn't quite control the pounding of her heart.

Elijah reached behind him, a casual, gentle gesture, and laid his hand on her arm. That small touch steadied her. She took a breath and forced herself to breathe normally, slowing her pulse. She couldn't be afraid of them. Her cat detested the scent of the two rogue leopards, yet recognized Conner's immediately, nearly purring at his closeness.

A stir at the door drew her attention. Isabeau peeked around Elijah and caught her first glimpse of Imelda Cortez. She wore a long, flowing gown of bloodred, matching her long nails and lipstick. Her hair, as black as a raven's wing, was swept up in an intricate knot so that the dazzling gems on her ears and at her throat were prominently displayed. The dress was slashed nearly to the navel so that the perfect globes of her breasts peeked out, making Isabeau feel drab and childish in comparison.

Imelda swept into the room on her spiked crimson heels, her dark eyes alighting instantly on Conner, her hungry gaze devouring him in a slow, greedy perusal that drank in the broad shoulders and thick chest. There was no missing the aura of danger he exuded, and Imelda actually inhaled sharply, her breasts heaving, in grave danger of spilling out of the dress.

Isabeau's cat went crazy, raking at her, clawing and growling, recognizing an enemy, desperate for the freedom to destroy her. For one terrible moment Isabeau was certain she wouldn't be able to stop her leopard from emerging and killing the woman in a fit of rage. Her muscles contorted. Her bones popped. Pain burst through her jaw and her mouth seemed overcrowded with teeth.

No! You will not! She fought the leopard back. *He needs us. Both of us.* She filled her mind with Conner, drew strength from him, from her love of him. And she did love him with every fiber of her being. She would do this for him.

Imelda Cortez was tall and thin, very fashionable, but she reminded Isabeau of a praying mantis, an insect ready to strike her prey the first chance she got. Imelda's gluttonous gaze slid dismissively over Isabeau once, but moved quickly on to the men in the group—a new supply of men for her voracious appetite. That told all of them that Imelda wasn't leopard, or even part leopard. She would have known Isabeau was close to the Han Vol Dan and therefore her biggest threat. The two rogue leopards would be consumed by her presence. Their duty to Imelda would be second to their need of mating with a female leopard in the throes of the Han Vol Dan.

Imelda moved across the room, aware all eyes were on her. She pursed her lips and made a little clucking noise, shaking her head. "This is no way to treat Philip's guests, Martin." She slid her fingers playfully down Conner's arm. "Who do we have here?"

Isabeau's cat gave a fierce snarl, but subsided under her

growing control. Conner didn't even so much as glance at Imelda. His gaze remained fixed and focused on Martin's. There was a threat there, very real, and Martin didn't dare move, not even with Imelda clearly giving him the signal to back off.

"Conner," Marcos said in a low tone. "I think he has the message."

Conner took a step back immediately, never taking his eyes from Martin. The rogue leopard stepped back as well and broke the stare, looking at his employer. There was a fine sheen of sweat on his forehead.

Imelda gave a sniff of contempt and handed him a handkerchief. "Mop up. You look ridiculous." She glided close to Conner, and ran her finger down his chest this time, a blatant invitation, her breasts nearly touching him, her perfume engulfing him, her eyes devouring him. "Very few men can get the better of my guards."

Martin stirred as if he might protest. Imelda's hand came up and she waved languidly. "Go away, Martin. You're boring me."

Martin glanced at Isabeau, his eyes glittering dangerously and then he looked once more to his boss. Hatred flared briefly, and he turned abruptly, signaling the other security guards, who dispersed to various spots in the room. Only then did Conner look down at Imelda. Isabeau held her breath. There was no expression whatsoever on his face.

"Excuse me, ma'am." He moved in silence back toward the wall where the shadows in the room swallowed him.

"Oh my," Imelda said, fanning herself. "You have good taste in protectors, Marcos. I'm Imelda Cortez."

Marcos bent gallantly over her hand. "A pleasure to meet you, Imelda—may I call you Imelda?"

"Of course. I believe we'll be great friends." She flashed him a lovely smile, all teeth and flirty pouting lips.

Conversation began cautiously around them once more. Imelda didn't seem to notice the chaos her men had caused. Or rather, she knew, Isabeau decided, but she didn't care what inconvenience there was to anyone else. She thrived on the drama she created.

"May I present Elijah Lospostos and his charming little cousin, Isabeau."

"*Cherished* cousin," Elijah corrected, making her instantly off limits to the attentions of Philip or any of her men.

"Elijah," Imelda murmured. "Your . . . reputation precedes you."

"All good, I'm certain," Elijah replied smoothly and bent over her hand, although he didn't pretend to allow his lips to brush her skin.

"Of course," Imelda agreed with a feigned smile and turned her attention to Isabeau. "My dear, what a lovely dress. Who is the designer? I must have one."

Elijah answered, taking Isabeau's elbow, his fingers sinking into her skin. Imelda's sharp gaze couldn't miss the signal to Isabeau not to speak. "I brought the dress for her from one of our little boutiques in the States. I travel quite often and saw this and knew it would be perfect for her. It's one of a kind and suits her less dramatic appearance."

Isabeau heard the small bite in his voice, implying the innocence of Isabeau's dress would never suit someone who wore the bloodred gown revealing half of Imelda's body. She held her breath, afraid Elijah was antagonizing the woman, but Imelda took it as a compliment. She ran her hand down her hip, smoothing the material and jutting out her breasts, turning her back on Isabeau as if she was of little consequence. Isabeau realized that was Elijah's intent, to make certain Imelda didn't see her as a threat in any way.

She tried not to let the byplay undermine her confidence in herself. She'd never considered herself beautiful. She was curvy, carrying a little more weight than was fashionable, but she had great hair and good skin. She didn't think she looked drab, but next to Imelda she probably did. Imelda's tinkling laugh irritated her, and the way she moved into the center of the circle of men as if she belonged there irritated her even more.

A hush fell over the crowd again and heads began to turn toward the door. Isabeau found herself following the gazes of the others. A guard, obviously one of Imelda's, pushed a wheelchair into the room. The occupant looked to be in his eighties, a thin, rather handsome man with thick silver hair. He wore his suit as if it had been made for him—which it probably had been. His smile was kind, even benevolent, and he waved to several people and greeted them by name as he was pushed through the crowd.

People reached out to touch him. Each time someone greeted him, he stopped and talked for a few moments before moving on. Couples smiled at him. He seemed to know everyone's name and asked about children or parents. Imelda sighed and tapped her foot impatiently.

"My grandfather," she announced. "He's very beloved."

It seemed to annoy her that her grandfather was so popular with the people. Isabeau guessed it took the attention that she craved away from her. The man suddenly looked up and she could see his eyes through the thick glasses. Old and faded, they were more a gray than a black, but he seemed genuinely interested in those around him. She couldn't imagine that a creature as immoral and malevolent as Imelda could possibly be related to this man.

"For heaven's sake, Grandfather," Imelda snapped and broke away from the group. "We have important guests," she hissed in his ear, shoving between his chair and the guard. She took control of the chair herself and pushed him through the remaining throng to their small corner of the room. "Come meet Marcos Santos and Elijah Lospostos. This is my grandfather, Alberto Cortez. He's a little hard of hearing," she apologized.

Marcos and Elijah both shook his hand and greeted him with respect and a deference they hadn't shown Imelda. Alberto smiled at Isabeau. "And who is this?"

"Elijah's cousin, grandfather," Imelda said, her tone waspish.

"Isabeau Chandler, my cousin," Elijah presented her with a small, courteous bow.

He took Isabeau's hand in both of his. Her cat hissed, her skin still too sensitive for contact. "Lovely dear, you outshine every woman here."

Imelda rolled her eyes. "Please forgive the old man, he's always been a charmer."

"You are very charming," Isabeau addressed him directly, not looking at Imelda, feeling a little sorry for him. Imelda treated him like a doddering fool, when it was obvious his brain was sharp and fully functioning. "I'm so glad you've come."

He winked at her, also ignoring his granddaughter. "Are they talking business again?"

"I think they were about to."

"The music is a bit wild, but the food is good and the women are gorgeous. What is wrong with men today that business is everything? They don't realize that time speeds by and they should take time to enjoy the little things." He looked up at the faces around him. "Soon you will be old with little time left."

Two red flags of color swept into Imelda's face. "Excuse him, please. He talks a lot of nonsense."

"No, no, dear," Marcos patted her arm. "He speaks the truth. I intend to enjoy myself immensely while I'm here. I agree, entertainment and enjoyment are very important." His gaze swept the room and lit on Teresa, who was carrying an empty serving tray back toward the kitchen. "Just a small amount of business and then we'll have fun with friends, right, Elijah?"

"Of course, Marcos."

Alberto frowned. "Forgive an old man, Elijah, but I knew your uncle. I heard he died in an accident in Borneo. Accept my condolences."

Elijah inclined his head. "I had no idea you two knew each other."

"Briefly. Only briefly. You and your sister were very young when I met him. Where is your sister? I had heard that she disappeared as well. Such a tragedy, your family."

"Rachel is alive and well. There was bad business." Elijah shrugged casually. His eyes were flat and cold. "An enemy stupid enough to try to use the threat of my sister against us."

"She is alive then? Good. Good. A beautiful girl. I hadn't heard what had become of her. I should have known you would take care of any problems."

Elijah sent him a cold smile. "I always take care of my own. And my enemies."

"May I borrow your beautiful cousin while you talk business? Just for a little while. We can walk in the gardens. My man will be with us to watch over her. And perhaps one of your men can accompany us as well, if you prefer."

Imelda scowled. "That's just silly, Grandfather. Philip has security everywhere. What could possibly happen to either of you?"

Elijah thought it over. The garden was fully visible from Jeremiah's position. There shouldn't be any problem. He brought Isabeau's hand to his chest. "I think that would be nice for you, Isabeau, much better than listening to boring business." He tucked a strand of hair behind her head. "I'll send Felipe with you."

"That's not necessary," Isabeau said. "I'd much rather he look after you."

Alberto gestured to his guard. "This is Harry. He's been with *me* for ten years." He emphasized the pronoun, making a point.

Imelda sighed and rolled her eyes. "Oh, for heaven's sake. Let's go. Philip, take us to your secure room. Grandfather and your little cousin can do whatever." Her eyes had already gone to the shadows, looking for Marcos's bodyguard.

Conner moved the moment Marcos did, falling smoothly in behind him. He didn't look at them, but his gaze moved restlessly through the room, taking in everyone. He gave the appearance of being able to describe in detail every single person—and Isabeau was certain he probably could.

"Come with me and make an old man's day, Isabeau," Alberto encouraged. "Let me show you Philip's garden. He's not a man you want to spend time with, but he does love beautiful things. His taste is impeccable."

She had to agree that the house and artwork and even his furniture all bore the stamp of someone who loved beautiful things. They passed the case filled with instruments of torture and she shivered, afraid those things had been used numerous times on real people.

Alberto reached out and patted her hand. Again her cat leapt and hissed and her skin burned from that casual touch. She was close to the emerging. Too close. And that was a frightening thought. She suddenly wanted Conner to hold her close. They were firmly entrenched in a house of deceit with ruthless killers pretending to be civil. The crowd seemed friendly enough, and very curious, but she couldn't trust any of them either.

She pulled her hand away gently, trying not to upset him. Alberto Cortez had been the friendliest face she'd seen. "Have you always lived here?" she asked, trying to make small talk.

"My family is one of the oldest in Colombia. Our holdings have expanded over time. My son was the first to have interest in Panama. I didn't agree with his decisions, but he was strong-willed and his daughter is very much like him." He looked up at his attendant. "Isn't that right, Harry?"

"That's right, Mr. Cortez," Harry agreed, moving easily through the crowd. His voice was good-natured and his tone affectionate.

"How many times have I told you to call me Alberto?" the old man demanded.

"Probably a good million, Mr. Cortez," Harry admitted.

Isabeau laughed. She liked the old man better for his easy camaraderie with his bodyguard.

Alberto drew his brows together. "And you, young Isabeau? Am I going to have the same problem with you? He makes me feel old."

"He's being respectful."

"He can respect Imelda. She seems to need it. I'd rather

just be plain Alberto, growing my favorite plants in my garden."

"You're a gardener?"

"I love working with my hands. My son and grand-daughter don't understand my need of the land and getting my fingers in the dirt."

"I love plants," Isabeau said. "Someday I'm going to have my own garden as well. Right now, I've been cata-loguing medicinal plants found in the rain forest. I've done so both here and in Borneo. I'd like to go to Costa Rica next. The plants are amazing with the various uses. Peo-ple have no idea how valuable they are for medicines, and we're losing the rain forests far too fast. We're going to lose those resources if we don't get researchers moving on . . ." She broke off with a small laugh. "I'm sorry. It's a passion of mine."

Harry reached around the chair to open the French doors leading to the garden. She held them open so he could take Alberto through. The garden was enormous, humid and vividly green. Trees shot up, sending umbrel-las of greenery shielding them from the night sky. She walked to the bench most visible to the side of the forest where she knew Jeremiah was secreted. He would have them in his sight and she felt a little more at ease, know-ing he was there.

A small man-made stream ran over rocks, winding through the garden to culminate in a series of small water-falls. Her body tightened just a little at the sound of water, reminding her of the feel of Conner's body moving inside hers. She took a deep breath and let it out, inhaling the scent of roses and lavender.

Lacy fronds of various ferns lined the stream, and flow-ers turned one sloping bank into a riot of color. She recognized most of the plants and was amazed at how beautiful the layout was. "Philip has an extraordinary gardener. Look at how everything is placed. It's beyond beautiful."

Alberto beamed. "I'm glad you approve."

She turned her head, astonished. "You? You designed this garden?"

He inclined his head. "A hobby of mine."

"You're very talented. This is art, Mr. Cortez."

Alberto began to laugh and Harry joined him.

Isabeau grinned at him. "I'm sorry, Harry paid me to say that."

Alberto roared with laughter. "You're very good for this old man, Isabeau. I think I spend far too much time alone. Take a look around and tell me what you think."

"You don't mind?"

"No, I've seen it all, remember? I just want to watch your face when you discover all the various plants. I think you'll appreciate this place more than any other."

Isabeau's weakness was plants. She couldn't resist the invitation. Besides, she was curious.

"The garden encompasses an entire acre. The stream winds through the entire thing, and the terrain is rolling, so I used that to my advantage when I was designing the layout," he explained. "I wanted everything to be natural but controlled."

"Do you have a garden at home like this one?"

"Not exactly. I didn't section it off from the rain forest. I just took what we had growing naturally and organized it a little."

Harry snorted derisively. "He isn't telling the exact truth, Miss Isabeau. You've never seen anything like it. His garden is much more beautiful than this. Orchids are everywhere. They hang from the trees like chains of flowers winding up and down the trunks. Even the trees and vines are kept shaped . . ."

Alberto patted Harry's arm. "I've made an enthusiast out of him."

"I had no choice," Harry admitted.

"He's my legs," Alberto said. "Once I was confined to the chair, I thought my gardening days would be over, but Harry found a way for me to keep going."

Harry shrugged. "I'm not going to tell him I enjoy it. He's been wanting me to admit that forever, but I have to have something to hold over him for my raises."

Isabeau laughed at his dry tone. "Okay, I'm going to take a look around and see what you've done. I'll bet I can identify most of the plants."

"I'll be interested in discussing medicinal plants with you for my garden," Alberto said. "But you go now, and we'll talk when you've had a chance to see everything."

It was obvious he was proud of the garden and wanted to share it with someone he hoped would appreciate it. Isabeau set out, moving down a well-worn path that took her to the southernmost end of the garden first. It was the most open and she wanted Jeremiah to feel comfortable with her walking around.

She took her time, taking Alberto at his word. She enjoyed the night sounds. She could hear the pounding music in the distance, but the insects and the flutter of wings were more prominent—and musical—to her. She found the garden soothing, and the farther she walked away from the others, the more safe she felt. Her cat settled and her skin quit itching. There was no longer the scent of intrigue and depravity. Freshly dug dirt, the fragrance of flowers and trees took the place of cloying perfume and malicious intent. Maybe Alberto had sensed her need of peace and sent her out to allow her space. He was a perceptive man in spite of his age.

She began to mentally name the various plants and their uses. Scarlet passionflower blooms attracted and were pollinated by the hermit hummingbird. The flowering bromeliad's nectar fed a variety of bats. An array of orchids grew both on the ground and up the trunks of trees, providing food for all kinds of birds and insects, including the orchid bee.

Isabeau stopped to admire an epiphytic blueberry, the bright orange flower and bulbs a favorite of hummingbirds. Although they were usually found high in the canopy, Alberto had brought them within reach of the ground, which in turn brought the various species of hummingbirds closer to inspection.

Many varieties of ferns grew taller than her, forming a beautiful, lacy jungle. All kinds of philodendrons in various shades of green, with different types of leaves, both split and variegated, towered above her as well. The winding path took her up a small slope where the brush was far thicker. Here, small animals made their homes. She could hear the rustling and even scent them in the burrows.

The next bank of plants was her favorite, all medicinal. Alberto Cortez even had the *Gurania bignoniaceae*, a plant that had extensive medicinal uses. The leaves and flowers could be crushed and the material applied to infected cuts or sores that refused to heal, something that often happened in the humidity of the rain forest. The leaves and roots could be brewed into a tea and taken as a potion to remove worms and parasites. The flowers could be crushed and made into a poultice and applied to infected sores. She knew of a half dozen more uses for the plant for various ills, although depending on where it was grown, the roots could be toxic.

She frowned when she saw the large variety of strychnos, used in making strong curare for blowguns. There were hundreds of plants, both toxic and medicinal, all mixed together. There was even the plant she knew Adan's tribe used for countering the frog's poison used in their darts when they accidentally managed to get the poison on their skin.

The garden had everything from small brush to exotic flowers. She even found a little bed of daisies that pleased her. It seemed a little incongruous beside the more brilliant bird of paradise, but the simple beauty of the daisies was not lost on her.

She found herself following the little bed of common flowers. Around it, the brush grew thick with variegated leaves and fronds. Some of the leaves were so large that when it rained, they formed little umbrellas and the water ran down in tiny streams to the beds below, eroding the dirt. She crouched closer to examine the beds to see if the plants below were getting damaged. Some of the stalks were brown and withered as if they weren't getting water— or had a fungus.

Something—an animal—had been rooting around the flowerbed, digging for roots. There was evidence of birds as well, as though something had attracted them to this area. She crawled through the dying flowers to the middle of the bed and caught a whiff of decay. Her cat recoiled from the smell. Compost? She'd never smelled anything quite like it. It almost smelled like death.

Her heart jumped and she looked around to make certain she was alone. The stench was overpowering and she could clearly see that animals had disturbed the area. She moved closer, her eyes examining the withered flowers. Around them, the dirt was freshly dug. Something small and white and shiny peeking out of the dirt caught her attention. Isabeau glanced nervously through the trees to see if Harry and Alberto could see her, but the foliage was too thick.

Inching closer, she crouched low. The smell of decay grew stronger and her cat rebelled, urging her to flee. She brushed aside the dirt around that small white object and nearly leapt back. When she turned over the dirt, hundreds of small insects wiggled and protested. Very delicately, she pushed at the object to reveal more. She was looking at a partially decayed finger. There was a human body in the garden.

Trying to breathe shallowly so she didn't take in the smell, she stood up and stepped back carefully, her heart pounding. Philip Sobre had his own burial ground. The garden was an entire acre. He could bury any number of people here. She swallowed hard and tried to think what to do. She didn't want any evidence of her discovery. With her hand, she carefully brushed over her footprints and made her way back to the main path, trying to cover up anything she might have disturbed.

Did Alberto know? Surely he hadn't deliberately sent her out looking, hoping she'd make the discovery. Was it possible he had his own agenda? That he wasn't the sweet old gentleman he appeared to be? But what could be accomplished by her discovering a dead body in Philip Sobre's private garden? This place was horrible and she wanted out of it as fast as she could go.

She made herself walk, not run, heading back toward the old man. Glancing over her shoulder for one last look at the burial ground, she hit something hard. Two hands caught her arms in a firm grip, steadying her, and the scent of an aroused male assailed her nostrils. She recognized him instantly. Ottila Zorba, one of the rogue leopards, and he was looking at her with a leopard's focused gaze—as prey. He stared down at her without smiling and slowly, almost reluctantly, released her.

Isabeau forced a small smile. "Hello. I didn't see you there. I should have been looking where I was going." She took a step as though she would go around him, but he glided in that fluid, silent way of leopards, cutting off her escape. He was a good-looking man, very muscular, with a raw-boned face and a firm, attractive mouth.

Isabeau felt a familiar itch running under her skin. Her cat stretched sensuously and all at once her body felt sensitive and achy, coiling tight in need. She had the sudden urge to rub herself all over his very masculine body.

Don't you dare! she threatened her cat. *I thought you didn't like him.*

It was hot in the garden, too hot. Her skin felt too tight. Her nipples peaked and rubbed against her bra. She felt sweat bead and then trickle down the valley between her breasts. She raised a hand to sweep back the heavy fall of hair spilling around her face. She was so sensitive that just the touch almost burned her skin, like the lick of a tongue. She swallowed and caught him staring at her throat with hunger in his eyes. The action of bringing up her hand to her hair was seductive. Had she done it on purpose? It brought attention to her breasts and beaded nipples.

Her cat moved, an alluring enticement, meant to tempt any male in her vicinity to help her mate prove to her she was choosing the right partner. Isabeau knew exactly what the hussy was doing too. She hissed, trying to show her displeasure to the male.

"You shouldn't have come out here unescorted."

"I'm not alone," Isabeau hastened to point out. "I'm here with Imelda's grandfather and his personal protector."

"An old man and his weak bodyguard? You think that's enough to stop me from taking what I want?"

She sent a quick, furtive glance toward the forest to see if Jeremiah had a clear shot. He didn't. Not unless he'd moved position. She moistened her lips. "I'm not ready."

"But you're close." Ottila moved his head toward her, the slow freeze-frame motion of a large hunting cat, and inhaled her, taking her charismatic scent into his lungs. "Very close." He reached out and ran his finger across her breast.

Her cat went insane, throwing herself forward, shrieking a protest, drowning out Isabeau's fear and replacing it with rage. She leapt back, swinging at him, claws bursting, skin burning as stiletto claws burst through her fingers and raked his arm. No male leopard touched a female until she was ready, even she knew that.

"Keep your hands to yourself." The claws were gone that quick, leaving her hands aching and feeling swollen.

Blood dripped down his arm. He looked at the claw marks and then smiled at her. "You marked me, *Isabeau*." Deliberately he hissed her name with a possessive curl of his lip.

"You're lucky I didn't kill you for touching me," she snapped. "You have no manners."

"I'm leopard. Same as you."

"And I'm protected. You touch me and even your boss will want you dead because my people will demand your head on a platter."

"She's only my boss as long as I want to work for her. And those men should know better than to let you wander around unprotected." He reached for her belly, undeterred by the claw marks on his arm, settling his palm over her womb. "My child will grow here."

She slapped his arm away a second time and retreated a couple of steps, trying to get out into the open, facing the trees where she was certain Jeremiah waited with his rifle.

13

"WHAT happened to your face?" Imelda asked as she caught up with Conner. He walked directly behind Philip as the man led the way to his private den. "You look as if you had a fight with a large cat." Her voice shook with excitement. She reached out as she kept pace to touch one of the long scars.

Conner caught her wrist and pulled her hand down. "I did. A leopard."

He felt her shiver. "Really? How frightening."

He shrugged. "It happened. I'm alive." He stepped in front of her, cutting her off before she could enter the room. "Wait here until I give the okay."

Her eyes glittered. "I'm not used to taking orders."

"Then your men aren't doing their job," he said and turned his back on her.

Philip held the door open and Conner went through, followed by Rio. Felipe and Leonardo stayed with Elijah and Marcos. Their movements were coordinated and efficient and no one spoke. Elijah and Marcos paid no attention, used to their team sweeping rooms. Imelda pressed her hand to her heaving breast.

"How long have you employed him?" she asked Marcos.

Marcos frowned. "Conner? Several years. He's a good man. I knew his family." Her leopards were nowhere close to smell the lie. Her security team had made their show and now, feeling comfortable in Philip's house, they'd scattered throughout the rooms to let the crowd know she was an important person and they were keeping an eye on everything. She had one guard, and he wasn't leopard.

Elijah glanced at Marcos, a little worried that both the rogue leopards were missing. Their primary concern should have been Imelda's safety. They didn't know Marcos or Elijah or their intentions.

"How long have you had your security?" Elijah asked.

Her lashes veiled her eyes. "About two years. They're . . . exceptional."

His eyebrows shot up. Marcos smirked. "Really?" Elijah said. "I don't see them here where they should be, watching out for you. They wouldn't stay in my employ for ten minutes."

"Nor mine," Marcos agreed.

Anger slithered over her face. She didn't like being embarrassed and she could see the point both had made was valid. She glared at her guard and snapped her fingers. He immediately began to speak into the radio, telling the two rogues Imelda requested their presence immediately.

"They've gotten sloppy," Elijah continued. "They should be on you every moment. Conner, or any one of these men, would never stand for being away from you, even if you wanted it. They would have made certain you signed a binding contract with them to that effect. If you refused, they wouldn't take you on as a client."

"Marcos, didn't you tell Philip that one of the guards was your nephew?" Imelda asked.

Marcos and Elijah exchanged a knowing look. She'd made a mistake and didn't realize it. The conversation had taken place before Imelda had arrived, which meant they'd been taped and she'd already viewed those tapes before her arrival—which they'd suspected would happen.

"That is correct. Two of them are. And one is related to Elijah."

Imelda shrugged one slim shoulder. "You see, your help is family and no one else can be fully trusted to do the job."

"Conner is not family, but is fully trusted," Elijah objected. "But of course, we obviously think differently. I know my men wouldn't betray me and I don't worry if they overhear business discussions. They would carry the details to their grave."

She couldn't miss the smirk exchanged between the two men. The head of her security team had made her look foolish in front of the two men she wanted most to impress. She would not forgive that easily. For a moment, black rage glittered in her eyes, and then she resumed her mask of congeniality.

Conner emerged, his expression unreadable. "That room is not suitable for a discussion, Marcos." There was finality in his words. A command, not a suggestion.

Imelda was clearly intrigued by the way he ordered his employer. Conner had studied every detail of her personality from information Rio had gathered and she wanted a strong male, but also wanted the control. Her men didn't last long. And her security detail probably went through

hell with her. A man like Conner Vega would appeal to her
in every way. He was clearly loyal to a fault, in complete
control and dedicated to serving his employer. And he'd
bested her leopards.

"That's ridiculous," Imelda argued, more because she
wanted to challenge Conner, make him notice her, than
for any other reason. "We conduct all our business in that
room."

Conner's impassive gaze flicked to her and then returned
to Marcos. "The room is hot."

There was a small silence. Marcos slowly turned his
head to stare at Imelda, his friendly demeanor dissolving.
Elijah put his glass down and faced her and there was no
trace of friendliness. Suddenly he looked every inch his
reputation. Imelda was very aware of the other bodyguards,
moving into positions where they could stop anyone from
coming in from any direction.

"I don't know what that means," Imelda said, trying
to stay calm. No one had ever challenged her authority
before—not and lived. Right at that moment she felt closer
to death than she ever had before. It was both terrifying and
exhilarating. The threat was in the burning gold of Conner's
eyes. He looked impersonal, yet so dangerous. Her body
flooded with adrenaline, but also with sudden hunger.

"It means," Marcos explained impatiently, "that the
room is wired."

"I thought we were having a friendly conversation," Elijah said. "Marcos assured me of that."

Comprehension dawned. Imelda had been the one
to suggest to Philip that he take advantage of his sexual
hobby and make his servants available to his wealthier and
diplomatic "friends." Videotaping indiscretions, especially
any fetishes or sadistic traits, made for instant obedience.

Money and favors poured in. Fury burned through her. She spun around on Philip.

"How dare you!" There could be no mistake that she didn't know he was taping their conversations. Imelda had her own sexual excesses. Whipping a man or woman and watching their skin stripe while they screamed in pain was such a turn-on, and she could rarely refuse herself the pleasure, especially if she was sharing it with someone who appreciated the sight, such as Philip. He was a connoisseur of torture.

He backed away from her. "Imelda. You know I wouldn't."

She looked from him to Conner's implacable mask. Who to believe? Would Philip really be that stupid as to risk everything they had together? She fed him clients. She shared his sexual proclivities. He was terrified of her with good reason. "Show me," she challenged Conner.

He didn't obey her command. Instead he looked at Marcos, who nodded. That put her on edge. This was her territory and between Philip and Martin Suma, her head of security, she looked weak. Damn them for this. She needed someone like Conner running her security.

Conner indicated for Philip to lead the way back into the room. Philip glanced at his watch. "I have guests. If you want to tear apart the room looking for nonexistent equipment, you're welcome to do so, but without me."

"Philip," Imelda hissed between her clenched teeth. "Get in that room." She wanted to kill him on the spot. Where the hell was Martin? Or Ottila? Damn them as well. She glared at her lone bodyguard. "Get them here now," she snapped.

Philip reluctantly went into the room, aware that Imelda would be furious when she found out what he'd

·done. He didn't understand how the security guard had
known. There was no evidence, there couldn't be. So
how? He despised Marco's personal protector. Smug
bastard. Imelda was already drooling over him like the
bitch she was. He stepped back to watch the man play out
his little drama. There was no way he could really know.
But uneasiness had set in. Even if the man wasn't able to
prove it, the seed of doubt had been sown in Imelda. And
that meant he'd have to leave fast. He'd built up millions.
He was prepared, but this place had been perfect for a
man like him.

Conner ran his hand, palm out along the wall, his expression still unchanged. If Imelda didn't know that the
conversations in the room were taped, and he was certain
she didn't know, he hadn't smelled a lie, then that meant her
rogues hadn't told her. Why not? Why hadn't her leopards
warned her? They had to have heard the click as the record-
ers came on at the sound of voices. There was a faint hum
as the conversation was recorded. What were the leopards
up to? And why weren't they protecting her now? They had
to have known the recorder would be discovered.

Isabeau. His stomach knotted. Were they after Isabeau?
She hadn't pressed the little panic button built into her
watch yet. He snapped a quick commanding look at Elijah,
uncaring in that moment if the others caught it.

Elijah waited a heartbeat. Two. He turned and looked
toward the door rather casually and then down to his watch.
"My cousin has been gone a long while."

"Your cousin?" Imelda echoed as if she'd forgotten
Isabeau.

Conner realized she probably had. She didn't notice
anything or anyone unless it pertained directly to her. Her
world was very narrow and self-involved.

"I want her found now," Elijah snapped at Felipe.

Felipe turned abruptly on his heel and left.

Imelda sighed. "This is insane. The girl is in no danger and there is no one recording our conversations. She's with my grandfather. He'll see that no harm comes to her."

Conner smashed his fist through the paneling, not bothering to find the hidden switch to reveal the audio equipment. It was much more satisfying and dramatic to rip through the flawless wall.

Imelda gasped and spun around to glare accusingly at Philip. "You treacherous worm," she snapped. "Just who were you planning on giving the tapes to? The police?"

"I imagine you have the police firmly in your pocket," Marcos said and sank into a chair, pulling a cigar from his pocket. "Do you mind, Imelda?"

She drew in a deep breath and forced herself back under control. "No, of course not, Marcos. Be my guest." She said it deliberately. There was no escape for Philip. He was a dead man already and he had to know it. He might be foolish enough to try to get his security force to go to war with hers, but he had amateurs for guards. Her men were combat trained. And she had the leopards. No one else had the leopards . . . unless . . . She really looked at Conner, speculation in her shrewd eyes.

Conner met her stare with burning golden eyes, leopard's eyes. He watched her gasp and then try to cover her pleased knowledge. He knew her brain was racing, trying to decide about the others. They had similar builds. They all carried that magnetic aura of danger. And she probably thought there was some kind of hierarchy in the leopard species and he was somehow superior to Martin.

Try loyalty. He felt contempt for a woman who wouldn't recognize that if a leopard was willing to betray his own people, he would be willing to betray his employer twice as fast. She should know that.

"Philip, do sit down," she snapped, tearing her gaze away from Conner. "You're not going anywhere until we sort this out."

"I had no idea that recorder was there," Philip whined. "Do you think I have a death wish? I sit in here and talk with you. Anything that condemns you, condemns me. You have more on me than any other living person on earth. What would be the point, Imelda? Someone set me up."

He was lying—he knew about the tape, but the setup was a possibility. If he hadn't thought of it on his own, and he was right, what would be the point, then someone else had persuaded him to tape the conversations. The police? Was someone not already in Imelda's pocket secretly investigating her? Conner turned the possibility over in his mind. Not likely. She had too many officials on her payroll and she would have gotten wind of it. No, it was someone else.

"Someone set me up," Imelda mimicked. "Do you expect me to believe that, Philip?" Now that she knew Marcos and Elijah believed she was innocent, she could enjoy watching Philip squirm. He loved controlling others. He loved watching them beg him, try to please him, crawl to him and kiss his feet while he held pain and death over them. She'd watched him kill numerous times. Once he'd acted so lovingly to a woman after marking her viciously with the whip that she'd believed his act, all the way to the moment that he'd cut her throat while he ejaculated in her. The woman's eyes had stayed on her the entire time and it had been . . . delicious . . . watching her die.

Imelda smiled at Philip. Cold. Pleased. She would show the world what happened to anyone who betrayed her. He broke out in a sweat, fear permeating the room.

"Perhaps we should close the door for privacy," she suggested to her lone bodyguard.

"Kill them," Philip screamed to his guard. "Kill them all." He dove behind his chair.

His guard brought up his automatic weapon, his face a mask of fear and determination. Conner killed him, swiping a claw across his throat and ripping the gun from his hand even as Rio and Leonardo took Marcos and Elijah to the floor, covering them. Both had drawn their guns, but they aimed at Philip and Imelda's lone guard.

She rose gracefully, stepped over the dead man and closed the door. "Very impressive. How did you do that?" She indicated the torn throat.

Conner didn't answer. He kept the others covered while Rio and Leonardo helped Marcos and Elijah to their feet. Rio yanked Philip up and all but threw him into a chair. Philip landed hard and pressed a trembling hand over his quivering mouth.

"Thank you," Imelda said, flashing Conner a coy smile. "You just saved my life."

He didn't point out that he'd saved his own as well as his entire team. He barely inclined his head and for the first time allowed his gaze to drift lazily, a little insolently, over her body. He saw her breasts heave and her red-tipped nail traced a line from her throat to the swell of her breast. She shifted in the chair, allowing her gown to slide up her thigh. There were no underwear lines anywhere on the gown. She smiled at him, her tongue touching her lower lip.

"I suggest we leave immediately," Rio said.

"Whatever for?" Imelda asked, still looking at Conner.

"There's a dead body on the floor, Imelda," Marcos pointed out. "I don't want my man questioned by the police, nor do I want to have anything to do with this. We can

meet another time—perhaps in a more appropriate setting."
He started to rise.

"No, no," Imelda frowned. "We can easily take care of
the body. It's no problem, is it, Philip?" She sent him a
poisonous smile. "Philip is a master at disposing of bodies,
aren't you, sweetie?"

The man was so pale he looked like a ghost. "Imelda . . ."

"Don't," she hissed, the smile vanishing. "You betrayed
me."

"I didn't."

She dismissed him with a wave of her hand and looked
pointedly at her bodyguard. He immediately went to Philip
and smashed the butt of his gun on the man's head.

Imelda smiled again. "I think we're okay to talk, Marcos. I'll handle the body and no one will ever know there
was a problem. Philip will be found dead and the police
will discover that he had quite the graveyard going. All
those missing women over the years just might be found."
She crossed one leg over the other and swung her ankle,
nearly kicking the dead guard where he lay on the floor in
front of her.

Conner had no idea whose bodies she was talking about,
but the thought that she knew women were being killed and
she did nothing about it sickened him. He had to leave soon
or he was going to blow it and kill her right there before
they ever got into her compound and found the children.
He considered it. If she was dead, would anyone in her
employ free the children, or kill them? It was too big of a
risk to take.

"No, no." Marcos held up his hand. "We have to go
now, Imelda. I'm not taking any chances with my man." He
pushed himself out of the chair and waved her off. "Elijah,
we have to go now."

Rio was already on the move, indicating for Imelda's guard to get out of their way.

"Come to my home, Marcos," she invited, desperate not to allow her opportunity to slip away. She could do business with both perhaps, and she wanted to see Conner again, have the chance to lure him away from Marcos. With Philip gone, she'd need a partner. He seemed cold enough, ruthless enough and just dangerous enough to be the one she'd been looking for.

Marcos hesitated.

"Both of you. And the little cousin. She seems to get along with my grandfather. He can entertain her while we talk."

While she spoke, her hand stroked her throat. Her eyes were on Conner, bright with promise. He didn't respond, but his gaze slid over her, dwelled for a moment on her breasts, as though judging her. She went hot, flushing, going wet with just that single almost contemptuous perusal. So offhand. Like she meant nothing, but he was interested, she was certain of it.

She softened her voice and forced herself to look at Marcos. "Come. You'll find the accommodations to your liking."

"It's a great distance to travel, Imelda," Marcos hedged, forcing her hand.

"I have plenty of room for your entire party. Bedrooms are empty and you would be welcome to stay a few days." She wanted the time with his bodyguard. "Don't think of it as work. You can play all you want. We have everything you can imagine or need."

Marcos turned to his friend. "Elijah?"

Elijah shrugged. "Give her a couple of days to take care of this business," he indicated the body and Philip. "I can see what Isabeau is up to and then we'll be free to take Imelda up on her offer." His cool black eyes met hers. "You can give directions to my men."

Imelda sucked in her breath, wildly excited. What could have been a disaster had turned out to be perfect.

Elijah looked at his watch. "Where the hell is Isabeau?"

She hadn't heard the man swear. Or worry edge his voice. Nothing had gotten to him, but that one little sentence betrayed his weakness. Isabeau. The silly nothing cousin. She should have been more careful to instruct her grandfather to really watch over her. Overlooking details like that could ruin one's plans. Isabeau, a potential fly in the ointment.

"Shane, please find out why Martin or Ottila haven't answered. I want to make certain that my grandfather and Elijah's dear little cousin are being looked after." She rose gracefully. "You stay here and lock the door, keep everyone out." She smiled up at the two men. "I'll take you to the garden and personally see you out. Don't worry about the mess."

"There was a young lady, a server . . ." Marcos broke off.

"Teresa," Imelda supplied, showing once again she'd had access to the video before she'd arrived.

"I'd very much like her to accompany us."

Imelda's smile was pure canary. "That can be arranged, Marcos." She started to step out into the hall, but Conner dropped a hand on her shoulder to prevent her leaving. She looked up at him over her shoulder, her expression coy, one eyebrow raised. Deliberately she looked at the hand on her shoulder.

"I go first." His voice was firm. Commanding, leaving

no doubt that he meant to be obeyed. The hand remained
on her shoulder. He waited until she felt the heat spreading. "To make certain it's safe for you." He added the last
two words deliberately to connect them. She'd repeat those
words over and over to herself, convinced he was sending
her a private message, convinced she had a chance to lure
him away from his employer. What better way than using
sexual attraction?

Imelda flushed and inclined her head, princess to peas-
ant. He removed his hand, but slowly, allowing his palm to
slide in a caress across the nape of her neck. She shivered.
His cat roared with rage, spitting and growling, prowling
close to the surface so that he felt the ache in his muscles
and jaw.

She caught the nightglow in his eyes as they went
completely cat, the burning, fixed stare unnerving her. He
forced his leopard under control. *Soon,* he promised and
moved past her into the hall. As he pushed past, he let his
body slide against hers, skin to skin. Her gasp was audible,
her gaze hot, no mistaking the sexual intent. He got a whiff
of her arousal and it sickened him. He felt dirty. How could
he go to Isabeau after touching Imelda, letting her believe
that he would take her to bed?

Cursing under his breath, he swept the area and announced it clear. He led the way to the garden, not looking
at Imelda again. He could smell her. Hear her breathing.
That was bad enough.

JEREMIAH swore softly and shifted position for the third
time, praying he could get a clearer line of vision. He'd
seen the rogue leopard. Ottila, the quiet one. Suma gave
all the orders, and strutted around like a big shot. Jeremiah

had been impressed with him, especially when he'd flashed all the money around. Now he wasn't so certain Suma was the one to watch, not after being around Conner and Rio and the others.

"Come on, Isabeau. Get out into the open," he whispered softly. "You know I'm here, right? Come on, honey, just get out of that little section."

He had a clear shot to almost any line on the southern side, with the exception of the area she'd chosen to enter. What had possessed her to go into an area so thick with brush he had no hope of coming to her aid? The moment he spotted Ottila slinking around the garden, deliberately avoiding the old man in the wheelchair and his guard, he knew the rogue was up to no good. Isabeau was too close to emerging. Even *he* had been affected, in spite of his moral code.

He wiped the sweat beading on his forehead onto his sleeve. "Come on, Isabeau. Show yourself. Get him out in the open."

The leaves of a large bush swayed slightly, giving him a direction, but he couldn't see his target. He waited, holding his breath, never taking his eye from his glasses. He knew the distance, the wind, every variable he might need, every calculation, but he couldn't actually get the target in sight. He knew he was there. He could visualize him. He could taste him. But he couldn't see him.

"Damn. Damn. Damn." He wasn't going to fail, not the first time he had a chance of proving himself. And if he failed, they'd lose Isabeau. Aside from the fact that Conner would kill him, he didn't want anything to happen to her. He liked her—like a sister, of course.

It was starting to drizzle—a steady, but fine rain that made the tree branch slippery. He shifted, trying to peer through foliage. His heart leapt. He caught a glimpse of blue. Isabeau definitely had been wearing a blue dress. He kept his gaze fixed on that small bit of material. She moved again, inch by slow inch.

"Good girl," he murmured. "Bring him to Papa."

Now he could see a vague shadow in the deep foliage. Black. Ottila was wearing black, but many of the security guards were. It seemed to be a popular color. Even Elijah had changed to a black shirt. Frustrated, he forced a deep breath. Most of his job was patience. He knew he could make the shot if he could just get a visual. He breathed away the fear for Isabeau and irritation that he didn't have a visual. It would come. She was working it.

"I'm here, honey," he assured. "Bring him to me."

The blue material was on the move again. She wasn't running. Good girl. She had courage. She took another step and this time he could see her profile. She hadn't removed the barrette from her hair, although her hair was messy, strands tumbling around her face. She didn't look toward him; she kept her attention focused on the man he was certain was Ottila following her.

A hand came into view and pressed, fingers splayed wide on her belly. He knew the significance of that with a woman in the throes of the Han Vol Dan. She slapped the hand away and retreated a few more steps until she was fully in the open. Jeremiah smiled and fit his eye to the scope.

"Now I have you, you bastard. Touch her again and you're a dead man."

The wind shifted and he caught the faint scent of cat. Without hesitating, he leapt, taking his rifle with him. Behind him, something hit the branch he'd been in hard enough to shake the tree. He landed in a crouch and sprinted fast, slinging the rifle over his shoulder. He managed to make it into the dense foliage before he dropped to one knee and fit the rifle against his shoulder. He let his cat take over, senses flaring out to read the night.

He was being hunted. Definitely leopard. Probably Martin Suma. "Come on, you bastard," he hissed between his teeth. There was no sound, but he wouldn't expect that. Leopards didn't make sound. They could creep into a house and select a victim in a bedroom, or even a living room where people were gathered watching television, and drag him out unnoticed. It happened more often than one would think at the edge of the jungle. He wasn't going to hear Suma. And he probably wouldn't smell him either.

He stayed low, keeping very still, making no noise. Suma had to know he was dealing with leopard. And he'd probably caught his scent. He wouldn't expect much opposition from an untrained kid. That was the only advantage Jeremiah had. He waited, his heart pounding, expecting any moment for Suma to drop on him from above. His gaze continually swept the trees overhead.

The scent of wet fur hit his nostrils and he turned, squeezing the trigger at the leopard emerging from the brush just to his left. He rolled, shot again from a prone position and kept rolling. The leopard grunted in pain, roared once, and thrashed. Jeremiah jumped to his feet, bringing up the rifle a third time, but the leopard crawled into the brush. He knew better than to follow. He could see a trail of smeared blood. He'd scored, but it was no kill shot. A wounded leopard was extremely dangerous.

Swearing, he shouldered the gun and went up the tree fast, grateful for the hours Rio and Conner had forced him to keep practicing. If anything had happened to Isabeau, he'd never forgive himself. Now he had to watch his back trail as well as try to keep her from being attacked and possibly kidnapped. Where the hell was everyone?

"I DIDN'T catch your name," Isabeau said, stalling for time. She'd drawn him out in the open and surely she was safe now. If she could stall him long enough, Alberto or Harry might come looking for her. Or she could try screaming, but she was afraid that might provoke him.

"Ottila Zorba." His eyes had gone mostly eerie green-yellow, a cat's eyes glowing in the night. He stepped closer. "Come with me without fighting. Don't make me kill the old man."

She swallowed hard. "I'm not ready. I would fight you to the death and you know I would. Why would you think your cat would allow that?"

He smiled. "Eventually your cat will emerge and when she does, she'll need a mate."

But not you. Never you. She wouldn't let that happen. She was gaining control of her cat. The little hussy was definitely feeling the effects of her heat, but she was obeying Isabeau more readily.

"And then what, Mr. Zorba? Do you think we'll live happily ever after?"

He smiled and it wasn't pleasant. "At least I'll be happy. Whether you are or not depends entirely on how much you choose to cooperate."

He reached for her, his hands curling around her upper arms with enormous strength. Instead of fighting, she reached up to try to yank the barrette from her hair. He laughed and leaned close. "Did you think your friend was going to shoot me? We swept the trees the minute we realized you were leopard. Of course you'd have someone in the canopy. He's probably dead by now. Martin doesn't miss."

She closed her eyes briefly, her heart squeezing down hard, afraid. "So he's helping you out." She tried to pull away from him but the movement only tightened his grip on her.

He leered at her. "We share. We always share."

She shuddered. "Isn't Imelda enough for you? She's just as perverted as you."

He laughed. "She liked it all right, but she's disgusting. And she isn't leopard. After a couple of times, we couldn't stomach her."

She stopped struggling and let him lead her a couple of steps. She breathed deep with both steps and summoned her cat. To her shock, the female leopard answered, roaring her rage, the sound echoing through the garden, claws bursting through her fingertips and strength coiling inside her, allowing her to twist free, raking and ripping through flesh. Twisting and turning with the cat's flexible spine, she fought her way out of his grip. Hot blood streaked across the trees and splattered over vines and leaves, droplets sprinkling over her dress.

"Fucking wildcat," he snarled, "you're going to pay for that."

She tilted her chin. "Go ahead and kill me. See what your friend says."

"Oh, I'm not going to kill you, but I have a lot of ways I can make you sorry. I've learned a thing or two from Imelda."

Her stomach lurched. She tried to remember what Conner had said. She'd backed away from Ottila earlier to get him to follow her out into the open. But backing away would draw him to her and she'd be off balance. She needed to step to the side, keep her feet under her shoulders, not be flat-footed. He wouldn't be caught by her cat twice.

Ottila reached for her again, and the sound of a cocking shotgun was loud. Ottila turned toward the sound without expression. He didn't bother to wipe the blood from his face or chest. It dripped from the claw marks on his arms. He smiled at Harry. "Are you sure you want to be a part of this, Harry? Just walk away and you'll stay alive. I won't only kill you, but I'll kill your boss as well. This isn't your business."

"She was put in my care," Harry said. "Isabeau, walk back to me."

"Don't you move, Isabeau," Ottila hissed. "I'll kill him before he gets a shot off and then I'll have to kill the old man."

"You kill Alberto, and Imelda will never let you live. She'll hunt you down, and nowhere will be safe for you. She'll kill every man, woman and child you care about," Harry promised.

Isabeau held up her hand. "Harry, I don't want you and Alberto in the middle of this. Elijah will come after me. And his team is lethal. I'll go with him."

"I don't think so, Isabeau."

A new voice came from behind Ottila. Confident. Accented. So very familiar. Isabeau looked past Ottila and saw Felipe and she couldn't help the relief bursting through her. She'd seen Felipe move and he was fast. Very fast.

"Harry, thank you. I can take it from here. Don't leave the old man alone," Felipe said.

Ottila whirled around and this time he held his palms out in surrender. He waited until Harry nodded and sauntered away before he addressed Felipe. "I can see I'm going to have to work a little harder to get my female."

"You can choose a different one."

"She has so many scents on her, I can't find one particular one. That tells me she isn't mated and therefore I have just as much right as any other to try to mate her."

"We're her family and we say stay the hell away from her."

Ottila moved into the brush, angling away from Isabeau. "She's a little hellcat."

"I see you didn't fare well with your courtship."

"Hellcats are the best kind," Ottila said. "They last longer and give you strong cubs." He looked Isabeau in the eye. "You haven't seen the last of me."

Isabeau met his gaze, letting her cat look at him. "I hope for your sake I have."

He saluted her and began to walk away, turning at the last moment to send a smirk to Felipe. "You'd better check on your boy in the trees. The little hellcat gave the signal to shoot and he didn't take the shot. Now what do you suppose that means?" He sounded smug.

Isabeau blinked back tears. The idea of Jeremiah in the hands of Martin Suma made her ill. He would have no mercy.

Felipe merely smiled back. "I think you'd better check on your partner. Shots were fired. The boy doesn't miss."

Felipe did a quick examination of Isabeau. "You all right?"

She nodded. "Shaken up, that's all. He didn't hurt me."

"You have bruises on your arms. And blood all over your dress." He took a step after Ottila, as if he might fight him after all.

"His blood." Isabeau caught his arm. "Don't. Let's just get out of here. I want to make sure Alberto Cortez is all right and I have to tell you what I found. This place is a burial ground. I'm not kidding."

"That doesn't surprise me. Nothing about this place or these people surprises me."

"Do you really think Jeremiah is okay?"

"He's a damn good shot, Isabeau. He'll be a huge asset with a little experience."

She noticed he didn't exactly answer her question. They continued along the path leading back to where she'd left Alberto. As they hurried, following the stream, Harry appeared around a sweeping bend, pushing Alberto's chair. The older man had the shotgun across his lap and looked prepared to use it.

"Where is that guard?" he demanded. "Are you all right, Isabeau?"

She nodded her head. "I'm fine. Thanks, Harry. I think this place gets to people. Everyone's acting crazy. Please don't shoot anyone on my account."

"I'm going home," Alberto declared. "Now that I know you're safe. I suggest you do the same. Harry, call my driver. I hope we meet again, Isabeau."

"Your garden was lovely," she said.

Felipe put a hand to his ear, listening to the voice coming over the radio. "We're leaving, Isabeau. Elijah said to take you out front to the car." He took her elbow.

To her dismay, the server, Teresa, was already in the car, looking as though she was going to cry. Isabeau climbed in wordlessly next to her, worried about Jeremiah, afraid for Teresa and wondering what exactly was going on.

14

ISABEAU stared out the window as the car moved rapidly down the long, winding drive, avoiding everyone's eyes. She knew they could smell Ottila's scent on her. There were spots of blood on her dress, impossible to hide in the close confines of the vehicle. She heard Conner's expletive when he saw the dark bruises marring her skin and the blood on her dress, but she didn't look at him. She knew she was at her limit and just needed space. They all needed to give her space—especially Conner. Philip Sobre, Imelda Cortez and the rogue leopards disgusted her. She felt dirty and just wanted to find a good, hot shower.

The vehicle slowed and Leonardo shoved the door open. Jeremiah exploded out of the thicker forest and raced through the thinner stand of trees and brush. He was about halfway to the SUV when something heavy dropped from the trees on top of him, slamming him to the ground. Fur and teeth and man tumbled and rolled, thrashing. The rifle went flying.

Teresa began to scream and Elijah leaned over very casually and clipped her, at the same time pressing his thumb hard into a pressure point so that she slumped forward unconscious, her face a mask of horror. A roar of fury shook the SUV, and Felipe slammed on the breaks even as Conner leapt through the open door, stripping as he shifted, the vehicle spinning around and coming to a halt.

Isabeau blinked, shocked at the speed with which Conner made the transformation on the run, shedding his clothes at the same time. She'd seen Jeremiah practicing and she'd seen Felipe working with him, but it hadn't prepared her for the actual dizzying speed. She wouldn't have believed her own eyes had she not known the truth about the species. He shifted into a leopard so fast she wouldn't have been able to process that he'd ever been a man.

Leonardo and Rio also jumped out of the car, nearly before it stopped spinning, but they were searching the trees for a sniper, back to back, sharp gazes examining every inch of the canopy, using their animal senses for knowledge, rifles ready.

Conner was on the leopard before it realized he was even there, swiping at the heaving sides with a huge paw, knocking the furious cat away from Jeremiah's torn body. Elijah sprinted through the trees as the two leopards came together, snarling, rolling, flexible spines nearly bent in half as they raked and tore at each other.

"Damn it, wake up, Isabeau!" Rio snapped. "Grab a rifle."

His voice jerked her out of her shock. She didn't hesitate, but yanked a rifle from the open trunk on the floor and jumped down. "Where?"

"Get as close as you can to them. If you get a shot, take it," Rio ordered.

She ran across the intervening space, her heart in her throat. Just in her line of vision, Elijah bent and lifted Jeremiah, shifting him to his shoulder in a fireman's carry. Blood dripped down his arm and back. Puncture wounds dotted his body. Elijah flashed past her and to her dismay it looked as if Jeremiah wasn't breathing.

A blood-streaked Suma leapt, twisting, using the leopard's flexible spine to turn in midair as Conner went up on his hind legs and anchored claws in the hindquarters, yanking the leopard down. Suma nearly folded in half, slamming powerful claws into Conner's neck and side. Conner rolled, ramming into Suma, knocking him off his feet so the two leopards were a tangle of fur, claws and teeth. The roar of the two male leopards filled the forest.

Isabeau put the rifle to her shoulder just as a shot rang out and bark splintered from a tree trunk where Conner had been a half second earlier. If he hadn't rolled, the shot might have hit his head. Her gaze jumped to the trees, trying to find where the shot had come from.

Instantly, Rio and Leonardo sprayed the canopy in the distance, obviously having no problem figuring out the trajectory of the shot.

"Shoot the son of a bitch, Isabeau," Rio yelled.

She jerked her attention back to the ferocious fight between the two leopards. They were locked together in mortal combat, rolling over and over, their tails lashing, the sounds horrifying. She felt almost surreal, as if she was in the throes of a nightmare and not real life. There was no way to get off a shot and not take a chance of wounding or killing Conner.

"I'm trying," she snapped back.

With the two bodies wrapped so tightly around one another, she couldn't distinguish one from the other.

They looked like a dizzying sea of spots, blurring as they slammed into one another, broke apart and came together again. The eyes appeared as simply two more rosettes lost in the midst of a thousand spots, except for the intensity. Smoldering fire. Shocking intelligence. Cunning. Rage such as she'd never seen.

This was the man who had killed Marisa Vega, Conner's mother. The sheer fury of Conner's leopard drove the other leopard off his feet repeatedly. The claws tore great rips in the sides and belly. Suma shuddered and tried to escape, but Conner's leopard would have none of it. He seemed oblivious to the rending tears in his own body; instead, he seemed determined to literally tear Suma to pieces. It was only Suma's strength and experience, a male in his prime, that kept him from being instantly killed. He seemed to know he was in trouble, and Ottila, who, despite the assault from Rio's and Leonardo's rifles, kept up his own intermittent fire, trying to aid his partner.

"Damn it, Isabeau, we're going to get caught out here. Fucking finish him," Rio snarled.

Leopard emotions were intense, and right now, she couldn't see how either was going to give ground. Blood ran down the sides of one of them, and she realized after the first heart-stopping moment that this was how to identify Suma. Jeremiah must have shot him. His own blood, and that of Jeremiah, coated the fur. The red streaks were beginning to transfer to Conner's coat, but he had nowhere near the same amount on him.

She took a breath and concentrated, blocking out everything the way Conner had told her to. At first she heard the roars, and growls, the shots, another bullet scattering leaves and dirt beside the two leopards. Then she was in a tunnel and there was only the leopard's blood-encrusted fur and

her. No one else. Nothing else. She aimed for the back of
the neck.

Her heart pounded. Her mouth went dry. She was terrified of hitting Conner. The two furious leopards moved so
fast, tangled, came apart, tangled again. So fast. Too fast. If
she shot the wrong one . . . She took another breath, willing the bullet to go exactly where she put it, and squeezed
the trigger.

Suma reared up, his eyes yellow and raging with hatred.
So much hatred. She shivered as Conner took advantage,
slashing at the exposed belly, ripping deep. Suma tumbled
over and lay still, his eyes open, staring at her. His tongue
hung out, his sides heaving. Blood bubbled around his
muzzle. Conner went for the kill, sinking teeth into the
throat and holding, suffocating the leopard.

A volley of shots rained down, clipping Isabeau's skirt,
throwing up dirt around her, striking along Conner's flank
so that he roared and whirled to face his new enemy. His
enraged gaze landed on her. Her heart skipped a beat and
then began pounding. The leopard, with one last act of hatred and vengeance, ripped open the exposed belly, turned
fully toward her and lowered his head into stalking mode,
his gaze burning through her.

"Calm him down," Rio shouted. "And both of you get
the hell out of there. We can't get to the shooter. The best
we can do is keep him off you."

"*Calm him down?*" she echoed, feeling a little faint. If
Rio had been standing in front of her, she might have considered violence. "Are you crazy?"

The leopard, covered in blood, fur and flesh torn,
crouched lower and took one step toward her in the freeze-
frame motion that struck fear in the heart of prey. She knew,
as long as she lived, she would never forget those piercing

eyes, burning with pure rage. His muzzle and face were smeared with blood, as were his teeth.

"Conner." Her voice shook. She lowered the muzzle of the rifle and held out her hand to him. "I'm so sorry, baby. It's over now. Let's get out of here. Come with me."

The leopard snarled, his nose wrinkling into a savage display. His powerful jaw opened, showing his four canines prominently, teeth used to stab and hold prey during a kill. She knew that the gap behind each of the canines allowed the leopard to sink his teeth deep during a killing bite. His incisors could easily scrape flesh from bones and the side teeth could shear through skin and muscle like the sharpest of blades.

With each slow step, that powerful jaw and mouthful of teeth came closer to her until she felt the heat of his breath blasting her face. Again she pushed aside everything until there was only the leopard and her.

"Conner." Deliberately she used his name, calling him back from the throes of black anger. There was no humanity in those eyes. No love, or recognition. "Conner." She chose love over fear or anger, reaching for him with trembling fingers.

Before she could connect with him to sink her fingers into his blood-stained fur, he swiped at her with a large paw. A streak of fire raced up her arm. She gasped, for a moment unable to catch her breath with the staggering pain rushing up her arm. Fear shook her, but she refused to break the stare, summoning her cat.

Now or never, you little hussy. Deserting isn't an option. Get out here and do your thing. Be alluring. Entice him into that car.

She tried to remember what she'd felt like in the garden when the wave of heat had rushed over her, leaving her desperate for a man between her legs. Right now, she wanted to run for her life, not stay facing this snarling beast. She didn't dare look at her arm, but she consoled herself with the thought that he could have just as easily made that warning a killing swipe across her very vulnerable throat.

Her leopard pushed closer to the surface, not in the throes of passion, but with a female's disdain of the male. She wasn't in the mood and she didn't want to be bothered. She leapt at the male, giving him a swipe of her own. As rebuffs went, it wasn't very impressive, but it shocked the male cat almost as much as it did Isabeau.

"Whoops," Isabeau withdrew her palm. It was stinging from the hard slap she'd delivered to the male's snarling face. *Sheesh! Are you out of your freaking mind?* she demanded of her cat. *Way to soothe him, smart one.* "Sorry about that."

The rage subsided a little in the burning eyes to be replaced by intelligence. She let her breath out, seeing that piercing, keen intellect was back. "Conner, there's a sniper in the canopy. We have to get out of here. Now."

He nudged her and she turned and ran, grateful for the covering fire Rio and Leonardo provided. She felt totally exposed with the leopard behind her and the sniper in the trees. She jumped into the SUV and scrambled all the way in to give the others as much room as possible. The leopard nearly crushed her, practically landing on top of her. He was already shifting, crawling into the third seat in the very back, where Elijah had Jeremiah stretched out, and was clearly breathing for him.

Leonardo entered and whipped around to help Marcos provide cover for Rio.

"Go!" Rio snapped as he slammed the door.

Before the word was out of his mouth, the SUV was fishtailing down the dirt road.

"How bad?" Grim-faced, Rio let himself look toward the very back. He couldn't see Jeremiah, but Elijah and now Conner were working on him.

"He'll need a doctor," Conner called out. "There used to be a doctor, one of ours, my mother would take me to, but it's been years. He lives about fifteen miles from the first cabin where we met."

Rio glanced at his watch. "What do you think, Felipe?"

"I can make it in twenty minutes."

"It will be close," Conner said. "Your call, Rio."

"He'd never be safe at a hospital. We know Imelda has too many people in her pocket. We just took out her number-one security. His partner is going to try to hunt us down. Jeremiah would be too vulnerable in a hospital. Do what you can to keep him alive."

Isabeau pressed a hand to her mouth to keep from protesting. They knew more about Imelda's operation than she did. They also knew the workings of a leopard's mind. She curled into a ball and shook uncontrollably, unable to stop the waves of nausea that swept through her.

"What about the woman? Teresa?" she made herself ask.

Rio sent the woman a quick glance. "We have to make certain she stays out. Leonardo, get the medicine kit. There's a knockout syringe in there."

"That's not what I meant. Why did you insist she come along?"

"She spent too much time with us and Conner defended her," Marcos explained. "First, she was in danger from Philip. Did you see his face when Conner interfered? I think he would have killed her after the party. If not, he certainly would have hurt her. And if Imelda was watching the tapes and this thing goes bad, she might very well think Teresa was a plant. Either way, it seemed safer to remove her from the situation and get her out of harm's way."

Isabeau remained silent, drawing up her knees and clasping her arms around them.

Marcos sent her a small smile. "Did you think I was a perverted old man?"

"You played the part very convincingly," she agreed, trying to smile back.

Rio looked at her for the first time. He made a sound, more leopard than human. "What the hell happened to you, Isabeau?" He yanked her arm out to look at the striped, welling blood. "Damn it, why didn't you say something? This is likely to become infected fast."

Conner raised up enough to look over the seat, his gaze narrowing on Isabeau's arm. "What happened?"

"You don't have any fucking control, you bastard," Rio snarled, "that's what happened."

"I need you focused, Conner," Elijah snapped. "We're not losing this boy."

Isabeau could see the anguish in Conner's eyes, the apology, and then he was back behind the seat, focused once more on Jeremiah. She was grateful that he wasn't looking at her. She needed to sort out all of her emotions. The entire evening had been horrendous.

She'd been the one to do this—to insist they go after Imelda Cortez. Nothing she'd seen tonight had made her change her mind—only strengthen her resolve—but she was unprepared for the level of immorality, the complete disregard for life, or even rights of other human beings. Imelda surrounded herself with despicable people. It was as though they recognized one another, gravitated toward each other in order to reinforce their own behavior.

She bit on her knuckles. She'd killed a man. Maybe Conner had finished him off, but she'd been the one to pull the trigger. She'd never thought, never imagined, in all of her dreams or nightmares, that she'd kill another living being. She'd watched the life go out of his eyes and it had sickened her, not thrilled her. Philip Sobre had all but come out and said he loved to torture and most likely kill his victims. For the thrill. She heard a sound, broken and lost, and realized it came from her own throat.

Rio leaned close to her with something in his hand. "This is going to hurt like hell."

He didn't wait, and the breath exploded out of her lungs as he pressed a cloth soaked in some fiery liquid to the streaks in her arm. He held it there while she focused on counting under her breath and struggling not to cry.

Marcos put a needle in Teresa's arm and she moaned softly. He patted her. "You'll be fine. You're safe," he reassured.

Isabeau wasn't certain any of them would ever be safe again. Imelda seemed as if she were a bloated spider, spinning a web that encompassed everyone. All the partygoers had been officials and high-ranking police officers and judges. They couldn't fail to see people taking the servers to the upstairs rooms. Now they were afraid to even take Jeremiah to the hospital.

Rio removed the cloth and, ignoring her protest, held on to her arm to examine the lacerations. "They aren't deep." He said it loud enough for Conner to hear. "I'm going to use an antibacterial cream." He said that to no one in particular, but when he began to apply the cream he forced Isabeau to look at him. "We have a poison in our claws, Isabeau. You can't let this go. Be meticulous about cleaning it and apply the cream several times a day. I'm going to give you a shot of antibiotics, a very large dose, and then you have to make certain to take the entire bottle of pills."

Her eyes met his. "Did Conner get an infection when I raked him with my claws?" Reminding him. Angry with him. He was team leader and it was his job to keep them all in line, even grieving leopards, but she was still angry with him.

He shrugged his broad shoulders, accepting her anger. "Yes he did, in spite of the antibiotics. But they saved his life, and they'll do the same for you."

She pressed her lips together. He'd gotten an infection. She hadn't been there for him. And if Rio was worried about some little scratches on her arm, what about Jeremiah and Conner? Both were covered in bites, claws marks and punctures. She'd caught a glimpse of Conner's body before he'd leapt over the backseat, and he'd looked torn up to her.

"Isabeau! Are you paying attention to me? This is serious."

She looked at him without really seeing him, but forced herself to nod. She could hear Elijah breathing for Jeremiah, slow and steady, but knew he was tiring.

"Get the IV to me," Conner said. "I need a vein. We can't take a chance of him crashing and losing his veins."

Rio turned his attention to the men in the backseat, passing Conner everything he needed from the medical kit. Marcos patted her leg. "Just breathe. You're in shock."

She had considered that. She'd felt a little this way when she'd realized Conner had seduced her to get close to her father—that he wasn't the man he'd pretended to be. Now, of course, she knew he was *exactly* that man. He might have changed his name, but he'd been dangerous and intense and wholly committed to what he was doing. He had the same sense of humor and the same dominant nature. He was leopard and all the traits that she'd fallen in love with were still there.

She looked down at her arm. He would suffer because of this. Small scratches, really. He'd already been on his way to controlling his cat. But her cat . . . She sighed. She'd failed at controlling her. *Maybe I'll never let you out.* But it was a false warning and both of them knew it. She wanted her leopard. She was ready to embrace her.

Rio turned back to her once Conner had the IV in Jeremiah. He came into her view, holding a syringe. "I need to shoot this in your butt."

That got her attention. She glared at him. "Well, choose a different location. I can assure you, it isn't going to happen." *A little backup would be helpful, kitty cat. I'm not dropping my drawers in front of all these men. I don't care about their lack of modesty. Sheesh. What good are you if you don't help a girl out when she needs it. Look badass or something.*

"Don't be a baby. We all have to have shots in the ass."

She leveled a cool stare at him. "Not me. You try it and you'll lose your eye."

Felipe snorted. Marcos smiled. Even Leonardo covered a grin.

"We can do it the easy way or the hard way. I'll have Leonardo hold you down."

Her eyebrow shot up. Her cat stirred. *Finally.* "You're pissing off my cat," she said with satisfaction. "I'm not good at keeping a leash on her yet."

"I'll give her the shot later," Conner said.

His voice was so neutral Isabeau was certain that in

spite of the life-and-death drama in the backseat, he and Elijah had exchanged a quick smile. She didn't care if all of them were laughing at her. She was drawing the line. Rio had put a gun in her hands, yelled at her—*yelled*—and forced her to calm a stalking leopard. She'd had enough of all the testosterone and male leopard domination. She gave Rio her most catlike glare, daring him to try it.

"Little she-cat," Rio muttered under his breath. "You're going to have to sit on her."

"I'll get it done," Conner assured.

"He can try sitting on me," Isabeau muttered in rebellion and felt her cat stretch languidly, unsheathing her claws.

Rio rolled his eyes. "Women," he said under his breath.

They were all leopard, they couldn't fail to hear him.

"Men," she retaliated childishly, under her breath.

"Where are we stashing Teresa?" Marco asked. "I feel responsible for her."

"Someplace they won't find her and she won't be able to contact anyone," Rio said.

"Adan has a cousin," Conner said, "not far from where we're going. If I can't persuade the doctor to help us, we can go to him."

"How well do you know the doctor?" Rio asked.

"Fairly well. He and my mother were friends. They played chess. He actually taught me chess. He would never betray our people."

"Switch places with me," Elijah said. His voice was strained.

Isabeau could hear rustling in the backseat.

"Down this road, Felipe," Conner called out. "The third farm. He practices out of his home now, he's retired."

The road was pitted with deep potholes. She could imagine a leopard choosing this spot to live. The forest encroached close to the houses, and there was a large distance between each farm, giving plenty of privacy. As they bounced past the first two farms, in both instances some-one came out to the porch to mark their passing. Obviously more than curious, she wondered if they were leopard as well. She found herself being nervous all over again, or maybe her anxiety hadn't had the chance to dissipate. It didn't help when the men all checked weapons and Rio slipped her a small Glock.

"Take it," he hissed. "Just in case."

Discovering how these men had to live was a revelation. She knew it was a choice, and that she was making that choice with them, because her choice was always and forever Conner. She took the gun and checked it to make certain it was fully loaded and safe to carry.

Elijah took over again for Conner so Conner could pull on a pair of jeans before Rio opened the back of the SUV. They went onto the porch together. Conner rapped on the door and waited. He could hear movement: one, no, two people. One had a heavier tread than the other. The heavier tread approached the door and swung it open, no small telling crack, rather a wide welcome.

"What can I do . . ." The voice broke off, taking in Conner's torn body. "Come in."

"Doc, it's Conner Vega. You remember me? I've got a kid in bad shape. Really bad shape. A leopard attack. We need your help."

The doctor didn't ask questions but motioned them to bring the boy inside.

"I'm sorry, Doc, but we'll have to know who's in the house," Conner said.

"My wife, Mary," the doctor answered without hesitation. "Bring him in, Conner. If your friend has to search, tell him to hurry if it's as life threatening as you're implying."

Rio went into the house and Conner ran back to the SUV, waving for the others to bring Jeremiah. Isabeau dropped back to protect Elijah as he carried Jeremiah into the house. Leonardo stayed on the porch. Felipe and Marcos drove away, taking Teresa with them, presumably heading to Adan's cousin, where they knew the tribesman would look after her.

"Puncture wounds to the throat. We've been breathing for him most of the time," Conner explained as Elijah laid Jeremiah on the table in the doctor's small office. They hung the bag of fluids on the hook and stepped back to give the doctor room.

"Mary!" the doctor called. "I need you. This is more important than your soap opera."

She came in, a small woman with graying hair and laughing eyes. "I don't watch soap operas, you old coot, and you know it." She smacked him with a rolled-up newspaper as she went past him straight to the sink to wash her hands and don gloves.

"Get out, Conner. But don't go too far. You're next and then the young lady," the doctor ordered gruffly. "And don't pace like you used to. Sit down before you fall down. There's hot coffee in the kitchen."

Mary glanced over her shoulder. "Fresh bread under the tea towel." She bent over Jeremiah.

Conner watched the two working so smoothly together, barely speaking, handing instruments back and forth with the doctor grunting occasionally and shaking his head.

Isabeau tangled her fingers with his and looked up into his face. She was exhausted and worried. He tightened his

hand around hers and pulled her with him out of the room.
Elijah followed reluctantly.

"He's good?" he asked.

Conner nodded. "All the leopards came to him. He might
be retired by now, but he knows his stuff. He won't let him
die if he can possibly save him. His name is Abel Winters.
Dr. Abel Winters. He was in our village for a while, but left
before my mother and I did. Of course he was very young
and probably had gone off to school. I didn't really remember him, when I was that young, but my mother did. She
knew everyone in our village."

He looked around until he found a towel to soak so he
could try to clean some of the blood off before he sat down.
"When we moved to the cabin, my mother would take me to
him for the normal broken bones. I shifted fairly early and
used to try leaping from the canopy and trying to shift on
my way down. I broke a fair amount of bones that way."

Elijah laughed. "I'll bet you did."

The tension eased a little. Isabeau took the towel from
Conner and he bent over the sink, holding on to the edge as
she tried to wipe the worst of the blood away.

"Damn, that hurts like hell. I'm going to find a
shower."

She wanted to go with him, but stayed in the kitchen
with Elijah, feeling awkward and out of place.

"You did well, Isabeau," Elijah offered, breaking the uncomfortable silence.

"I was scared." She didn't look at him, but out the window. "Really scared."

"We all were. I knew I was running a gauntlet, trying to
get to Jeremiah, and I expected the sniper to shoot me at
any moment. I imagine you expected the same thing."

She shook her head. "No, I expected him to shoot Conner. He had the same problem I did. He didn't want to hit his friend. I didn't want to hit Conner." She wiped back the tendrils of hair spilling around her face.

"What does 'marking' mean, Elijah?"

He frowned. "In what context?"

She avoided his gaze again, staring uneasily at the floor. "Like the marks I accidentally put on Conner's face. What does that mean in the leopard world?"

He shrugged. "He's your mate, so it's no big deal. You put your mark on him. More than skin deep. You have a certain chemical in your claws. You can transfer that chemical into a man's body. You did that when you raked Conner. You didn't know what you were doing, but your cat did. She made certain he would want her. Usually a female won't do that unless she's in the throes of the Han Vol Dan. I won't say it never happens, as evidence by your cat marking Conner, but that's probably the biggest danger during the emergence."

"So what happens if she marks someone *not* her mate?"

Elijah straightened slowly, the silence stretching painfully until she was forced to meet his eyes. "Did that happen, Isabeau?"

"Did what happen?" Conner asked, striding into the room, toweling his hair dry. His jeans rode low on his hips, the deep lacerations, bite marks and torn flesh very evident.

She bit her lip hard. She had a very bad feeling that Elijah was going to reveal something she didn't want to know.

"Isabeau wants to know what would happen if she marked someone other than her mate."

There was that silence again, stretching until her nerves were raw.

"Isabeau?" Conner asked. "Did that happen?"

She avoided the question. "I found a dead body in the garden. I think Philip Sobre is a serial killer." To keep from looking at either of them, she went to the other side of the table and lifted the tea towel from the freshly baked loaf of bread.

Silence greeted her statement. Feeling his eyes on her, she turned around. Conner looked stunned. "You found what?"

She sliced the bread and put it on a plate. It was warm and smelled like heaven. "A body. Alberto told me about designing the garden and planting it. Apparently he's a gardener, a very good one. He invited me to look around. He waited for me by the pond."

"Get to the body, Isabeau," Elijah said.

"And the marking another man," Conner encouraged.

She took a dish of butter from Elijah and applied it to two slices, pushing the plates across to them before pouring coffee. "Does anyone take cream?"

Conner put the coffee cup down and went around the table to wrap an arm around her waist. "Stop what you're doing and sit down. You need to tell us what happened."

Isabeau let him pull out a chair and put her in it. The two men sat down with her. She shook her head. "I don't know if Alberto knew the body was there and wanted me to find it. Maybe he wanted me to call the police on Sobre."

"Are you certain it was a body?" Conner asked.

"Positive. I got close to it. Something—an animal—had been digging. There were insects and the smell of decomposition. I saw a finger. It was a body. I backed off and removed all evidence of my presence. I didn't know what to do. I didn't trust Alberto or his guard. He didn't give any indication that he was anything but a nice old man, but my cat didn't like him touching me and I just had this feeling . . ." She pressed her hand to her stomach and looked helplessly at Conner.

He reached for her hand and brought the tips of her fingers to his mouth. "I'm sorry, honey, I should never have allowed you to get mixed up in this. If I'd been thinking, I would have stashed you somewhere safe until it was over."

"I wouldn't have gone. I started this, Conner, and I'm going to see it through. Someone has to stop them."

Elijah took a sip of the coffee and made an appreciative sound. "She's done great, Conner. She walked right up in the middle of a leopard fight and shot the son of a bitch. She found a dead body in a garden and didn't scream her head off. She kept her cool and removed all evidence of being there."

Elijah's assessment of the situation steadied her. She flashed him a quick smile. "I was leaving and Ottila showed up. He cut off my escape. We were in deep brush and I was pretty sure Jeremiah didn't have a good shot at him. What I didn't know until later is that the two rogues had assumed you'd put a shooter in the canopy, and Ottila was the bait to draw Jeremiah out while Suma did the hunting."

Conner covered her hand again to still her fingers as they tapped nervously on the tabletop. "No one could have known, Isabeau."

"Maybe, but you probably would have caught on to what he was doing. He talked instead of acted. He knew Harry and Alberto might walk up at any moment but he kept talking to me. I should have put it together. I didn't know until he taunted me with where Suma was. I tried drawing him into the open by talking and taking little steps backward. He followed, but then he grabbed me, and when I gave the signal, Jeremiah didn't take the shot."

She bit down hard on her lip, the memory of that moment terrifying her. At the time, she couldn't give in to fright, but now, safe with Elijah and Conner, and far away from Ottila, she found herself trembling. She lowered her eyes, ashamed, but determined to tell Conner everything. "And then *she* got all amorous on me."

Conner straightened in his chair. Elijah took another sip of coffee. "Keep going," Conner encouraged.

It was only his fingers on hers that gave her the courage. "He got really ugly, and then she—my leopard—swiped at his arm when he tried to force me to go with him. She marked him. He said something about it that made me think I'd done something wrong—that it was more than just protecting myself. It was the *way* he said it."

Conner's eyes met Elijah's over her head. He lifted her fingers to his mouth again and bit down gently on the tips. "It's all right, Isabeau. You got away. You used whatever means you could and you didn't panic."

"But what does it mean?"

"He has the right to challenge me for you."

Her heart jumped. Ottila was strong. He had confidence in himself. She thought it was significant that he hadn't shot her. She'd been out in the open. The two leopards were rolling together in a wild scramble, but she'd been the one exposed most of the time. She had a rifle in her hands and he had to have known she was trying for a shot at Suma, yet Ottila hadn't shot her.

She leaned her head into the heel of her hand. "I'm tired, Conner. I just want to lie down for a few minutes. Maybe take a shower first. I swear those people made me feel dirty just being in the same room with them."

"Back in the forest, there's a resort owned by the doctor's son. Mostly leopards stay in the area because it isn't well known, they don't advertise, it's mostly word of mouth. We can stay there tonight. They have individual cabins. We'll be close enough to Jeremiah to keep an eye on him and yet still be safe. This road looks as if it dead ends, but there's a small side road about a mile up, swinging deeper into the woods. Most of the time it's passable. Not always after a good rain."

The doctor walked into the room, looking tired. He drew up a chair and sank into it. "He's going to live, but he'll have a very different voice. And he's going to have to do some swallowing therapy. He's breathing and that's what counts." He sighed and looked directly at Conner, his eyes demanding. "Do you want to tell me what you've gotten yourself mixed up in? You didn't do that to that boy, did you?"

Conner looked a little shocked. "No. I should have known it would look that way. He was attacked and I jumped in. Elijah pulled him out. You don't want any part of this, Doc."

"You made me a part of it by bringing that boy here."

Conner shrugged and glanced at Elijah. "Imelda Cortez kidnapped children from Adan's village. She took my half brother as well and killed my mother."

"Ah." Few things shook the doctor, but he was visibly shocked. "In that case, let me call my son and get you a place to stay. Your other men are going to need something hot to keep them going while I clean you up."

15

THE cabin Conner chose was the greatest distance from all the others and deepest in the forest. He needed to feel the safety of the trees around Isabeau. Her leopard had marked another man, and that gave that man the right to step forward and challenge his claim on her. Their species was an old one and they followed the higher law of the wild. It wasn't Isabeau's fault. She hadn't been raised leopard and she didn't know how it all worked. She didn't yet know how to fully control her leopard. The girls living in the villages were taught from the time they were little so when the Han Vol Dan occurred, they had a better chance of keeping their leopards under control.

His father had taken advantage of that law. His mother had been young and impressionable. An older, handsome man, strong, a village leader, she'd been flattered that he'd courted her. When he pushed his suit before her time, she'd made the mistake of marking him. There was no one capable of challenging him for her hand, and wherever her true mate was, if he was even alive, he hadn't been in the village to save her.

He could hear the water turn off abruptly in the shower. The scent of lavender drifted to him through the open door. He sat waiting for her on the bed. She was exhausted—so was he—but there was one more task he had to finish tonight. He smiled as he looked out the large picture window. Moonlight barely managed to make it through the high canopy, but there were breaks where the trees had been cleared to make room for the cabin, and beams burst into the room, spilling silver across the tiled floor.

He leaned back and stared at the high ceiling, a light wood with darker knots scattered all through it. The cabin's walls were wood and covered in rake marks. He could see deep furrows decorating each of the four sides and the ends of his fingers tingled with the need to leave his own mark. He should have left his mark on Isabeau.

He'd been saving that ritual for marriage, but he should have done it. Any male would have thought twice before trying to force a claim. Ottila had judged correctly that she was innocent and wouldn't have knowledge enough, or control enough, to elude his trap. He swore under his breath. It was his fault. Any other male would have made certain she was marked. It was just that . . .

He sighed. He'd betrayed her by seducing her while he was working a job. She hadn't even known his real name. He wanted choices for her. He wanted to be certain *he* was her choice—Isabeau—the woman—not her leopard. He wanted all of her to be his.

"Damn it." He raked his fingers through his hair, angry with himself.

"What's wrong?"

She leaned one slim hip against the doorjamb, a towel

wrapped like a sarong around her body while she towel-dried her hair. The shower had done her good. Her skin wasn't quite so pale, although the bruises on her arms stood out.

His breath suddenly caught in his throat. "Did he put his mark on you?"

She frowned. "Like how?"

"Did he bite you? Claw you?" He leapt up, one fluid movement, swift and purposeful, but obviously intimidating. She retreated into the hall, her eyes wide.

"No. He didn't get the chance. Felipe came and scared him off." Her frown deepened. "He wasn't exactly scared. He actually was very confident. I don't think Suma was the dominant between them. I think it was the other way around."

He leaned down and pressed a kiss to the dark blemishes marring her upper arm before taking her hand and leading her into the bedroom. "Thank you."

"For what?"

"For having the courage to kill the man who murdered my mother. I know that wasn't easy for you. And for braving a leopard in the throes of madness." He turned up her arm to examine the four marks there. They matched the scars on his face, although they weren't deep, more like scratches than lacerations. Still . . . He kissed each red streak, his mouth gentle.

Isabeau leaned into him until he was surrounded by her scent, until he surrendered to it and took her into his arms, holding her close to his chest. Her towel slipped a little, but that was all right with him. The feel of her breasts rubbing along his skin helped revive his body. Every nerve, every cell came alive.

"Marisa was my friend, Conner. But honestly, all I was

thinking about was you." She tilted her head to look up at him. "Well, you," she hedged, "and maybe shooting boss-man Rio. Sort of accidentally on purpose. I think if he yelled at me one more time, I might have gone psycho on him."

He took a step, forcing her backward toward the bed. "And then he had the audacity to threaten you with a syringe."

"In front of everyone. He was lucky he didn't try it," she added.

His next step put the backs of her legs against the bed. He took the damp towel from her hand, gave her hair a slight rub as though he was drying it and then simply tossed it away.

"If I don't dry my hair, it curls everywhere. Little ringlets." She made a face. "And it's so long and thick, it takes forever to actually dry."

Isabeau made a movement as though to retrieve the towel, but he bunched her sarong in his fist and tugged until it slipped off her breasts, spilling them into his sight, before he took the entire towel from her. "I don't really think it matters, do you?" he asked, and bent his head to her breasts.

Her nipples peaked and she gasped as his hot mouth closed over one tip and drew it deep. His hand drifted down to the junction between her legs. "I like your curls. All fiery. The way you are inside." His fingers teased at the dampening entrance.

He sank down slowly until he was sitting on the bed, and tugged until she followed him. At the last moment he spun her around and bent her over his knees, yanking so that she fell over his lap, facedown, her buttocks exposed. He placed one hand on her upper back to hold her position while he surveyed her thrashing bottom.

"Very nice." His hand rubbed and massaged her firm cheeks until she was squirming breathlessly, her breasts jiggling with every movement, an added enticement he hadn't considered. His cock was being massaged with each thrash of her body, and her long, damp hair brushed like living silk against his thighs. "I could get used to this."

"Well don't," Isabeau advised.

But he could tell his hands were already working magic. He could see the evidence of her desire, her receptiveness gleaming between her legs. He worked his hand down the curve of her butt to the crease between her thigh and buttocks and rubbed as well, inserting his hand to force her legs farther apart.

She softened more, became pliant for him. He bent his head to nip at the soft flesh, several little love bites, all the while continuing his massage. She moaned softly when his fingers slid through damp heat. Her stomach muscles bunched and her body flushed.

"Does this feel good, baby?" he asked, spearing two fingers into her hot core.

Her body shuddered, inner muscles tightening around him. She was so responsive, so open to him, always indulging him and any fantasy he had. He hadn't started out thinking this was going to be anything but accomplishing an end, but now he couldn't have stopped his explorations if he wanted.

His hands moved over her possessively, paying attention to her thighs and buttocks, and then plunging his fingers deep. He found her most sensitive spot and teased and circled until she was lifting her bottom and riding his hand.

"Does it feel good, Isabeau?" His fingers stroked and caressed, exploring every hidden secret recess and shadowed hollow of her body. "Tell me."

Isabeau's breath came in ragged gasps. "Yes. Everything you do always feels good." She was truthful. The more she let him know what she liked, the better each time together was. She could never resist him. When he touched her, she felt alive. She'd thought to fall on the bed and just go to sleep for as long as she could, but the moment his hands touched her body, all she could do was want.

She never expected there would be something terribly erotic in lying over his lap with his hand holding her down and her buttocks being massaged and fondled, but there was a guilty thrill, a pleasure she had never considered. She could feel his heavy erection, hotter than a brand against her stomach. She knew this new position was arousing to him as well.

She wasn't surprised when his hand lifted and came down experimentally on her bottom. The sting sent warmth coursing through her. The smack wasn't hard, and she knew he'd test her response. She was as shocked as he was at the flood of liquid heat bathing his fingers. Every inner muscle clamped down around his fingers. His hand rubbed and caressed over the heat.

"What does it feel like?" He whispered the words, his voice a sinful temptation. "You have to tell me everything."

"Hot. The nerves spread straight to my clit. I can't explain it exactly, but there's so much heat, like a fire building that I can't stop."

"Do you like it?"

"As long as it's not really painful. I wouldn't like that." But she loved the massage and the way his fingers moved in and out of her—the way he explored her body without reservation, with his hands and mouth. He was cat, and it showed in his oral need to lap at her skin, to tease with the edge of his teeth and massage tactilely.

"Then I'm sorry, baby, but I have to do this." He withdrew his fingers, reached behind him to get the syringe. He pulled the cap with his teeth, put the syringe in his mouth and brought down his hand a little harder, hoping the sting would momentarily numb her skin. He plunged the needle in and pushed the plunger to dispense the antibiotic.

She hissed, a long, slow promise of retaliation. He wasn't a male leopard for nothing. He recognized a female cat's displeasure and he wasn't about to let her up until he soothed her and made her forget such an indignity.

"I'm sorry, beloved, but you refused even the doctor."

She turned her head to glare at him. Her eyes had gone cat, taking on the fiery glow of the night. In the moonlight she looked incredibly exotic, her pale skin soft and enticing, the perfect globes of her butt tempting and her red hair tumbling around her furious little face. His entire body tightened, his shaft painful and full.

"There was a reason for that, you dimwit. It's called a needle phobia."

"You told him you weren't allergic when he asked you," he pointed out. His hand began a circular massage to ease the ache and, if he was lucky, start a new one.

"A phobia isn't an allergy," she explained. "Now let me up."

She was becoming receptive to his attentions again but her voice said she didn't like it, she wanted to keep her "mad." He stroked his tongue across the sore spot and slid his fingers deep inside her again.

"You're so wet, honey." He withdrew his fingers just as she was pushing back against his hand to draw him deeper. "See?" He held them, gleaming with moisture, in front of her face. "Like nectar." His hand was back, massaging and rubbing. "I want you, Isabeau, are you going to tell me no?"

She shivered at the dark promise in his voice. The hand on her back eased and he allowed her to slide off his lap. She sat on the floor gingerly, afraid of sitting squarely on the offending sting. She looked up at him. The moonlight spilled across his face, giving him a softer edge in spite of the scars. She lifted her hand and cupped the side of his face, her thumb sliding along the groove of the deepest scar.

"Rio told me you got an infection."

His hand covered hers, and then he turned his head and pressed kisses into the center of her palm. "I've gotten them before and will again." His golden gaze burned into hers. "I took my shot of antibiotics without whining."

"You're just so big and brave," she answered, her smile faint and mysterious. Her gaze dropped to his groin, to the heavy erection, thick and standing up against his flat belly. Trailing her fingers with a light delicate touch over his shaft, she found her way to the sac hanging below, watching him shiver as she did so. "Yet one touch and you're trembling."

Isabeau stroked the pads of her fingers over his soft velvet balls, before she cupped them, rolling and squeezing gently, all the while keeping her eyes focused on the center of his body, as if his every reaction was the most important thing in the world to her. His breath exploded out of his lungs when she leaned into him and licked gently, over and over, lapping at his balls and the base of his shaft while pleasure flooded his body and he hardened impossibly.

She sucked on him, again her mouth infinitely gentle. Everything she did was designed to please him. Her hands were back, caressing and stroking as she removed her mouth and went back to watching his reaction.

Conner absorbed the feel of her touch on his skin. She

could transport him instantly to another realm just with her fingers. He observed her through half-closed eyes, watching the rapt attention on her face as she closed her fingers around his thick shaft, forcing a gasp of pleasure from him. She pumped experimentally. Once. Twice. Her gaze never left his cock. She studied the way it pulsed in her hand, reacted to the warmth of her breath on the mushroom head. When small pearly drops appeared she licked them off as if she was clutching an ice-cream cone.

Every touch, every stroke was feather-light, barely there, designed to torment him. There was a look on her face that shattered him—truly shattered him. She understood him. She *saw* him, the man and the leopard. She understood his drive to dominate and she accepted him for who he was. She enjoyed giving him pleasure. And she trusted him completely. Trust was in her eyes every time she gave herself to him without reservation.

She leaned forward and curled her tongue around the underside of the broad head, teasing his most sensitive spot, and looking pleased when his cock responded with a quick, pleasurable jerk, throbbing and pulsing in her hand.

He groaned, swore softly and buried his fists in her glorious hair, pulling her head forward, bringing her a little off balance, until his cock was poised at her mouth. He smeared her lips with those small pearly drops, and his heart nearly stopped when her tongue slid out to capture his essence, drawing him in.

"Open your mouth," he commanded softly. Needing her. Wanting her. Loving her. God, but she was brutal, a woman to hold forever.

She looked up at him then—her gaze meeting his, and his heart went into overdrive, pounding with the force of a sledgehammer. He watched her eyes change, go slumberous, drowsy, so sexy he groaned again and pulled her head right down onto him. Her mouth opened under the pressure and she sucked his cock into a tight, hot cauldron.

Her tongue began flicking and dancing around his burning head, stroking the underside until he swore he was going blind. The room actually blurred and little explosions went off in his brain. Electrical currents sizzled in his bloodstream, causing his body to shudder and another deep groan to escape. She lapped at him, sucked and flicked, never staying to one thing but changing constantly so he was always off balance and the sensations just piled, one on top of the other. She showed no sign of getting tired, but drove him to the very edge of his control over and over and then pulled back until he thought he might explode.

Breathing heavily, using the silken reins he held, he pulled her head up. "Get on your hands and knees."

Still holding him deep in her mouth, tongue working up and down his shaft, she shook her head, her eyes telling him he was ruining her fun. He pulled her off of him, holding her still, hands still buried tight in her hair, until she complied. She shivered as he knelt behind her and placed his hand between her shoulder blades, pressing her head to the floor.

The action raised her buttocks, those perfect globes and he curved his palms over her ass possessively. He massaged and kneaded and then slipped his fingers between her legs where moisture glistened. "I love how wet you get for me, honey." He rubbed the head of his cock back and forth through the soft folds, feeling her steaming heat, prolonging the moment, wanting her to push back against him. "What do you think? Should I tease you the way you were teasing me?" He bent over her, letting her feel his weight while he pressed his cock into her burning entrance.

She shuddered and made a strangled sound in the back of her throat. He felt the vibration run down her body and straight through her feminine channel. His hips surged forward and he felt her body give way for his invasion. Tight. Scalding hot. Always that little bit of reluctance as though she might not allow him entrance and then . . . paradise.

He just breathed her in, let her take him over, surrendering to her completely. It always amused him that she thought she was the one who surrendered. He was the strong one, the dominant male leopard, aggressive, taking her whichever way he wanted. Yet it was this moment, this first joining when love for her overwhelmed him. It shook him so badly that he always needed this one moment after he buried himself in her, to just give himself up to her—to the enormity of what he felt for her.

He began to move, a little shaken at the strength of his love for her. When he was like this, feeling as though he was touching the edge of a miracle, he preferred to be behind her where she couldn't see his face. Each stroke sent flames rushing over his body, licking at his skin, burning through his cock and spreading like a wildfire out of control until the sensations were so strong he couldn't think.

She moved her hips back to the strength of his rhythm, a hard, fast pace that was nearly brutal. She winced once and he immediately forced himself to stop, holding still in that exquisite cauldron of fire. "What is it, beloved?" he managed when his entire being wanted—*needed*—to continue.

She shook her head and wiggled. "Please," she managed, "keep going."

"What hurt?" His voice was rougher than he intended, his throat nearly closing with the burning fire rolling through his body. Every instinct demanded he plunge deeper and harder.

She gave a small laugh. "My butt. The shot hurt."

He instantly shifted his angle so his body wouldn't slap against that small injury. "Next time," he said through clenched teeth, as he pushed deep, feeling her tight folds stretch around his invasion, gripping, making the friction exquisite. "Next time, tell me immediately when you're uncomfortable."

Isabeau suppressed her sassy comment, not wanting to risk a smack on her butt when she just happened to be in a vulnerable position. Besides, right now she didn't want him to ever stop moving. His fingers were hard on her hips, guiding the rhythm, setting the fast pace, rocking her with every stroke. She always lost herself in him, every amazing moment they came together.

She could feel her body building, always building, the sensations stronger and stronger until she was stretched as far as she could possibly go without breaking, wound so tight she thought there could be no more without snapping into a million pieces. Her body shuddered, every muscle quivering, contracting, gripping at the invader as he thrust deep again and again.

He buried the full length of his thick shaft, over and over into her aching, needy body. Her head tossed, hair flying in all directions, when his hard hands gripped her hips and held her still while he pounded into her, sheathing himself until there was nothing but the sound of their bodies coming together, their combined harsh breathing and the building fire at the center of their bodies.

She clenched her muscles around him, gripping him tight, stroking his shaft with hot velvet caresses. His cock, silk over steel, was like a spike driving into her deep, so hard, so hot, dragging over the bundle of raw nerves again and again as he stretched and filled her.

He suddenly slowed, his stroke pushing inch by fiery inch through her tight folds, a slow relentless piercing that had her moaning brokenly. She could feel every vein on the thick length of him pushing through her body until the large head bumped her womb and lodged like a burning brand.

"Damn, Isabeau," he hissed.

She couldn't stop herself from rolling her hips, tightening her muscles around him, squeezing and milking, twisting herself on that thick spike of pleasure invading her.

His breath exploded out of his lungs. He swore and gripped her hips hard. That was her only warning. He began thrusting like a jackhammer, impaling her over and over, driving deep, sending ripples of mind-numbing pleasure spreading through her, the intensity growing and growing until it was all encompassing.

She cried out hoarsely, the sound strangled as she felt his release, hot and thick, explode deep into her, against her spasming, throbbing womb. For a moment her entire body locked down, every muscle contracting, clamping down hard, and then the release tore through her like a firestorm, building in intensity. She could hear the roar in her head, feel the scorching flames rush over and through her, her body quaking from toes to head.

He held her, whispering softly. "I'm sorry, baby, this has to be done."

His teeth sank into her shoulder, not the teeth of a man, but that of a cat, holding her still while his body trapped hers, still rocking with pleasure. Pain streaked through her shoulder right under his mouth, and then his tongue lapped at her, taking away the sting. She shuddered under that rasping tongue and turned her head to look over her shoulder. His eyes were all cat, golden and focused, so intense she felt another spasm in her womb.

Conner dropped his face against her back and rubbed, skin on skin, the shadow along his jaw grazing her skin roughly, sending more ripples through her core. He pressed kisses down her spine and slowly straightened until he was kneeling upright behind her, still holding her. "I love you, Isabeau. More than you can know."

He eased out of her body and sank down onto the edge of the bed, his legs shaky. She turned and crawled to him, her face flushed, her eyes glazed, her breath coming in ragged little gasps. She sat on the floor in front of him, looking up at him. Their gazes locked.

Her expression was so loving it humbled him. He didn't deserve the way she felt, that all-encompassing love, almost adoration, but he resolved never to lose it. He bent toward her and she immediately tipped up her face to let him take possession of her mouth in a long, satisfying kiss.

"I'll do everything in my power to make you happy, Isabeau."

"You do make me happy, Conner. When we're alone like this, and I have you, I know what I feel and what you feel. It's here in this room and it's enough for me."

He looked around the small rustic cabin. This would be her life with him, at least for a long while. Always traveling from one assignment to the next. He could never be far from the forest, he knew he could never live in a city. He'd spent time in the United States on a large ranch, a beautiful place, but not for him.

"Can you live like this, Isabeau?"

She smiled at him. "With you? This is exactly where I want to be."

Conner shook his head. "I want you to give it some thought, beloved. You have to really think about what it would be like day in and day out. I'm a demanding man. I like my way. I've tried to be honest about what I want with you and I look around and see I'm not exactly offering you the world. At times it will be dangerous, and the intensity of those moments can be overwhelming in a bad way."

She frowned at him. "Are you trying to get rid of me?"

His hands framed her face. "No. Of course not. I just want you to be very sure of the reality of loving me. It won't always be wonderful."

"Like finding dead bodies in a garden or having to kill someone?" Her voice cracked and she scowled at him. "I know exactly what I'm getting into, Conner. You haven't exactly soft-soaped it. I met you while you were on an assignment, remember? That didn't turn out so well for me. I'm not a princess caught in a fairy tale. I'm a real-life woman who has a brain and can figure out consequences."

"Have you figured out what it will be like living with me? The man? The leopard?"

She reached back and touched the bite mark on her shoulder with trembling fingers. "That's one thing I do know. You're not a mystery there, Conner. You like your way when it comes to sex."

"In all things."

She laughed at him. Amusement sparkled in her eyes. "Really? In all things? I don't think so. I think you care about what I want, what makes me happy. Even in sex, you want me thinking of your pleasure, but while I am, you're thinking of mine. You don't see yourself nearly as well as I see you."

"I know I love you, Isabeau, with every breath in my body, and I wouldn't survive you leaving me. I had an endless fucking year without you, and I never want to go through that again."

Isabeau smiled and leaned into him, her tongue sliding

over his shaft. She took her time, lapping at him lovingly, while his hands settled in her hair and stroked caresses. She was answering him in a way no other woman would think to do and his heart nearly burst with love for her.

She took her time, making certain that he heard her—that he knew exactly what she was saying—shouting—in silence to him. She was aware of every shiver of his body, every tiny nuance, as she took care of him, bringing him back to his semi-hard state. She sank back and smiled up at him. "I'm going to go clean up and fall into bed and sleep for hours. Do *not* wake me up."

He knew he would. And he knew she knew it. Her smile was like the cat that ate the canary. She knew exactly what she did to him with that mouth of hers. With the way she loved him. He watched her walk away, and for the first time, she seemed comfortable with her nudity in front of him, her hips swaying provocatively, enticingly.

"Little minx," he whispered and lay back on the bed, lacing his fingers behind his neck, satisfaction humming through his veins. She made him feel on top of the world. She made him feel—magic.

He contemplated the ceiling, his body languid and sated, stretching like the cat that he was. She came back into the room, her body fluid and graceful, very feminine, and both he and his leopard admired her as she crossed to his side and sank down onto the bed.

Conner lay on his side, one elbow propping him up while his other hand stroked caresses through her wild mane. She was right about her hair. The strands had dried into a riot of curls he found intriguing. She usually wore her hair sleeker, hiding her untamed look. He liked her wild side.

"I've been thinking, Isabeau," he murmured, watching

the moonlight play across her face. "Neither of us have family anymore."

"You have a brother."

It was an unexpected body blow. "I do. I didn't think about that aspect—of what I'd be asking of you."

Her lashes veiled her eyes. "And what would that be?"

"Well, of course I have to take the boy in. Raise him myself. He's only five years old. If you were with me, I'd be asking you to be a mother to him."

She made a small sound, much like a sigh. "I'm way ahead of you, Einstein. Of course we'll raise him, what else would we do? Your mother would haunt us forever if we didn't. Besides, I've met him. He has your eyes and mop of hair. He's a darling boy. Now go to sleep."

He continued to play with her hair, watching her breathe. The long expanse of her skin looked soft and tempting in the moonlight. The ache in his groin was pleasant, not painful, and he rather enjoyed just lying there, his body spooning hers, his cock tight against the crack of her butt, his thighs pressed against hers. This would be his nights. Isabeau in his bed. He looked down at her breasts, the nipples soft and inviting. Someday a child of his would nestle there and feed and it would be the most beautiful thing in the world.

"Marry me, Isabeau." His hand left her hair to cup her breast, his thumb brushing lazily back and forth across her nipple, knowing he was sending tiny sparks of arousal straight to her clit. He kept his touch gentle and undemanding.

She kept her eyes closed. "I already said I would. Now go to sleep."

"Marry me tomorrow, Isabeau," he whispered, his hand

stilling, his palm curling around her breast to just hold the soft weight.

Her lashes lifted then. She blinked and turned her head enough to look over her shoulder at him. "Tomorrow?"

"I want you to be my wife. Neither of us has family—other than the boy. The team is our family. The doc could arrange it for us. My guess is this valley is made up of leopards. The doc would only settle where his expertise would help his own people. I want to know that you're waiting for me at the other end of this thing."

She rolled over slowly and pressed her hand to his face. "Conner. I love you. I know what you have to do to get those children back. And I know it makes you feel dirty and not worthy of me, but it makes you more so. Don't you see that? You're an extraordinary man to risk what we have for the safety of others. I meant what I said when I told you I stand behind you one hundred percent. You tell me what to do to help you and I'll do it."

"Marry me tomorrow. Be my wife. That would help me."

She swallowed. He watched the motion of her throat, intrigued that she would be nervous when he knew she was so committed to him. He stroked his fingers down her throat and felt that convulsive swallowing and then traced her lips with the pad of his thumb and felt them tremble. "What is it, baby?" He kept his voice soft and low, intimate. "Are you afraid?"

She blinked rapidly again. "I just have a difficult time sometimes . . ."

"With . . . ?" he prompted, his hand shaping her breasts again and then sliding down to rub small circles on her belly.

"With believing that a man like you could really be satisfied with a woman like me."

His hand stilled. He stiffened. "What the hell does that mean, Isabeau?"

Isabeau turned onto her back and stared up at his face, scarred and tough, experience and danger in every line. Although the moonlight spilled across her, he was still hidden in the shadows, something she equated with him. He would always be that shadow man. Rugged. Tough. A little mysterious. And so—so experienced in every way she wasn't. "Way out of my league."

His mouth quirked, his smile slow in coming. "You have it backward, honey. I've always known you were way out of my league with your innocence and your trust. You're the most beautiful thing in my life, and I'm not talking about your exceptional body, which I'll admit I'm quite fond of. You're everything I want, Isabeau, and you should never feel like you can't keep up. If anything, it's the other way around."

"I'm not talking about intellect here, or even courage. I feel I can be an asset to you, Conner, but here, in bed, I don't have *any* experience, other than what you've taught me."

His shaft jerked against her bottom, grew hotter and thicker. He laughed softly. "Feel that, baby? That's what you do to me. You're so willing to please me and you follow instructions beautifully. A man wants a woman who gives him her trust and her body without reservation. You do that. I can't ask for anything more. You aren't afraid to tell me—or show me what you like. You don't think that's a turn-on? To watch you enjoying my body is the biggest turn-on there is. Sex is just sex, Isabeau. Love is different. Love is both mind and body, heart and soul. I don't know how else to say it. When I'm with you, it isn't just about my body being satisfied. I've had love—your brand of love—and I don't ever want anything else."

She rolled back over onto her side and scooted her round, firm bottom tighter into his lap. "Fine then. I accept. Now go to sleep."

Conner stared down at her, at the long lashes once more veiling her eyes, and he started to laugh. "You're going to be hell to live with, aren't you?"

"Absolutely."

"Well, aren't you going to talk about dresses and suits?"

"I don't have a dress."

"Are we getting married naked then? It has its possibilities."

She laughed softly. "You would think that. No. We're wearing clothes. Now go to sleep. Talking makes you hard."

"*You* make me hard. Looking at you makes me hard. Lying beside you gets me hard. The sound of your voice, the touch of your skin . . ."

She pushed back into him and wiggled, rubbing her buttocks back and forth across his shaft. "Stop! I get the point."

"So you want to wear clothes. What clothes? We didn't exactly pack much and your dress has blood all over it. I shredded my clothes when I went to help Jeremiah."

"I'll wear my jeans. I brought a change of clothes, jeans and a T-shirt. Well, a tank top, but it will be fine. The point isn't our clothes, right?"

"So a dress then. And a suit. We'll have to ask doc where we can come up with something that will work."

Her laughter was muffled against the pillow. "You're impossible. I have no idea where we're supposed to come up with a dress and a suit, but whatever." Her eyes opened and she looked at him again from over her shoulder. "And I can tell you're going to go through a lot of clothes. Perhaps you should practice stripping on the run without ruining what you're wearing."

"Extreme circumstances call for extreme reaction."

"Not if I'm the one having to try to repair said clothes. And if you go around ripping your clothes to shreds, what do you think your little brother will do? He's going to follow your example in all things."

"Do you think so?" He rolled her over onto her back and swept his hand from her breasts to her thighs, slowing along her flat belly and mound before traveling lower. "I love the feel of your skin."

"I'm not moving, Conner. If you're going to . . ." She broke off with a little cry when he dipped his head and swept his tongue along the same path as his hands, this time stopping at the junction between her legs.

She laughed and caught his hair in her hands, holding him there.

16

ISABEAU took the cup of tea from Mary Winters with a small smile. "Conner wants me to find a dress to wear. For some reason it's really important to him."

"And it isn't to you?" Mary asked gently.

Isabeau looked down into the steaming cup. "I don't want it to be. It isn't like I have family. My mother died so long ago I barely remember her and my father . . ." She broke off. It wasn't like she had anyone to walk her down the aisle. The wedding was going to be taking place in the doctor's backyard right on the edge of the rain forest. White, flowing, traditional dresses wouldn't make sense anyway. "I think every girl dreams of this day, walking down the aisle with her father, surrounded by family and friends." She shrugged. "I want to marry Conner, of course, but I pictured it all happening quite differently."

Mary reached out and sympathetically patted her knee. "Don't be depressed, Isabeau. You can make this day anything you want. When Abel asked me to marry him, we had no one either. Now . . ." Her smile was warm. " . . . our family is very large and we're blessed with several grand-children. I remember the day we got married as if it were yesterday. You want your day to be like that. Your man is so excited. I can see joy on his face."

Isabeau's smile lit her eyes. "Me too. That's why I've agreed to this. It's such an imposition for you."

"Did you know Marisa?" Mary asked, placing her cup carefully on the white-laced tablecloth.

Isabeau nodded. "I met her a short while ago, right be-fore she was killed. She was a good friend to me. At the time, I didn't know she was Conner's mother."

"But she knew you were Conner's chosen mate," Mary said. "I know because I always knew with my sons. Moth-ers have that extra sense about them."

"I hope she knew. I hope she approved."

"Marisa was an accepting person. The man she chose when she was young and impressionable wasn't her true mate, but she remained loyal to him in spite of the fact that he was so wrong in the way he treated her. She raised her son to be a good man, and she would have raised the boy she took . . ." She broke off when Isabeau gasped.

Mary nodded. "Yes, dear, we knew about little Mateo. Marisa brought him to us when she needed a doctor for him. She was a good woman, and she would be so happy that you are going to be the one to share her son's life. I know she would."

"You're very kind," Isabeau said.

"I knew Marisa very well, Isabeau, and she would want me to help you. I'd like to do just that if you don't mind. I never had a daughter—only sons. Fortunately I love all of their wives, but they have their own parents to handle things like weddings. Marisa and I often talked about that—how as a mother we both had dreamt of creating a wonderful day for our daughters. She had no daughter either, so she pinned her hopes on Conner's wife—you. She isn't here, but perhaps you would be willing to fulfill both our dreams."

Emotion nearly choked Isabeau. Tears burned behind her eyes and she had to bite down hard on her lip to stifle a sob. "I don't know what to say. You make me feel like anything is possible."

Mary's face lit up. "Anything is. I just happen to have this trunk and it will be a treasure chest for us, I think." She assessed Isabeau's size, drawing her out of the chair and making her turn in a circle. "Yes, I think we'll be just fine, and if not, well, I'm pretty handy with a sewing machine. Let me just make a few phone calls. I have friends who will come help us."

"Conner might be concerned about strangers around, especially with Jeremiah in a bad way," Isabeau pointed out reluctantly.

"Jeremiah is doing much better. Go have a look in on him and let your man know what I'm doing. Remind him that Abel and I have known those I'm calling for over twenty years. I've got a million things to do. Go reassure yourself that your friend is doing better and then get right back here."

Isabeau felt her heart leap in her chest. For the first time, she felt lighter, as though there was a chance she could make the day special and memorable. Most likely, she realized, because she had someone to share her happiness with, someone to talk to while she got ready. Conner had Rio and the others, even Doc, but she didn't know anyone that well. Mary made Isabeau feel as if she was being fussed over: Not only did she want to help with the preparations, but she looked forward to it.

She nodded and went on through the house to the back room where Jeremiah was resting. Conner and Rio were in the room with him. Jeremiah looked pale, bruises and lacerations marring his body. An IV fed him and she noted a bag of antibiotics dripping into his arm.

"How is he?" she asked.

Conner wrapped his arm around her waist and drew her to the side of the bed. "He's fighting an infection, but Doc says he'll make it. He's going to have an interesting voice for the rest of his life."

Rio sighed. "I shouldn't have used him. He wasn't ready."

"I don't think you could have stopped him," Isabeau said. "He felt guilty for listening to Suma in the first place. He had the need to make it up to himself and maybe to me. He would have just followed you."

"He handled himself well," Conner pointed out. "He didn't panic and in spite of encountering an enemy, he went back to the original mission, trying to protect us. Suma was experienced and a fighter. I had a few bad moments with him myself. Isabeau shot him, remember? I just finished the job."

"You would have taken him," Rio said, "but it was going to take time we didn't have."

"I think Ottila is going to be more dangerous than ever," Isabeau ventured hesitantly. "He appeared to take a backseat to Suma, but I didn't believe it after encountering him. I think he was the brains. And I think his number-one priority will be seeking revenge for Suma."

Conner shook his head. "It will be acquiring you."

She frowned. "Suma and Ottila seemed like close brothers. He said they . . ." She bit her lip and forced herself to continue, although she found it embarrassing. "They shared everything—including women. He was willing to share me with Suma, although he said I would carry his child."

"That alone speaks to who is the dominant," Rio said. "He would have taken her in her heat, not allowing Suma access to her, to insure the child was his. She's right, Conner, it was Ottila, not Suma, who was calling the shots."

"And we know they aren't entirely loyal to Imelda," Conner added. "Or they would have told her Philip Sobre was recording their conversations. My guess is, they pushed Sobre to do it. Ottila probably had Suma approach Sobre and lay out a plan. They would pretend to work for Imelda, but really be working for him. They most likely suggested he tape the conversations, probably even told him how. Sobre isn't the brightest man on the planet."

"Wasn't," Rio corrected. "Did you see the newspaper this morning?"

Isabeau snuck a quick look at Conner from under her lashes. They hadn't looked at a newspaper or done much else other than enjoy each other's body. She had lost count of the times he woke her and still, when the morning light crept into the room, he'd already be moving inside her. She wasn't certain she could walk normally and definitely was a little sore.

"Philip Sobre was found murdered. He was hanging in a closet with his entrails wrapped around his cut throat. His tongue had been pulled through the opening in the traditional 'Colombian necktie.' He had obviously been tortured extensively. The party was mentioned, but the guests were all seen leaving, and Philip waved good-bye from the door, kissing the ladies, even Imelda on both cheeks," Rio said. "They have video surveillance to prove it."

Isabeau pressed a hand to her stomach. "That's just sick. Did Imelda do that?"

"According to the papers, she was devastated. Philip Sobre was a former lover and a wonderful, close friend. She'll
miss him terribly and will not stop hunting his killer. She
looked right into the camera when she uttered that lie with
such complete sincerity. She had no comment on the find-
ings in his private garden," Rio added.

Isabeau inhaled sharply. "What did they find?"

"Bodies. More than thirty so far, both female and male.
There is speculation that Philip Sobre could be Panama's
biggest serial killer in the history of the country," Rio told
her.

"I believe there's only been one or two that have ever
been acknowledged or known about," Conner said. "This
will be extremely uncomfortable for law enforcement, especially as so many officials knew him."

"What a mess. Imelda just couldn't wait," Rio said. "My
guess is, she took that place apart hunting for those tapes.
By now all evidence against her is destroyed."

Isabeau grew hot and uncomfortable, her mouth aching
as if someone had punched her. Even her teeth hurt. The
conversation made her sick.

"Maybe," Conner said, "but if Ottila was the one who
put the idea of taping the conversations in Sobre's head in
the first place, there's a good chance he has them stashed
somewhere. And if he was the one who searched the house,
he'd have no reason to find them. Imelda has no idea he
isn't loyal to her."

"Why am I his first priority?" Isabeau asked. "Isn't
money his true motivator?" Unexpected tears welled up
and she had to blink them away rapidly.

"An unmated leopard has trouble resisting a female in
the throes of the Han Vol Dan. I think the instinct to mate
overcomes all good sense. You introduced a chemical into

his bloodstream. It will be like a building fever in his body. He'll have to come for you," Rio said.

Her breath caught in her lungs. Her gaze jumped to Conner for confirmation. "Is that what I did to you?" She reached up and brushed the pad of her finger along the groove in his cheek. "When I did this?"

Conner caught her fingers and brought them to his heart. "Yes. But that has nothing to do with my falling in love with you. I was already far gone before you took a swipe at me."

"Do claws always release the chemical?" A wave of heat rushed over her, leaving her sweating. Maybe she was running a fever from the claw marks on her arm in spite of the shot.

He shook his head. "It's usually deliberate. Your cat probably marked me because of a combination of things. Your anger, which was righteous by the way, we're mates, and we had fallen in love."

"And Ottila?" She couldn't keep humiliation and pain from her voice.

"She's in heat, emerging. She's not in control of herself any more than you're in control of her. It's a learning process. Most of our women have the advantage of parents teaching them how to deal with their cat instincts from the time they're little. You didn't even know you were cat." He brought her fingers to his mouth and scraped back and forth with his teeth, his gaze locked with hers. "Don't worry about it, Isabeau. I can handle Ottila."

She wasn't sure. Conner seemed invincible. Confident. Experienced. But there was something very frightening about Ottila. Her heart pounded at that thought of him hunting Conner—and her. She couldn't seem to stand still, her legs restless, her nerves jumpy.

She touched her tongue to her bottom lip and then nodded, changing the subject. "Mary is going to help me with
the wedding preparations. She's making calls to some
friends of hers right now and before you protest—and she
knew you would—she said to remind you, she's known
these people for over twenty years."

Conner bit back his protest, seeing the happiness in Isabeau's eyes. He glanced at Rio over her head. Rio smiled at
him and shrugged. It was her wedding day and they were
just going to have to be vigilant.

"You know the doc and his wife," Rio pointed out.
"We're already trusting them with Jeremiah."

"Doc wants to make certain you have all the necessary
vaccinations and medical tests required. In our society
it's much easier to get married, but we want to be legal in
all countries. I filled out the license for us. It just so happens the doc has a friend who is a judge here. They know
they have to hold the paperwork before filing until this is
over. He was willing to juggle dates a bit for us, knowing
Imelda's reputation, but he assures me it will be legal and
binding. It was easy enough to get my birth certificate, and
we're searching for yours. The judge has been very helpful. You need to sign a certificate stating you've never been
married in front of the judge."

She scowled at him. "Have you already done all that?"
For some reason she was angry at him. Her out-of-control
emotions made no sense at all.

"I'm not letting you escape."

She forced a smile when she really wanted to swipe at
him again. She hated the way she was feeling and no longer
trusted herself, so she touched Jeremiah's shoulder and left
the room.

"I don't know what's wrong with me, Mary," she said,

entering the kitchen and rubbing at her arm. "I'm all over the place today. Conner just told me about the various things he's been doing, certificates, making it legal, and I suddenly had this mad desire to cry." She sighed and went to the window, ashamed of herself. "My skin feels too tight and itches uncontrollably. My emotions are completely out of control. I either want to cry or I'm angry and then I'm wildly happy. Does every bride feel this way on their wedding day?"

Mary turned around from where she was mixing cake batter in a bowl, her gaze speculative. "If the bride's cat is close to the emerging, then yes, I'd have to say those emotions all make sense. Those are all classic signs, Isabeau. Has anyone talked to you about what to expect?"

"A little. My cat is a hussy."

Mary laughed. "During the Han Vol Dan, all the females are hussies. And it's the only time your male is going to be tolerant of flirtations. Our men are very jealous." She laughed again and looked through the open door toward the den where Doc's voice murmured in low tones. "Even old silly men." There was affection in her voice. "He still finds me attractive, even in this old body."

"You're not that old, Mary."

"Seventy-one, child. I look younger, but I don't move as spryly as I used to." She poured the batter into a cake pan and scooped out the last of it carefully. "As for you and your leopard, it's an exhilarating experience. Are you afraid?"

"Nervous. Well . . . a little afraid. Does it hurt?"

"Some, because you can feel the transformation, but in a good way. Don't hesitate. Just let it happen. You won't be lost. You'll be there fully, just in another form."

"And she'll want to mate with her leopard?"

"Yes. And you'll have to let her." She laughed, her expression dreamy. "She'll only make you wilder for your man."

"If that's possible," Isabeau muttered. "I'm pretty wild for him already and he knows it."

"He wouldn't be leopard if he didn't know it, honey," Mary said. She pushed the pans into the oven and stepped back, dusting off her hands. "Come on, let's go take a look into the treasure chest and see what we can find."

Isabeau's heart jumped. She wasn't going to hurt Mary's feelings no matter what. The woman was being so kind. Isabeau felt her cat close, stretching, pushing, almost purring with need. Her breasts began to ache, and when she walked, her jeans rubbed along the junction between her legs. *Not yet. I'm a little aggravated with you,* she cautioned her cat.

The female leopard didn't seem to care. She rolled, making Isabeau want to arch her back. She was feeling a little desperate for Conner. The burning between her legs grew stronger with every step she took.

"I was married in 1958 and had a very daring wedding dress for those times. I had to make my own wedding dress, as we didn't have access to dresses. Doc was from a different village, and many of those in my town treated me as if I was a scarlet woman. I was quite the flirt back then, and very defiant of tradition." Mary laughed as she climbed the stairs to the attic and shoved open the door. "A friend drew the design and basically did the actual sewing for me. She's remained my best friend for all these years and lives just down the road. In her time, she was a wonderful designer, always raising the bar. To me this dress represents adventure, a deep-abiding love and everything romantic and magical."

She glanced at Isabeau over her shoulder. "I loved Doc with all my heart when I married him, and I love him a thousand times more now. I would be honored if you wore this dress and perhaps passed it on to your daughter some day. Each time a new way to preserve it came out, I had it done. It's as fresh now as it was fifty-two years ago."

Mary knelt in front of a chest made of cedar and slowly opened the lid. Reverently she took out several items until she came to a large sealed box. Isabeau held her breath while Mary broke the seal and pulled out the dress.

"Mary." Isabeau breathed her name, staring in awe at the dress.

The dress was champagne and ivory, the color less traditional than stark white. The nearly form-fitting gown had a silky slim skirt that dropped dramatically to the floor with Belgium lace swirling around the hem.

"Back then, the style was full skirts, and lots of lace. Neither suited either my personality or my figure, and so Ruth adorned the hem and bust with the finest Belgium lace, but left the rest plain. The bust is beaded over the lace. Few designers were doing beads then, but Ruth had always incorporated beads into her drawings. Of course the strapless bust was totally risqué. Some designers were doing it, but they covered the shoulders with a small jacket or lace so the bride would be decent in church."

Isabeau laughed. "Mary, you were a rebel."

"No one back then paid much attention to Ruth's designs. They told her she would never amount to anything. Only men could have their own businesses. Women were supposed to stay home and mind the children. It made me angry. So I asked her to come up with the design, and our friends helped to find the right materials. We had to send away for everything, and it was so expensive. Now the money would be laughable, but then, it was a pretty penny and with the way we lived, difficult to find."

"Were you a sensation in it?"

Mary grinned at her. "Doc couldn't take his eyes off of me. The ruche satin made my waist incredibly small. I thought I looked like a princess."

"Who wouldn't in such a beautiful dress?"

"Turn it around. I love the buttons."

Isabeau carefully turned the dress around to expose the back. Tiny satin buttons adorned the back all the way down to the bottom of the small train.

"At first Ruthie was only going to put them to the waist but she wanted to accent the line of the dress, so in the end, she attached them all the way to the hem. Just so you know, sitting isn't all that comfortable. You have to position the dress just right, but it's so beautiful, who cares?"

"It *is* beautiful." Isabeau had to blink back tears. "What if it doesn't fit me?"

"It will fit. And I can take it in or let it out if I have to, but I think you're very close to what my size was back then. And Ruthie is on her way over to help, so if I can't do it, believe me she can."

Isabeau frowned, a thought occurring to her. "You aren't talking about Ruth Ann Gobel, the famous designer, are you?"

Mary laughed. "That would be Ruthie. She'll love that you recognized her name. Her dresses—now considered vintage—have grown popular over the last few years. She barely made a living in her day."

"Mary, this dress is worth a fortune. If it's the first dress she ever designed and sewed, with the condition it's in, the dress is priceless. I can't accept . . ."

Mary patted her hand. "I insist. What's it going to do,

stay in a box? It was meant to worn, to be special, to make a woman feel wonderful. You wear that dress today and you'll be making two old women very happy."

Mary was a very slender woman now, her bones small, her hair gray, but her eyes were bright and the few wrinkles looked more like laugh lines. Isabeau could see a timeless beauty in her, the bone structure, the skin, the ready smile. Or maybe it was her inner spirit shining through.

"Are you absolutely certain?" Isabeau was afraid Mary didn't understand the treasure she had. "Perhaps a granddaughter . . ."

Mary shook her head. "This is for Marisa. I *want* to do this. We spent so many hours talking about it and planning it, and if I do this for me, I'm doing it for her as well. And Ruthie was so pleased when I told her you might wear the dress."

Conner's mother had touched so many hearts. She was an exceptional woman and she'd raised an exceptional son. Isabeau felt humble that she was reaping the rewards of Marisa's friendship with Mary.

"Thank you, Mary. I accept gladly."

"Let's try it on then."

Isabeau couldn't wait. Suddenly she was very excited about her wedding day. She wouldn't be wearing jeans and a tank top, she'd be wearing the first dress the famous designer Ruth Ann Gobel had ever made. She knew she would feel like she was in the midst of a fairy tale.

Mary led the way to the back of the house to an empty guest room. Isabeau was extremely careful, half afraid that she might rip the dress. The material felt alive under her hands. She stripped and stepped into the dress, wiggling until she could pull it over her breasts. The moment Mary began to close the buttons, Isabeau could tell it fit like a glove, as if it had been made for her alone. Knowing the history of the dress only made it all the more special to her.

Very slowly, nearly holding her breath, she turned around to face Mary. She felt magical, beautiful, even extraordinary, and she hadn't even seen herself. Mary's eyes grew bright as she blinked back tears.

."Oh, my dear, thank you for this moment. You're stunning. I knew I'd feel as if I had a daughter, and I do. Look in the mirror."

The looking glass was full length on a wooden stand. Mary turned it slowly until Isabeau's reflection stared back at her. She gasped and brought both hands to cover her mouth. "Is that really me?"

Mary brushed a hand through Isabeau's hair. "You're so beautiful. I think your man is going to be very happy that he wanted an actual wedding ceremony for you."

Isabeau's fingers creased in the dress. "Don't tell him about this." The dress made her feel more than romantic and beautiful—she felt sexy. Really sexy. A wild temptress. Maybe Ruth Ann Gobel had woven in a spell the way some of the newspapers claimed when they talked about her work. Women felt different in her designs. Isabeau certainly did.

"Oh Mary!" Another voice chimed in from the doorway, and Isabeau whirled around to see another woman. She looked a little more worn than Mary, was a little heavier, but her eyes were kind, and right now she was staring at Isabeau with rapt attention. "So this is our little bride. Isabeau Chandler? I'm Ruth Ann Gobel. Mary tells me you may need some alterations, but can't tell where. Let me look."

For the next two hours, Isabeau was spun around, poked,

prodded, her hair washed and redone in preparation for some "do" Mary and Ruth both felt was necessary to complete the look. The two decorated the cake with surprising flourish, and other women began to arrive with platters of food.

"Go out onto the back porch and have tea with your man. We put out fruit, crackers and cheese, and you should eat something," Mary said. "You've got a couple of hours to rest before everyone begins to arrive."

Isabeau looked around the kitchen at all the women. "There's more?"

"The entire valley is coming, dear," Mary said with a sweet smile. "A chance for a celebration, you know. We're all on the other side of sixty and we could use something fun like this. No one is going to miss it."

Isabeau shook her head. Conner had no idea what he'd gotten them all into with his sudden idea of marriage. She felt a little light-headed herself, the talk swirling around her until all the words ran together and there was just the roar of need in her head. Need of Conner. Need for freedom. Need to let her cat out.

She ran her nails lightly over her arm. At least for a little while the other women had managed to drown out the needs of her leopard, but after a while, the close proximity of so many females—even though they were no threat to her mate—made her leopard cranky. Isabeau sighed and wandered out to the back porch, stopping abruptly when she saw Conner sitting at a table with Rio. A long, jaunty red-and-white cloth hung to the ground around the circular table, and an unlit candle adorned the center, along with plates of strawberries and raspberries mixed with cheese and crackers, a pitcher of lemonade and another of ice tea. The ladies had already been here.

She studied Conner through half-closed eyes, the width of his shoulders, the heavy muscles of his chest and arms, his firm jaw and straight nose, the four scars that only made him look tougher. Her entire body reacted to the sight of him, and something wholly mischievous and very sexy took hold of her. She moved up behind Conner and deliberately leaned over his shoulder, allowing her aching breasts to push against his body. At once her nipples tingled with arousal. Her head was against his, her mouth close to his ear. She breathed warm air onto the side of his neck and pressed her lips right against his ear. "I wish we were alone."

She felt his reaction, the small ripple of awareness sliding down his spine, the slight rise in his temperature. She smiled with satisfaction and sank into the chair quite close to his, pulling it close to the table so the cloth draped down. If she had to suffer, so could he.

She took a strawberry from the bowl and bit off the end, letting the juice gleam on her lips as she kept her gaze steady on Conner. He shifted, easing the tightness of his jeans, and she nearly purred. Her gaze flicked to Rio. "I was just wondering, although we did go over all the contingencies, thinking up everything that could go wrong . . ." She swiped her tongue over her lips to get the juice of the strawberry off. "Remember when Jeremiah said Suma came to his village in Costa Rica and talked to the youth? Did anyone ask Jeremiah if any others took Suma up on his invitation?"

She dropped her free hand into Conner's lap, her palm cupping the thick bulge, just holding still for a moment. His thigh muscles bunched. His body tensed. She took another bite of strawberry and smiled at Rio. "We could be facing a little army of leopards in that compound, right?"

Rio frowned and tipped his chair back. "I should have

thought of that." He glanced at Conner. "We both should have."

Conner's croak of agreement was a little strangled as she began to rub slow, caressing circles along that hard, thick bulge. His hand covered hers, pressing her palm tight against him and holding it still.

"I'm going to ask him, see if I can get an answer," Rio said. He pushed back his chair.

Isabeau watched him leave with a small smile.

"What do you think you're doing?" Conner hissed.

She lifted one shoulder and sent him her best siren's smile. "Playing with fire. I like how it burns."

"You keep it up and you'll be crawling under the table and giving me a little relief."

She shook her head. "Not this time. This time, I'll be insisting you find a way to give me some relief. My cat won't let up."

He sat back in his chair, his eyes going golden. "Really? She's giving you trouble, today?" His gaze grew hot.

Flames licked over her skin. She tried rubbing him again, but his fingers tightened over hers. He pulled her hand out of his lap and bit the ends of her fingers, sending a spasm of liquid heat rushing to her melting center.

"It's hot as hell knowing you need my cock buried inside your burning little body. I should torment you a little bit and wait until you're begging me."

She leaned close to him, licking at his ear with the tip of her tongue. Her teeth raked the side of his neck. "Or maybe you'll be the one begging."

He groaned softly. "You're killing me, baby, with all these women surrounding us. And believe me, they're sneaking peeks. I can hear their whispers and their laughter."

"I'm just obliging them. They want to know what kind

of package my man is delivering," she whispered and tugged at his earlobe with her teeth.

"I think they're judging whether or not I have enough strength to resist a little temptation from a she-cat."

"Or enough manhood to do something about it," she countered.

He rose so fast he knocked the chair over. With one swift motion he picked her up, rolled her over and deposited her on his shoulder, head down his back. One hand clamped tight just under her bottom as he stepped off the porch and headed toward the barn. Laughter followed them, the sounds of both men and women.

"What are you doing?" Isabeau grabbed his shirt with both fists and hung on as he strode across the uneven terrain.

"Proving my manhood, beloved. I certainly don't want you—or that pack of women—to think I can't handle the job."

"No one's replacing you, crazy leopard man, that was called teasing."

"Totally foreign concept to me," he said and yanked open the barn door. "Proving manhood I understand."

She was laughing so hard she could barely hold on. "Put me down, cave man."

"I am the ruler of the forest and I've captured my mate."

Rio stepped in front of him, Doc at his side. "You can put your little captive there down, Tarzan, and back off."

Conner whirled around to face Felipe and Marcos coming in on his left. Felipe shook his head and snapped his fingers. "Give me the girl, ape man."

Conner growled a warning and spun to his right, only to be blocked by Leonardo and Ruth Ann Gobel's husband, Dan.

Leonardo held up his hand. "I don't think so, not on her wedding day. Give us back our sister."

Conner whirled around in circles, Isabeau laughing uncontrollably as they were surrounded by the men. Most were sixty or seventy, but they looked stern and uncompromising.

"Hand her over," Doc ordered.

Conner reluctantly put Isabeau onto her feet, holding her body in front of his, his arm curled around her waist.

"You don't understand," he said as the mob pressed closer. "The women challenged my manhood. I had no choice."

Rio crooked his finger at Isabeau. "Come here to me, little sister."

Isabeau couldn't keep a straight face. Rio managed to look scary, but his eyes were laughing as were most of the older men. Leonardo and Felipe were just plain snickering. She slid one hand behind her back and continued a slow massage over his thick erection all the while pretending to struggle against Conner's arm. "He won't let me go."

"I'm going to have to take him out behind the barn and teach him some manners," Doc declared. "You let that girl go."

"Not happening, Doc," Conner said, holding her to him. Her fingers were pure magic. He'd forgotten fun. Maybe all of them had. Abel and Mary reminded them what life was all about—sharing with family and friends. Laughter and hope. Love. And he loved Isabeau Chandler with everything in him.

"He's just too strong, Rio," Isabeau claimed and then reached her arm up and behind her to hook around the nape of Conner's neck and draw his head down to hers.

Her lips were velvet soft, firm and far too enticing to

resist. Her mouth was hot, her tongue sensually tangling with his. For a moment he forgot their audience and their silly game and just lost himself in the wonder of her kiss. He tasted love and it was the most addictive spice there was.

"Hey there!" Rio said. "Little sister, I think you're worse than he is. Let her go, Conner, or we're taking you out behind the barn to give you a little lesson in respect."

"Actually," Conner said, without a hint of remorse, "I am being respectful. I'm trying to spare you and your women from seeing what your shortcomings are. If I don't keep Isabeau right here, we could have a riot on our hands."

She spun around and pushed him away from her with both hands flat on his chest, color flooding her face. "You're terrible." She marched over to Rio, her nose in the air.

Doc intercepted her path, catching her arm. "Young lady, I think you need to come with me. It's obvious I need to put you in protective custody."

She turned her head to watch the men close in on Conner. They were laughing as they advanced menacingly. She had the feeling her bridegroom was about to be subjected to some ancient ritual. She went back to the house with Doc. The women were gathered on the porch, watching the men's antics, laughing together.

Mary snapped a tea towel at her. "Naughty girl." Amusement sparkled in her eyes. "Sign the documents for Abel and let him complete your health certificates and then we've prepared you a nice bath. Claudia will do your hair for you. She's a wonderful hairdresser. Leopard hair grows so thick and fast and yours has curl to it. She'll be able to put it up beautifully."

"I brought jewelry," another woman said. "I'm Monica, a jewelry designer. As soon as Mary called me and said

you were Marisa's daughter-in-law, I knew I had found the
perfect person for my most special design. It's just been
sitting there. I've never even displayed it. I just knew it was
for an important occasion. This is my present to you on
your wedding day."

She held up a box. Champagne diamonds sparkled in a
swirl of glittering white diamonds dropping in tears from
a chain of white gold. The earrings were small teardrops
matching the necklace. It was the most beautiful jewelry
Isabeau had ever seen. She stepped back, shaking her head.
"I can't accept that."

Monica smiled at her. "I'm eighty-two, Isabeau. I have
no children and this is my work. I'm grateful for the opportunity to give it to someone who will treasure it."

Isabeau felt tears choking her. The kindness of these
people, the sheer generosity was amazing. She let her
breath out, struggling not to cry. "Then, thank you. I'll
never forget any of you. You make me feel as if I really
have a family."

The women smiled at one another and ushered her into
the house, out of Conner's sight.

17

CONNER was nervous. He hadn't expected to be nervous. He was also excited and he'd expected that, but suddenly, standing up in front of the judge with a much larger audience than he'd counted on was a little disconcerting. Rio kept grinning at him and he found it was just better not to look at Leonardo or Felipe. Even Elijah had shot him a quick smirk before going off to patrol. He ran his finger around his collar and adjusted his tie one more time. Admittedly this was all his idea, so he couldn't exactly run.

He wanted to marry Isabeau. It wasn't that making him nervous. But what if she changed her mind? He shouldn't have pushed her so hard. She was young. Nearly ten years younger than he was, and she'd been sheltered. What had he done? Come into her life, exposed her father, revealed she'd been adopted and then dragged her into a very dangerous situation. He took a breath and ran his sweaty palms down his thighs. Okay, she'd been the one to seek out the team for the present job, but truthfully, if he'd ever found out about his brother, he would have gone anyway, and he could have—*should* have protected her more . . .

The music started. Hushed murmurs rose and he turned his head. His heart stopped beating. The breath stilled in his lungs. Isabeau stood framed in the doorway, her gloved hand tucked into the crook of Doc's elbow. She was in a floor-length gown that emphasized the curves of her body to perfection. Diamonds sparkled at her throat and ears. She looked ethereal, a princess in some fairy tale. She looked so beautiful his eyes burned and his throat felt raw. His heart managed to kick-start again, this time hammering in his chest. A roaring started in his head and muscles knotted in his stomach. Her wild hair looked elegant, and yet maintained her untamed appearance, adding to the throb in his groin.

He realized his mouth was open and he was devouring her with his eyes, but he couldn't stop. There was no way to look away from her, a vision, walking toward him. He felt a mixture of emotions, humbled by the fact that she could love him after what he'd done—and what he might have to do. She was everything to him and he knew that emotion was raw and stark on his face for everyone to see, but he couldn't mask it. He didn't even want to try.

Mary sobbed in the front row and several other women dabbed at their eyes. One of the men blew his nose loudly. And then she was moving, walking toward him, her gaze on his, and his love grew with every step she took until he felt as if he might burst with it. He didn't know if every groom felt this way, but in his world, where everything was life and death, where he saw the worst in people, this moment, surrounded by friends and good people, was perfection.

He glanced once at Rio to make certain he had the all-important ring. Doc's friend, an older woman by the name of Monica Taylor, had brought him several boxes to allow him to pick out a ring for his bride. He'd never seen such beautiful work, and when he realized the jeweler was Monica, he was even more impressed. Her hands were twisted and gnarled with arthritis, and when she showed him the rings, she'd trembled.

Rio seemed to understand his concern and he nodded his head and made a show of touching his pocket, leaving Conner able to concentrate solely on his bride as she walked up the aisle to him. He wanted the moment to last forever, that image of her moving toward him. Everything else in the yard disappeared. Even his sense of self-preservation. He'd been raised to always—*always*—be on the alert for danger. There was a part of him aware of his surroundings, constantly vigilant, but in that moment, he was wholly focused, even his cat's entire attention was completely centered on Isabeau.

He heard the judge asking who gave this woman to this man as if from a great distance. Doc's voice murmured an answer and then he was placing Isabeau's hand in Conner's. He closed his fingers around hers and drew her hand to him. He leaned down, his gaze holding hers.

"You're so beautiful, Isabeau. Thank you for this."

Her lashes fluttered. She actually looked shy. He felt her fingers curl in his and his heart jumped again. He'd never felt so protective of anyone in his life. He pulled her close to him as they turned to face the judge. He wanted his body heat to envelope her, his scent, so that he filled her senses in the same way she filled his.

He could hear the man speaking about the sacred bond of marriage and at last he understood what he was really feeling. This was his other half. He was complete with her and she with him. They had chosen one another to share it all—both good and bad. They knew bad. They knew the worst of humanity—and the best. And they had chosen to walk a path together. He wanted that path to be the best he could make for her.

She looked into his eyes as she stated her vows in a soft, firm voice. He was clearer, confident, knowing his choice was right. With every passing moment of the binding ceremony, he felt the threads tying them together grow stronger until they were unbreakable bonds. She looked a little shocked when he removed her glove and pushed the ring onto her finger. She blinked up at him with a little gasp and then turned her head to search out and find Monica with a small happy smile and a nod.

Then he was enfolding her in his arms, drawing her against his chest and sealing their vows with his kiss while everyone stood up and clapped. Rio clapped him on the back and Felipe and Leonardo followed suit, nearly knocking the breath out of him.

He kissed Isabeau's fingertips. "I can't believe how beautiful you look." He inhaled her fragrance; she smelled of cherry blossoms and fresh forest after a rain.

"The women helped me. They've been so wonderful."

She looked so happy Conner kissed her again, vowing silently to try to find a way to repay the people of the valley. They'd turned this day into something magical. Their generosity seemed boundless. As the guests congratulated them, they each pressed a small gift into their hands. Each item was made with loving hands. All seemed priceless. A sharp hunting knife, the metal folded and honed into an edge that gleamed. A knitted pullover sweater for Conner. A cardigan and scarf for Isabeau. The wool had been spun and dyed right there in the valley. Isabeau's personal favorite was a small bronze statue of two leopards, one a fierce male standing protectively above a female who nuzzled his throat. The beauty of the piece brought a lump to her throat.

Talk swirled around them and music started. The buffet tables were filled with wonderfully smelling food, and several of the women took turns taking plates and coffee to Elijah as he prowled the grounds and nearby forest to keep them all safe. Marcos flirted outrageously with the women, and laughter rang throughout the valley.

Conner pulled Isabeau into his arms, the music pounding through his veins in time to the beat of his heart. She fit perfectly, and the scent of her drifted through his lungs like fine wine. He rested his cheek against the soft silk of her hair, content to sway gently to the rhythm.

"I can't believe they did this for us, Conner," Isabeau said. "I was afraid I'd feel lonely and sad, and they've transported us into some magical realm." She tilted her head to look at him. "They did this for your mother, for Marisa. She's here with us. They all loved her and they took us in and made us family because of her."

"She was magic," Conner agreed. "She had a way of making every person feel important, maybe because, to her, they really were. I never really heard her say an unkind word. She took in Mateo and raised him as her own. And when I say "as her own" I mean she would love him the way she loved me. With everything in her." His arms tightened around Isabeau. "I'm glad you had a chance to meet her."

"I see her in you, Conner."

"Do you?" He was really asking. Really hoping. "I was afraid I was all my father." Hard. Mean. A man others would avoid.

"She's in your eyes, Conner. And in the way you love.

You didn't hesitate to take Mateo in, even if it meant losing me. You would sacrifice for a small boy you don't even know. Her kindness lives in each of the people she touched, in you and hopefully in your brother."

He brushed kisses along the corners of her mouth. "We'll see to it."

"You aren't worried, are you, Conner?" she asked. "We'll find him and we'll bring him out safely."

"I've never thought about being a parent. First I was worried that I might not measure up as a mate to you, and now I have to worry about what kind of father I'll make."

She snuggled against his chest. "I don't think you have to worry. You had a great example in your mother and, although my father did many things very wrong, he was a good parent to me. He loved me and made me feel important to him. He made certain I had a good education and always felt loved. I might not have had a mother, but I did have a father. You didn't have a father but you had a great mother. Between the two of us, we're bound to have picked up a few things."

Conner looked around him at the men and women who had established a retirement valley. They grew food on their farms and most still worked at their occupations, but were now committed to the good of the community. "We have a wealth of knowledge right here," he whispered against her ear. "Look at them all. They've already fought their battles and learned their lessons. We'll settle somewhere close to them. You can still work with your plants in the rain forest, we can raise Mateo and any children we have nearby."

"What about your work?"

He shrugged. "It isn't that difficult. Rio sends for us when we have a job."

She scowled at him. "I don't think I'm going to be so

willing for you to seduce a woman after this. I'd like to say my leopard wouldn't be jealous . . ."

He laughed softly. "Your leopard would be spitting jealous. She'll turn ferocious if she finds her mate near any other woman. Don't worry, I gladly give up my job to one of the others. When I go"—because she had to know this was his life's work—"I'll go as one of the team, not the front man."

Elijah passed by on his shifting patrol and one of the women handed him a strawberry lemonade. His smile was genuine, but she couldn't imagine what he was thinking. Did they know about his past? Probably. The men and women in the retirement valley seemed to know about everything—leopard or human. They were accepting, tolerant people who were willing for anyone to live out their lives. No one asked him questions and he was treated with open friendliness.

Isabeau inhaled sharply, wanting to remember every detail, the setting sun turning the sky into an orange-red flame, the forest a silhouette of dark trees and brush and especially the fragrances mingling in the air. She could sort them all out if she chose, the food, the forest and each individual. She knew exactly where Mary and Doc were at any given moment. She threaded her fingers through Conner's as they strolled around the yard talking to the various guests.

Mary, Ruth and Monica insisted they cut the cake and feed each other a slice, and Isabeau did so, laughing at Conner's wry expression. The wedding had been his suggestion, but he hadn't counted on the women of the valley pulling off a traditional wedding. She rested her back against him and looked around her, committing her magical wedding to memory.

A wave of heat poured over her unexpectedly, nothing

at all like the other times. This was hot and fast and robbed her of breath. She nearly dropped her plate with the slice of cake. There was no mere itching beneath her skin, but a strong pushing, the pressure tremendous. Very carefully she put the plate on the table, each motion precise. She tasted fear in her mouth. She knew the leopard was not going to wait much longer. Her skin felt too tight and her mouth and jaw ached, teeth sensitive. Her eyesight blurred, eyes aching.

"Conner," she whispered his name like a talisman.

"What is it, beloved?" he asked, and looked down into her face.

She saw the instant recognition. Her eyes had taken on the glow of the cat at night, wholly leopard now. There was panic on her face, something she couldn't help. She knew it was different this time. Her heartbeat was different. Her skin burned, the weight of the dress painful. She wanted to tear it off her body, dig her nails into her own skin and shred it, peel it away. The heat came in waves, washing over her so that she could barely breathe.

He put his cake plate beside hers, just as carefully as she had. "Don't be afraid, Isabeau. I'll be with you. You'll experience running free, feeling nearly euphoric. There's nothing to be afraid of."

She breathed deeply, great gulps of air, trying to suppress the urge to rub herself all over him. She'd thought her addiction to his body was powerful before, but now, with the leopard's needs surging to the surface, she couldn't stand still. She stared into Conner's face, despair in her gaze. She didn't want to ruin their perfect time by ripping the priceless dress from her body, her leopard emerging to leap on the buffet table and smash the cake. For one awful moment, she envisaged the carnage.

"Keep breathing, baby," he whispered, wrapping his arm around her waist and all but pushing her through the back door into the house. He glanced over his shoulder. "Mary!" His summons was sharp. Imperative.

When Isabeau tried to reply, no coherent sound emerged, not with the way her throat felt closed and swollen. She was acutely conscious of the mechanics of her body. The way she took in air, the way it moved through her body. Each individual strand of hair on her head. Scents grew stronger, flooding her system until she feared it might shut down. Her body burned, tension coiling tighter and tighter, the itch growing not only through her skin, but through every cell in her body.

"I've got you," Conner assured, thrusting her into the first room he came to.

She was moving continually, unable to stay still. The perfumed heat from the interior of the rain forest called to her. Walls seemed oppressive. She felt caged and claustrophobic. Her breasts felt swollen and achy, her nipples hard and so sensitive that with each step she took, as they rubbed against the material of the bodice, nerve endings sizzled and electrical charges raced straight to her core. She was melting from the inside out. Conner's masculine scent overwhelmed her, his body heat making her catch fire as his fingers fumbled with the buttons of her wedding dress.

Mary pushed open the door, took in the sight of Isabeau's flushed face and apprehensive expression and slid into the room, closing the door behind her. "You get everything ready that you'll need," she told Conner. "I'll help Isabeau. I've been through this." Her hands replaced Conner's on the buttons. Although she was older, she moved each satin-covered button deftly, quickly opening the back of the dress.

Conner leaned over to give Isabeau a quick kiss. "Give me five minutes, beloved."

Isabeau honestly didn't know if she had five minutes. The house was too stifling, and even Mary's presence, so close to Conner, sent her cat into a frenzy. She exerted control over her cat, annoyed that a woman who had treated her as a mother with such kindness could trigger bad behavior in her leopard.

"It's all right," Mary assured. "You'll handle her. She's emerging and her every instinct is centered on Conner. Let her run with him and flirt until she's worn out. She'll want to mate with his cat. She'll *need* his cat. And that's the way it's supposed to be. Once she's aware no one is going to take her mate from her, she'll settle down." She held the dress so Isabeau could step out of it.

"Does it hurt?"

Mary smiled at her. "It's a relief. By the time she emerges, you're going to want to be with anything that resembles a man. When she starts, just let it happen. You won't disappear, but it feels, the first time, as if she's swallowing you. The faster you let it happen, the less of a wrench. Your man will be there with you and he won't let anything go wrong."

Isabeau couldn't stand the feel of clothes on her skin, but she couldn't run across the expanse of ground to enter the forest naked in front of her guests. Mary thrust a thin robe into her hands and she put it on without even looking at it.

"You've been so good to me," Isabeau told her—or tried to do so. Her voice had turned to gravel, but she was determined to let Mary know what she had done for her, what this day had meant to her. "I don't remember my mother— either of them, my birth or adopted mother, but if I have children, I'm going to try to be like you." Ignoring her cat raking at her, she hugged the other woman, refusing to panic. If this calm, steady woman told her she would be all right, then she'd face this exciting, exhilarating moment with courage. "Thank you, Mary, for everything."

She could barely speak with the ache in her jaw and mouth. Her skin felt raw, every nerve ending inflamed. Her womb clenched, and feathers of arousal teased her thighs and belly. The roaring in her head nearly drowned out the sound of Mary's voice. She could barely hear her, as if from a great distance. Her vision was fully cat now, her hands curling until she was afraid to wait for Conner.

"I have to go." Her voice was no longer her own, strangled and growling, her throat reshaping.

Fur rippled and receded along her arms, down her legs and left her body crawling with sensation. Flames licked over her stomach as her muscles rippled as if alive. The burning increased until she was nearly squirming. The light robe hurt where it touched her skin. Everything hurt.

Conner thrust his head in the door, took one look at her and caught her hand, yanking her under the protection of his shoulder. "Let's go."

"Wait!" Mary caught at them. "Her jewelry. Put it in your bag."

Conner took her ring while Mary unfastened her necklace and earrings. When they were safely in the pack, Isabeau breathed a sigh of relief.

"Thanks for everything, Mary," Conner said.

"It was a pleasure," Mary replied. "Have courage, Isabeau," she added.

Conner was barefoot, and shirtless, wearing only light jeans and a pack slung around his neck. They hurried out the back door and began sprinting for the forest. Isabeau caught the low murmurs behind them, yet nothing mattered but her strange vision and the acute hearing, the myriad of unfamiliar sensations coursing through her body.

She felt as if she had a fever that kept rising until she was going to burn from the inside out. Everything felt too tight, especially her skull. The trees swallowed them and they kept running deeper into the darkness, but she wasn't blind. There was no fear of that dark interior; instead, her body embraced the brush of leaves, the rustles of the insects, the constant, never-ending hum of the cicadas and the flitting of birds and monkeys from tree to tree overhead.

Her legs went rubbery and she found herself on the forest floor, her muscles contorting. Her hands curved and knotted, knuckles extending. Muscles contorted and once again a wave of fur raced over her body and disappeared. Bones and joints popped. She cried out, the sound foreign, her vocal cords nearly crushed under the changes in her throat.

Conner was beside her in an instant, framing her face with his hands. "Let it happen, Isabeau, don't fight her. There's nothing to fear."

Tears burned in her eyes. She wanted this—she did, but the sensations were so frightening. The fear of the unknown. The twisting and gut-wrenching turning of her body inside out. Her spine bent, that long, flexible instrument that allowed her to twist and leap, to turn in midair. She breathed deeply, trying to call to her cat. Yes, she wanted this. This was part of her life with Conner, and she wanted her life with him, no matter what was thrown at them. She could do this, lie on the forest floor, her body contorting, the roaring loud in her head and the fear shimmering in her belly—for Conner. She could do anything for him.

Conner crouched beside her, shaking his head as she reached for him. "This is for *you*. This is who you are."

She heard his words as if far off. Already the night was rushing at her, the sights and sounds as her body reshaped, tendons and muscles protesting and aching. Sharp stabs of aching pain cut through her, but now she could barely acknowledge the transformation as her body reshaped. She *felt* her cat, her other half. The lithe, compact body, the heightened senses, the raging needs, but most of all, she would never be alone. The sense of oneness was gone as her cat emerged, the body rolling for a moment in the thick vegetation, but she leapt gracefully to her feet and let out her first purring chuff.

The leopard stretched languidly—seductively—and looked over her shoulder at the large male emerging beside her. At once she moved, enticing him, rubbing her scent on trees and brush, leaving him in no doubt how very alluring she was. The male followed at a more cautious pace, knowing females had their own time line and only when she was ready would she submit to his possession.

She deliberately enticed and seduced him, rolling in the leaves, rubbing her long, beautiful coat along the bark of the trees, sending leaves scattering with a brush of her paw. Conner could see she was enjoying her newfound freedom. Living wild was a lure all of them had to face. The natural law of the rain forest was easy to follow in comparison to the human world. Greed and deceit had no place here.

Conner widened his eyes and pressed his ears forward, signaling her leopard he wanted to play. All cats enjoyed playing—even the large ones. Within moments, they were chasing one another, wrestling, and tumbling over and over in the thick carpet of leaves. They played a long game of hide-and-seek. Isabeau hid and Conner stalked and ambushed her, pouncing on her, rolling her over in a tangle of tails and legs, and then leapt away laughing.

All the while, the female leopard continued to entice the male with her seductive vocal communication as she rolled and stretched. Conner came close, staring into her eyes in the way of the leopard male. At first she reciprocated, gazing deeply into his eyes, but when he moved slightly toward her, she rebuffed him with a growl, spitting and hissing her refusal even as she leapt away in a seductive move, inviting chase.

Conner ran beside her, rubbing his scent from one end of her fur-clad body to the other. He found her beautiful and sensual, a heady mixture to his male leopard. She moved ahead of him along the narrow trail, winding in and out among the trees, heading to the river. Every few minutes she would stop and crouch in front of him. He approached her warily. A female not ready was dangerous. He waited for her to be very certain. Each time he approached, she'd leap away, hissing, swiping at him with a paw.

He loved the wild sight of her. Her scent, calling to him, was overpowering, a heady aphrodisiac as they continued deeper into the forest. Night creatures called back and forth. The continual flick of bat wings signaled the creatures hunting insects in the night sky. This was his world and he ruled. He approached her again, this time coming in straight behind her as she crouched. She stayed in position and everything in him settled.

His mate. *His.* He roared a challenge once to any male in the vicinity, and then he was on her, his teeth sinking into the back of her neck to prevent her moving, his body blanketing hers. All males were possessive and attentive when their female was in heat, and sex between cats could be rough. The large male leopard took his time with her, the drive to claim his mate overpowering. She cried out when he withdrew, spinning around to threaten him with her sides heaving and a grimace on her face, but when he rubbed his muzzle over her, she calmed.

They lay together in a heap of fur, tails twining around one another while he rested, and then he was on her again. They spent several hours together, but the male kept them moving slowly but steadily back toward the small cabin where their human counterparts were staying. They mated frequently and ferociously as was the way of the leopard.

As they neared the cabin, the female began to realize where they were and she tried to turn back to the forest and the freedom of living wild. The male, knowing the tremendous lure, prevented her, using his shoulder and upper-body strength to push her back toward the house. The reaction was very common for the first emergence, but it was necessary to curb it fast. Staying in leopard form for long periods of time could be dangerous, increasing the traits of the leopard in the human.

Isabeau smelled civilization and knew Conner was forcing her home. Already the change was beginning. The moment she recognized intellect, she knew her brain was already functioning as a human. The change started there, in her mind, a reaching for her human body. Almost immediately there was a reaction, a wrenching of muscle and bone. A small cry escaped, half human—half wild.

She felt the night air on her skin and she found herself facedown on the porch of their cabin, completely naked, her body in a terrible state of arousal. It made no sense when her leopard had been fully sated, but apparently the violent need manifested itself in the human—at least in her as well. She lifted her head to look at her husband.

Conner crouched a foot away from her, his golden eyes fixed on her face. He made no attempt to hide the stark, raw need burning through his body. With deliberate intent he reached for her, rolling her over onto her back, right there on the secluded porch. His gaze was fierce, almost as wild as his leopard as he came over her, his mouth seeking hers. He was ravenous for the taste of her, his hands moving, shaping, exploring, starved for the feel of her soft skin.

She lifted her head to meet him, their mouths fusing, welding, fastening together, tongues dueling while his hands kneaded and massaged her breasts, tugged and rolled her nipples until those soft little sobs of desperation began in her throat. Until neither could breathe and they were forced to break a scant few inches apart, drawing the air harshly into burning lungs and devouring one another with their eyes. His hands never stopped, moving down her belly until his fingers plunged inside her and she bucked helplessly against him. She felt as if she was so hot her center was melting.

"Hurry, Conner. Please hurry," she pleaded.

He knelt between her legs and lifted her hips, hesitating a moment at her entrance. She squirmed, her head thrashing, not wanting to wait, trying to impale herself on him. He surged forward and she cried out, a broken, whimpering sound of intense pleasure as she felt him drive deep inside. Her tight sheath gripped him hard, reluctant to open, forcing him to push through those hot folds so that she could feel every inch of his heavy thickness.

The floorboards had no give, and when he held her still and pounded into her, the flames licked over her like a fire out of control, sweeping her up into a vortex of pleasure. Each time he entered her, he seemed to stretch her to capacity, his heavy erection burning like a brand between her thighs and then deep, so deep, until she felt as if he was lodged in her stomach. She could feel her body pulse and throb around his, grasping greedily, reveling in the wild pleasure he brought her.

Isabeau writhed and bucked under him, her hips tuned to his wild, jackhammer rhythm. Her breath came in ragged, harsh gasps and she pushed with her heels, wanting to take him even deeper. That thick shaft, so hot, pounded into her, stroked caresses, varied the tempo until she was shuddering over and over with such pleasure she could only gasp his name and dig her nails into his arms to anchor her there. The tension grew, her body winding tighter and tighter as he thrust into her, his hands anchoring her to him. He adjusted the angle of her body, bending over her, driving harder.

Her soft, keening cry drifted from the porch to the forest, the sound of their bodies coming together in a rhythmic, frenzied mating as molten fire poured into her body, and the pleasure burst through her like the rush of a drug. She began to thrash under him, her breath now a sob as the building pleasure increased until she thought she might not survive.

Conner's face was a mask of harsh lines, lust etched deep, love blazing in the golden eyes as he furiously claimed her, jerking her legs over his shoulder, pounding ever deeper until she stiffened, her body clamping down like a vise on his. Her orgasm tore through her, taking him with her, so that she could feel the hot splash of his release in the midst of the ferocious waves ripping through her. She screamed, a loud, long wail of pleasure as the release gripped her and refused to let go, a fiery inferno that burned both of them alive.

Conner collapsed over her, his breathing as harsh as hers. She could hear his heart beating wildly as she linked her fingers behind his neck. She would have told him she loved him, but she couldn't find enough air. He smiled and knelt back up, very slowly and deliberately running his hands from her breasts to belly and lower, and she knew it was a claiming. *His.* She loved being his.

She smiled at him, drinking him in there in the darkness. It felt to her like the perfect day. She had a fairy-tale wedding, and her leopard had finally emerged. She'd experienced running free as well as the kindness of strangers. They'd made love until neither could move and now they were here in their own little world where the ugliness of someone like Imelda Cortez couldn't touch them.

"Some days are just perfection," she whispered.

He leaned down again, kissing her mouth, nibbling on her lower lip and then licking his way down her throat to the slope of her left breast. "You are so beautiful to me, Isabeau. When I saw you walking toward me in that dress, my heart stopped." He couldn't bear to separate his body from hers. He knew her mouth would create miracles if he just gave her the chance, but her body was a cauldron of fire surrounding his. The little aftershocks rippling through her sent waves of pleasure spiraling through his belly and down his thighs.

"They were all so kind," she said. She reached up to stroke his cheek—the four scars adding to the masculine perfection.

"I don't want this to be over." He threw his head back and looked up at the night sky. Stars were so thick the inky dark appeared milky.

"Silly man." She pushed at him. "I love keeping you happy."

Just her response was enough to send a surge of heat through his body. Leopards often could hear lies, and Isabeau never lied to him. She loved attending his body and she lavished him with her attention.

She laughed softly, feeling his erection thickening, growing harder as he gently pushed deeper into her. His fingers tightened on her hips as he lifted his head to the sky. The wind shifted just a little and Conner's head snapped around, his eyes blazing as he scanned the tree line and canopy. Very slowly, he straightened, still on his knees, his body buried tight in hers. Deep inside his leopard snarled and raked, fury bursting through him.

He inhaled deeply and scented—*enemy*. It was a brief, barely there scent that disappeared almost immediately, as if the male leopard had shifted position with the wind. There was no warning from the canopy, nothing to indicate there was an enemy close, but Conner knew he wasn't mistaken—he had scented another male leopard briefly. He remained still, his gaze sweeping the surrounding forest.

"Is something wrong?" Isabeau asked, recognizing the stillness in him. She started to turn her head, but he dug his fingers into her hips and surged forward, sending ripples of aftershocks spreading through her.

"Don't move. Just look at me."

"Oh my God," she whispered. "Is someone watching us?" She shivered, suddenly frightened. The rain forest had never scared her, yet now shadows seemed to be lurking behind every tree.

"He's out there. Watching us."

She didn't have to ask who "he" was. Ottila Zorba. "How long has he been there?"

"I have no idea. We're going inside. I want you to lock yourself in. You know how to shoot. I'll call for backup and then I'm going to shift and hunt him."

She wanted to shake her head, afraid for him. He pulled away from her and moved his body to block Ottila's view of her while he helped her up and yanked open the door, nearly shoving her inside.

Ottila hadn't cut the communication off, probably not wanting to tip them to his presence. Conner made the call to Rio and then began to move through the cabin, preparing to leave her.

"Wait for Rio, Conner," Isabeau cautioned. "There's something about him that's just plain scary. I'll feel better if you wait."

His leopard wouldn't let him. He doubted if the man would. She had no idea how much nature and instincts played a part in their lives, dominating even good sense at times. His cat raged, a black, jealous haze spreading through his mind. He dragged weapons out and showed each to her, taping one beneath the tabletop, putting another in a drawer, hiding four guns and two knives for her.

"He'll be too busy trying to kill you," Isabeau pointed out. "He doesn't want to kill me, but he wants you dead. If that's really him—and we don't know for certain . . ."

"It's him," Conner said with certainty. "My cat knows it's him. Lock the doors, Isabeau. Stay inside and keep the lights out. I'll call out when I return, otherwise you shoot anything that tries to get in."

She clung to him. "Please just listen to me this once. It's you he's after. He wants you dead. He wants you to go into the forest after him. Otherwise, why tip you off to his presence?"

"No one can predict the wind shifting like that. He was caught and he's probably halfway to the next village by now, running like a rabbit."

She knew better, knew Ottila had no intention of running. Her heart pounded with fear for Conner. He was supremely confident, but he hadn't actually met Ottila as she had. The rogue leopard changed his spots continually, and she had a feeling he was hiding something.

Conner gently put her from him, leaned down and kissed her just once. Then he lifted the back window and shifted as he dove through. He disappeared almost at once into the shadows. Isabeau closed and locked the window, and then drew the shutters, making certain all of them were in place and no one would be able to come through a window.

With shaking hands, Isabeau dressed, putting on her clothes like armor. Layers of them. Underwear, jeans, heavy socks, a T-shirt, before wrapping herself in Conner's sweater. She sat down to wait, her heart beating fast and hard and the taste of fear in her mouth. She had no idea how long she actually sat there, but she realized tears blurred her vision. She couldn't just sit still. She paced for a while and finally opened the shutters overlooking the front porch and stood staring out, trying to see what was happening in the rain forest. She could hear the sounds of the insects and night creatures—the forest had its own music at night, but there was no disruption, no fight between leopards and no warning from the animals that leopards were in the vicinity.

By now, she consoled herself, Rio would have joined Conner in the search. And maybe he was wrong. Maybe he hadn't really caught the scent of a male leopard—although she didn't really believe that.

After a time she realized how hopeless that task was of looking into the rain forest, straining her eyes when there was nothing to see, so she carefully closed and locked the shutters again before she put the kettle on. Tea might combat the shocky way she was feeling. At least the ritual of making tea kept her busy. Once the water had boiled, she poured it into the small pot over the tea leaves and placed a towel over it to steep. She needed something to revive her. There was no way to relax, not with Conner in danger.

She turned to go back to the window. Her heart jumped. Began to pound. Fear made her mouth go dry. Ottila Zorba stood not ten feet from her, his eyes glowing in the darkness, his stare fixed on her as if she was his prey. He'd obviously just shifted. She had no idea how long he'd been there, but his stark naked body, all roped muscle and obvious strength, was very aroused.

18

OTTILA Zorba cocked his head to one side and inhaled, drawing Isabeau's fragrance deep into his lungs. "He made certain to leave his scent all over you," he greeted.

Isabeau wrapped Conner's sweater closer around her body for protection. "What do you want?"

His green-yellow eyes drifted over her from head to toe. "You left your mark on me."

She bit her lip hard. "I wasn't raised with the leopard people. I didn't know what was happening to me."

"Your cat knew and she wanted me."

Isabeau gasped. That couldn't be true. Conner was her mate. She knew he was. She shook her head in denial. "I made a mistake and I'm sorry for that, but you deliberately provoked me. You knew I didn't know what it meant."

He shrugged and took a step toward her.

"Don't." Isabeau retreated, moving toward the table where the gun waited. "I don't want to hurt you, but I will if you give me no other choice."

He smiled, baring his leopard's canines, and held a weapon up. "Are you looking for this? You stared out into the night and all the while I prowled the room, removing your weapons under your nose."

Her heart jumped painfully. Who could do that? She'd heard of leopards dragging victims out of their homes before even those sitting beside them knew what had happened, but she couldn't conceive of anyone being that stealthy. She glanced toward the door, trying to judge the distance. To make it easier, she took another step toward the table, to keep it between them. As she figured, he stepped around toward the other side, giving her that extra step or two.

Isabeau ran for the door. She ran like a human, he leapt like a leopard, clearing the table and landing right beside her as her fingers twisted the lock. She tried to yank open the door, but he slammed it shut with a vicious slap of his palm, trapping her body between his and the wood. She cried out, shaking, feeling small and lost against his enormous strength.

"Ssh, don't scream. Just stay calm," he said. "I'm not going to hurt you."

His arms went around her and Isabeau shuddered, keeping her head down, afraid of what he might do.

"Please," she said softly. "What I did was an accident."

"Ssh." He kept her upright with his strength, when she was trembling, her legs rubbery. "Get yourself a cup of tea and sit across the room, away from the table." He indicated a chair. "Put sugar in your tea. It will help."

His voice was steady. Pleasant even. And that somehow made it worse, but when he removed his hands, she could at least breathe again. She forced herself to walk to the counter where the tea was steeping.

Isabeau glanced over her shoulder, trying to pretend he was a guest. "Would you like a cup as well?"

His smile was all male amusement. "I don't think it's a good idea to put temptation in your path. You would try to throw boiling water at me and then I'd have to retaliate and you'd get hurt. I don't want that and I don't think you do either."

Isabeau concentrated on keeping her hands from shaking as she fixed herself a cup of tea. She waited until she sipped at it before walking to the chair he'd indicated and sitting in it rather gingerly. Had Conner put a knife beneath the cushions? He told her not to panic and she was definitely on the verge of panicking. She made herself take another swallow of the hot liquid and breathe.

"Why are you here?" Her voice was back under control and she let herself feel triumphant. One small victory at a time.

"To give you a chance to come with me. Right now. Before anyone dies. Come away with me. You don't need anything but the clothes on your back. I've got money. Everything Imelda paid me was in cash." He smirked. "Between what Suma and I took from both Sobre and Cortez, we'll be able to go anywhere."

His offer was the last thing she expected. He seemed so reasonable. He didn't move toward her, which helped her maintain her composure.

"Even if I left a note trying to convince them that I went voluntarily with you, they'd come after us," she said. "You know that."

He shrugged, and it was impossible not to see the ropes of defined muscle ripple across his chest, arms and belly.

"So really, you know you'd still have to kill him. I wouldn't be saving his life by going with you, only causing him distress." She tilted her head and regarded him steadily over the top of her teacup. "I'm in love with him."

"You'll get over that in time." His gaze didn't leave her face. "If you come voluntarily, I'll give you a little time to forget him. Your cat will help by accepting me."

She could see he thought he was making a huge concession to her. It was frightening, walking a tightrope, trying to placate him, stall him and keep from triggering a violent outburst. He was too controlled and she was terrified of him. She moistened her lower lip with the tip of her tongue and set her cup aside, dropping her hands to her sides on the pretext of hiding her trembling fingers. She knew he caught the shaking, he was too focused on her not to, but she had to find a way to check the cushions.

He shook his head and sprang again, the leap taking him to the side of her chair. "I told you, I removed the weapons. The knife was down the right side. Do you think I'm stupid?" There was an edge to his voice.

"No. But I'm very scared," she admitted, shifting a little from him as she tried to find the right words to reach him.

His hand anchored in her hair, preventing her from moving even an inch from him. "This is your chance to save him, Isabeau. I'm offering it once because it will be more difficult for you to forgive me if I kill him, but I will."

His face was inches from hers, a snarling mask of determination and absolute confidence. The lines in his face were cut deep, a tough man with much experience. Looking into his eyes, she knew she'd been right about him: He'd been the brains, the one running Suma, yet he'd hidden it well. He didn't need the accolades. He wasn't hurting her, but the threat was there. In fact, the pads of his fingers were rubbing strands of her hair back and forth as if savoring the feel.

"Go take a shower," he said abruptly. "If you argue with me or you put anything of his on, I'll scrub you myself and you're not going to like it much. Do it fast. I want you back out here in five minutes smelling like you and not him."

He tugged on her hair just enough that she rose and rushed out of the room. He followed her at a more leisurely pace. She was stripping off her bra when he sauntered in and she stopped abruptly, shaking her head. "I'm not taking my clothes off in front of you."

A muscle ticked in his jaw. "I watched you letting him fuck you in the forest and then again on the porch. I'm well aware of what your body looks like. I want his scent gone. Now. I'll scrub you down myself if you don't move. You've got four minutes now."

She told herself she was leopard and there was no modesty in that world. She didn't want to provoke him into showering with her and possibly raping her. If she could, she would stall enough to allow Rio and Conner to pick up his trail and realize he'd circled back to the cabin. She wanted to keep her back to him as she stripped, but she needed to see him. Because if he moved to touch her—she wasn't going down without a fight.

She got under the water, her gaze on his, fixed and defiant, daring him to try to come near her as she soaped off under his intense scrutiny. He reached for the water at the same time she did, his fingers brushing hers, and she jerked her hands back, both coming up defensively.

That seemed to amuse him. He handed her a towel. "Do you really think you can fight me and win? Don't be silly. I'm not a man who would deliberately hit a woman. There has to be a very good reason."

"Why in the world did you ever work for Imelda Cortez, let alone kidnap children for her?" she asked, rubbing the water—and Conner's scent—as best she could from her skin. *Keep him talking and calm,* she reminded herself. *Be interested in him.*

She pushed past him and found her backpack, jerking out a pair of jeans and yanking them on quickly. She glanced at him over her shoulder. "You sold out your own people."

He watched her with the unblinking eyes of a cat. "They aren't my people. They threw me out. I owe them no loyalty."

She frowned as she pulled a T-shirt on and turned to face him, doing her best to look a little sympathetic. "Why would they do that?" She was interested, that part wasn't a lie. She hoped she was staying close to the truth. She'd admitted she was scared of him. Maybe he'd make allowances.

He shrugged, but for the first time a ripple of emotion crossed his face. "Our laws are archaic and make no sense. If a hunter kills one of us in leopard form—even though it's against the law of man—we're to just allow them to get away with it. One killed my baby brother. I hunted him down and killed him. The elders called it murder and banished me. In other words, I'm dead to the village. I figure if I'm dead to them, they are to me and I owe them no loyalty."

"How terrible." And she meant it. If a family felt there was no justice in a killing, how did they go on? "That still doesn't explain someone as evil as Imelda Cortez and why you would choose to reveal your species to her."

He stepped back to allow her to proceed him through the door into the next room. "Cortez offered me a living and I took her up on it. Eventually I knew I'd kill her, so what the hell difference does it make what she knows? She can't prove it and if she tells anyone, they'll think she's insane—which she is. I can smell it on her."

She swallowed fear. He said it so casually. *Eventually I knew I'd kill her.* "Is that what you're going to do to me eventually? Kill me when you get tired of me?"

He shook his head. "It doesn't work that way." He caught her wrist, jerking her around, forcing her palm to circle the hard length of him, his fingers fisting tight around hers. "You put this there. I go to bed like this and get up like this. It isn't going to go away until we're together. And I imagine it will be back often, every bit as painful."

She stomped as hard as she could on his instep and spun, slamming her elbow into his ribs, continuing around as he freed her hand, aiming a back-fist at his face. He was already on her, taking her to the floor, dropping hard so that she slammed into the wood, cracking her head, his superior weight on top of her. She saw stars, and had to fight to keep from passing out. Struggling wildly, she tried to throw him off. He drove a knee into the small of her back and pinned her wrists together, his strength enormous. She lay crushed beneath him, tears burning in her eyes and throat.

"You don't know much about men, do you, Isabeau," he said softly. "Some men get turned on by a woman fighting him. Lie quietly. Just take a breath. I said I wouldn't hurt you if possible, and I meant it."

She let herself weep for a moment before making an effort to pull herself back together. His free hand stroked her hair as if soothing her. When the tension drained out of her, he got off her and pulled her to her feet, forcing her across the room to the same chair. Once she was seated in the chair, he put both hands on the arms of the chair and bent his face close to hers.

She gathered herself. Head-butting might work. Or punching him hard right in the middle of that very large erection.

His eyes met hers and he shook his head slowly. "The first time, I let it go because you're frightened of me. But you attack me again and I'll retaliate."

She blinked up at him, one hand going defensively to her throat. "Today's my wedding day," she admitted. "I married him."

His expression didn't change. "I don't really give a damn. You knew better, or at least you should have."

She studied his face, that strong, masculine face. She needed to keep him talking because it was the only defense she had. The sound of their voices, the passage of time. Conner had to come back soon.

She drew in her breath. "Did you tell Imelda about all of us being leopard?"

"Why would I?" He picked up her teacup and moved across the floor to the teapot.

Isabeau covered her sigh of relief with a small throat clearing. He was so *big*. Intimidating. He seemed invincible to her. And where was Conner? Surely he must have unraveled Ottila's trail and should be back.

"Imelda should never have taken those kids. I tried to tell her, but she likes being the boss. I knew Adan would never sit still for it. She's so arrogant she doesn't listen to her advisors, not even her security advisors."

"So you've left her on her own."

From the small pack he carried around his neck, he drew a small vial and, thumbing it open, poured it into the cup of tea right in front of her. Her entire body tightened up. She half rose, but he gave her a stern look and she subsided.

"I'm not drinking that."

"Then we'll do it the hard way and pour it down your throat. It really is all the same to me, Isabeau."

"What is it?"

"Not a date rape drug. I haven't stooped so low that I'd rape a woman. When I take you, it will be because you can't help yourself, you'll need me."

She wasn't going to argue how illogical that was, not when he was coming at her with the teacup. She leapt out of her chair, this time remembering her cat, calling on the lazy hussy to help out. Why wasn't she outraged? Why wasn't she fighting for their survival? For Conner's survival. And, God help her, where was Conner?

Deep inside her, her cat stirred, scented the air and found her own mark on Ottila. Another rival for her affections. She stretched languorously. Isabeau hissed at her to subside. Where was the famous leopard loyalty? She cursed herself for not knowing the rules.

"What is that?"

"Choose for him, life or death."

She couldn't look away from his eyes. It was difficult not to believe him. He seemed invincible and absolutely sure of himself. She touched her tongue to her lip, for one awful moment considering going with him. By why hadn't he just knocked her out and taken her out of the cabin? This wasn't about choice, it never was. It was about something altogether different. Her brain went *click, click, click* as pieces fell into place.

"You were always going to kill him, right from the beginning, weren't you?"

He caught her around the throat, letting her feel his immense strength. Isabeau didn't struggle. There was a warning in his eyes she heeded. "He's been inside you. His mark is on you. He can't live."

She swallowed hard. "You were never going to share me with Suma."

"Not in a million years.

She lifted her chin and indicated the tea. "Tell me what's in that."

"I don't want you to feel what I'm going to do to you."

Her heart slammed so hard against her chest she was afraid it would burst. Fear breathed through her like a living entity. He said it so matter-of-factly, not blinking, no sympathy, no remorse.

"What are you going to do to me?"

"Not you. Him. He has to be made to suffer. To be off his game. His leopard will go into a rage and he won't be able to control it. I've studied him. He's methodical. And good. I don't believe in being stupid. I need an edge and the only way I'm going to get it is to hurt you, or crawl into the doctor's house and savage his young friend. Either would set him off."

She knew he deliberately threatened Jeremiah to coerce her to drink the drugged tea. "You're going to hurt me?" she echoed. He was right, Conner would never forgive himself and he'd turn the rain forest inside out looking for Ottila. He'd follow him right into a trap. She looked into Ottila's eyes, forcing courage into frozen muscles.

"You need to punish me, don't you?" In his own sick way, he felt she'd betrayed him—betrayed their relationship. She'd been deceived by his absolute calm.

"Drink the tea, Isabeau," he instructed softly.

She took the cup from him, her fingers trembling, looking down into the dark liquid. He'd made certain the water wasn't hot enough to burn him if she threw it at him. He actually expected her to obey him and drink his drug. She brought the mixture to her mouth and flung the contents into his eyes, carrying the cup on through to smash it against the arms of the chair. She kept moving, whirling around as she slashed at him with the shard. It wasn't like she had much to lose, he was going to hurt her on purpose.

The piece of glass cut a thin line across his chest, but he didn't even wince. His gaze burned into hers, a fierce promise of retribution. Isabeau refused to be intimidated. She held the shard like a knife, down low, the jagged edge pointed up toward the softer parts of his body. Ottila side-stepped and then moved in on her, fast, so fast for a big man. His hand slapped her wrist away, turning aside the glass as he spun her around, trapping her body against his.

His hand controlled hers, slamming it hard against the wall. "Drop it," he ordered. "Drop it right now."

When she hesitated, he drove her hand a second time into the wall. The jagged edges cut into her palm and the force of the blow sent pain shooting up her arm. Tears burned in her eyes and she blinked them rapidly away, not wanting to show weakness. She was terrified of letting go of her only weapon, but he was just too strong.

"Drop it, Isabeau," he ordered again.

There was no change in his inflection. He might have been talking about the weather. Shivering, she complied. He held her for a few more moments, his arms strong, hold-ing her up when she might have collapsed.

"That was stupid. What did you gain from it?"

"I had to try."

"I guess so."

His hands were gentle as he put her away from him. So gentle, in fact, that when he struck her, she was more shocked than hurt. Blows rained down on her body, hard, fast jabs that had her doubling over and sliding down the wall. He kept hitting her, methodically, over and over. She tried crawling away from him, fighting back, using her arms to defend herself, but the blows kept falling all over her body. He never touched her face and when she curled into the fetal position to try to protect herself, he crouched beside her and continued.

There was no way to protect herself from the blows. They seemed to go on forever. She closed her eyes, sobbing, holding up her hands to try to block him. Just as abruptly as it started, he stopped hitting her.

"Open your eyes," he commanded softly.

Tears swimming in her eyes, she obeyed him reluctantly. He bent his head toward her, shifting as he did so, until a male leopard in his prime held her pinned against the floor, his teeth sinking deep into her shoulder directly over the mark Conner had put there. At the same time, his back claw raked down her thigh. She felt the gash, the blood run free, and she also felt the burn spreading through her system. She could hear her own screams of anguish, but the leopard ignored her pleas, rolling her over so that she was on her back, her soft belly exposed to him.

His claws sank into her breasts, deep punctures that drew blood. She heard herself scream, but he wasn't finished. His claws raked the insides of her thighs and then sank deep into her feminine mound. The pain was excruciating. She nearly passed out, the edges of her vision darkening, bile rising.

He lifted her onto her hands and knees, holding her head down to keep her from fainting. She was going to be sick, her stomach cramping and heaving in protest. He appeared just as patient, his hands stroking her hair, soothing her as if he hadn't been the one to cause such damage in the first place.

Sobbing, Isabeau tried to crawl away from him, but he simply drew her into his arms and rocked her back and forth. She didn't fight him. Any movement caused pain to rip through her body.

"We're tied together, Isabeau," he said softly, looking down at her shredded, bloody jeans. "You'll need an antibiotic. He's going to be so enraged he may forget, so you'll have to be the one to remember." Again he spoke matter-of-factly.

"Why?" she asked.

He didn't pretend to misunderstand. "When you think back on your wedding day, it will be me you remember, not him." His hand stroked her hair, trying to soothe her when she was shaking uncontrollably. "And to prove a point. You'll never be safe with him, neither will your children. I got to the kid right under the noses of his guards, and I got to you. I can do it again, anytime, anyplace. You need to think about what you want in a partner. We live by the law of the jungle, Isabeau, and if he can't protect you, what use is he to you?"

"Did you kill Jeremiah?" She pressed her trembling fingers to her mouth. Any movement was painful and she desperately wanted to remove her jeans and top and press a cool cloth to the throbbing puncture wounds.

"His death would have accomplished very little. I needed the kid alive to delay your man. Now he'll have to live with the fact that he made the wrong choice in helping the boy. Each time he tries to touch you"—the pad of his finger slid over the wounds on her breast—"he's going to see my mark, my brand."

She wanted to slap his hand away, but she was too cowed. She'd never been beaten in her life. He'd done it with such objectivity, as if he was completely removed from the act. She tried to crawl away from him, finding the wall to lean against, the only way to hold herself up.

His fingers circled her ankle like a shackle. "Make certain you don't get pregnant with his baby. I'd hate to have to kill a cub, and it would be much harder for you to forgive me."

How could he think she could forgive the beating he'd given her? He'd terrorized her on purpose, a punishment that in his twisted mind she deserved. "Tell him to meet me and to come alone. If he doesn't, I'll be back periodically to visit until he does."

"Where?" She whispered the word.

"He'll know."

She slid down the wall when he let go of her, crying softly, terrified for herself—for Conner. Ottila stood over her, once again taking his human form. Both were intimidating. "I can get to you anywhere. Anytime. If he tries to run with you, you'd better believe he can't protect you, no matter where he takes you, I'll find you. You tell him that."

She bit down hard on her lower lip and stayed very still, afraid to move. He leaned into her, his mouth finding hers. She held herself very still, trying not to sob as he explored her mouth with his tongue, taking his time, his hands once again gentle. It was disconcerting, to have him go from violence to almost loving. He didn't protest when she remained passive. He pulled back and looked into her eyes.

"Next time, you might remind him that leopards like to go high."

He shifted right in front of her, a male leopard in his prime, his tail switching as he leapt up into the beams with casual ease and disappeared into the small attic. She didn't hear him after that, but she remained huddled against the wall, terrified that he hadn't really left and would come back.

SHE jammed her fist into her mouth and wept as quietly as she could. She didn't want to see anyone, not Conner—especially not Conner. She felt bruised and battered. Ottila had completely broken her. She had no idea what to feel, only fear, intense fear. He'd stripped her down until she couldn't recognize herself. She had to get her clothes off and treat the puncture wounds. He'd wanted to mark her, not maim her, so they couldn't be as bad as they felt. But she couldn't move. She stayed still, huddled against the wall, weeping quietly.

"ISABEAU! We're coming in," Conner's voice made her jump, but she didn't move, making herself as small as possible there against the wall.

CONNER waited uneasily when Isabeau didn't answer him. He glanced at Rio, who was still pulling on his jeans. The cabin was dark, just as he'd told her to leave it. All the shutters were closed. There seemed no good reason for his uneasiness, although after tracking the large leopard back to the doctor's house and into Jeremiah's room, he could believe the leopard capable of anything. The boy had been helpless, lying hooked to an IV, fighting for every breath, and Ottila had raked deep claw marks in his belly. He could have disemboweled him. The general consensus had been that he'd been interrupted by Mary or the doctor as they'd looked in on him.

Many guests still remained in the house and Elijah
patrolled outside, yet the leopard had managed to locate
Jeremiah's room and enter with so much stealth, no one
had even known he was in the house. Conner knew the
leopard could have killed all of them—Mary, Doc, his
friends and certainly Jeremiah. He knew the others were
wrong, Ottila hadn't been interrupted, he hadn't wanted to
kill Jeremiah.

Conner put his hand on the door and inhaled. Was there
a faint scent of a leopard? "I'm coming in, Isabeau, don't
shoot me."

He unlocked the door and the smell hit him hard,
waves of it. Leopard and blood. The mixture was potent.
He whipped his head around, examining every inch of the
cabin until his gaze found her huddled and bloody in the
darkness.

"Is he here?" he asked. She looked in shock, her face
starkly white. It took every ounce of control not to leap to
her side and gather her up.

For a moment she was silent. *Traumatized.* He didn't
want to think about what had happened here. Not with her
clothes bloody and that look of terror on her face.

"Isabeau," he hissed, putting a flick of command in his
voice.

"I don't know. He went up there," she pointed to the
beams overhead. Her tone was so low he barely caught the
words, even with his acute hearing.

Rio moved into the room, his bare feet silent on the
wooden floor as he studied the rafters above his head. He
leapt, catching one of the beams and swinging his body
into position.

Conner crossed to Isabeau's side, crouching down beside her, gently reaching for her. He made certain to keep

his movements slow and deliberate. "Tell me, Isabeau," he instructed.

A sob escaped and she pressed her fingers to her trembling mouth, moving back to make herself smaller. Conner let his gaze slide over her, looking for the worst of the injuries. She had blood on her shirt over her breasts and more was seeping through the material at the junction of her legs. His heart began to pound in alarm.

"Can you tell me what he did?"

She moistened her lips and pressed back against the wall, needing the stability of the structure. "He said he wanted you to meet him. He said you'd know where."

"He's gone," Rio announced. "He got in through a small screened vent in the attic. He had to have planned this very carefully." He swung down and stood next to Conner, observing her pale face and bloody clothes. "I'll call the doc." He reached for the light.

Isabeau shook her head, alarm spreading across her face, so much so that Conner held up his hand to stop Rio.

"I don't want anyone to see me like this. Don't turn on the light."

"I have to take a look at you," Conner said, his voice gentle. "I'm going to pick you up, beloved. It may hurt." He had no idea of the extent of her injuries, but the scent of blood was strong. There was a hint of lingering musk, as if Ottila had been aroused, but he didn't smell sex.

"There's broken glass on the floor," Isabeau warned.

It seemed so inconsequential to him given the circumstances. "We'll be careful." He reached for her, afraid of hurting her when she shuddered in his arms. The scent of blood was stronger, but even more so was the scent of Ottila's leopard. He'd marked her deliberately, wanting to insult Conner, wanting him to realize he could take his woman at any time. Conner read the challenge for what it was.

"Would you mind starting a bath, Rio?" he asked, more to get the man out of the room than for any other reason.

He had no idea where to start. He just knew that he couldn't make this about him, about the rage burning like a wildfire in his belly. This had to be about Isabeau. She was dazed, confused and looking at him with fear in her eyes.

Shaken, Conner gathered Isabeau to him, cradling her against his chest, feeling her wince when her body pressed against his. "What did he do?"

"He beat me," she said, suppressing another sob. "He wasn't angry. He just beat me, like it was a job to him. And then he used his claws on me, on my . . . body." She buried her face against his shoulder and clung to him.

So close to her, the scent of the other leopard was overpowering. His cat went wild, raking and clawing, demanding to be set free to kill his rival. He wanted the scent off of her. "I need to look at the damage, Isabeau."

She shook her head, refusing to meet his eyes.

"Would you be more comfortable with a woman? With Mary?" He kept his voice gentle.

Again she shook her head. "I don't want to see anyone."

He had to ask. "Did he rape you?"

She pressed her forehead tight against his shoulder. His heart pounded hard in his chest, but he made no movement, staying still, just waiting.

"He said he would never rape a woman." She began to weep a little wildly. "He was so cruel, Conner. And all the while, he acted like I deserved it, like I had betrayed him."

He tightened his arms carefully around her, trying not

to choke on the other man's smell. His leopard was insane, pushing close to the surface, raging at his enemy, trying to rip through flesh to get to the hideous, offensive smell.

"We're going to get you in the bathtub where I can inspect the damage. You'll need painkillers, Isabeau, and antibiotics . . ."

She lifted her face to look at him for the first time and there was a hint of pride in her gaze. "He said you'd be too upset to remember the antibiotics, but you didn't forget. "

"Of course I didn't," he brushed a kiss along her forehead. "You're my first priority, always, Isabeau."

"He thought I'd be upset that you went to help Jeremiah," she said. "But I'm glad you did." She couldn't keep the edge of hysteria from her voice. "He did everything he could to drive a wedge between us."

Conner's stomach knotted. He heard the uncertainty in her voice. She wasn't aware of it, but Ottila had done damage to Isabeau by shaking her confidence, not only in him—that he could accept another man's mark on her—but in herself. He lifted her, taking her on through to the bathroom. Rio had thoughtfully lit candles to keep the light muted and soft.

"Should I get the doc?" he asked.

"She's already on antibiotics. Give me some time to assess the damage," Conner said. "He planned this out very well. He let me catch a whiff of him, laid a trail straight to Jeremiah, hurt him enough that we'd stay there and help, left us another trail into the forest leading away from the valley and from here, and all the while we were chasing him he was terrorizing Isabeau."

"Is it possible he's doing Cortez's bidding?" Rio ventured. "We have to at least take a look at the possibility that she knows about us."

"No." Isabeau raised her head, her gaze meeting Rio's steadily. "He deserted Imelda and is coming after Conner. He's got a twisted sense of right and wrong. It was okay to beat me, but not okay to rape me. I should accept him and we can live happily ever after, although he might have to kill Conner's and my child. I think he has enough money to be satisfied and he's already moved on to his next agenda. I made the mistake of marking him." Her voice wobbled but she kept her gaze steady. "This isn't about Imelda. We're still clear to go."

"You're betting our lives on that," Rio said. "A good way to kill Conner is to lure him into Imelda's compound."

"He wouldn't do that," Isabeau denied.

"Why?" Rio asked.

"He has a sense of honor," she replied.

The knots in Conner's belly tightened even more. He didn't want Ottila Zorba anywhere near Isabeau. "Listen, baby," he crooned softly. "This isn't your fault. None of this is your fault."

"I did something to him." There was a frown in her voice, but she wouldn't look at him. "He said my cat would accept him. And she didn't come out to help me. She didn't protest what he was doing."

"We have venom in our claws." He brushed kisses over her temples. "Zorba is trying to confuse you, to make you think that what you did entitles him to you, but he saw you and in his twisted mind, like any other common stalker, he thinks you have a relationship with him. He knows you're my mate. He knows you're married to me, but it doesn't matter to him. Mates are sacred. No one touches another's mate."

He took her through to the bathroom and allowed her legs to drop to the floor, one arm holding her steady.

"I don't understand, Conner. You said he has the right to challenge you."

"You chose, but yes, an unmated female certainly has the right to choose her mate. She isn't restricted to one single male until that choice is made. Ordinarily, mates look for one another, life cycle after cycle, but they don't always. Your cat indicated she found his cat attractive, that's all. But you are mated, and he has no rights at all to you. He knows that."

"Then what does the venom do?"

He was afraid she'd ask. He busied himself tugging at her shirt, which she didn't want to give up. She kept pulling the hem back down. Finally she covered her chest with her arms, preventing him from removing her top.

"I'll do it myself, when I'm alone."

Defiance crept into her eyes. Shame. His heart contracted. He caught her arms and dragged her to him, his mouth coming down on hers. His kiss was long, tender and filled with as much love as he could pour into it.

"You have to believe me, Isabeau. This isn't your fault. Did you think because all the people in this valley are so kind, that leopard people are always good? The danger of our business is that we see the worst of people, not the best, as we have in this valley. But I've seen the worst in leopards and the best in humans. Ottila is a sick man. You didn't give him an opening, he fixated on you all by himself."

She refused to meet his gaze. "He did this so you wouldn't want me. I know he did. The wounds will heal, but they'll scar. Right now, his scent and his marks are all over me. He wanted you to find me distasteful—repugnant."

"Well, guess what, he didn't succeed."

Her gaze leapt to his face. "My cat can smell your lie."

"Not a lie. My cat is raging. As he should be. As, deep

down, I am. I don't want another man touching you." He kept his gaze steady on hers, never flinching. Yes, his cat was snarling, hating the smell of the other man—but never her—never his mate. He raged at himself for not protecting her, but the blame was on his shoulders, not hers, if there was blame to be had by one of them. "I could never be repulsed by you, Isabeau. You're my heart. My soul. This man can't drive a wedge between us. Let your cat smell whether I'm telling you the truth or a lie. Now let me take your clothes off and see what damage he's done."

"He was careful not to really injure me."

"He's a first-class bastard who gave no thought to your feelings. Possession isn't love, Isabeau, no matter how possessive a man feels. And I do feel possessive, but I know I don't own you. And I don't have the right to hurt you or take away your choices. I put my mark on you to protect you from him, not to brand you as mine. I think my leopard may have that idea, but I'm not just my leopard and I refuse, as every man should, to use our cat's instincts to guide us into animalistic behavior. And don't get me wrong, Isabeau, Ottila's behavior was an abomination against animals."

For the first time a faint smile crept into her eyes. "Did you think he dazzled me with his show of strength? He terrified me. I never want to see him again."

This time she let him remove her clothing. His fingers brushed her skin and she jumped a little, but remained still. There were puncture wounds on her breasts and at the junction of her legs, a strike at him, Conner was certain, but the real damage was the mottled bruising coming up under her skin.

He closed his eyes for a moment, breathing deep, breathing away the combined rage of the leopard and the man. He waited until he was completely under control. "You know I'm going to kill him."

She sank into the heated tub, shivering, the blood slowly turning the water pink. "That's what he wants. Let's just get the children and leave."

"You aren't coming with us, Isabeau. It's too dangerous and you're in no shape. Tomorrow you won't be able to move."

Her gaze jumped to his face. "You're not leaving me alone. Not again. And I'll be even more of an asset to the team. Imelda and her crew will think Elijah did this to me and they'll be happy that he's like them. It will be one more thing to make her let down her guard enough to give us a little rein in her territory. Besides, I'm the one her grandfather talked to about gardens. He said he had one. That's outside. He'll expect me to go out with him and see it. My cat can smell as well as yours. I'll find them while Elijah and Marcos talk alliances and you look tough."

Pride burst through him along with the desire to weep. Isabeau was down, but not out. Ottila had shaken her, but she had never lost sight of what she was about or who she was. He hoped she could move in the morning, but he doubted it. Watching her shivering, trying not to weep while he cleaned the wounds and treated them, he knew Ottila was a dead man.

A man capable of doing such damage to a woman just to prove a point would come at them again and again. It would never be over until he was stopped permanently. There was no point in stating the fact to Isabeau. She was too afraid of the man—but Conner wasn't.

19

"ARE you certain Isabeau can handle this?" Leonardo asked Conner as they drove down the narrow road along the edge of the rain forest. He studied Conner's grim features in the dim light streaming in through the tinted windows.

Imelda Cortez's sprawling compound was found at the end of a very long, windy road that switched back and forth up a mountain and dead-ended at her property. The rain forest surrounded her on three sides. The team had already run through their routes over and over, and the most promising was on the southernmost tip of the estate. If they could get the children to that side of the compound, the forest was practically reclaiming the fences.

They came in two vehicles. Marcos, Conner and Leonardo were in the first one. Elijah and Isabeau with Rio and Felipe arrived in the second. The others had been shocked when they saw Isabeau. Her face was untouched, her skin flawless but pale. She moved like a much older woman, unable to stand straight, obviously in pain. She'd taken a painkiller, but it hadn't seemed to help much.

"If Isabeau says she can do this, then she can," Conner said, his voice terse. He hadn't been able to dissuade her, not even when she'd rolled over onto her hands and knees, pushing up as her stomach heaved, protesting the severe beating. He didn't know if it was her fear of Ottila returning, or her determination to see their mission through that got her on her feet, but she somehow had managed to get herself dressed and ready for the trip to Imelda's.

Weapons were stashed in two secret locations just inside the rain forest. Without the rogue leopards guarding Imelda's compound, it had been fairly easy to place the caches without detection. They had more stashed in the two vehicles, hidden from sight so it didn't look as if they were going to war.

The gates loomed up before them, heavy ironwork designed to keep out anyone, or keep someone prisoner behind the eight-foot fence that surrounded the rolling grounds. Guards with dogs patrolled the fence and several more guarded the gates with automatic weapons. Conner was certain Imelda wanted a show of force for her visitors. He kept his dark glasses in place and spent most of his time looking indifferent as he studied the layout of the compound and the close proximity of the forest.

Had he been the head of the security force, the first thing he would have done would be to move back the forest. The fence itself was a security nightmare. Imelda wanted the top flat and wide enough for guards to use it, but she should have had it built so no one could climb it. Some of the lower branches actually touched the fence. The branches were often used as a highway for the animals, and both Suma and Ottila would have known that. They really hadn't cared much about their job, or maybe they'd grown lazy, as no one ever challenged Imelda's stranglehold on the Panama-Colombia border.

He glanced briefly at Isabeau as she was helped from the car by a solicitous Elijah. He swept his arm around her, bringing her under his shoulder, ignoring her wince with every step she took. She was still walking gingerly, a little bent over, but she stood, eyes apparently downcast, the picture of a woman under a man's complete control. Elijah looked satisfied and even arrogant, his gaze boldly sweeping the estate as if comparing it with his own.

Imelda came out to greet them, shaking hands with Marcos and Elijah. Conner saw her gaze rest thoughtfully a few moments on Isabeau. She took off her sunglasses and smiled.

"How are you . . . Isabeau, isn't it?"

Isabeau played her part perfectly, glancing nervously up at Elijah as if asking permission to speak. His cool gaze swept her face and he barely nodded, the gesture nearly imperceptible, but just enough for Imelda to catch it.

"Fine, thank you," Isabeau intoned, her voice barely audible.

"I'm so glad you came with your . . . cousin." Deliberately Imelda linked her arm to Isabeau's and swung her around toward the house, calling out over her shoulder, "Do come in. I'm so pleased to have guests."

Conner knew she couldn't fail to feel Isabeau's wince, and she deliberately set a brisk pace to force Isabeau to keep up with her. She was enjoying not only Isabeau's humiliation, but her pain. His gut twisted as Imelda sent him a smoldering look that promised all kinds of things he didn't want. He could see Imelda's fingers touching Isabeau and wanted to tear his wife away from the woman who was so deliberately cruel. He realized he didn't want Isabeau to work with him in this business, seeing the worst of people. He wanted her somewhere safe where she would always keep her faith in humanity.

He fell in behind Marcos, taking in the position of every guard and each structure. There was a large water tower with a narrow wooden staircase. He figured it was more of a convenience for a sniper to see everything than an actual needed tower. There appeared to be another water tank, near a pump house. Guards moved in three places on the wall, in small cubicles built on top of it. There were several of those where a soldier who was a good shot would have command of the forest around him, yet have good protection.

He entered the house. It was long and low and cool, built like a Spanish mansion. The verandah wrapped around the front and two sides, shaded by a roof held by thick columns. Inside the sprawling room was comfortable furniture and wide spaces he realized accommodated a wheelchair. Imelda didn't seem the type of woman to accommodate anyone, least of all her aging grandfather, but Conner could feel the influence of the man in the house. There were large banks of sunny windows, although bars covered each of them. Plants grew tall and bushy inside as well as out. He could see the plants not only were beautiful, but in a way they would be functional in a battle. They were large enough to screen windows and provide cover for those inside. They'd also provide fuel for a fire should one happen to be started.

The older man sat waiting, a smile of welcome on his face. It slowly faded as he watched Isabeau walk toward him.

She brightened immediately when she saw him. "Mr. Cortez. How wonderful to see you again."

Alberto Cortez held out both hands to her, forcing Imelda to drop her arm. Isabeau took his hands and leaned in to kiss both cheeks.

"I'm so glad you've joined us, my dear. I had hoped you would come."

"I didn't want to miss seeing your garden. The plants in here are magnificent."

Imelda hissed out a long, annoyed sigh. "Grandfather. We have other guests." She sent a small, apologetic smile to the men over her shoulder.

The old man smiled at the group of men. "Forgive me," he said. "Isabeau is an enchanting woman. Welcome to our home."

Imelda rolled her eyes but refrained from issuing another reprimand as both Marcos and Elijah shook hands with her grandfather.

"It's good to see you again, sir," Elijah said. "Isabeau is indeed an enchanting woman."

"I trust you keep her well in hand," Marcos said.

Elijah ran his gaze deliberately over Isabeau. "She managed to make her way here to the rain forest, far from our home, but I've come to collect her."

As a chess move, Conner had to admit, Elijah's simple statement was brilliant. He managed in that single sentence to imply he was ruthless enough to control his family with an iron hand and collect any strays who managed to slip away. Given that his sister had disappeared some time earlier, but had been recovered, Imelda would assume Elijah was very much like her, a cruel, possessive dictator who squashed rebellion immediately.

Isabeau played her part to perfection, actually moving a little toward Alberto, almost for protection, her eyes downcast, avoiding Elijah's domineering gaze.

Alberto patted her hand absently. "You won't mind me showing Isabeau the garden, will you? I had hoped to show off for her."

There was a small silence while Elijah clearly debated.

"Oh for heaven's sake. It will get them out of our hair while we talk business. Nadia! Get drinks immediately," Imelda called to a young servant girl.

Elijah refused to be pushed. "I allowed her to go off with your grandfather and she was accosted by one of your security men. An issue I would very much like to address before we go any further. I made it quite clear she was protected and off limits." There was a chill in his voice, ice in his eyes. "I wish to see this man."

Imelda's mouth tightened. She clearly didn't like to be thwarted in even a small way. "I heard from my grandfather that this occurred, but Harry was there with his shotgun to make certain she was safe." There was a hint of impatience in her tone and she tapped her foot, frown lines etched deep into her forehead and around her mouth. "She was never in any danger."

"The bodies buried there?"

"Clearly Philip Sobre's. My security man had nothing to do with the bodies. Unless you're implying my grandfather had his own burial plot there." She laughed gaily as if she'd made a wonderful joke. "It was so sad about Philip, don't you think? The police are questioning everyone, but they think a parent of one of the women got to him. The guests saw him throughout the rest of the evening and even after I left. He locked up his house after the party ended, and they believe his killer was hiding inside."

"How terrible," Marcos murmured approvingly. "Although if he did kill the young men and women they're finding in his garden, I can hardly blame the parent."

Isabeau shivered and Alberto patted her hand again.

Elijah frowned. "Still, Imelda, it would be a good faith gesture to allow me to have a word with your security man."

Imelda scowled. "He's gone."

Elijah's eyebrow shot up. "Gone?" He sounded skeptical.

"He threatened to kill my grandfather," Imelda said, her face revealing her true personality. All trace of beauty was gone, leaving a mask of twisted malevolence. "Did you think he would stay around to see what I would do to him? I have a certain reputation for protecting my own. The man worked for me and he betrayed me over a . . ." She bit off an obvious insult.

Two spots of color appeared high in Isabeau's cheeks, but she didn't raise her head. Elijah, however, took a threatening step toward Imelda. Instantly Rio and Felipe moved with him, facing Imelda's security guards.

Alberto rolled his chair between his granddaughter and Elijah. "Imelda had no intention of insulting your family, Elijah, or anyone you care about. She's very distraught that a man we trusted betrayed our family. She gave you her word your woman would be safe with me, and we both believed it. Zorba not only betrayed us, but it appears he killed his partner as well. I apologize on behalf of our family and assure you that everything that can be done to find this man and bring him to justice is being done by my granddaughter."

Imelda, for the first time, sent a small smile toward her grandfather. "He always reminds me of my manners. Living the way I do, running such a big business, I tend to lose the small courtesies that count. I'm sorry, Elijah." She inclined her head like a princess.

Elijah allowed a small smile to slip out, bowing slightly

in a courtly manner. "I have the same problem, but with no grandfather to remind me."

"Please sit down and make yourselves comfortable. Your men can relax a little." Imelda gestured toward the most comfortable chairs.

Conner, Felipe, Rio and Leonardo spread out, covering the entrances, stationing themselves where they had a good view of every direction through the windows.

"My men are the best," Marcos said. "I like to use family, men I know who are loyal to me and mine. Men with a stake in my success."

Imelda sank into a chair, her greedy gaze on Conner's face, devouring him with her eyes. "You should count yourself very lucky, Marcos. Unfortunately, I have no family left other than my grandfather." She picked up an ivory fan and coquettishly began to fan herself, using an idle indolence that was purely feigned for Conner's benefit. She wore a skirt and blouse that showed off her figure and when she crossed her legs, allowed her thighs to show off to their best advantage.

"Come, my dear," Alberto said. "With Elijah's permission, we'll go out to the garden. Bring your drink with you." He turned his head. "Harry."

The man came striding in, shooting Isabeau a wide smile. "He's going to take you to his little paradise, is he? Prepare to hear a dissertation on every plant."

"Elijah?" Isabeau turned to him.

Elijah tapped his finger on his chair and then looked at Conner, indicating he follow her to the garden before nodding his permission. Imelda looked instantly dismayed, while a wide, grateful smile curved Isabeau's mouth. Elijah shrugged. "Neither of us will be distracted while we talk. I

always find when I have someone's full attention, there are
no mistakes."

Imelda snapped the fan closed and placed it carefully
on the table. Her eyes were cool and shadowed. "You definitely have my attention, Elijah."

Isabeau shivered at the sound of Imelda's voice. There
was a distinct threat, as if the woman's thin veneer of civility had finally worn off. Isabeau had to walk slowly and
was grateful Harry pushed the wheelchair at a leisurely
pace. Conner followed at a polite distance, not looking at
them, very intimidating in his bodyguard mode. His shoulders looked broad, his glasses dark, and the wire in his ear
sensitive. It was clear he was armed, and the other guards
looked at one another uneasily. Harry ignored him.

"What happened?" Alberto asked, his voice low, a whisper of conspiracy. "Do you need a doctor?"

Isabeau glanced around, looked at Conner as if judging the distance. He was leopard. He could hear a whisper
with no problem. The shake of her head was barely perceptible. "I've seen a physician." Deliberately she reached
in what could only be taken as a nervous gesture to push
back the heavy fall of hair. The action lifted her short shirt
just enough to reveal the mottled bruising on her skin. A
glimpse only, before she put her hand down, looking un-
aware that she'd confirmed Alberto's suspicions. His gasp
had been overloud and hastily muffled.

She was beginning to think Ottila's beating had turned
into a useful prop. She glanced up to see Alberto exchanging
a quick look with Harry, who frowned. She still didn't know
what to think of Alberto Cortez, but his son and granddaughter were both ruthless killers who enjoyed the pain of others.
They had to have gotten that legacy from somewhere. So

far, she couldn't imagine that such traits were possible in the
wonderful old man who told her stories and was unfailingly
courteous, but she wasn't going to take chances.

Harry cut through a courtyard that had beautifully kept
beds of brightly colored flowers. Orchids wound around
every tree trunk, and stepping stones meandered through
the green lawn. Benches were scattered at strategic points,
shaded by the thick foliage overhead. Isabeau widened her
eyes and looked everywhere, peering beyond the plants to
try to find outbuildings large enough to house a group of
children. They would need enough space to allow the children some play, or at least to eat.

"Your house is large, Mr. Cortez," she observed. "This
courtyard is so spacious. And the smells coming from just
over there are delicious." She pressed a hand to her stomach. "I just ate a little while ago but it's making me hungry
all over again."

"We have a wonderful chef," Alberto said. "As you can
see, his kitchen is quite large. The garden is just on the
other side of it, so the entire time we're working, Harry's
stomach growls. And call me Alberto."

"Does it, Harry?" Isabeau asked. At his nod she laughed.
"Then I won't feel so bad."

She wanted to stay in sight of the kitchen and was glad
when they rounded a corner and saw the garden. Her mouth
fell open. In the tradition of English gardens in the large
estates with castles, the hills were rolling green and the
bushes made up a labyrinth. Trees dotted the slopes, the
branches twisted into looping shapes where orchids spilled
down the trunks and rose upward in every conceivable
color.

Alberto laughed with pleasure at her reaction. "I've had
years to work on it."

"It's lovely. More than lovely. Unbelievable, Alberto."
She forgot about her sore body and took a few steps down
the path obviously put in for his wheelchair, moving a
little too rapidly and having to gasp and wrap her arms
around her midsection. As she did, she turned away from
the others, hoping they wouldn't see her wince. She felt
a little sick and pain stabbed through her left side. The
worst was as she'd lengthened her stride, she felt the protest in her groin where the wounds rubbed against the
material.

Swallowing hard, she glanced back toward the house.
A servant came out of the kitchen with a covered tray—a
large tray. Isabeau turned back toward Alberto, took a step
and gave a little hop, as if she had a pebble in her shoe.
Instantly, Conner was there, allowing her to use his body to
hold on to while she removed her shoe.

"I think she's taking food to the children," she murmured low, and then aloud, "thank you." She left his side
without looking at him to crouch beside what amounted to
a field of bird of paradise. "Alberto, these are amazing. I've
never seen so many together like this." It was important to
keep them where Conner could follow the progress of the
female with the tray.

Harry rolled Alberto's chair back to her as Conner
moved away from her, into a position better suited to watch
their surroundings, supposedly for any threats, in reality to
follow the progress of the servant.

"This is the best soil," Alberto said, bending to scoop
some of the rich dirt into his palm. "Right behind the
kitchen, I have an entire bed devoted to herbs, so the chef
always has fresh herbs. We have a vegetable garden just
over there, inside that building. I can't grow vegetables
very successfully out in the open because of the insects.

They eat everything before we have a chance to harvest, so we built a greenhouse."

Isabeau glanced in the direction he pointed to see the servant with the tray through the glass walls disappearing into a jungle of green foliage. Her heart jumped. "That's an enormous greenhouse. Is it hydroponic or did you use soil beds?" She made the interest in her voice plain. Either the servant was taking a shortcut through the greenhouse to get to the children or they were in that very large building.

"Soil beds. I'm old-fashioned. The joy for me is in working with my hands," Alberto explained. "I doubt I'd get the same satisfaction from any other way of growing plants." He straightened and dusted off his hands, before turning them over and over for her to see. "I've worked with the soil all my life."

"Then you couldn't fail to notice the insects in Sobre's garden," Isabeau said. "You knew he buried bodies there." She removed her dark glasses and stared him down. "You knew I'd recognize the signs."

He had the grace to look ashamed. "I'm sorry, my dear. Your knowledge of plants and soil was such an asset. I should never have put you in such a position. I didn't count on putting you in danger. I thought you'd scream and the guests would all come running. Philip's dark secret would be out and it would put a stop to the killings once and for all."

"That's why you wanted me to explore on my own. You didn't want it to look like you were leading me to the bodies."

He shook his head. "No, that wouldn't do at all."

She took a few steps in the direction of the greenhouse, trying to lead them in that direction. It enabled Conner to have an excuse to get closer and allowed them to see more of the insides of the buildings, although the plants were so overgrown it was difficult. "Did your granddaughter have anything to do with those bodies?"

"Imelda?" Alberto looked shocked. "Of course not. How could you think such a thing?"

She inhaled. Her cat snarled and her heart sank. He was lying. He looked so innocent sitting there in his chair, but he was lying to her. She took a breath, let it out and tried again. "You then?" This time she put a little disbelief in her voice. "Did you have anything to do with those bodies?"

His hand fluttered against his heart. He gasped. Wheezed. Harry bent over him solicitously, but Alberto gallantly waved him away. "Me? How would I be able to do such a thing? No, Isabeau, it certainly wasn't me. Philip Sobre needed to be stopped and you managed to do it by telling your family."

He was lying about the bodies. He not only had known about them, but some of the dead belonged to him. She could hear her heart pounding in her chest, the blood roaring in her ears. This beautiful garden most likely hosted many bodies as well. Adan had once told her that those who worked for Imelda rarely—if ever—left the compound. He'd meant that literally. Once a servant for the Cortez family, you lived your life here. And you died here. The money earned could be sent to family, which was why many did it, but their families never saw them again.

"Why did you want me to find the bodies instead of just telling the cops your suspicions?" Isabeau asked. "Perhaps you could have stopped him sooner."

Alberto shook his head, the picture of sorrow and guilt. "I could not. I couldn't take a chance on our family name being involved in any way. You understand with your family."

She frowned at him. "It was pretty ugly to make that kind of discovery."

"I know. I'm sincerely sorry."

If she hadn't been leopard, she would have believed him. He was one of the best actors she'd ever run across. He delivered his lines with absolute sincerity and looked so sad and guilty she had the urge to reassure him even though she knew he was lying. She sighed. "What else can I do but forgive you? At least he's been discovered, although what a horrible way to die."

"Thinking of all those young girls and their families," Alberto said, "I can't say I'm surprised. And all the times he went out with Imelda . . ." He shuddered. "It could have happened to her."

Isabeau found she couldn't speak, so simply nodded, trying to look understanding. She suddenly realized why the old man had taken such an interest in her. She was their leverage, their hostage. She had been a hostage at the party and she was now. They hadn't been able to keep Elijah from sending a bodyguard with her this time, but she was, in effect, the Cortez's prisoner. They could kill her at any time if Elijah or Marcos made a hostile move.

She had to assume that not only Harry was armed, but Alberto as well and that both were ready to kill her at a moment's notice. Was Conner close enough to stop them? Did he know? He was making them believe he thought any threat might come from an outside source, not them. Harry had backed away from Ottila the other night because he knew just how dangerous the man really was. He knew the truth, just as Imelda did—that Ottila and Suma were leopards. Imelda had shared her knowledge with her grandfather and his trusted bodyguard.

Alberto waved toward a looping path. "Harry, this way, I want to show Isabeau my favorite spot."

"If you don't mind, Alberto," Isabeau said, "it's getting difficult for me to walk. I thought we could take a look at the greenhouse and get off the uneven surface. Besides, I'd love to see the size of your vegetables if you're using this soil."

Alberto smiled at her. "I shouldn't have even considered you coming out to the garden. I just wanted to show it to someone who would really appreciate it. We can go sit on the verandah and visit. The greenhouse has recently been sprayed and no one can go in for twenty-four hours."

"How disappointing," Isabeau said. She'd managed to get them within thirty feet of the building.

Conner was much closer, but seemingly disinterested, although he was talking into his radio. His gaze continually swept the rooftops and the fenceline. She took a cautious sniff of the air, testing for the scent of leopards. If Alberto and Harry knew, had others been hired as well? "I used to grow vegetables when I lived at home with my father, but now that I travel so much," she shrugged, but took another few steps toward the greenhouse.

"Another time, perhaps," Alberto said as Harry pushed the chair toward the house.

The door to the greenhouse swung open and for one moment there was the sound of a child crying, hastily cut off as the servant slammed the door closed. The woman whirled around to see them all staring at her, Alberto furious. He swore at her in the local Indian dialect even as he reached beneath his lap blanket, as understanding dawned. Alberto was a shrewd, cunning man who had put together the Cortez empire. In that split second he realized he'd fallen into a trap and that they'd come to find the children, not negotiate deals or friendships. Isabeau saw the knowledge on his face.

Conner suddenly moved, his speed blinding, as he rushed them. Simultaneously, the scent of leopard filled her lungs. She screamed and threw herself toward Conner, terrified as she recognized the overpowering smell of her worst nightmare, barely registering that the old man was aiming a gun at her head.

Harry whirled to face the large cat dropping out of the tree above their heads, his shotgun bucking in his hands. The shotgun boomed, a deafening sound that exploded through the air just as the sound of gunfire erupted from the direction of the house. Alberto's deceptively sweet mask had been replaced by a twisted, cunning killer, lips drawn back in a snarl as he whipped up the gun and fired several shots at her just as Conner took her to the ground, covering her body with his.

Alberto was far too late. Ottila was on him, driving the chair over backward, spilling the body onto the ground. A powerful swipe of the paw sent the gun skidding across the ground out of the old man's reach. Harry swung his shotgun on Conner and Isabeau in an attempt to complete the job Alberto had started. Bullets spat into the trees and ground around them as men began firing at anything and everything in the yard, unable to tell what was happening either in the house or out in the yard. Without someone in command, chaos broke out and the guards began to panic.

Conner fired his gun from his hip as he burst off the ground, drawing fire away from Isabeau, the bullets cutting a straight dotted line across Harry's chest. Harry tried to bring up the shotgun again, but he went to his knees, the weight too much for him with the blood pumping from his body.

Isabeau sprinted for the greenhouse, ignoring her screaming body. She caught a glimpse of the leopard turning his attention back to Alberto as the old man dragged himself through the dirt toward the gun. The leopard's expression stayed the same, focused completely on his prey, all the while the mind beneath those spots was working a cunning, savage plan. The eye contact, laser-sharp, never left Alberto. Ears flattened, belly close to the ground, the leopard crept closer. Alberto screamed and gestured wildly for the cat to leave him, but those merciless eyes never blinked.

The leopard rushed forward, lightning fast, and grabbed his prey with extended claws. The hind legs were firmly on the ground as the suffocating bite was delivered. The cat's canine teeth forced apart the two neck vertebrae, breaking the spinal cord.

Isabeau hadn't realized she'd stopped and was staring while a hail of bullets struck just a few short yards from her. Conner grabbed her hand and yanked her into motion, practically dragging her to the greenhouse. When he tried to pull the door open, it was locked from the inside. He simply shot the lock and jerked it open, thrusting Isabeau behind him. He rolled in first, going right, clearing the room before he called to her.

Isabeau hurried inside and stepped behind him, trying to stay small and not make noise as he threaded in and out among the plants, making his way toward the back of the building. There was another door, clearly leading to a small room, probably originally a potting or tool room. There was the sound of a scuffle. A curse. A yelp of pain. Conner put his hand on the doorknob and slowly turned it.

Isabeau flattened herself against the wall at his gesture
to stay back as he eased the door open. At once bullets
smashed into the door and zipped past into the greenhouse.
Conner kicked the door all the way open, standing to one
side back behind the doorjamb. A very scared-looking man
held a boy in front of him like a shield. Isabeau gasped. It
was Adan's grandson, Artureo.

Conner called out in the Indian dialect, his arm flashing
up, gun extended. He pulled the trigger as the boy jerked to
his right. The bullet took the man behind him dead center
in the middle of his forehead.

"Nice to see you," Artureo greeted. "You took longer
than I expected." He stepped over the body and waved to
the other children to come out into the open.

Isabeau was proud of him. He'd taken leadership just as
his father and grandfather had always done. He'd kept them
calm and hopeful.

Conner frowned as his gaze swept the children. "Where's
the boy? Mateo?"

"She took him," Artureo said. "Last night. She came
in with one of the mean ones and they dragged him out
of here." He glanced at the other children and lowered his
voice. "I think she suspected he was different. I followed
them over to the water tower."

"You followed?" Conner's eyebrows shot up.

Artureo nodded. "Did you think we were just going to
sit here and wait until she killed us? Or took the girls? She
and the old man are devils. We've dug our way out of the
tool room, but hadn't figured out how to make it to the fence
without being shot."

Conner flashed him a grin. "Let's get out of here. Keep
them together, very tight. No talking. We're going to make
for the southernmost wall. Get them into the rain forest,

Isabeau. Start on the trail. Rio and the others should be close behind you or already waiting for you." He pushed a gun into Artureo's hands. "You know how to use this?"

Artureo nodded. "My grandfather taught me."

"I expect you to protect them. Isabeau, I'll lead you out, but you take over when I get to the water tower."

"I can do it," Isabeau assured him, feeling slightly sick.

It was difficult to keep from staring at the dead body slumped on the floor, blood pooling around his head. So like her father's death. She realized this was exactly how her father had died, only Rio had been the shooter, and her father had tried to kill Conner. Her stomach lurched at the memory and she pressed her hand there hard.

Conner's fingers curved around the nape of her neck. His mouth brushed her ear. "Are you all right? Are you up for this? I can take you all and come back."

She forced a smile. "I'm good. Let's do it."

Conner went first, breaking the padlock on the back entrance and cautiously opening the door to peer out. The yard was in chaos. The sound of gunfire was sporadic, but men ran in all directions. The main house had turned into a wall of flames, the fire burning ferociously. Heat poured off the roiling conflagration so that it was impossible to get too close to the inferno.

Conner found a niche inside a particularly thick bushy area and he waved to Isabeau. She sent Artureo first, and the teenager held hands with the youngest. They formed a chain with Isabeau bringing up the rear, hurrying as quickly as they could while hugging the walls of the building and staying in close to the hedges until they crammed like sardines into that small spot.

Isabeau looked toward the garden. Many of the trees and bushes were already on fire as the wind, mostly created by the fire itself, sent sparks flying through the air. Two bodies lay sprawled in the dirt, and the wheelchair was still tipped over on its side. She couldn't help herself, she began searching above their heads for any sign of the leopard. The large cats preferred to be up high and often dropped down on the unwary prey. Systematically she searched the rooftops and trees. Her gaze landed on the water tower and she froze.

Conner signaled again and they followed the winding flowerbeds, staying low and stopping whenever Conner held up his hand. "Rio's waiting by the wall," he told Isabeau. He stepped out to get a better look at the terrain between the children and their destination.

"Conner!" Isabeau shouted a warning.

He ducked back into cover and looked up just as a bullet kicked up dirt inches from his foot. Imelda held a squirming Mateo in front of her, his feet right on the edge. "Get back, all of you, or I'll drop this little bastard."

"Isabeau, I'm going to shoot toward the tower and drive her back. Take the children and run as fast as you can for the rain forest. Get them over the fence. I've called up the others to help me here. Leonardo will guide you, Marcos and the children."

Before she could reply, Conner was firing, the bullets carving chunks of wood from the tower around Imelda. She screamed, swearing, and stumbled backward, dragging the boy with her. Isabeau took off running and this time Artureo brought up the rear. She didn't look back—or up—she just ran for the fence.

The high fence loomed in front of her far more quickly than she'd bargained for and at the last second she gathered herself and leapt for the top. Her body shrieked a protest, every muscle cramping. She might have missed on her own, but Marcos caught her outstretched arm and dragged her onto the thin plank that was the top. She forced herself to keep going, landing on the rain forest side, trying not to feel the terrible burning in her body. Leonardo jumped off and began tossing children to Marcos. The man caught each one with amazing dexterity, handing them down to Isabeau.

Conner didn't dare risk a glance to see if Isabeau had made it to the fence safely. He kept up the volley of shots and then sprinted to the bottom of the water tower out of Imelda's sight. Rio took up where Conner had left off, spitting bullets around Imelda to keep her away from the edge of the tower with the boy.

Once under the water tower and hidden from sight, Conner removed his shoes and stuffed them into the pack he always carried along with his weapons. He tied the pack securely around his neck and began to climb fast, staying inside the wooden structure for most of the way up. He used his enormous strength to take his body up quickly in an effort to get to the boy before she threw him over— because he knew Imelda was going to fling him off just because she could.

He heard the boy hissing like a small leopard cub and wondered if the cat would emerge to help the child. Imelda slapped at the struggling boy. She screamed suddenly and the slaps grew louder and more frantic. The boy must have hurt her. He heard a thud as she dropped him on the platform and began kicking him.

The sounds and smells triggered the leopard's survival instincts. He felt his muscles begin to contort and he allowed it to happen, welcoming the shift, tearing his clothes off in strips even as he tried to keep moving upward. Just as he had almost completed the change, he heard Rio shout a warning and he looked up.

Mateo came hurtling over the edge, the boy's face a mask of terror—that same look he'd seen on Isabeau's face the night before. Conner leapt into empty space, completing the shift, his hands forming outstretched claws. The boy hit hard and cried out as the leopard's mouth came around his body. Conner twisted in midair, righting his body, knowing they were high enough up that even his cat could be injured. He did his best to protect the boy as they landed. The shock went up his legs, but he kept his mouth soft and the boy high enough to prevent him from striking the ground. The moment he could move, he opened his mouth and Mateo dropped.

He turned back to the tower.

20

UNDER Rio's covering fire, Elijah raced across the open yard to the water tower. Flames began to lick along the bottom of one of the legs of the wooden structure. Elijah scooped up Mateo.

"We're rescuing you," he said as the boy began to fight, hissing and spitting and digging sharp nails into Elijah's arm. "That's your brother, Conner, Mateo. He's come for you. Your mother must have told you about Conner."

The boy went quiet in his arms and peeked over his shoulder to see the leopard moving fast up the framework toward the top where Imelda crouched, shouting orders to her men in the hopes of taking command. It was impossible to make out her exact words over the roar of the flames, but her shrill voice was punctuated by the firing of a gun.

Mateo began to wiggle again. "I go help him," he stated.

Elijah laughed. "You would. But not this time. He wants you in the forest taking care of his wife, Isabeau. He said

to tell you to look out for her until he can get there. She's
got an enemy—a leopard. Only another leopard can protect
her."

The boy pushed out his small chest. "I can do it."

"Let's go then." Elijah anxiously assessed the fire. In
a few more minutes it was going to cut off their escape
route. They had to go. He signaled to Rio that he was moving with the boy. He shifted Mateo to his back. "Hold on.
We're on the move," he barked into his radio, not wanting
his own men to accidentally shoot them.

The fire was becoming a larger threat than the erratic
gunfire. Rio signaled to his men to follow Elijah and get
out. They couldn't wait any longer. He tried to warn Conner that the base of the tower was on fire, but the leopard
had already made it to the top and was just beneath the
platform. He didn't want to give Imelda any warning of
the cat's presence, not when she seemed to have a small
arsenal at her fingertips.

The smoke rolled into the air, turning everything grayish black, dropping visibility. It was helpful to Elijah as he
took the boy out of the compound into the safety of the rain
forest, but the smoke was nearly choking Rio. He covered
his mouth with a handkerchief as he strained to see what
was happening above him on the tower. He no longer could
see Imelda, but she had to be aware of the crackling flames
greedily rushing up the supporting legs of the tower.

THE smell of the fire was overpowering to the large
leopard. Every survival instinct he possessed urged him to
run for his life. The leopard snarled as the smoke stung his
eyes, but he kept climbing, determined to put a stop to the
gunfire as Imelda continued to fire into the hazy yard below

her. Conner's leopard dragged himself onto the platform in absolute silence.

Through the swirling clouds of billowing smoke, he could see the woman, lying on top of the tower, weapons strewn around her, an automatic gun sweeping the yard below with no regard for who she might hit. Below, the men broke under the assault, abandoning their tries to put out the fire, running instead to get out. The ground below was in chaos.

Imelda screamed at them, swearing and hurling curses, most directed at Elijah and Marcos. She must have believed that they had deceived her in order to take over her drug routes. It obviously didn't occur to her that they had come to rescue the children. She swore vengeance and death to their families as she continued to shoot at anything that moved below her.

The leopard fixed his stare on her, focusing completely on his prey. He began the slow, freeze-frame stalk that took him step by slow step across more than half of the tower platform. He went to his belly and moved even slower, not making a sound as he neared her.

Imelda suddenly stiffened. She turned slowly, her eyes widening in terror. "Ottila. I would never tell anyone." She lifted her hand, palm out, as if that would stop a charging leopard. "I'll double your pay." Even as she said it, she whipped up the gun, finger already on the trigger, spraying bullets across the platform as she tried to bring the weapon up into position against the leopard's charge.

Conner felt the stings just before he hit her, one near his hip and one just grazing his shoulder, and then he was using his powerful legs for the spring, hitting her with the force of a freight train. Filled with loathing, he drove them both over the edge—the same one she'd thrown Mateo over. He heard the air rush from her lungs, felt everything break apart inside of her. Her mouth stretched wide in a scream, but the sound was torn from her, disappearing into the smoke.

It was much more difficult righting his body, somersaulting in midair. His back legs crumbled when he hit the ground. She landed hard, the sound like a pumpkin smashing and spilling contents across the ground. He crawled to her, using the cover of the smoke. She was still alive, her eyes wide, her body unmoving. She gasped. Wheezed. Fought for air.

The leopard put his giant paw on her belly. She tried to move, but with a broken back it was impossible. The leopard's hot breath fanned her face. She stared at death, the long canines, the fierce eyes lost in a sea of spots.

"Conner!" Rio's voice called out of the smoke. "Move!"

Shots could be heard in the distance, coming from the direction Isabeau had taken the children. He saw sudden recognition in Imelda's eyes. Not Ottila. Fury burned. Hatred. Then, as his head moved closer and he drew back his lips in a snarl, fear. He delivered the killing bite, severing her spine, not out of mercy—he felt none—but with the knowledge that evil often found a way to survive and he wouldn't permit it, not this time.

The leopard took several experimental steps. His back leg dragged a bit, but he could walk. Pain crashed through him after the first few feet, the numbness wearing off.

"You need help?" Rio came up on his left side, his gun ready as they hurried through the swirling smoke toward the fence. His face was grim, eyes bloodshot, always moving, searching through the smoke for an enemy, but his hands were rock steady.

Conner shook his head, grateful he had a friend who

watched his back. Blood coated his hindquarters and the pain in his back hip and leg was becoming unbearable.

Around them, it looked as if the world was on fire. Flames rolled and spun, reaching high, greedy for something to consume and finding it in the buildings and plants throughout the compound. Already, the tall fence surrounding the estate was on fire in several places. The smoke choked lungs, burned eyes and throats. The loud roar pounded through their ears, driving out nearly every other sound. The conflagration created its own wind, a fierce, hot breath that scorched anyone it touched.

Conner kept going, forcing the pain to the back of his mind, afraid for the children and Isabeau. He kept telling himself Elijah and the Santos brothers were with them. The fence loomed up in front of them, a fiery wall that seemed to surround the entire complex now. Bullets spit into the dirt near him and someone shouted hoarsely. Rio dropped to one knee and began firing.

Conner gathered himself and forced his cat to leap through the flames. Heat seared him, singeing whiskers and fur. For a moment the heat was so intense, he thought he was on fire. He landed on the other side and crouched, panting, his sides heaving as his leg gave way and he staggered and fell. Rio landed beside him, already reloading.

"You need medical attention. Get to the trees and let me take care of that," Rio said. When the leopard shook its head, Rio's mouth tightened. "That wasn't a request."

Conner snarled, showing teeth, but reluctantly followed his team leader's order. Rio rarely put things as a command, but he ran the team when Drake wasn't around—and Drake hadn't been around in a long while.

They hurried away from the heat and roar of the fire. There were a few men running away from the flames, so they avoided them. The ones hunting the children and Isabeau were a different matter. The leopard sank down into the thick vegetation, while Rio withdrew his medical kit and found what he needed.

"I think the bullet's still in there, Conner. I'm going to have to take it out."

He injected the cat with painkiller to numb the area before feeling around to see where the bullet was lodged. Leopards could be unpredictable in the best of times, and digging around for a bullet was not something most would allow. Rio wouldn't have tried it with just anyone. Conner was strong and held his cat in check through most difficult situations. And they had little time.

Rio could feel the leopard tremble as he probed the wound. Once he nearly had the slippery bit of metal with the tweezers, but the cat flinched. "Damn it. Hold still. The light's no good here and I'm working blind." Mostly the cat's teeth were too close, making him nervous.

It took a few more minutes of digging before he managed to grasp the bullet enough to pull it out. The cat shuddered and hissed out a long protest, but resolutely kept its head turned away from him. Hastily, Rio cleaned up the wound site and injected him with antibiotics. "Don't do anything crazy and that should hold until you can shift again. Let's go."

Conner tested the leg. With the painkiller, he could put more weight on it, but he was weak and a little disoriented. The two set out at a run. Rio slung his gun over his shoulder and tried to keep up with the wounded leopard. The men had set a fast pace with the children. Elijah was obviously carrying Mateo, his footprints were deeper than the others. They came across two bodies, both guards from Imelda's compound, shot.

There were smears of blood after that, indicating someone had been injured. Deep inside the leopard, Conner's
heart pounded in fear for Isabeau.

"Not her," Rio said. "Felipe or Leonardo I think." He
pointed to a broken stride. "Right here."

Both inhaled deeply. "Definitely Felipe," Rio said.

They took off running again. The sound of a gunshot
reverberated through the forest. Beside the leopard, Rio
suddenly jerked and went down on one knee. Blood splattered across the rotting vegetation as Rio fell facedown,
sprawling out limply.

Conner used his powerful claws to grip a leg and pull
the body into the deeper cover of the trees, sinking down
beside his friend to gently roll him over. He was losing too
much blood. Conner shifted, uncaring of the vicious pain
slamming through his leg and hip as he crouched beside
Rio, working fast to stop the blood.

There was both an entry and exit wound. The bullet had
passed through Rio's body, close to the heart, but it hadn't
hit it. He had no idea of what damage it had done, but Rio
was breathing shallowly. Conner had no doubt who had tar-
geted them. Just as they had stashed supplies and weapons
in the forest, so had Ottila.

He worked on Rio for twenty minutes before he was
satisfied he'd done all he could. Rio stirred, lashes fluttering several times. Conner leaned close to his ear. "Lie still.
He's out there hunting us. I'm putting the gun in your hand.
It's fully loaded. There's water next to your other hand. I'm
going to kill him, but it may take some time. I don't want
you getting all impatient on me and trying to move. You
understand, Rio. Don't move around."

Rio's nod was barely perceptible. Conner put his hand

on his friend's shoulder and bowed his head, looking for a
little help. He didn't want to come back to a dead body.

Shifting, he slunk low to the ground and bellied his way
through the thick brush. He crept slowly. Patience on the
hunt was essential. He couldn't think about Rio or Isabeau.
He had to turn his instincts completely over to his leopard.

He circled the area around Rio, stealthy and silent on
his cushioned paws. The man would have to be protected.
Ottila would certainly try to kill him, to make certain there
would be no interference during his challenge for Isabeau.
Conner had to be able to see Rio at all times, and to be able
to get to him quickly.

His cat found a tree with a multitude of sweeping
branches and went up. He was up against an enemy who
was cunning and quick, one determined and very familiar with the territory. He was hunting in Ottila's backyard.
But, Conner decided, Ottila had no idea Conner had been
born and raised in the Panama rain forest and he also was
familiar with it. Granted, he'd been away five years, but he
wasn't one to forget.

He curled up on a branch and went still, relying on his
heavy coat to camouflage him, fade him into the background. Now it was a waiting game. Ottila would feel the
pressure more than Conner. He would think that Elijah and
the others might backtrack and come looking for them if
they took too long to catch up. Ottila had no idea orders
were to see to the safety of the children before anything
else. No, the leopard would come with his evil intentions
and he would be forced to make the first offensive move. A
game of chess then. The stakes were life for Rio and Conner and Isabeau, or death for them all. Ottila had a battle
on his hands.

Conner had spent hundreds of hours as a sniper, locked

into a position simply waiting for that perfect target. He felt the familiar calm that always seeped into his veins. Ice water, Rio called it, but it flowed through him bringing peace. He became aware of every nuance of the rain forest. The birds, the constant calls back and forth, the monkeys, all frightened and fleeing the heat and flames of the fire. The wind was carrying the fire toward the east, away from them now, but the smoke had settled in the trees like a gray, choking blanket.

There was no sound, nor did Conner think Ottila would make such a mistake. He watched the brush around Rio until he saw what he was looking for. A low branch on a bush shifted slightly when there was no breeze. That was all the warning he got—all he needed. His gaze locked on to the ground and brush. His tail twitched and he stilled it. Waiting.

The snarling face of a male leopard in his prime pushed through the foliage and froze. Conner could see the fur was darker than his own golden pelt—more of a tan or tawny base, with a sea of black rosettes covering his body. Ottila looked a strong brute, large with roped muscles and cunning intelligence burning in his yellow-green gaze. His ears lay flat on his head as he crept forward, never taking his eyes from the motionless boot sticking out of the bushes just yards from him.

The path chosen by the stalking leopard would take him close to the tree where Conner lay in wait. Conner gathered himself, every muscle coiling tight in preparation. Inch by inch, Ottila crept forward. The foot never moved. The body never shifted. Conner was afraid Rio had passed out again and wouldn't be able to defend himself if he missed the initial attack.

He kept his gaze focused on the leopard, watching each

freeze-frame step that took him closer to his prey. He waited until he could see the bunching of the muscles beneath the thick fur, the gathering as Ottila prepared to charge. With the darker leopard so focused on his prey, Conner launched his own attack, striking with the blurring speed of the leopard. At the last moment, Ottila must have sensed his presence, breaking off his focused stare to look up.

Conner hit him hard, knocking him off his feet. They rolled, a tangle of teeth and claws, raking at one another. Tails lashed as both rose up on their hind feet, digging deep into the ground for leverage as both tried for a suffocating hold on the throat. Ottila hissed and snarled his hatred of his rival, the roars reverberating through the forest, so that the birds rose screaming from the trees. Howler monkeys threw twigs and sticks down on the two leopards.

The cats separated, circled and met again in midair, eyes locked, both savagely ripping at the other. Ottila arched into a half-circle, his flexible spine enabling him to nearly fold into two. Conner timed his swipe perfectly, raking hard at the belly, ripping deep even as the darker leopard tore open his side. They landed, sides heaving, blood smearing the leaves around them both as they once again circled warily.

Ottila tried to take the fight closer to Rio, but Conner cut him off, refusing to give ground, springing once again and driving the other leopard off his feet. Ottila rolled over, spun, nearly somersaulting, his powerful front paw swiping with tremendous force across Conner's injured back hip. Conner tried to get out of the way enough to at least lessen the blow, but the claw connected, sending fire shooting down his leg and rolling in his belly. His leg collapsed and he went down.

Ottila leapt on him, claws raking at his belly, breath hot in his face, the malevolent eyes glaring into his as they struggled, nose to nose, Ottila trying to sink his teeth into Conner's throat. Conner slammed his legs into Ottila's softer belly, ripping at the fur to draw blood, trying to go deeper while the leopard slashed and bit at his throat. With one last desperate heave, Conner managed to roll his body over and out from under the other leopard. He tried to stand and went down again.

Ottila circled, snarling, lips drawn back, exposing the bloody canines. There was blood smeared over his muzzle, turning the tawny color muddy. His eyes were red flames, shining with hatred and resolve.

Conner stayed in position, only expending the energy it took to stay facing the other leopard. His hind end was barely working, the leg weak, with a tendency to crumble beneath him if he put too much weight on it. He was careful to hide the weakness as best he could. Ottila was strong, too good and too experienced for Conner to give him any edge.

Ottila charged him, a burst of speed, striking with so much force that he not only drove Conner over, but it carried him past the golden leopard as Conner went down, the only thing that really saved Conner's life. His insides felt broken, smashed to pieces, but he resolutely rolled over and regained his feet, shaking himself. Ottila rose, whirled back, snarling. Conner began limping toward the other leopard, his sides heaving, blood coating his hips, legs and now his sides.

Rio groaned and shifted position, drawing the enraged leopard's attention. Ottila snarled again and, dismissing Conner as too injured to be much of a threat, crawled on his belly toward the body lying so still in the brush, now only feet from him. He didn't want a bullet in his head when he went to finish Conner off. Rio raised his head, his eyes locking with the leopard. The rifle lay loosely in his hand, seemingly forgotten, or Rio was too weak from blood loss to even lift it.

The tawny leopard pulled back his lips in a grimace of hatred. He looked evil in that moment, using his claws to pull himself inch by inch closer to Rio, prolonging the agony, knowing the man was utterly helpless.

Conner followed the leopard grimly. As Ottila picked up speed on the ground, Conner struck, a desperation move, driving his two front claws as deep as he could into the leopard's hips. He dug his back legs into the ground and pulled with every bit of strength he had, dragging the leopard away from Rio.

Ottila roared with rage and twisted, ripping a razor-sharp claw across Conner's muzzle. Conner kept dragging him, back-pedaling, his grip relentless. Blood ran down the darker leopard's legs, and each time he twisted, Conner dug deeper, refusing to allow even that flexible spine to interfere with his determination to remove the threat to Rio.

Ottila began to panic as the claws kept adjusting, puncturing deeper and deeper, the grip relentless, merciless, unbreakable. Conner sank his long canines into the spine and Ottila's terror spread like a disease. He twisted and snarled, throwing his weight sideways in an attempt to roll, his claws ripping everything he could touch. He slashed at the golden leopard frantically, chest, muzzle, shoulders and front legs, but he couldn't dislodge the other animal sawing through his backbone.

Ottila needed leverage, but the golden leopard countered every move. He seemed to anticipate every move before he made it. He knew Conner was weakening. His continual slashes were taking their toll. He raked the face, the chest and shoulders and arms, long, deep slices that spewed fountains of precious blood. He couldn't get to the throat, although he'd come close, twisting and turning, and still those claws and teeth were relentless, hanging on, dragging him away from the man on the ground.

Conner began moving up, inch by inch, using his claws to crawl up the body, blocking the burning pain as the other leopard fought back with slashing swipes of powerful paws. Conner knew he had no choice but to hold the tawny leopard. He needed to find a way to deliver the killing bite, but his strength was waning fast. His back leg was on fire, the pain excruciating. He blocked out everything, the sounds of the battle, the pain, the thought of Rio lying helpless, the smoke swirling inches from the ground and veiling the trees, everything but Isabeau. This was for Isabeau. He had to defeat Ottila.

Deliberately he brought forth every image of her mottled, purple bruises, the terror in her eyes, the deep puncture wounds this animal had inflicted on her just because he could. *There is no way you're going to live.* Not even if it meant both of them died there. Ottila Zorba's life was over. Conner yanked hard with his claws, dragging the other leopard beneath him with renewed strength, walking up the spine until he was at the thick neck. His claws dug into the heaving sides so that he was riding the other leopard.

Ottila rolled, desperate to remove him from his back, desperate to get away from those wicked teeth and razor-sharp claws. He smashed Conner into the ground, deliberately landing hard on Conner's injured hindquarters, but the golden leopard refused to be dislodged. Like a demon, he hung on, slowly moving up the back, until those terrible teeth closed around the nape of his neck in a punishing bite.

The canine teeth sank deep, seeking to separate the

spinal cord. Ottila tried to flip, fear suddenly filling him. He actually felt the sudden, spreading paralysis, his legs stiffening, his body going limp. The leopard held him for a long moment until Ottila's eyes glazed over and the air left the lungs. He held him even longer, waiting until he was certain the heart had ceased beating.

It was almost too much effort to release the leopard from his grasp. Conner collapsed on top of him, bleeding from too many places to count. He knew he had to get back to Rio, but he didn't have any energy left. He could only lie over the other leopard, his body consumed with such pain it was impossible to tell what part of him hurt the worst. It took minutes—or hours—he didn't know which, to gather enough strength to begin what seemed like a mile-long journey of dragging himself across the ground to Rio's side.

Rio raised his head slightly and sent Conner a sickly grin. "Don't you look a sight?"

Conner grimaced. He had to shift and it was going to hurt like hell. He couldn't chance being caught as a leopard, not if they were to call in help in the form of a helicopter. And both of them needed medical care. He didn't wait, didn't dwell on it—he simply willed the change. Pain crashed through his body, his vision went red, then dark. His stomach lurched and nothing seemed to work. He found himself sprawled facedown in the rotting vegetation and wondered if the insects would eat him alive.

He woke up sometime later. Time had to have passed, as the smoke had dissipated near the ground, although the smell of the recent fire was strong, and clouds of it still hung in the trees. Something moved close to him and he managed to turn his head toward the rustling leaves. Rio pushed a canteen of water into his hands.

"Drink. You've lost a lot of blood."

His vision was blurry. Everything hurt. *Everything.* There didn't seem to be a place on his body that wasn't slashed to ribbons. "Do I have any skin left?"

"Not much. I don't think you're going to be such a pretty boy anymore," Rio cheerfully informed him. "The bastard did some real damage."

Conner peered at him through bloodshot eyes. "I was never a pretty boy."

Rio snorted. "Oh yeah you were. Your lady's going to give you hell for getting all torn up that way."

"And yours is going to be happy?" Conner raised his head enough to drink. The water was warm and brackish, but tasted like heaven. "You were dumb enough to get yourself shot."

"I've had plenty of time to think about how I can spin this to my advantage with her," Rio said. He stared up at the canopy and the birds gathering there. If they thought they were about to have a meal, they had another think coming. "I'm the hero, see, taking a bullet for you."

Conner choked on the water and smeared blood across his face when he wiped his mouth. "It didn't happen that way."

"But the point, my friend, is that it could have. And now it did."

"What a load of crap."

"It could have happened that way." There was amusement in his voice. "I don't actually remember it all that well. But I'm lying here with a hole the size of a baseball through me."

It was Conner's turn to snort. "Slight exaggeration. You really are trying to think up stories to make your woman sympathetic."

"I've been married longer than you. You come home all

beat up, you're in for a lot of trouble. I'm imparting wisdom here, rookie. Listen up."

Conner tried to smile but it hurt too much. "I don't think we have too much to worry about. I'm getting eaten alive by these damn bugs. Another hour and they'll have picked my bones clean."

Rio managed a soft laugh. "I activated our 'come and get us, we're fucked' button."

Conner worked at turning his head to survey their surroundings. "We're not exactly at the clearing where they can set down a helicopter. No road to drive to us. I'm going to let the bugs take care of me. I swear I'm not moving."

"Pansy. I always knew you were a wimp."

Conner laughed and immediately began to cough. He touched his mouth, and his hand came away with blood smeared on it. "Damn leopard. He did a number on me."

"I was worried there for a few moments. Fight lasted nearly thirty minutes. He was strong," Rio said. "What the hell went wrong with him?"

"Who knows?" Conner closed his eyes. "That poor kid. Mateo. First his mother throws him away like a piece of garbage because his father can't bear the sight of him, and then he loses his adopted mother—murdered right in front of him."

Rio was silent a moment. "I'm sorry about your mother, Conner." He paused again. "You taking the kid in?"

"He's my brother."

"Half," Rio pointed out. "You're under no obligation."

"He's my brother," Conner said stubbornly. "I know what it feels like to be unwanted, but my mother, rather than kick me out, left the old man and gave me a good life.

I'm not letting that bastard ruin this boy. I want him," he said fiercely. "Isabeau is with me on this."

"And if she wasn't?" Rio asked.

Conner looked at him. His eyes burned bright gold behind the red. "Then she wouldn't be the woman I thought she was. I'm not leaving him behind."

A slow smile softened the hard edge of Rio's mouth. "You're a good man, Conner."

"That's bullshit."

"Well. Probably." Rio grinned at him. The grin turned into a moan, and Rio put his head down. His face was gray-white.

"You planning on dying on me?"

"If those idiots take much longer," Rio said. He groaned again. "Damn this hurts."

Conner didn't like the way he was breathing. He couldn't push himself up onto his hands and knees, so he dug his toes into the vegetation and propelled his body forward an inch at a time, using elbows and toes to push himself along the ground to get around Rio to the medical bag. It was the first time he wished certain parts of his anatomy were smaller. Dragging his very sensitive cock along the ground wasn't a great idea.

He wasn't that far away from the medical kit, but the distance seemed like miles. He had to rest frequently. Sweat broke out to mingle with the blood covering his body. There was a roaring in his head, his pulse thundering loud enough to drown out the natural sounds of the forest. His mouth was dry and his arms like lead.

He left a trail of blood behind him, but he managed to make it to the kit. It took longer to push himself into a sitting position. His hip screamed a protest and for a moment, everything swam in a dizzying circle. He rummaged through the bag, searching for the field IV equipment and more painkillers. Rio was trying to stay focused, but it was obvious he was becoming disoriented.

"You fucking decide to die on me, and I'll put a bullet in your head," Conner muttered.

"That's helpful," Rio pointed out.

Conner's hand trembled as he tried to wipe Rio's arm over the vein. He smeared blood on Rio's forearm and cursed.

"I'm thinking that you could be just a little more sanitary about this," Rio added.

"You have bugs crawling all over you. You're lying in dirt and rotting leaves."

"Thanks for letting me know." Rio coughed. The effort to talk was beginning to weigh on him. "I was trying to ignore the bugs."

Conner poured water over his hands and wiped them, afraid they were so slippery he wasn't going to be able to get the needle in. "Hold still. And don't whine while I do this."

"Ow. Quit poking me."

"You sound like a girl. I told you not to whine." Conner took a breath and let it out in an effort to steady his hands. He was weaker than he'd thought. The two of them were very likely going to die there, bleeding out slowly, and the bugs were really going to pick their bones clean.

He felt sluggish and found it hard to concentrate. Once again he wiped sweat and blood from his forehead with his arm, trying to keep his hands clean. Rio had good veins, but Conner's eyesight kept blurring.

"Just do it," Rio encouraged and let his head loll back.

Conner didn't like the shallow way he was breathing, as

if he labored for every breath. He was as gentle as he could be with his blurred vision and shaky hands, but he got the needle into the vein. With a sigh of relief, he hastily set up the IV to give Rio fluids.

"Come on, man, hang in there."

"Hurts like a son of a bitch," Rio admitted.

"A few minutes and you'll be feeling better."

"If something goes wrong . . ."

"Shut the fuck up."

"No listen to me, Conner. If anything happens to me, you and the others take care of Rachel. She's got money. Elijah saw to that, but she'll need all of you."

Conner swore and bent over Rio. "Look at me. Open your eyes and look at me, Rio."

Rio's lids fluttered with the effort, but he managed.

"You. Will. *Not*. Die." Conner enunciated each word individually so there could be no mistake. "I'll get you out of here if I have to pack you out on my back."

Rio searched his face a long time and then a faint smile crept into his eyes. "I believe you would. You're a stubborn son of a bitch."

"Watch what you call my mother. I'm the son of a bastard. Get it right."

Rio managed another smile and nodded his head.

Conner pressed his hand to Rio's shoulder and took another swallow of water. He meant what he said. If he had to crawl, he'd get Rio to help. It was a matter of finding the strength.

He rested, drinking water to try to hydrate while he waited for the painkiller to take effect. Rio moaned a few times and grew restless, but eventually he quieted. Conner prepared for the journey slowly and with deliberation. The first thing to do was clean as many of his own wounds as possible. He used the Betadine, which burned like hell. Once he was certain he passed out, but as soon as he came around again, he sewed the worst of the wounds closed to keep from leaking more blood.

He had to pause several times, his body shuddering with pain, shaking so uncontrollably at times he couldn't work the needle through his skin. He continued doggedly until he thought he'd done enough repairs to stay alive. The next step was to drag jeans over his lacerated legs. That was a hell of a lot harder than he'd imagined and hurt so much more that he actual rolled over onto his hands and knees and was sick.

He gathered weapons next, methodically preparing for the journey. He had to get Rio to a clearing where a helicopter could come pick him up. The others would be looking at the coordinates on the map they'd used for every contingency including this one. They'd be coming, but they needed a place to set down.

It took three tries to get Rio on his back. Each time Conner tried to heft him up, his legs turned rubbery and threatened to give out. Both men were sweating profusely by the time he managed to lift Rio up. Conner began with one step. One foot in front of the other. At first he was conscious of hurting Rio and tried to keep his stride smooth and even to jar him as little as possible, but within a matter of minutes, Conner realized it was going to be a long, bone-jarring journey for both of them.

He walked, or more accurately, he staggered as far as he could go toward his destination until his strength gave out and drove him to his knees. He put Rio carefully on the ground, gave him water and drank himself, both lying down until the air stopped burning in his lungs and he could push himself again to another effort.

By the second hour, Conner realized the others were long gone and no one was coming to relieve him. They were sticking to the plan and meeting at the rendezvous point with the helicopter. He really wasn't all that certain he and Rio were going to make it there.

Rio was mumbling, his eyes glazed, his breathing shallow. Real fear bit at Conner with every step he took. He didn't want to risk taking any more breaks. He forced each leg to work, concentrating on foot placement, calling on his leopard's strength and endurance to help him put one foot in front of the other.

He was still two or three miles from the agreed-upon meeting place when his legs simply gave out. The ground rose up to meet him faster than he would have believed. As he toppled over, he thought he saw a tribesman standing just in front of him, the hallucination very vivid. The Indian carried a blowgun and was dressed in the more traditional loincloth to hunt in the rain forest. The absence of clothes was normal. Clothes only got in the way, growing damp, clinging to the skin and adding to the heat and humidity.

The tribesmen had it right, he decided, he shouldn't have worn clothes. They were so heavy on his skin. What good were they? Conner smiled and gave an odd salute from where he lay on the ground to the vision of the Indian. Rio's bulk weighed him down, nearly crushing his chest into the ground, but he didn't have the energy to ease the man off of him. He just lay there, watching the tribesmen.

He looked familiar. Older. A worn face with faded eyes. The eyes crinkled and the tribesman came closer. He crouched beside Conner. "You don't look so good."

Conner didn't like the idea of hallucinations speaking. Not when he was too weak to protect Rio. He tried to find the knife at his side, but the older man stopped him.

"It's Adan, Conner. The men of our village met Isabeau and your team in the forest. There was a bit of a battle with those following them, but my men are very accurate. We've been backtracking them to find you."

"The children?"

"All are alive and well."

Several tribesmen lifted Rio gently from Conner's back. Conner made a lunge for his partner, but Adan caught him in his strong grip. "They'll take him to the helicopter. Both of you look a little worse for wear."

"There's a leopard dead a few miles from here," Conner said. "The carcass has to be burned in a hot fire, enough to reduce the entire thing to ashes. Leave no evidence of our species."

"It will be done. Let my men take you to the helicopter. And, Conner . . . don't knife anyone. They're on your side." Adan grinned at him as his men laid Conner on a cot and began hurrying in the direction of the clearing.

21

THE old wooden rocking chair creaked in time to the breeze blowing through the trees. Boughs shivered and leaves swirled in the air as the wind rushed through the valley. A second chair groaned and rasped in counterpoint to the first one. A third one added a slight squeak to the symphony. Conner leaned heavily on his cane and surveyed the three men rocking on Doc's porch in the sturdy, hand-carved rocking chairs.

"Well," Conner said, "we burned her house to the ground. Imelda can't hurt anyone anymore. We should at least feel good about that." As he spoke he turned his head to look at the little boy throwing rocks with enough force to make dents in the wooden fence.

"As far as we know, no one left alive knows about our people," Rio said. "And Adan's tribe should be safe enough."

"Until the next monster comes along," Felipe said gloomily.

Jeremiah stirred. "We'll cut their head off all over again." His voice was husky, low, barely there, as if he whispered rather than spoke. His expression, as he looked at the others, was belligerent. "I'm joining your team."

Rio flashed a small grin. "Wouldn't have it any other way, kid. Welcome to hell."

Conner studied the three drawn, gaunt faces. "Aren't you three a sorry sight," he observed. "Gossiping old biddies."

Jeremiah, Felipe and Rio looked at one another.

"I don't think you're looking much better," Rio pointed out. "In fact, you look worse than any of us."

"The scars add to my rakish appearance."

"You're going to scare the kid," Jeremiah said.

Conner sighed. "Isn't that the truth?"

Rio frowned. "Conner, the boy wants you to like him. He's trying as hard as he can. He watches you all the time."

Conner snorted. "He runs from me. He's watching me, because he's afraid I'm going to eat him for dinner."

"Try smiling," Felipe offered helpfully.

Conner turned his head to observe the little boy talking so earnestly to Isabeau. Mateo hadn't smiled once in the three weeks since they'd rescued him. He was a beautiful little boy, his body compact in the way of the leopard people, his eyes large and more gold than yellow, much like Conner. In fact, with his shaggy, unkempt head of hair and his bone structure, he looked very like Conner.

Conner sighed. He had no idea how to talk to children. The boy avoided him. He was a sober little child with big eyes holding too much sorrow and a terrible rage. Conner understood the intensity of both emotions, but didn't know how to reach the boy. He kept his eyes on Isabeau. She reached her hand down toward Mateo. Conner held his

breath. A heartbeat. Two. Willed the boy to take her hand—
to make human contact.

Isabeau never moved. Never said a word. If anyone was
going to get through to him, it would be Isabeau, not him.
She was so patient. She never took his rebuffs personally.
She never stopped trying with him. The boy took her hand
and Conner let his breath out.

Mateo didn't want to love again. Or trust. He'd lost too
much in his young life. He had nightmares almost every
night, and it was almost impossible to comfort him. Conner knew the leopard in the boy was close, trying to protect
him with the sheer force of anger, building a wall around
the boy. He didn't know how to bring that wall down.

"It will work out," Rio said softly.

Conner shook his head and began the slow, rather hum-
bling journey, limping across the yard to Isabeau and Mateo. He had to keep reaching out, hoping to find a way to
the reach the boy—to let him know he understood and that
the child could count on him to see him through the coming years.

Mateo didn't turn his head, but by the slight stiffening
of his body, Conner knew he was acutely aware of him. A
shadow slid over the boy's face as he approached. He felt
the hesitation. Should he disturb them? Leave them alone
to let the boy have a little peace? Or should he continue to
try to insert himself into the boy's life? How did his mother
always seem to know the right thing to do? Isabeau had
finally gotten Mateo to hold her hand; maybe this was the
wrong time.

Before he could turn away, Isabeau halted, the boy's
hand firmly in hers. "You look so sad, Conner."

Isabeau. Sweet Isabeau. She was giving him an opening.
Willing him to be strong enough to talk about his mother to

the child. She had brought up the subject late in the night, while lying in bed, holding him close. She thought the darkness would help him cope better, but he couldn't talk about his mother or her death. Tears had threatened to choke him. He wasn't the kind of man to talk about things like losing one's mother. He didn't cry. He didn't acknowledge pain if he could help it. Yet Isabeau was convinced that if he could let down his guard, it would allow the boy to do the same.

Mateo's expression was closed off, yet so very vulnerable. Conner was a man, and Mateo expected rejection from Conner. Those eyes. He looked at those every day in the mirror. So much pain. So much rage. So much vulnerability.

You're like her. Your mother. Not like him. Isabeau's soft words from the night before reverberated through his mind. *You're like her. She left you such a wonderful legacy, Conner. She taught you what love really means.*

He looked into those upturned eyes so like his own and he felt the shift inside him. Something hard seemed to melt into a softness he didn't quite understand. Marisa had left this child with him, believing he would give the boy the same gifts she had given Conner. Unconditional love. A sense of belonging. Freedom. Family. He looked at Isabeau. His woman. His wife.

He knew now why Isabeau made him feel whole. It wasn't the laughter—or the sex. It was moments like this. Moments that counted for a lifetime. That trust in her, that faith, the serenity on her face. As if she knew without a shadow of a doubt that he was like his mother—like Marisa—and he would find the way to unlock this boy's heart.

"Let's walk over here where I can sit down," Conner suggested. Because he couldn't choose his words carefully when his inflamed hip protested just standing. Or maybe, he was putting a confrontation off for as long as possible. The boy looked so frightened.

He turned without waiting, not giving Mateo a chance to protest. He simply headed to the barn where he knew Doc had a bench—and kittens. Isabeau followed with Mateo. He could hear them walking behind him. The boy was surprisingly adept at walking quietly, although Marisa had probably used the same tactics with him as she had with Conner—allowing him to sneak out, thinking he was getting away with it so the boy could practice.

He sank down onto the bench and waited until the boy was standing in front of him. Isabeau took the seat next to him. He could see Mateo brace himself for rejection.

"It's been a tough few days, hasn't it?"

Mateo blinked. Nodded. Remained silent.

"The thing is, Mateo, we were lucky. It doesn't feel that way right now, but we had a mother who loved us and left us each other. When I'm feeling alone without her, I'll always know I have you and Isabeau. When you're feeling alone, you'll have Isabeau and me."

Mateo hissed, sounding exactly like a leopard cub, spitting mad. His golden eyes flashed and he shook his head violently, stepping back. "She's gone."

"Did she talk about me to you, Mateo?"

The boy's chest heaved and he blinked rapidly, trying to cover up his deep agitation. He nodded, not trusting himself to speak.

"What did our mother tell you about me?"

Mateo set his jaw. "That you were my brother." His voice broke. "That you would want me. She said . . ." He pushed a fist into his eyes and shook his head.

Conner circled the boy's wrist with gentle fingers. "For a

very long time after I figured out that my father didn't want anything to do with me, I thought it was because something was wrong with me. That it was my fault." He shook his head. "It was his fault. There's something wrong with him."

The spiked, tear-wet lashes lifted and the boy looked at him solemnly. "That's what my mom said."

"You know she never lied, Mateo. We're leopard. We can smell a lie. She told you the truth. About him. About me. I do want you. Isabeau wants you as well. We're family."

The boy's mouth tightened and he shrugged.

Conner glanced helplessly at Isabeau. She brushed her hand along his thigh. A soft commitment of faith. "I hunt bad guys. That's what I do. I get in fights and sometimes I win and sometimes the other guy does . . ."

"Mostly you win," Isabeau interjected.

Conner nodded. "I have to win if I want to live. But the point, Mateo, is that for a long time I thought to be a strong man I couldn't show emotion. I couldn't ever lose control. Certainly I could never cry, no matter what the circumstances. But I was wrong about being emotional and not being a man. A real man knows it's okay to show when he's hurt. I'll never get over our mother's death. Not ever. I'll think about her every day, and at night, I cry when I'm missing her. Isabeau puts her arms around me and then I don't feel so alone."

Mateo pulled his wrist away and wrapped both arms around his middle, as if hugging himself. "I don't cry about it."

"About what?" Conner prompted.

"My mom leaving."

"She didn't leave you, Mateo," Conner said. When the boy remained stubbornly staring at the floor, Conner put a thumb under his chin and forced his head up. "Look at me."

The eyes flashed at him. Anger. Unbearable sorrow. Fear. Conner's heart contracted. "She didn't leave us, Mateo. Someone took her from us. Isabeau and I killed him."

Isabeau gasped, pulling her hand away from his thigh. Conner didn't look at her, knowing she would disapprove of his methods, but he had been this very little boy with that same rage, that same fear. And he felt the same unbearable sorrow.

"We're leopard, Mateo, and it isn't always easy to contain that much hatred and rage, even though our mother told us we should be forgiving. We can never justify taking a life because we're angry, but sometimes it's necessary, we have no choice. Do you understand? Our mother wouldn't want us to harm others, not even when we're hurting, but we have the right and the obligation to defend ourselves and our families."

"I hate him."

Conner nodded. "I hate him too. But that won't bring her back to us. She left us each other, Mateo. When I look at you, I see her in you. I hope when you look at me you can see her too. We'll make her proud of us. When I'm having a hard time, when I'm so angry I want to hurt someone, I'll talk to you about it and you will remind me what she would want. When you're feeling angry, you talk to me and I'll remind you. We can get through this together."

Mateo looked him steadily in the eye, and Conner could see the leopard there, judging, weighing him, wanting to believe he could entrust the child to the man. Conner opened his arms. Mateo's eyes went liquid, drenched in tears, and he stepped into Conner's arms.

Conner enfolded him tightly and just held the sobbing boy. There was so much pain in that little frame, and Conner felt that same emotion deep inside. "We have a bond no one can ever take away from us, Mateo. Our mother. She'll always tie us together, our love of her, our memories of her. It will always be us, you and me and Isabeau."

Mateo sobbed out his anger and sorrow, hiding his face against Conner's chest. Conner just held him close and remembered all the times his mother had done the same for him. Eventually he stroked the boy's hair, waiting for the hiccups that signaled the storm was over.

"Isabeau told me Doc rescued some kittens from a poacher. Did you want to show them to us?"

Mateo nodded and sniffed. "He said they were on a freighter, stuffed in a box with sawdust, and their lungs were messed up."

"Doc can't keep them all," Isabeau said helpfully.

The boy looked up at him with a glimmer of hope in his eyes. "Someone has to help him out."

Conner's eyebrow shot up. Now he knew what parents felt like when their child gave them that look. His heart did some kind of funny melting thing and he found himself looking a little helplessly at Isabeau. She laughed softly and took his free hand.

"Come on. These kitties are pretty big, Mateo. You'd have to help us with care and feeding and exercise."

"I would. I really would." Mateo skipped ahead of them to the corner of the barn where four little clouded leopards snarled and spit.

Conner limped after the boy, Isabeau at his side. "Funny what I'm already feeling for him."

"Me too," Isabeau acknowledged.

"I checked on Teresa, that servant girl you were worried about," Conner said. "She's a single mother and was desperate for money, so she went to work for Sobre in spite of the rumors. She sent the money home to her mother, who was taking care of her son. She was happy to be reunited with them. Adan found her a job."

She smiled up at him. "Thanks. I couldn't get her out of my mind." Her gaze followed Mateo as he sank down near the tumbling, squirming bodies of small leopards, watching their antics with enormous eyes. "I can see why she'd do anything for her child. Mateo's already getting to me, and I didn't even give birth to him."

He bent his head to the temptation of her mouth. Once he touched his lips to hers, it was the same flaring heat, lighting a match to an explosive. His fingers curled around the nape of her neck to anchor her to him while he lost himself in the exquisite taste of her.

"Oooh. That's gross," Mateo said. "Are you going to be doing that all the time?"

Conner grinned at him. "All the time," he confirmed.

Mateo's answering grin was slow in coming but when it did, it reached his eyes. "Guess I can live with that."

"Guess I can live with one of those kittens then," Conner conceded and watched the joy burst across the boy's face. "But I don't know about Isabeau. It's a family decision, right?"

Mateo turned his attention on Isabeau, and there was glee there, as if he already knew he had her wrapped around his finger.

Isabeau winked at him and turned her face up to Conner's. There was love shining in her eyes. "I think the family is all in agreement. We definitely need one of those kittens."

Mateo flung his arm around her leg and one of Conner's. Conner dropped his hand on the boy's head as he kissed Isabeau again. Somehow it felt like Marisa was right there, in the barn with him, sharing his happiness.

Keep reading for a special preview of
the upcoming book in a new series
from #1 *New York Times* bestselling author
Christine Feehan

WATER BOUND

A Sea Haven Novel

Available in August 2010 from Jove Books

FLAMES raced up the walls to spread across the ceiling. Orange. Red. *Alive*. The fire was looking right at her. She could hear it breathing. It rose up, hissing and spitting, following her as she crawled across the floor. Smoke swirled through the room, choking her. She stayed low and held her breath as much as possible. All the while the greedy flames reached for her with a voracious appetite, licking at her skin, scorching and searing, singeing the tips of her hair.

Chunks of flaming debris fell from the ceiling to the floor, and glass shattered. A series of small explosions detonated throughout the room as lamps burst from the intense heat. She dragged herself toward the only exit, the small doggy door in the kitchen. Behind her the fire roared as if enraged by her attempt to escape.

The fire shimmered like a dancing wall. Her vision tunneled until the flames became a giant monster, reaching with long arms and a ghastly, distorted head, crawling after her on the floor, its hideous tongue licking at her bare feet. She screamed but the only sound that emerged was a terrible choking cough. She turned to face her enemy, felt its malevolence as the flames poured over her, trying to consume her, trying to devour her from the inside out. Her scream finally broke past the terrible ball blocking her throat and she shrieked her terror in a high-pitched wail. She tried to call out, to beg for water to come to her, to save her, to drench her in cool, soothing liquid. The shriek of the sirens in the distance grew louder and louder. She threw herself sideways to avoid the flames . . .

Rikki Sitmore landed hard on the floor beside her bed. She lay there, her heart racing, terror pounding through her veins, her mind struggling to assimilate the fact that it was just a nightmare. The same old familiar nightmare. She was safe and unharmed—even though she could still feel the heat of the fire on her skin.

"Damn it." Her hand fumbled for the clock radio, fingers slapping blindly in search of the button that would stop the alarm that sounded so like the fire engine of her dreams. In the ensuing silence she could hear the sound of water, answering her cry for help, and she knew from experience that every faucet in her house was running.

She forced herself to sit up, groaning softly as her body protested. Her joints and muscles ached, as if she'd been rigid for hours.

Rikki wiped her sweat-drenched face with her hand, dragged herself to her feet, and forced her aching body to walk from room to room, turning off faucets as she went. At last, only the sink and shower in her bathroom were left. As she went through the bedroom, she turned on the radio and the coastal radio station flooded the room with music. She needed the sea today. Her beloved sea. Nothing worked better to calm her mind when she was too close to the past.

The moment she crossed the threshold of her bathroom, cool sea colors surrounded her with instant calm. The green slate beneath her feet matched the slate sea turtles swimming through an ocean of glossy blue around the walls.

She always showered at night to wash the sea off of her, but after a particularly bad nightmare, the spray of the water on her skin felt like a healing wash across her soul. The water in the shower was already running, calling to her, and she stepped into the stall. Instantly the water soothed her, soaking into her pores, refreshing, her personal talisman. The drops on her skin felt sensual, nearly mesmerizing her with the perfection of shape. She was lost in the clarity and immediately zoned out, taken to another realm where all chaos was gone from her mind.

Things that might ordinarily hurt—sounds, textures, the everyday things others took for granted—were washed away with the sweat from her nightmares or the salt from the sea. When she stood in the water, she was as close to normal as she would ever get, and she reveled in the feeling. As always, she was lost in the shower, disappearing into the clean, cool, refreshing pleasure it brought her, until, abruptly, the hot water was gone and her shower turned ice cold, startling her out of her trance.

Once she could breathe without a hitch, she toweled off and dragged on her sweats, not looking at the scars on her calves and feet. She didn't need to relive those moments again, yet night after night the fire was back, looking at her, marking her for death.

She shivered, turned up her radio so she could hear it throughout the house, and pulled out her laptop, taking it through the hallway to her kitchen. Blessed coffee was the only answer to idiocy. She started the coffee while she listened to the radio spitting out local news. She dropped into a chair, stilling to concentrate when it came to the weather. She wanted to know what her mistress was feeling this morning. Calm? Angry? A little stormy? She stretched as she listened. Calm seas. Little .wind. *A freaking tsunami drill?*

Not again. "What a crock," she muttered aloud, slumping dejectedly. "We don't need another one."

They'd just had a silly drill. Everyone had complied. How had she missed that they had scheduled another one in the local news? When they conducted drills of this magnitude, it was always advertised heavily. Then again . . . Rikki sat up straight, a smile blossoming on her face. Maybe the tsunami drill was just the opportunity she'd been looking for. Today was a darned perfect day to go to work. With a tsunami warning in effect, no one else would be out on the ocean—she would have the sea to herself. This was the perfect chance to visit her secret diving hole and harvest the small fortune in sea urchins she'd discovered there. She had found the spot weeks ago, but didn't want to dive when others might be around to see her treasure trove.

Rikki poured a cup of coffee and wandered out to the front porch to enjoy that first aromatic sip. She was going to make the big bucks today. Maybe even enough money to pay back the women who'd taken her in as part of their family for the expenses they'd incurred on her behalf. She wouldn't have her beloved boat finished if it wasn't for them. She could probably fill the boat with just a couple of hours' work. Hopefully the processor would think the urchins were as good as she did, and would pay top dollar.

Rikki looked around at the trees shimmering in the early morning light. Birds flitted from branch to branch and wild turkeys were walking along the far creek where she'd scattered seed for them. A young buck grazed in the meadow just a short distance from her house. Sitting there, sipping her coffee and watching the wildlife around her, everything began to settle in both body and mind.

She'd never imagined she would have a chance at such a place, such a life. And she never would have if not for the five strangers who'd entered her life and taken her into theirs. They'd changed her world forever.

She owed them everything. Her "sisters." They weren't her biological sisters, but no blood sister could be closer. They called themselves "sisters of the heart," and to Rikki that's exactly what they were. Her sisters. Her family. She had no one else and knew she never would. They had her fierce, unswerving loyalty.

The five women had believed in her when she'd lost all faith, when she was at her most broken. They had invited her to be one of them, and although she'd been terrified that she would bring something evil with her, she'd accepted, because it was that or die. That one decision was the single best thing she'd ever done.

The family—all six of them—lived on the farm together. One hundred thirty acres, which nestled six beautiful houses. Hers was the smallest. Rikki knew she'd never marry or have children, so she didn't need a large house. Besides, she loved the simplicity of her small home with its open spaces and high beams and soothing colors of the sea that made her feel so at peace.

A slight warning shivered down her body. She was not alone. Rikki turned her head and her tension abated slightly at the sight of the approaching woman. Tall and slender with a wealth of dark wavy hair untouched by gray in spite of her forty-two years, Blythe Daniels was the oldest of Rikki's five sisters, and the acknowledged leader of their family.

"Hey, you," Rikki greeted. "Couldn't sleep?"

Blythe flashed her smile, the one Rikki thought was so endearing and beautiful—a little crooked, allowing a glimpse of straight white teeth that nature, not braces, had provided.

"You're not going out today, are you?" Blythe asked, then nonchalantly went over to the spigot at the side of the house and turned it off.

"Sure I am." She should have checked all four hoses, darn it. Rikki avoided Blythe's too-knowing gaze.

Blythe looked uneasily toward the sea. "I just have this bad feeling . . ."

"Really?" Rikki frowned and stood up, glancing out at the sky. "Seems like a perfect day to me."

"Are you taking a tender with you?"

"*Hell* no."

Blythe sighed. "We talked about this. You said you'd consider the idea. It's safer, Rikki. You shouldn't be diving alone."

"I don't like anyone touching my equipment. They roll my hoses wrong. They don't put the tools back. No. No way." She tried not to sound belligerent, but she was *not* having anyone on her boat messing with her things.

"It's safer."

Rikki rolled her eyes. How was having some idiot sitting on the boat not diving alone? But she didn't voice her thoughts; instead, she tried a smile. It was difficult. She didn't smile much, especially when the nightmares were too close. And she was barefoot. She didn't like being caught barefoot, and in spite of Blythe's determination not to look, her gaze couldn't help but be drawn to the scars covering Rikki's feet and calves.

Rikki turned toward the house. "Would you like a cup of coffee?"

Blythe nodded. "I can get it, Rikki. Enjoy your morning." Dressed in her running shoes and light sweats, she managed to still look elegant. Rikki had no idea how she did it. Blythe was refined and educated and all the things Rikki wasn't, but that never seemed to matter to Blythe.

Rikki took a breath and forced herself to sink back into the chair and tuck her feet under her, trying not to look disturbed at the idea of anyone going into her house.

"You're drinking your coffee black again," Blythe said, and dropped a cube of sugar into Rikki's mug.

Rikki frowned at her. "That was mean." She looked around for her sunglasses to cover her direct stare. She knew it bothered most people. Blythe never seemed upset by it, but Rikki didn't take chances. She found them on the railing and shoved them on her nose.

"If you're diving today, you need it," Blythe pointed out. "You're way too thin and I noticed you haven't gone shopping again."

"I did too. There's tons of food in the cupboards," Rikki pointed out.

"Peanut butter is not food. You have nothing but peanut butter in your cupboard. I'm talking real food, Rikki."

"I have Reese's Pieces and peanut butter cups. And bananas." If anyone else had snooped in her cupboards, Rikki would have been furious, but she just couldn't get upset with Blythe.

"You have to try to eat better."

"I do try. I added the bananas like you asked me. And every night I eat broccoli." Rikki made a face. She dipped the raw vegetable into the peanut butter to make it more edible, but she'd promised Blythe so she faithfully ate it. "I'm actually beginning to like the stuff, even if it's green and feels like pebbles in my mouth."

Blythe laughed. "Well, thank you for at least eating broccoli. Where are you diving?"

Of course Blythe would have to ask. Rikki squirmed a little. Blythe was one of those people you just didn't lie to—or ignore, as Rikki often did others. "I've got this blackout I found and I want to harvest it while I can."

Blythe made a face. "Don't speak diving. English, hon. I don't have a clue what you mean."

"Urchins, spine to spine, so many, I think I can pull in four thousand pounds in a couple of hours. We could use the money."

Blythe regarded her over the top of her coffee mug, her gaze steady. "Where, Rikki?"

She was like a damn bulldog when she got going. "North of Fort Bragg."

"You told me that area was dangerous," Blythe reminded.

Rikki cursed herself silently for having a big mouth. She should *never* have talked about her weird feelings with the others. "No, I said it was spooky. The ocean is dangerous anywhere, Blythe, but you know I'm a safety girl. I follow all dive precautions and all my personal safety rules to the letter. I'm careful and I don't panic."

She didn't normally dive along the fault line running just above the Fort Bragg coast because the abyss was deep and great whites used the area as a hunting ground. Usually she worked on the bottom, along the floor. Sharks hunted from below, so she was relatively safe, but harvesting urchins along the shelf was risky. She'd be making noise and a shark could come from below. But the money . . . She really wanted to pay her sisters back all the expenses they'd covered for her, helping her with her boat.

Blythe shook her head. "I'm not talking about your safety rules. We all know you're a great diver, Rikki, but you shouldn't be alone out there. Anything could go wrong."

"If I'm alone, I'm only responsible for my own life. I don't rely on anyone else. Every second counts, and I know exactly what to do. I've run into trouble countless times and I handle it. It's just easier by myself." And she didn't have to talk to anyone, or make nice. She could just be herself.

"Why go north of Fort Bragg? You told me the undersea floor was very different and the sharks were more prevalent there and it kind of freaked you out."

Rikki found herself wanting to smile inside when just seconds earlier she'd been squirming. Blithe saying "freaked out" meant she'd been spending time with Lexi Thompson, the youngest of their family.

"I found a shelf at about thirty feet covered with sea urchins. They look fantastic. The fault runs through the area so there's an abyss about forty feet wide and another shelf, a little smaller, but still packed as well. No one's found the spot. It's a blackout, Blythe, uni spine to spine. I can harvest a good four thousand pounds and get out of there. I'll only go back when no one's around."

Blythe couldn't fail to hear the excitement in her voice. She shook her head. "I don't like it, but I understand." And that was the trouble—she did. Rikki was both brilliant and reclusive. She seemed to take her talents for granted. Blythe could ask her to program something on the computer and she'd write a program quickly that worked better than anything else Blythe had ever tried.

Everything about Rikki was a tragedy, and Blythe often felt like holding her tight, but she knew better. Rikki was very closed off to human touch, to relationships—basically to anything that had to do with others. She had allowed each of the other five women into her world, but they could only come so far before she shut down. She was haunted by her past—by the fires that had killed her parents and burned down her foster homes. By the fire that had taken her fiancé, the only person Rikki had ever let herself love.

"You had another nightmare, didn't you?" Blythe asked. "In case you're wondering, I turned off the three other hoses around your house."

She didn't ask how the water had gotten turned on. The entire family knew water and Rikki went hand in hand and strange things happened when Rikki had nightmares.

Rikki bit her lip. She tried a causal shrug to indicate nightmares were no big deal, but they both knew better. "Maybe. Yes. I still get them."

"But you're getting them a lot lately," Blythe prodded gently. "Isn't that four or five in the last few weeks?"

They both knew it was a lot more than that. Rikki blew out her breath. "That's another reason I'm going out diving today. Blowing bubbles always helps."

"You won't take any chances," Blythe ventured. "I could go with you, take a book or something and read on the boat."

Rikki knew she was asking if there was a possibility she would get careless on purpose, that maybe she was still grieving, or blaming herself. She didn't know the answer, so she changed tactics. "I thought you were going to the wedding. Isn't Elle Drake getting married today? You were looking forward to that." *Another reason why the ocean would be hers and hers alone.* Everyone was invited to the Drake wedding.

"If you won't go to the wedding and you need to go to the sea, then I'll be happy reading a book out there," Blythe insisted.

Rikki blew her a kiss. "Only you would give up a wedding to go with me. You'd throw up the entire time we were out there. You get seasick, Blythe."

"I'm trying gingerroot," Blythe said. "Lexi says there's nothing like it."

"She'd know."

Lexi knew everything there was to know about plants and their uses. If Lexi said gingerroot would help, then Rikki was certain it would, but Blythe was *not* going to sacrifice a fun day just because she feared for Rikki's safety. Rikki's life was the sea. She couldn't be far from it. She had to be able to hear it at night, the soothing roll of the waves, the stormy pounding of the surf, the sounds of the seals barking at one another, the foghorns. It was all necessary in her life to keep her steady.

Most of all, it was the water itself. The moment she touched it, pushed her hands into it, she felt different. There was no explanation for it. She didn't understand it, so how could she explain to someone else that when she was in water, she was at peace, completely free in her own environment.

"Blythe, I'll be fine. I'm looking forward to going down."

"You're spending too much time alone again," Blythe said bluntly. "Come to the wedding. All of the others are going. Judith can find you something to wear if you'd like."

Rikki had a tendency to go to Judith for advice on what

to wear or how to look if she was going to anything where there would be a large group of people, and Blythe obviously mentioned her on purpose in the hopes that Rikki would change her mind.

Rikki shook her head, trying not to show a physical reaction, when her entire body shuddered at the horror of the thought of the crowd. "I can't do that. You know I can't. I always say the wrong thing and get people upset."

She had met Blythe in a grief counseling session and somehow, Rikki still didn't know how or why, she'd blurted out her fears of being a sociopath to the others. She never talked to anyone about herself or her past, but Blythe had a way of making people feel comfortable. She was the most tolerant woman Rikki had ever known. Rikki wasn't taking any chances of doing anything that might alienate her or any of her other sisters. And that meant staying away from the residents of Sea Haven.

"Rikki," Blythe said, with her uncanny ability that made Rikki think she read minds. "There is nothing wrong with you. You're a wonderful person and you don't embarrass us."

Rikki tried desperately not to squirm, wishing she was already at sea and as far from this conversation as possible. She adjusted her glasses to make certain she wasn't staring inappropriately. Sheesh. There were so many freakin' social rules, how did people remember them? Give her the ocean any day.

"And you don't need to wear your glasses around me," Blythe added gently. "The way you look at me doesn't bother me at all."

"You're the exception, then, Blythe," Rikki snapped, then bit down on her lip hard. It wasn't Blythe's fault that she was completely happy or completely sad, utterly angry or absolutely mellow. There was no in-between on the emotional scale for her, which made it a little difficult—whether Blythe wanted to admit it or not—for her to spend time with other people. Besides, everyone annoyed the hell out of her.

"I'm different, Blythe. I'm comfortable being different, but others aren't comfortable around me." That was a fact Blythe couldn't dispute. Rikki often refused to answer someone when they asked her a direct question if she didn't feel it was their business. And anything personal wasn't *anyone's* business but hers. She felt her lack of response was completely appropriate, but the individual asking the question usually didn't.

"You hide yourself away from the world, and it isn't good for you."

"It's how I cope," Rikki said with a small shrug. "I love being here, with you and the others, I feel safe. And I feel safe when I'm in the water. Otherwise . . ." She shrugged again. "Don't worry about me. I'm staying out of trouble."

Blythe took a swallow of coffee and regarded her with brooding eyes. "You're a genius, Rikki, you know that, don't you? I've never met anyone like you, capable of doing the things you do. You can memorize a textbook in minutes."

Rikki shook her head. "I don't memorize. I just retain everything I read. I think that's why I seriously lack social skills. I don't have room for the niceties. And I'm not a genius; that's Lexi. I'm just able to do a few weird things."

"I think you should talk about the nightmares with someone, Rikki."

The conversation was excruciating for her, and had it been anyone but Blythe, Rikki wouldn't have bothered making an effort. This conversation skirted just a little too close to the past—and that was a place she would never go. That door in her mind was firmly shut. She couldn't afford to believe she was capable of the kinds of things others had accused her of: setting fires, killing her own parents, trying to hurt others. And Daniel . . .

She turned away from Blythe, feeling almost as if she couldn't breathe. "I've got to get moving."

"Promise me you'll be careful."

Rikki nodded. It was easier than arguing. "You have fun at the wedding and say hello for me." It was so much easier being social through the others. They were all well liked and had shops or offices in Sea Haven—all a big part of the community. Rikki was always on the outside fringe, and was accepted more because she was part of the Farm than for herself. The residents of Sea Haven had accepted the women of Rikki's makeshift family when they'd moved here just a few short years earlier, all trying to recover from various losses.

She forced a smile because Blythe had been the one to give her a place to call home. "I really am fine."

Blythe nodded and handed her the empty coffee cup. "You'd better be, Rikki. I would be lost if something happened to you. You're important to me—to all of us."

Rikki didn't know how to respond. She was embarrassed and uncomfortable with real emotion, and Blythe always managed to evoke real emotion, the heart-wrenching kind better left alone. Rikki felt too much when she let herself feel, and not enough when she didn't. She pushed out of her chair and watched Blythe walk away, angry with herself for not asking Blythe why she was out running so early in the morning, why she couldn't sleep. Instead, she knew she'd hack into Blythe's computer and read her personal diary and then try to find a way to help her.

Rikki didn't mind invading privacy if she thought she had good reason. The fact that she was inept at meaningful dialogue with those she cared about gave her all the reason in the world. Blythe, of all the women, was an enigma. Rikki was an observer and she noticed how Blythe brought peace to all of them, as if she took a little bit of their burdens onto herself.

Rikki sighed and threw the rest of her coffee out onto the ground. Sugar in coffee. What was up with that? She glanced up at the clear sky and tried to concentrate on that, to think of her sea, the great expanse of water, all blues and grays and greens. Soothing colors. Even when she was at her stormiest and unpredictable, the ocean brought her calm.

She went back into her house, leaving the screen door closed but the back door wide open so she wouldn't feel closed in. She polished the cupboards fast where Blythe had touched them, leaving undetectable prints, washed the coffee mugs, and carefully rinsed off the sink around the coffeepot.

She hummed slightly as she packed a lunch. She needed high-calorie foods, lots of protein and sugar. Peanut butter sandwiches, two with bananas—even though there was an old saying that bananas were bad luck—and a handful of peanut butter cups and two bags of Reese's Pieces would keep her going. Her job was aggressive and hard work, but she loved and reveled in it, especially the solitary aspects of being underneath the water in an entirely different environment—one where she thrived.

Extra water was essential and she readied a cold gallon while she prepared and ate a large breakfast—peanut butter over toast. She might not like sugar in her coffee, but she wasn't stupid enough to dive without taking in sufficient calories to sustain her bodily functions in the cold waters.

She ate, toast in hand—she didn't actually use her dishes. Her sisters had given her the most beautiful set with seashells and starfish surrounding each plate. She carefully washed the entire set on Thursdays and her wonderful set of pots and pans on Fridays—but she always had them displayed so she could look at them while she ate her sandwich.

She'd washed and bleached her wet suit the night before and made certain that her gear was in repair. Rikki repaired all her own equipment religiously, waiting for that one moment when all her senses would tell her there'd be a calm and she could go diving. Her gear was always prepared and stowed at all times so the moment she knew she could make a dive, she was ready.

Her boat and truck were always kept in pristine condition. She allowed no one else to step on her boat except the women in her family—and that was rare. No one but Rikki touched the engine. Ever. Or her baby, the Honda-driven Atlas Copco air compressor. She knew her life depended on good air. She used three filters to remove carbon monoxide, which had killed two well-known locals a few years earlier.

She knew the tides by heart thanks to the Northern California Tidelog, her bible. Although she'd committed the book to memory, she read for fun daily, a compulsion she couldn't stop. Today she had minimum tide ebb and flood with hopefully no current—optimum working conditions where she wanted to dive.

Despite Blythe's concerns, Rikki really did consider safety paramount. Rikki stowed her wet suit and gear in the truck along with her spare gear. Divers—especially

Rikki—generally kept a spare of every piece of equipment on the boat on hand just to be safe, in an airtight locked container that she checked periodically to make sure it was in working order. Moments later she was driving toward Port Albion Harbor, humming along to a Joley Drake CD. The rather famous Drake family lived in the small town of Sea Haven. The Drakes were friends with her sisters, particularly Blythe and Lexi, but Rikki had never actually talked to any of them—especially not Joley. She loved Joley's voice and didn't want to chance making social mistakes around her.

Strangely, she'd never been bothered by others' opinions of her. Friendships were too difficult to manage. She had to work too hard to fit in, to find the right things to say, so it was easier just to be herself and not care what people thought of her. But with someone she admired—like Joley—she was taking no chances. Better to just keep her distance entirely.

Rikki sang along as she drove down the highway, occasionally glancing at the ocean. The water shimmered like jewels, beckoning to her—offering the peace she so badly needed. She'd had a few months' reprieve from her nightmares, but now they were back with a vengeance, coming nearly every night. The pattern was familiar, an affliction she'd suffered many times over the years. The only thing she could do was weather the storm.

Fire had destroyed her family when she was thirteen. Definitely arson, the firefighters had said. A year and six months later, a fire had destroyed the foster home she was staying in. No one had died, but the fire had been set.

The third fire had taken her second foster home on her sixteenth birthday. She had awakened, her heart pounding, unable to breathe, already choking on smoke and fear. She'd crawled on her hands and knees to the other rooms, waking the occupants, alerting them. Everyone had escaped, but the house and everything inside had been lost.

The authorities wouldn't believe she hadn't started any of the fires. They couldn't prove it, but no one wanted her after that. No one trusted her and, in truth, she didn't trust herself. How had the fires started? One of the many psychologists suggested she couldn't remember doing it, and maybe that was the truth. She'd lived in a state-run facility, apart from the others. Fire-starter, they'd called her; the Death Dealer. She'd endured the taunts and then she'd become violent, protecting herself with ruthless, brutal force when her tormenters escalated to physical abuse. She was labeled a troublemaker and she no longer cared.

The moment she turned eighteen she was gone. Running. And she hadn't stopped until she'd met Daniel. He'd been a diver too.

Rikki turned her truck down the sloping drive leading to the harbor, inhaling the fragrance of the eucalyptus trees lining the road. Tall and thick, the trees stood like a forest of sentinels, guarding the way. The road wound around and the Albion Fishing Village came into view. She drove on through to the large, empty dirt parking lot and then backed up to the wooden guard in front of the gangway connecting to the dock.

As she unpacked her gear, the last remnant of her nightmare faded. Now, here, in the daylight beside the calming influence of the ocean, she could almost be grateful for the nightmares. They always heightened her awareness of safety on the Farm, and the recent spate reminded her it was time to check all the fire alarms, sprinklers and extinguishers. She could never risk growing complacent again.

Even if she was not the one who somehow started the

WATER BOUND   477

fires, someone else had. It seemed clear to her that someone wanted her and everyone near her dead. She'd almost
run from Blythe and the others in order to protect them,
but she'd been so beaten down, so close to the end of her
rope, she couldn't have survived without them. And despite
everything, Rikki wasn't ready to die. Thankfully her newfound sisters had realized how important fire safety was
to her, and they had spent the extra money on everything
she'd asked for.

Rikki walked along the dock until she came to her
baby—the *Sea Gypsy*. She didn't buy clothes or furniture,
her home was stark, but this—this boat was her pride and
joy. She loved the Radon, all twenty-four feet of her. Everything on her boat was in impeccable condition. No one
touched her equipment but her. She even did her own welding, converting the design of the davit to make it easier to
haul her nets on board.

The river was calm, and the boat rocked gently against
the bumpers, a soothing mixture of sounds, water lapping and birds calling back and forth. There was one lone
camper trailer in the park and no one in sight. The harbor
was nearly deserted. She went through all her checks and
started the engine. Rikki untied the lines and cast off. A
familiar eagerness raced through her veins as she pushed
the *Sea Gypsy* from her dock.

For Rikki, no feeling on earth matched the thrill of
standing on the deck of her boat, the powerful engine,
a 454 MerCruiser with Bravo 3 outdrive and two stain-
less steel propellers, rumbling under her feet and the river
stretching out in front of her like a wide blue path. The
wooden bridge—with metal spanning the river, stretched
above her, sandbar and rocks to the sides—was her gate-
way to the ocean. The channel was narrow and impass-

able in low tide or heavy swells. With the wind on her face, she maneuvered the boat out of its slip, kept a low throttle as she moved along the channel. The sandbar to her right could present problems, so she kept to the center as the *Sea Gypsy* swept around the curve to enter the actual sea.

Double-crested cormorants vied for space on the closest sea stack, a small island made of rock where the birds nested or rested. She sent them a smile as she judged her mistress. She never fully trusted the weather reports or tide books—she had to see for herself exactly what mood the ocean was in. Sometimes, in the protection of the harbor, the sea felt and looked calm, but the waters beyond the land mass could betray her angry mood. Today, the ocean was calm, the water smooth and glistening.

The *Sea Gypsy* swept out into open water and Rikki relaxed completely. This was her world, the one place she was truly comfortable. Here, she knew the rules, the dangers, and understood them, in a way she could never understand social situations and human interactions. The sky overhead was blue and clear, the surface as smooth as the California coast ever managed to be, as the boat rushed over the water. She had a great engine, built for speed—a gift from her sisters, one she could never begin to thank them for.

She rushed past caves, sea stacks and cliffs—from here the coast appeared a different world altogether. Pelicans, cormorants and osprey shared the skies with seagulls, sometimes diving deep, their bodies sleek and streamlined as they plummeted into the depths after fish. Little heads popped up here and there as a seal surfaced close to shore, hunting for a meal. Two seals played together, somersaulting over and over in the water.

Spray burst up the cliffs in a display of power as the sea met land. She lifted her face to the salt air, smiling at the touch of water on her face. She began to sing, one hand weaving a dancing pattern in the air as she maneuvered the boat with the other. It was almost a compulsion, each time she found herself alone where no one could see or hear her. An invitation. A language of love. The notes skipped over the surface to the side of her boat as she rushed over the water.

Tiny columns began to form, sparkling tubes that danced over the surface like mini-cyclones. The sun gleamed through them, lending them colors as they twisted and turned gracefully. Some rose high, leaping above the boat in thin rainbows to form an archway. Laughing, she shot through it, the wind and water on her face and ruffling her hair like fingers.

She played with the water, out there in the safest place she knew, the shore in the distance and the water leaping all around her boat, drawn to her in some mysterious way she didn't understand, coming when she beckoned, saving her life numerous times, making her feel at peace when everything and everyone she loved had been taken from her. Under her direction the water plasticized, forming shapes. The joy bursting through her there on the water where she was so alive, could never be duplicated on shore where, for her, there was only vulnerability and emptiness.

She anchored the *Sea Gypsy* just off the shelf, but gave herself plenty of scope just in case a large wave did come at her out of nowhere. She checked her equipment a final time. Eagerness rose inside her, unmarred by any hint of fear. She loved to be in the water. Being alone was an added bonus. She didn't have to try to adhere to conventional social customs. She didn't have to worry about hurting someone's feelings, embarrassing her chosen family or having people make fun of her.

Out here, in the water, she could be herself and that was enough. Out here she couldn't hear the screams of the dead, feel the scorching heat of a blazing fire, or see suspicion on the faces around her.

After rubbing herself down with baby shampoo, she warmed her suit by pouring hot water from the engine in it before putting it on. Once again, she checked her air compressor—her lifeline. She'd spent a great deal of money on the Honda 5.5 horsepower engine and her Atlas Copco 2 stage air compressor with the three extremely expensive filters, two particulate filters with a carbon filter on top. Divers had died of carbon monoxide poisoning, and she wasn't about to go that way. She had a non-locking Hanson quick release on her end of the main hose so she could detach quickly if necessary. She carried a small bailout of 30 cubic feet—her backup scuba tank—on her back. Some divers dove without one, but since she usually dove alone, she wanted the extra protection. Rikki didn't care to be bent by an emergency ascent. She wanted to always be able to come up at the proper speed should anything happen, such as a hose getting cut by a boater who did not see her dive flag.

Donning her weight belt and then the bailout, she put on the most important instrument: her computer, which kept track of her time so there was no chance of staying down too long. She had a compass to know where she was and where she wanted to go. Grabbing her urchin equipment, she slipped into the water, taking four five-hundred-pound capacity nets with her.

The massive plunge felt like leaving earth and going into space, a monumental experience that always awed her.

The cool liquid closed around her like a welcome embrace, bringing with it a sense of peace. Everything inside of her stilled, made sense. Righted. There was no way to explain the strange sensations others obviously didn't feel when being touched. Sometimes fabrics were painful, and noises made her crazy, but here, in this silent world of beauty, she felt right, her chaotic mind calm.

As she descended, fish circled her curiously and a lone seal zipped past her. Seals moved so fast in the water, like small rockets. Normally, they would linger, but today, apart from a few scattered fish, the sea seemed empty. For the first time, a shiver slid down her back and she looked around her at the deserted spot. Where had all the fish gone?

The San Andreas fault line was treacherous, a good nine hundred feet deep or more, a long, black abyss stretching along the ocean floor. At around thirty feet deep, a high shelf jutted outward, the extensive jagged line of rock covered in sea urchins. The dropoff was another good thirty feet across where a shorter shelf held an abundance of sea life as well.

Rikki touched down at the thirty-foot shelf and immediately began to work. Her rake scraped over the urchin-encrusted rocks along the shelf wall, the noise reverberating through the water for the sea creatures to hear. She worked fast, knowing that below her sharks could hunt her, where when she normally worked on the floor she wasn't in as much danger.

The feeling of dread increased with each stroke of her rake. She found herself stopping every few minutes to look around her. She studied the abyss. Could a shark be prowling there in the shadows? Her heart rate increased, but she forced herself to stay calm while she went back to work, determined to get it over with. The sea urchins were plentiful and large, the harvest amazing.

She filled her first net in a matter of twenty minutes and, as the weight increased, she filled the float with air to compensate. In another twenty minutes she had a second bag filled. Both nets floated just to one side of her while she began working to fill the third net. Because she was working at thirty feet, she knew she had plenty of bottom time to fill all four five-hundred-pound nets, but she was getting tired.

She hooked the bags to her hose, and stayed on the bottom while she let the bags go to the surface, holding the hose to slow the urchins' ascent and so the air didn't leave the float once it reached the surface. She climbed her hose a foot a second until she hit ten feet, where she stayed for five minutes to be good and safe before completing her ascent.

Working in the water was exhausting, with the continual flow of the waves. The wash could push forward and back against a diver, and exposed as she was, having to be careful not to fall into the abyss, harvesting the urchins had made her arms feel like lead. At the surface she hooked both bag lines to the floating ball and climbed onboard to rest and eat two more peanut butter sandwiches and a handful of peanut butter cups, needing the calories.

The strange dread that had been building in her seemed to have settled in the pit of her stomach. She sat on the lid of the urchin hold and ate her sandwich, but it tasted like cardboard. She glanced at the sky. It was clear. Little wind. And the sea itself was calm, yet she felt threatened in some vague way she couldn't quite comprehend. As she sat on her boat, she twisted around, looking for danger. It was silly, really, the feeling of impending doom. The day was beautiful, the sea calm and the sky held no real clouds.

She hesitated before she donned her equipment again.

She could pull up another two nets filled with sea urchins, bringing her total to several thousand pounds, enabling her to pay a good amount of money toward the Farm. She was being silly. This part of the ocean had always given her a bad feeling. Resolutely, Rikki put on her weight belt and hooked her hose to her belt before reaching for her tank.

The air around her suddenly changed, charging, pressure pushing on her chest. She turned, still reaching for her tank, when she felt the tremendous swell building beneath her. Rikki turned her head and her breath caught in her throat. Her heart slammed against her chest as she stared at the solid wall of water rising up out of the sea like a monstrous tsunami, a wave beyond anything she'd ever witnessed.

Don't miss the brand-new series from
#1 *New York Times* bestselling author

CHRISTINE FEEHAN

WATER BOUND

A Sea Haven Novel

*In the swirling tides of the ocean
she found a handsome stranger . . .*

The last thing Lev Pravenskii remembers is being lost at
sea, off the coastal town of Sea Haven. Just as quickly,
just as miraculously, he was saved—pulled ashore by a
beautiful stranger. But Lev has no memory of who he
was—or why he seems to possess the violent instincts of a
trained killer. All he knows is that he fears for his life, and
for the life of his unexpected savior.

Her name is Rikki, a sea-urchin diver in Sea Haven. She
has always felt an affinity for the ocean and felt the seductive pull of the tides. And now she feels drawn in the
same way to the enigmatic man she rescued. But soon they
will be bound by something even stronger: each other's
tantalizing secrets, which will engulf them both in a
whirlpool of dizzying passion and inescapable danger.

M615T1209